Foolish Cravings

An April May Snow

Southern Paranormal Fiction Thriller

By

M. Scott Swanson

April May Snow Titles

Foolish Aspirations
Foolish Beliefs
Foolish Cravings
Foolish Desires
Foolish Expectations
Foolish Fantasies
Foolish Games

Prequel Series

Throw the Amulet

Throw the Bouquet

Throw the Cap

Throw the Dice

Throw the Elbow

Throw the Fastball

Throw the Gauntlet

Throw the Hissy

Never miss an April May Snow release.

Join the reader's club!

www.mscottswanson.com

Author's Note- This is a work of fiction. Character names, businesses, locations, crime incidents and hauntings are purely imagination. Where the public names of locations are used please know it is from a place of love and respect from this author. Any resemblance to actual people living or dead or to private events or establishments is entirely coincidental.

I got heartaches in my pocket
I got echoes in my head
And all that I keep hearing
Are the cruel, cruel things that you said

I'm a thousand miles from nowhere
Time don't matter to me

Dwight Yoakam-
"A Thousand Miles from Nowhere"

Chapter 1

Mama says the best prescription to keep my mind off my troubles is work. Lucky me, when my need for distraction is its greatest, I've got all the hay in the barn.

Our caseload at Snow and Associates is presently nonexistent. With the notable exception of Jared Raley, our cuckold car dealer. He can't decide to poop or get off the pot regarding divorcing his cheating wife, Crystal.

Jared is keeping us on retainer. I'm not delusional enough to believe he'll request we serve Crystal divorce papers anytime soon.

My brother, Dusty, is sweating the deadline for submitting the next volume in his wildly successful *Thirteen Ghost Haunts* series. He'll have no need for field research until he satisfies his editor, Mara Dearth.

Dusty claims they have a love-hate working relationship. Mara loves to hate on him.

He's sore because Mara is the only person capable of coercing my genius brother into completing a project—before beginning a new, shinier adventure. Her diligent task-management skills made Dusty a multi-millionaire before his thirtieth birthday.

I tug at the band on my silk shorts which have become noticeably tighter since I moved home. I've decided against moving up a size. There's a chance the constant reminder is the motivation I need to do something about the extra fifteen —twenty—pounds I'm carrying. My goal is to be the most sought-after defense attorney in the Southeast, not a five-hundred-pound reality TV star.

Leaning forward, I drizzle diet coke my first weight concession, into the water near the head of a circling catfish. The leathery gray fish smacks its tail on the surface, turns, and swims off.

I can't say I blame him. If I can't have a Dr. Pepper, a *real* Dr. Pepper instead of this chemically sweetened version, I don't see the point.

Bless it. I'm so bored. Yet, all I can manage to do is sit here like a bump on a log while I melt in the North Alabama sun. It must be a hundred degrees today, and the air is so muggy it's like inhaling fish-scented steam.

It's typical summer weather on Guntersville Lake.

Daddy says the humidity does wonders for the skin. That's good to know. I'll be a beautiful corpse when I die.

The creaking noise from the boathouse door catches my attention. "Chase?" Chase is my other brother. I assume it's him since Dusty is supposed to be editing his manuscript.

"Yo." He muffles a snicker.

His odd laugh piques my curiosity. But, before I can muster the energy to stand, another bead of sweat trickles down my back. The heat saps my desire to know what has Chase so amused with himself.

I'm not supposed to be here. In Guntersville.

No, really. I'm supposed to be in Atlanta or another major metropolitan city earning my bones as a pit bull defense attorney. Instead, I'm stuck in the town I spent twenty years escaping, cobbling together enough income to pay my monthly mortgage-sized student loans.

Why am I stuck in Guntersville rather than living the dream life I sacrificed so much to attain? In a nutshell, because my life bites and the world isn't always fair.

I force myself to stop my mental tailspin into the abyss of self-pity that would come with listing all the things gone wrong recently in my life. I'm working on a newly improved April May Snow. A positively optimistic April.

Acting like the glass-half-full girl I want to be, I smile and focus on the fact it is the Fourth of July. The Fourth of July plays second in holiday status only to Christmas on the lake.

If you asked me last Wednesday, what I now refer to as "black Wednesday," I would expect to still be curled up on my bed with the lights out today. I should be in mourning from obliterating a promising relationship with an incredible guy in the most unforgivable manner.

But look at me. I am the model of resiliency.

Standing, I pull my damp shorts back into place. If I sit out here, I'll have a case of swamp butt when we ride out to watch the fireworks show tonight.

Puppy barks. It sounds like it comes from the boathouse, and someone says, "Shh."

My limited mommy hormones kick in as I march toward the boathouse. "What are you doing with my dog?"

"Quick, get him in here," is followed by a bunch of goofy laughter.

That sounds suspiciously like my author brother, who is supposed to be working in his office today.

Rounding the corner, I grab the boathouse door handle and yank it open. The crooked door digs a rut in the gray dock boards, stopping half-open.

"Get the line."

My eyes won't adjust from the sun. I see two tall, shadowy figures in the boat.

The boat engine starts. I move inside, my vision still unsatisfactory. "Did I hear my dog?"

"It was his idea." The silhouette behind the wheel points to the thicker of the two men.

"You can't just—" I nearly step off the dock into the water. With a disgusted huff, I pull my sunglasses up, and my vision miraculously corrects itself. "Take my dog without asking."

Dusty and Chase share a look, laugh, and declare in unison, "We're his uncles."

This is a common occurrence. My brothers saying the same thing in concert, not the dog nabbing.

I stab a finger at them while my other hand clutches my hip. "I said no."

Dusty, who is tall, round, and as furry as my keeshond puppy, laughs as he jumps on the low-slung stern of the boat. The boat's bow lifts as it floats forward bumping the dock's rubber bumpers.

"Kick it, Chase!"

Rage builds up from my toes to my scalp, and I tremble with anger. Their goofy pranks always get my goat. "I said no!"

I stomp to the side of the boathouse. Placing my hand over the winch switch, I threaten to lift the boat out of the water. Raising my eyebrows, I lock eyes with Chase, daring him to back the boat out.

His lips thin and his chest heaves as he resigns to the better part of valor. "Why can't he go with us? He is a water dog, you know."

"Because I can't trust you knuckleheads to watch after him."

Dusty stops rubbing Puppy's ears and frowns, "What did you call us?"

His unexpected question makes me stutter, "Kn-knuckleheads."

Chase leans against the captain's seat while crossing his arms. "What does that even mean?" he asks Dusty.

"It's an archaic term for idiot. It's from the depression era," Dusty says.

"I knew I had never heard it before."

Dusty shrugs. "You might have heard it from Grandpa Snow before he passed. It would be from his generation."

"No"—Chase sucks in his lips—"Grandpa Snow would never have been so rude as to call anyone an idiot."

I stomp my barefoot on the dock. "Give me my dog," I growl.

"Why?" Dusty asks as he rubs Puppy's belly, who has now rolled onto his back.

"Did y'all even think to get the floatation device Daddy bought him? No, you didn't. You know he could drown out there. How would that make you feel?"

Chase lifts a small orange vest. "One extra-wide puppy vest. Check."

I should be grateful they care enough to prepare for Puppy's safety, but it makes me angrier. "Give me my dog."

Dusty lifts his hands off Puppy. "Fine. You don't have to go all she-devil on us."

"You ought to just come with us, April." Chase flashes his naturally brilliant white flawless smile that goes perfectly with his movie-star tanned body.

Tilting my head forward, I narrow my eyes. "I don't want to go on a boat ride, Chase."

"Let her be, Chase. She still wants to mope around about you-know-what, that happened with you-know-who."

They need to give me my dog, pronto. I'm fixin' to yank a knot in both my brothers' tails.

"It's not the dog's fault," Chase grumbles.

Dusty stands to pick up Puppy. Before he can put his arms around him, Puppy hops off the back bench seat and leaps onto the passenger captain's chair.

My dog is a traitor. I'm adding him to my list.

Dusty's shoulders slump. "Oh, come on, April. Look at him. I can't kick him off the boat now. He'll never trust me again."

"You should have thought about that before you decided to kidnap him. Now hand him to me. I'm not playing around with you two anymore."

Chase taps Dusty on the shoulder. "I'll do it. You take the wheel."

My brothers are incredibly tight. I assume that should be expected of twins.

In the case of my brothers, their personalities are as different as their looks. Dusty is the brainiac of the family, but Chase is Prince Valiant. He can surprise you with sweet gestures of empathy.

Having won the argument with my brothers and saved my dog's life, I relax as my heart rate slows.

Chase jumps onto the dock in a blur of motion, throws me over his shoulder, and jumps back into the boat. "Go!"

The boat lurches into reverse. Chase leans forward, precariously off-balance, threatening to send us both tumbling to the fiberglass floor. I hammer at his back with my fists anyway.

He catches his balance, dumping me onto the back bench seat as we clear the boathouse. The bright sun blinds me.

They make a whooping noise, and I see the silhouette of the two lugs giving each other a high-five.

"You made me lose my sunglasses!"

Chase reaches above my line of blurred sight. "These?"

I grab the glasses he pulls off the top of my head. "You're a jerk, Chase Snow."

"I've been told that before, but I know you don't need to be by yourself. You'll spend the entire day in your head replaying the dumpster fire that is your love life."

Puppy turns in his seat and yaps twice at me. I'll deal with him later.

Straightening the sunglasses on my face, I give Chase my best "you'll pay for this later" look. He takes the hint. Since Puppy claimed shotgun, Chase takes a seat on one of the benches at the boat's nose.

I get they want to cheer me up. But I'm not ready to bring my mourning to a conclusion. It's not been a week since the world knocked me to the ground and tinkled on me for good measure.

My plan to hide out all day in my room with Puppy was a solid one, since celebrating Independence Day and watching the fireworks on the lake didn't fit my present dark mood.

I love my brothers to pieces. It's not their fault they don't understand me. We are nothing alike.

They can't imagine a better place in the world to live than Guntersville, Alabama. I, on the other hand, have done everything in my power to escape.

Sadly, to date, I have been unable to break the gravitational pull of my birthplace.

If I don't leave town soon, I'm going to do something stupid. Like accidentally go and set down roots.

With Dusty driving the boat, we're going along at a comfortable clip without any harsh bumps. The wind swirls through my hair, and the sun caresses my skin pleasantly enough. I'm still too miserable about what I have done to relax and enjoy myself.

And why shouldn't I be melancholy? I recently had my heart crushed. Worse, I caused it with a foolish, knee-jerk reaction.

If I could only go back in time. I only need to change one poor decision that took all of ten seconds to sabotage a relationship I desperately wanted.

The loss of Patrick's love numbs all my senses. I feel hollowed out on the inside like a watermelon used for melon balls.

I buoy my bruised psyche with the possibility that it wasn't me but divine intervention. Twenty years from now, I'll be a senior partner at an immense law firm pulling down millions of dollars a year as the most coveted defense attorney in the state.

I'll look out my high-rise corner office window and remember the night I fell in love with Patrick McCabe. The night I convinced myself I could settle down in Guntersville and start a family with a man who fixes air conditioners for a living.

Bless it. That's awful of me.

What Patrick does for a living is necessary and admirable. He is a fantastic air conditioner technician.

It does highlight how disparate our life goals are from one another. No matter how much sexual heat we naturally generate, our marriage would be doomed to fail.

I'm a big enough girl to admit it's not him. It's me.

I do wish my skin would stop yearning to feel Patrick pressed against me. It would also be helpful if I could simply clear from my mind the vision of his cute butt in jeans with his work belt slung at a low angle.

The image that never leaves me. The one I would pluck from my memory and burn like a discarded photograph if I had the ability.

I blame my overwhelming disappointment on my parents. Mama and Daddy have been married for thirty-five years. They met at the ages of fifteen and fourteen when Mama started her freshman year in high school.

By the end of the year, they were going steady. Even through college, they never dated anybody else.

Seriously. How am I ever supposed to compete with that? They're like the gold bar standard for marital relationships.

They didn't pass the relationship bliss on to any of their children.

Chase had a steady girlfriend, Barbara, all through high school. She was such a fixture in our lives I thought of her as a big sister.

Their relationship died a quick and silent death during their senior year of high school. Fourteen years later, I'm yet to drag the tawdry details out of Barbara or Chase, who remain devoted friends.

Dusty hooked up with a winner right out of college. Bethany seemed okay at first, but as soon as Dusty's first book made a nice sum of money, she filed for divorce and claimed the book's format was her idea. She sued for fifty percent royalty rights into perpetuity.

Luckily, she doesn't live in town. That's fortunate. I wouldn't want any of the Snow clan to have to fix their fenders from hitting the cow if we happened to see her crossing Gunter Avenue.

Me? I don't understand what my issue is lately. I'm fond of male companionship, but I have always taken care to look at those relationships through the lens of "April will be headed off to be a big-shot lawyer soon." Which means I keep it flirtatious, light, and most of all, temporary.

Even while guarding my heart, since I graduated from law school, I've had a string of hot, attractive men nearly pull me away from my goals.

I know the circumstances are not necessarily related. Still, at the same time, my career has taken a nosedive into the mud. Now, the nagging feeling my carefully constructed life plan will slip away from me forever is my constant companion.

Face it. I'm pathetic. I'm twenty-seven years old, living in what used to be the party room above my parents' boathouse. I can't even begin to explain how I got here.

More importantly, for the first time in my life, I don't have a clue how to move forward. But "feel sorry for April time" ends today.

It's time to create my new life plan.

Chapter 2

Chase taps my arm while hollering over the roar of the boat engine, "Jacob's boat is over there. We're gonna go see what he's up to."

Dusty idles the motor as we pull alongside Jacob's metallic navy-blue ski boat.

Jacob and I were terrific friends in high school. Now he's an outstanding police officer who has helped me out of several professional jams.

In high school, he never took his shirt off. He played right offensive tackle for the football team and was always embarrassed by the tummy that hung over his belt.

His shirt is off today. The twenty-five pounds he used to carry in his gut is spread out nicely across his pectoral muscles and arms.

He better not be using steroids. His mama would roll over in her grave.

My eyes break away from the tease of hair on Jacob's flat stomach above the drawstring of his swim trunks. There are two ponytails in the back of Jacob's boat. I focus my full attention on them as I wonder who they are, and my curiosity slips into overdrive.

Full disclosure, my curiosity is incessant. I wish I could turn it off. Like right now.

It's none of my beeswax who's riding in Jacob's boat. Yet I'm craning my neck like some jealous lover to identify the women.

"I figured you'd be stuck at the marina today, Chase," Jacob says as they put the bumper guards out and tie the boats together.

"Jenny and Wilson have it. Besides, if they need me, they know how to reach me."

Who is Jenny? It occurs to me I haven't been out to our family's marina once in the month I've been back home.

My mama inherited the marina from her granddaddy. Chase runs it for the family now.

Chase jumps over the side of his boat into Jacob's and immediately turns into his natural state—a social butterfly. "Hey, Becky. I like that bathing suit."

My brother, the charmer, at work. Since he is incapable of being embarrassed, I'll be embarrassed for him.

I'm surprised when the short, thick brunette in the yellow one-piece stands and gives Chase a sideways hug. Sheriff Becky Gray—Becky Bucktooth—I would never have imagined her to be a hugger.

Of course, she'll never offer me a hug with our history. By successfully solving a case together last week, I hope we put our childish differences from middle school behind us.

"You better be saving one of those hugs for me."

A tall girl who can't be a day over twenty saunters up to my brother. Her auburn ponytail is so thick and long the tip bounces against the middle of her back. Her breasts spill out of her double D hot pink bikini top. Below her flat belly and an improbably small waist, the bikini bottoms are a narrow slash of Lycra. I don't like her one bit.

She raises onto her tippy toes and clamps my brother with both arms. She squishes those huge melons against his chest.

I try to be good. But I have a brief vision of me grabbing the brazen harlot by the red horsetail coming out the back of her head and slinging her off the boat.

"You're gonna give an old man a heart attack, Kimberly,"

Chase jokes.

I sidle up to Dusty. "Who's that Kimberly chick?"

Dusty raises his eyebrows and grins. I despise the fact he can read me so easily.

"Kimberly Meeks. Remember, she and her mom stayed at our house when her parents were going through that thing. She's police dispatch now."

It can't be. The Kimberly Meeks I remember is an eight-year-old, scrawny, freckle-faced girl afraid of her own shadow.

I don't like this getting old thing. It just doesn't suit me.

"Do you plan on going for a swim or just catching some sun and relaxation?" Chase asks.

"I thought we might float on the rafts, let the girls kill a six-pack, then take the long way to Dockside to have an early lunch," Jacob says.

"That's what I love about you cops. Y'all take all the details into consideration," Chase says.

"Everyone else has family in town to see the fireworks with tonight." Becky makes a circling motion with her finger. "We three losers don't, so we're going to be a makeshift family."

"You three are part of my family," Chase says.

I hear Dusty's laugh coming from the front of the boat. "He likes it."

Wait a minute. Where's my dog?

I do a quick scan of the boat, and Puppy is nowhere to be found.

Running to the front of the boat, I look over the edge where Dusty is sitting. I gasp in horror.

My furball is paddling in the lake water. Puppy doesn't have his float vest. "He's going to drown!"

"He's a natural. Look at that stroke."

"You're going to give me a stroke!" I lean out over the edge reaching for Puppy. He's just out of my grasp.

"Leave him alone. He'll come to us when he gets tired."

"If he doesn't sink first, you bonehead." I stretch out further and get a pinch of fur between my thumb and forefinger for my trouble. As I try to pull Puppy closer, I lose my balance and flip over the edge of the boat.

The freezing water shocks my senses, temporarily paralyzing me. I struggle to move my limbs. A jolt of energy mobilizes them again, and I pop to the surface madder than a wet hen. I wasn't prepared to go for a swim.

Dusty roars with a gaping mouth howl of laughter.

"You will pay, Dusty Snow," I say in tandem with what I'm sure is a scalding death glare. That is if I don't have raccoon eyes from my mascara running.

Puppy's paws scratch the back of my shoulder, and I swivel to face him. I pull him to my chest and backstroke to the back of the boat. I push my dog onto the boat stern and use the short ladder to pull myself out of the water.

Puppy shakes himself dry, slinging a mixture of lake water and fur to plaster my face.

"Thanks, but I wasn't looking for a shower, dude."

Puppy yaps at me, turns, and walks through the back-hinged door resuming his VIP seating. He's not even six months old, and he is already backtalking me.

Some mom I would make.

I plan to read Dusty the riot act for attempting to drown my dog. But I'm the only one on the boat. Human.

Looking over the side rail, the five of them are already situated on the lounge floaters with beers and cokes in their cup holders.

"Hey, like don't wait on me." This day is even worse than I imagined it could be.

Jacob lifts a thickly muscled arm and points toward his boat. "There's an extra float and your cut of the beer in my boat."

Fine. Whatever.

I thought I was going along for a quick boat ride. I never had intentions of going for a swim today. But since that Rubicon has already been crossed, I might as well join the rest of the Romans. Besides, a couple of beers could help the rest of the day go by smoother.

One thing is for sure, I am begging off the firework display tonight. I think dogs fear fireworks. Puppy will be my excuse for missing the festivities.

By the time I've settled into my raft and had a few sips of a beer, I'm convinced Jacob, Becky, and Kimberly are no more than friends. Two things about Jacob, he's an incredibly thoughtful guy, and he is not a loner. It makes perfect sense he would invite two women, with no family in town, for a ride on his boat.

Regarding Jacob, I can put my green jealousy monster back in its cage. My brother Chase is an entirely different subject.

Kimberly is taking full advantage of her raft having floated next to Chase's. She's sliding her toes, with their hot pink pedicure to match the too-small bikini, up and down the back of Chase's leg. She's acting like it's a recurring accident due to the close proximity of their rafts.

Chase is either too thickheaded to realize her game, or he is ignoring her clumsy seduction. Knowing my brother, my money is on the prior.

I hope Kimberly's sunscreen washed off when she jumped into the lake, and her creamy smooth skin turns cherry tomato red by the end of the day. What does she have to use on her luminescent white skin anyway? Two hundred SPF? Vampire sunscreen?

I seethe and chug. Seethe and chug. I don't have the same mindset to be happy as the rest of this crew. I have significant issues to mull over, and this happy little outing isn't helping my frame of mind.

The beer can I lift to my lips is empty. That was short-lived. I'll obviously need something more potent than light beer to get through this day. I settle back and close my eyes. The other five have drifted away from me. I can hear their voices, but I can't make out their conversation.

I need to call Nana Hirsch. After what took place during the team's last paranormal excursion, I'm left with no choice.

Nana is my maternal grandmother. Nana is outhouse rat

crazy and the scariest person I know. That's on her good days.

Scary or not, I need to seek her out for help. According to the rest of the paranormal team members, I generated an itsy-bitsy amount of Wiccan magic on our last assignment. Calling it Wiccan most likely is not one hundred percent correct. But it wasn't spiritual in nature—a.k.a. miracle—it was magic.

Creating magic isn't necessarily the issue. Especially since the unexplained shield saved my team members' lives.

Not knowing how I created the protective bubble is the concern.

Nana, an animist, has never hidden her magical abilities. In fact, I'd say she celebrates them. Which is fine, I suppose. It makes her happy, and she's not hurting anybody. Still, all the spirit catchers, hex bags, and insanely complex potions she creates make me nervous.

My relationship with Nana was better before I believed in magic. When I still had plausible deniability by not having first-hand knowledge rogue spirits exist.

The last thing I want is to be caught up in Nana's crazy world where witches and ghosts walk the earth.

I'm struggling enough trying to put my life back together. It would be so much easier if I were normal like everyone else.

Therein lies the rub. I'm not normal, and no amount of whining or complaining appears to ever lessen that truth. The best I can hope for is to control my "gifts" effectively and reliably.

Nana is the only person who can help me.

I open my eyes and watch the five talking and laughing without a care in the world. Their lives are so uncomplicated. I squash my envy and strive to be happy for them.

"The last one out gets the anchor," Chase says as he hand paddles to the boat.

During my contemplations, I have floated yards away from the boat. Of course, I'll be the last. Why would I expect anything different?

Chapter 3

Despite my pleas, Dusty concedes the wheel to Chase. I suppose Dusty doesn't have much of a choice because the boat belongs to Chase.

I clutch the railing with one hand and crush Puppy to my chest with the other. Wind rushes up my nostrils making it impossible to breathe. In response, I tuck my head and curl low against my seat. Searching for an effective windbreak.

We skip over the water with a sway to the left and a jerk to the right. I close my eyes and pray we will make it to Dockside before the boat becomes a wing and takes flight.

My fear of Chase driving a boat has been earned. I swear I'm still suffering from post-traumatic stress disorder from when Chase hit a log at top speed in March. His boat disintegrated on impact, throwing the two of us through the air.

True to Chase's personality, since we both lived and the insurance company bought him a new boat, all was well. It was just a one-off coincidence to him.

Me? I consider anytime I'm forced to seek medical attention to be a teachable moment.

The rush of the wind increases improbably as the nose lifts higher in the water. My curiosity wins out, and I open my eyes. Jacob's blue ski boat is streaking alongside us, doing its own dance on the water.

In my world, women become adept at reading our men's facial features at an early age. It's a necessity for survival.

Jacob rotates his head in the direction of our boat. I can make out the set of his jaw and the hint of a smile. The transformation of his expression is subtle. Only my years of practiced study allow me to discern the change so swiftly.

Please no. Not "crazy eyes!"

Jacob turns his attention back to his path, cutting across the rippled surface as he folds his bulky frame behind the windshield. His elbow jerks back, his boat squats further in the water and shoots past us like a blue streak.

I scream, "No!" but my voice is lost in the roar of the motor. Our boat's nose lifts, rolling me off my right hip on the bench seat. I tumble onto my side clutching Puppy against me.

Pushing myself upright, I brace against the momentum with my legs.

Puppy squirms free and plops his butt down well out of my reach. Fur flying, he raises his nose to the wind as his tongue lolls out his mouth. He appears to enjoy this walk on the wild side.

Phenomenal, even my dog has the danger-junky gene. Figures.

Our boat's tail swings further to the side with each skip, which are becoming less frequent. This is never a good thing. It means we are traveling at imminent danger speed.

My stomach cramps in response to our approaching calamitous death by drowning or fiery crash. Probably both simultaneously.

Each landing clacks my teeth together with such force I worry I'll crack a molar. Now acting like a buckboard, the bench seat repeatedly catapults me upward into the jet stream —the hurricane-like wind threatening to blow Puppy and me overboard.

Chase pulls even to Jacob's ski boat. Jacob's sleek navy blue boat slices through the water on a perfect line, its tail steady and straight, the nose hardly scratching the surface of the lake.

I have an epiphany. The two maniacs aren't going to stop until one of the boats has flipped over. I knew I should have put Puppy's float vest on him.

Jacob glances in our direction. I hold my breath, hoping the attention taken from his steering does not culminate in the catastrophic collision I'm envisioning.

They're gone. Jacob's crazy eyes have transformed into an expression of concern.

Bless it. That's what I love about Jacob. He knows when enough is enough.

Chase? That's a different story.

Jacob's boat slows, and the hull bites into the water as we fly past them.

"Yes!" Chase bellows triumphantly.

The boat lurches as Chase cuts the motor to quarter speed. He pumps his right fist into the air—my big, beautiful, crazy brother.

Dusty and I exchange an uneasy glance. We both worry about Chase. But what are you going to do? We are who we are? Right?

I'll miss Chase when he inevitably takes his *last* dare too far over the line.

"You buy the first round, Jacob!" Chase hollers as the boats float closer together.

"Heck, that was my plan before you tried to kill us, you maniac," Jacob replies with a practiced grin. His eyes do not share the humor his smile feigns.

"Ha. You drive like my grandma. You should have stayed on the porch with your rocking chair."

"Knock it off, Chase," I snipe.

"What?" he says with a roll of his shoulder.

"At least I'll make it to the porch," Jacob counters.

True that. Even as a child, Chase was wild. But now it's different. His actions often have an all-out, over-the-edge desperate feel to them. As if he has lost a sense of where the line between fun and actual danger is drawn.

We wait for two dock spaces to open at Dockside's pier. We are not the only boaters who thought it would be an ideal day to take a boat ride to the restaurant.

Dockside has changed hands more times than I can remember. Over the years, it has been a steakhouse, twice a barbecue joint, a meat and three, and even briefly a Chinese restaurant. Presently it bills itself as a "surf and turf" whose best item on the menu is a ten-inch burrito aptly named the Moby Dick. I suppose that's the surf part of the menu since there is not a single seafood entrée to be found otherwise.

Regardless of all the venue and name changes, one thing has consistently stayed the same at the restaurant: alcohol and atrocious service.

Alcohol being available during its stint as a meat and three always seemed peculiar to me. Although some people swore a Bloody Mary went well with meatloaf and mashed potatoes. I was too young to drink at the time, so I can't vouch for that opinion.

My mama likes to say Dockside only has two things going for it. It's the only restaurant on the lake, and it's the only restaurant on the lake.

She's right. Nobody can resist the idea of tying off their boat to a restaurant where they eat a meal. There is something extraordinarily cool about the experience.

Jacob wasn't kidding about buying the first round. True to his word, as Jacob always is, he instructs our waitress the first round will be on his tab.

I'm fortunate. I suppose deep down, I know that.

It's eighty-five degrees with light cloud cover and a refreshing breeze. I'm surrounded by family and friends as we prepare to enjoy a meal shaded under an umbrella. Later tonight, we will have a barbecue feast sure to leave my stomach tight as a drum. After dinner, we'll ride to the middle of the lake and be entertained by the spectacle of fireworks—as we have every year I can remember.

I know, it's a special kind of privilege. It's perfect.

Yet I'm fighting every moment to bring myself out of this dark chasm I created. While my margarita sweats, I lean over and scrunch my hand into Puppy's fur. I've been doing that a lot during the last week.

He had settled in for a nap but sits up and angles into my hand. His reciprocation of my touch brings tears to my eyes.

I want to do better and be a better person. How do I accomplish that when I'm relegated to giving myself pep talks every hour just to have my spirits slide back into the dark hole in my heart?

If someone could tell me when this lonely ache will end, I'm confident I could get control of my emotions and move forward with my life.

Everyone keeps telling me it's just a matter of time. "Give it time, April." Right, give it time. But how much will it take?

My life is based on schedules which are large blocks of days, hours, and minutes. Tell me how long something takes, and I can endure anything if the goal is something I want to accomplish.

I get an undergraduate in four years, I can do a law degree in another three; that's easy. I can accomplish anything as long as I know how long it's gonna take. But nobody, not a single person yet, has been able to tell me how long it will be before I am over Patrick McCabe.

What concerns me—the scary possibility that keeps me awake at night— is that no one will say how long because they know I'll never be over Patrick. That I will go to my grave ruing the day I walked out of his house and so thoroughly embarrassed myself.

I did what Mama suggested, alright demanded, the morning after when I finally had a reprieve from my sobbing.

It took me two days to raise the courage, but I called Patrick and explained myself the best I could. I made no excuse and didn't float the first white lie. My actions were inexcusable, I should have handled the situation with far more care, and I'm not prepared to be a mother yet.

Patrick sounded as devastated as I felt. He was kind and understanding, which made it all the worse. I wanted him to yell at me, curse me, tell me I was a shallow, selfish woman and proclaim he never wanted to see me again.

Instead, he said he fully understood. Being a parent is a big responsibility, and if I'm not ready, he certainly didn't want me to try and fake it.

The worst part of the conversation was he wanted to take the blame for the situation. He apologized and said he wished he had found a better way to tell me. Claiming he had fallen head over heels for me and the relationship had progressed too quickly for him to find the appropriate moment to discuss his parent status.

When Patrick said he was head over heels, I had to hold back another bout of sobs. I feel the same about Patrick.

Patrick and I are only part of this story. There's a young man that would expect me to be his stepmother. A challenging job I am hardly qualified to do. I haven't even mastered how to be a good mother to a keeshond.

End of love story. Hard stop.

I know I'll survive this romantic tragedy. Few people genuinely die from a broken heart.

Work will get busy again. There'll be things to take my mind off him.

I stare down at my hand clutching Puppy. He has gone back to sleep. I have a handful of hair for my fretting. Now I need to wash my hands.

Excusing myself, I make my way to the ladies room.

Gawking at my reflection in the mirror, I'm horrified. I look worse than I imagined. My frizzed-out blonde hair is in a permanent windswept 'do that rivals the bride of Frankenstein. The raccoon eyes effect from my mascara triggers my funny bone, and I laugh hysterically at my "hot mess" reflection.

A woman bedazzled in diamonds, who must be an out-of-town weekender, comes out of the last stall. She gives me a wary glance and decides to skip washing her hands. Nasty.

There isn't anything to be done about my hairdo. I do make a few futile swipes at my eyes with some tissue. I could really use some cold cream or Vaseline about now.

The random giggles left over from my maniacal laughter subside, and I take a deep breath. It's time I get back to the rest of my group and soldier through lunch with a smile. I can do this. I don't desire to be the wet blanket on everyone's fun today.

Chapter 4

I exit the bathroom and start down the narrow, shadowed hallway. Turning left toward the dining area, I decide I need to go to the fireworks display tonight with my family. If I'm serious about getting my life back on track, I need to return to some semblance of normal.

Staying in my room and sulking tonight would not be normal. Besides, despite being exceptionally proficient at beating myself up for things I can't change, remaining in a constant state of agitated sadness is getting tiresome.

It's true. I don't know how long before the Patrick thing is a distant memory. I do know waiting for it while I'm in my room pouting will make it seem like an infinitely extended timeline.

The force of the collision nearly knocks me down. Cold liquid hits my chest causing me to shudder. I'm looking at the huge wet spot on my T-shirt, and a napkin held by a furry hand pats the top of my breasts vigorously.

Vodka vapors burn my nostrils. I freeze in horror. The distinctly male hand continues to paw at me.

"I'm so sorry. I wasn't watching where I was going."

That makes two of us. I take a step back and clear the hand from my breasts with a swipe of my arm. My eyes come up to see who has been mauling me. I frown at the familiar face I can't place with a name.

His alcohol hooded eyes open wide. "Wow. April, is that you?"

"Yes." My answer sounds more like a question. I know I should remember his name. I think we even went out on a date once—I think—but not memorable enough to be sure.

The mauler slams his chest with his fist so hard it sounds like a body blow. "Chuck. Chuck Davis."

His tone is quite insistent, but my mind remains blank.

"You were a freshman at Alabama, and we went out. I was a senior from the SAE house."

That Chuck Davis? No wonder I didn't recognize his face. I spent most of the night focusing on his hands.

On our one date, I made more successful blocks than the average NHL goalie makes in a successful night's work. "Oh yeah. Hey, how are you doing?"

"What are you doing here? I mean other than eating. Are you down for the weekend?"

So many questions, so many words, especially from somebody I thought I had successfully left in my past. "I'm visiting my parents for a few weeks. You?" Why did I ask that pointless question? If it were physically possible for me to kick myself in the butt, I would do it right now.

"After school, I took over my dad's cleaning solution company. I told you about it, remember?"

No. "Yeah, I seem to remember something like that."

He crowds in closer to me. He is one of those people who doesn't understand the bubble principle when talking to folks.

"And then I married Carolyn Digby. You remember her. She was in Phi Mu."

Boy, that's just not ringing a bell. But then I didn't much care for the Phi Mu. "I think I know her."

"Biggest mistake in my life. I'm positive she only married me for my money."

I look out the screen door longingly at my group. Now I wish I had just eaten a hamburger with Puppy's fur all over my hands. Why am I the only one in my party concerned with clean hands? I need one of them to pass by on the way to the bathroom so I can escape this unsolicited conversation.

"Day one, she begins nitpicking me. Doesn't like the fact I'm traveling, doesn't like what I'm wearing, thinks I should be making even more money, that we should get a vacation home —It was like one constant gripe session."

I wonder if her feelings were mutual about the griping.

"Then, after two and a half years, she comes up pregnant."

"Oh, that's nice. Congratulations," I toss out numbly.

"Hardly, she took glee in telling me it was her ex-boyfriend's. I didn't even know he was still around. They broke it off back in high school."

On the one hand, I don't care a bit about Chuck's stupid marriage recounting. I want him to shut up so badly I visualize punching him in the mouth. On the other hand, Chuck makes me feel surprisingly good about the dystopian romance that is my love life. I don't have it as bad as I think I do.

"Carolyn wants a divorce. Which to that, I'm thinking good riddance. Until I get papers saying she wants half of my dad's company. She says she deserves it for all of her pain and suffering caused by living with me."

Alright, enough is enough. I can't take any more negativity. "So, you decided to come down to the lake for the weekend and enjoy the festivities?"

"Heck no. I hate this podunk town. I'm only here because I have to go to circuit court tomorrow for the first hearing on the divorce decree."

I don't care. I really don't. But my curiosity makes me ignore my better judgment. "Why is your divorce being done in Marshall County?"

Chuck lets out a laugh that sounds like it hurt. "Ask my useless attorney that question. Somehow my wife got the proceedings moved to Marshall County because it would be more convenient for her. Given her condition and everything."

"Condition?"

"Because she's nine months pregnant. She wants to get the

divorce done so she can marry that piece of garbage she was cheating with."

"Which judge?"

Chuck curls his lip. "Some Italian dude named Rossi."

Oh boy, Margaret Rossi will enjoy this stupidity being in her courtroom. However, she might get a kick out of someone thinking she is Italian.

The sudden hand on my shoulder makes me snap to attention. Dusty glares over my shoulder with his "I'm a hungry bear" expression.

"Is there a problem here, April?" Dusty growls.

"No worries, man," Chuck says with a sheepish grin. "I wasn't hitting on your girl. I've got my own."

I follow the direction of Chuck's finger. A teenager wearing what looks like a tube top stretched into a skirt is sitting by herself. Thankfully, she has her legs crossed.

Her left foot, clad in four-inch platform sandals, twitches in the air with an impatient tick. She must be fifteen years younger than Chuck.

"Best of luck with your case, Chuck," I say as I take my cue to escape.

"You're a lawyer, too?" Dusty is usually my perceptive brother. It is all I can do not to elbow him in the gut.

"Too? Are you a lawyer?" Chuck asks Dusty.

Dusty laughs. "No. But April is. She's undefeated as a homicide defense attorney."

It is adorable the way my brothers have taken an interest in my career. But right now, Dusty needs to shut his mouth.

"No kidding?" Chuck appears to recalibrate his opinion of me. "I can see that. You always seemed amazingly intelligent, April."

"Thank you"—I gesture with my thumb over my shoulder —"it's been great catching up with you, Chuck. But I really need to get back to my friends."

His brow furrows as he waves his hand. "Of course, my bad. It was good catching up with you. And again, I'm sorry I wasn't paying attention earlier when I spilled my drink on you."

"Don't think twice about it."

Dusty holds the screen door for me to exit to the outdoor dining area. "He seems like a nice guy," he says as I pass.

I'm glad Dusty can't see my eyes roll.

Chapter 5

At the Snow house, the only thing Christmas has on the Fourth of July is presents. Both holidays feature a feast that would make King Arthur envious. But let's be honest, baby back ribs, fresh silver queen corn, fried okra, and potato salad will put turkey and cranberry sauce to shame every day.

Everyone knows it's not even close.

Once you add in the warmer weather with an opportunity to ride in the boat and watch fireworks, you better be getting some fantastic gifts at Christmas.

Jacob, Becky, and Kimberly had to leave by three thirty to make their shifts. Mama wouldn't let them go without taking a plate with them.

I'm pleased most of Dusty's paranormal team accepted the invite. We're only short the Early brothers, whose parents also do a big Fourth of July meal. The marina closed for the night, and Wilson brought the new girl Jenny with him to our celebration dinner.

Granny Snow arrives as we begin to fill our plates. She isn't always a guarantee to show since she can tend to be a homebody. I make a quick scan to confirm Nana hasn't decided to make a rare appearance. Those two are like fire and ice.

I fill my plate, as usual, with twice what I need. The thinking is I will stop eating when I'm full. If celebrations past are any indication, I will only stop when my plate has been polished to a shiny clean with the last bit of bread on my dish.

My parents had set up three eight-foot tables on the deck and pulled two of the dock picnic tables to the base of the deck. Without thought, I sit down at the picnic table farthest from everyone else.

As I pick up my fork, the weight of the picnic table shifts.

"Do you mind if I keep you company?"

Liza, the only other female on my brother's paranormal team, isn't the biggest talker in the world. However, she is an excellent listener. "That would be nice."

We eat in companionable silence. When we are finishing our meal, Liza says, "You're so lucky everybody in your family is such a good cook. In my family, if it doesn't come in a can, it's too difficult to cook."

My face flushes with guilt. "It would be better if I could do it myself. I'm a lousy cook."

Liza laughs at me.

"What?"

"I'm a lousy cook," she mocks me and follows it with a smile.

"What? I am."

"I'm not arguing with you. But if you are, it's because you choose to be. I can't think of a single thing you couldn't do if you wanted to. Besides, cooking is overrated."

"You just got done saying you wish you could cook."

"No, I implied I wished someone had cooked for me when I lived at home. I don't want to do the cooking." She flicks her wrist. "Plus, it always tastes better when somebody else prepares it. It makes me feel special they cared enough to cook for me."

Fair. There isn't much to argue about with Liza's statement.

"Have you had any interesting cases lately? Has anyone else gone vigilante on home intruders or driven a nail through their husband's skull?" Liza quips.

Liza is referencing two of my recent bizarre court cases. She tends to find humor in things I find appalling. I suppose we all cope with shocking events in our own way.

"No. It's been kinda dead the last week."

"It *is* a holiday. Somebody will do something stupid before the end of the night."

I know Liza's statement is all too true. Somewhere in Marshall County, a guy or gal is enjoying a family meal unaware. They will do something moronic tonight to land their butt in jail. Possibly, an act they won't remember doing when the sun rises.

It's more common than unusual when it comes to Independence Day. Celebrating one's fortuitous freedom while mixing alcohol and fireworks is an explosive concoction of adrenaline and lowered inhibitions. Never a good mix for those who fail to moderate their behavior.

"Did you talk to your Nana yet?"

Liza's question hardly surprises me. After our last research project, I promised her I would seek Nana's council regarding the weird blue light I manifested. We were being attacked by a power-crazed warlock at the time.

Of course, I haven't. I've been too busy.

Check that, not true. I'm procrastinating. The thought of visiting Nana gives me the heebie-jeebies. When I'm around her, I can't even pretend my paranormal affliction doesn't exist.

Liza's role on Dusty's team puts her on the tip of the spear for sensing spirits. Dusty and the guys call her an expeller. It's a loose term they use to describe her spiritual training that allows Liza to expel spirits and demons possessing a human's body.

Liza is much more than some Father Damien Karras-like priest.

Her milky white skin is covered by beautifully detailed, colorful tattoos of spiritual emblems and mysterious scripts. I've only had brief glimpses of the intriguing artwork while we roomed together.

To date, I've only seen her animate one of the drawings. Liza saved my life with that animation.

I slouch my shoulders. "Not just yet."

"You know you need to."

"I know," I say in a high-pitched, whiny tone. Liza raises her eyebrows at me. I turn away from her.

"I'm not trying to harass you. It's just dangerous if you don't know what you're handling," she continues with a kind tone.

It could also be dangerous to *know* what I'm handling.

I have known since the age of eight that I'm a clairvoyant. I was carefully instructed on the best ways to limit the "gift" from interfering in my daily life. I had also been warned about the dangers of using the powers willy nilly. Paranormal powers are hungry and can change or even replace the personality of the gift holder if used in excess.

This new casting magic revelation has me wigged out. Mostly because clairvoyance is usually a passive power for me.

Only rarely, under the direst of situations, do I push out with my clairvoyance. When I use it in this manner, I still feel in control, and I am fully confident in what I am doing.

The magic I created on our last trip, I have no clue how I made it—the possibility of me owning a power that powerful scares the tar out of me.

It would also mean, if I accept that I possess the "gift," I'm even further from the "normal" life I so desperately crave. Y'all, I don't want to be a shunned old lady living out in the woods in a double-wide like Nana. I just can't.

"I know. I didn't say I wouldn't, I just said I haven't yet." I swallow hard after the half-lie.

"Thank you."

"For what?"

Liza grins. "For saving my butt with that beautiful blue shield-thing you manifested. I realized this morning I never thanked you."

Her sincere gaze makes me fidget on the bench. I can't take credit for saving Liza—us. It just happened.

Discussing that terrible day at Sloss Furnaces brings the

events of the day rushing to the forefront of my mind. The screams of Montel Bryant as the spirit of Lloyd Smith pulled him into the furnace is a sound I'll never clear from my memory. Two nights this week, I sat up out of a sound sleep swearing I heard Montel's screams in the distance.

"You're welcome." I try to make light of her expression of gratitude. "At least you won't need my super-duper magic for a while since Dusty dragging his feet on finishing the last book puts the kibosh on our research projects."

Liza rolls her eyes. "Dusty waiting until the last minute to deliver the final draft is standard operating procedure. He's never happy until he has Mara foaming at the mouth. I don't think he takes it seriously until she threatens him with bodily harm.

"The show still must go on, though. Miles, Luis, and I get our best future site scouting and culling done while the boss is trapped in his office finishing edits."

None of the team has mentioned this before now. "Like site authentication?"

"Sure. You could call it that. It's the best way to confirm a high probability of documenting a story worth publishing before we go through the expense of a thorough investigation."

I'm not sure why, but my feelings are bruised. If I were smart, I would retire from my paranormal hunting career. It's gotten way too dangerous for me, and it never fails to make my skin crawl.

Even though that is all true, it would have been nice for Dusty to ask if I wanted to be part of this scouting team. I believe I at least earned the right of refusal. "I wonder why Dusty didn't even mention the scout team to me?"

"You're joking. Right?" Liza snorts. "Have you seen yourself?"

I smooth my hair down with my hand. "What?"

"You are moping around like the world has ended. I'm sure Dusty believes you're not mentally up to the rigors yet. Given your compromised state."

"You don't know what you're talking about."

Liza shrugs. "I know it's tough being a woman. And it's tougher being a woman when you can't have the man you want."

I begin to object but hold my tongue. It is true. Liza is the only person who can say that to me without offending me.

"Do you three have anything planned soon?"

Liza narrows her eyes. "We are preparing a scouting trip to a cave up in Kentucky."

I know better; I should disengage from the paranormal world if I want to allow my "gifts" to subside.

This could also be a blessing in disguise for me. I'm so bored all I can think about is Patrick. Lord knows nothing is going on at the law office to distract me. A traipse through a cave listening to bogus stories from a lonely octogenarian museum curator looking for some attention might be what I need to get Patrick off my mind.

I'm putting it together as I go. But mentally, I put another task on my new and improved life plan draft.

I plan to approach Dusty about a position on the site scouting team. If I'm going to put this malaise I have been struggling through behind me, I'll need work, and lots of it, to distract me.

Chapter 6

We load up on Daddy's Whaler and Chase's ski boat as the orange sun dips below the top of the pines and water oaks. My attitude, because of connecting with Liza about the fireworks, continues to improve. I look forward to the event with the same childlike anticipation that usually fills me when it's time to travel into the main channel for the cacophony of noise and color.

I'm torn on leaving Puppy in my room or taking him on the boat. The explosions won't sound as loud in my apartment as they will on the open water. But I also don't want him to be alone in the event he becomes scared.

Being the responsible mommy I try to be, I bring him with me and take the necessary precaution of strapping his float vest on him. He doesn't appear to appreciate the fashion statement. I swear he is pouting.

"It's for your own protection. I don't want anything bad to happen to you." There's no telling what drunk idiot will decide to drive their boat tonight. It's dark out on the water at night. If some maniac crashes into our boat, Puppy will appreciate his safety gear. "You'll understand when you get older."

Puppy gives a short growl that sounds uncannily like a human grumble.

Turning his furry butt to me, Puppy walks across the boat

cushions to plop down next to Granny's thigh. That's gratitude for you.

The boats pull away from the dock, and we ride into the inky darkness. The pace is slower than this morning as other boats are now tiny dots of green and red lights on the black surface against the black night.

Turned crisp and moist, the summer air traces slowly across my skin, caressing goose pimples into existence. I'm ageless. This is how this ride felt when I was seven, seventeen, and now. The same anticipation builds in me—the sense of family and community. Collectivism, as we travel into the darkness toward the center for the spectacle we have faith will awe and delight us.

I lean back, tilting my face to the sky. The moon, a sliver, barely illuminates the silver edges of the high-flying clouds. Through the gaps in their billowing cover, the glitter of stars shine fiercely.

Few things in life hold the same intense magic as they did the first time I experienced them.

I've heard some friends talk about feeling young again when visiting a nationally known theme park with cartoon characters recognized worldwide. They've told me how they can't resist taking a selfie with their favorite childhood heroes despite being in their late twenties.

Other friends say kayaking a river or hiking a trail they did in their youth with their parents can heighten their energy level. They become rejuvenated by the familiar physical challenge, often forgetting they are now much older.

Those unique places all enjoy a common element. For the individual cleaving to a particular memory made in those places, it is part of their identity. It is as if a time portal opens, and age no longer holds meaning.

In your special place, you are just you. You are the essence of you. And you are your happiest, you are at peace, and you are at your best.

The ride out to the fireworks barge each year and the twenty minutes of dizzying explosions and colors are my unique time portal.

I know. All day, I debated whether I would make the trip or not. It was never genuinely in question. The fireworks are too much of a touchstone to my essence for me to purposefully skip.

I will enjoy myself tonight. I'm committed to the goal.

Do I believe I deserve to be happy tonight? Not in the least.

I'm finding it difficult to forgive myself for being a shallow, shortsighted person who humiliated herself. Still, no amount of self-flagellation will correct the past.

My self-loathing is like a boil afflicting my attitude. Tonight, I will lance the negativity I've allowed to fester in my heart. Moving forward is an impossibility without me owning my mistake and forgiving myself.

I do on both counts.

Real life is a lot harder than anyone led on. Or, more likely, I wasn't listening because I didn't want to hear their warnings.

Gazing into the inky dark night, I see an increasing concentration of green and red signal lights as well as a few white cabin lights. The further we move toward the center of the lake, the more lights come into view until it looks like someone has strewn Christmas lights across the lake.

The barges, where the fireworks are prepared for the show, are illuminated by portable road construction lights, making the barges shine like fallen stars floating on the lake.

From our vantage point, it reminds me of a concert stage. We are still back in the cheap seats, and Daddy is working his way through the maze of pontoons and ski boats. We glide by leaving no wake.

We draw near one of the large boats my daddy likes to call a "redneck yacht." Loud music is thumping while people my age and younger dance in bathing trunks and bikinis while balancing red Solo cups in their hands. All I can think is they must be freezing and need to put some clothes on.

One of the boys rushes the railing and doubles over it. I

assume he will yell something lewd at us which is not entirely uncommon. Instead, he projectile vomits his dinner. His regurgitation plummets fourteen feet and makes a sickening slapping sound as it breaks the water's surface. He follows this up with a dry heave, making me cringe.

"Classy!" Mama yells at the sick young man.

He lifts his head up, smiles, and lifts his Solo cup into the air. "You want some, baby!"

Mama waves back at him. "I'm good, but thanks for asking."

He has a moronic amused look plastered on his face as he disappears from our view.

I struggle to contain a giggle. My mama. The only woman I know who can cut a man down and leave him smiling. I've never been able to put my finger on how she manages it. I don't know if the men pay too much attention to her natural beauty instead of what she is saying or if it's her perfect delivery. I hope someday I can emulate her skill.

Daddy cuts the motor, and Wilson drops the anchor for us. Chase floats his ski boat up next to us. Dusty and Miles put the bumpers out and tie the boats together as they drop anchor too.

Chase stands up and waves in my direction. "Hey, Ms. Wanda, Mr. Bruce."

I feel icy fingers climb up my spine as my shoulders creep toward my ears. No. Please, not Ms. Wanda.

Ms. Wanda is the head nurse at Albertville Memorial Hospital. Recently, I accidentally told her a fib. I was scheduled for a charity workday at the women's shelter where she and my mama volunteer. I sort of forgot about my scheduled workday.

I've neglected to get in touch with her to apologize and to reschedule my workday—one more thing on my to-do list that just caught up with me.

Wanda's baritone voice grates over the top of me from behind, "Hi Chase, Dusty, Ralph, Howard, Viv... Is that you, April?"

I turn around and offer her a meek wave. "Hi, Mr. and Mrs.

Neal." I can't stand how that woman makes me feel like a five-year-old child.

"I'm surprised your schedule permitted you time to come out and enjoy yourself tonight, dear." Wanda's voice drips with false honey. "I know how dreadfully busy you are with your career."

"She's actually gotten through that busy patch, Wanda." Okay, Mama still has some maternal instincts. She isn't going to let the big bad wolf devour me.

"That's wonderful to hear. We were talking about repainting the offices a week from Saturday. I know how eager you were to help last time we talked, April."

The statement hangs in the air uncomfortably. Coming from a Southern woman, it isn't a statement as much as a veiled command. Mama remains silent this time. She must be done saving me this evening.

Reluctantly I answer, "Yes, ma'am. That sounds like a wonderful opportunity for me."

"Bullfrog time," Daddy says in Mama's direction.

Mama glares at Daddy and then Howard. "I told you two, not this year."

"You didn't really mean it," Daddy says.

Howard walks to the back of the boat, removing a tarp revealing a twenty-gallon cooler commonly seen on football sidelines on Friday night. "Besides, it's a tradition."

"You boys have always been the worst influences." Mama is scolding, but there is no fire in her voice, and I can see the edges of her lips ticking up.

"Give me one of those, and easy on the ice, son," Granny says as Howard produces our own red Solo cups.

"And the boys obviously didn't fall too far from the tree," Mama continues.

Granny takes the drink from Howard and turns to Mama. "Oh, Vivian, quit trying to act like a stick in the mud. It doesn't suit you."

"She's just doing it because the kids are here," Daddy

grumbles.

Granny takes a long draw from her cup and smacks her lips. "Vivian, they're all adults now. They probably can handle seeing their mama drink, and probably figured out you and Ralph have had sex at least three times, too."

Mama shakes her head as a smile blooms across her face. She motions to Howard with her fingers in a "come here" motion, and he puts a drink in her hand.

That's one thing about Granny. She can just shut a conversation down by going all scorched-earth nuclear.

Uncle Howard can't play barkeep quickly enough for me. I swear I can still feel Wanda Neal's eyes burrowing into the back of my neck.

The first sip clears my sinuses, and I cough. By the third sip, I've grown fond of the lemon-lime burn.

Howard offers bullfrogs to everyone in Chase's boat as well. Dusty and Wilson declare themselves designated captains for our return trip.

Daddy and Chase tune the boat radios to the local station playing patriotic music. Lee Greenwood's familiar voice comes through the boat speakers. By muscle memory, I stand with my family and hold my red Solo cup to the sky while yelling, "I'm proud to be an American," badly off tune.

I feel sorry for any nation that doesn't have a holiday like the Fourth of July. There's nothing quite like hearing all the patriotic songs while you hang out with your family and get ready for the fireworks.

The digital clock on the dash reads nine, and the emcee announces the fireworks are about to be launched. I have a healthy buzz. But it isn't all alcohol. I believe I'm gaining spiritual strength with every passing second.

Let's face it, I'm a strong woman. I've earned my law degree from a prestigious university, am prepared to pass the bar on my first attempt, have dealt with pissed-off homicidal spirits, and am an undefeated homicide defense attorney. You think you can keep me down? Go ahead and kid yourself. I am April

May Snow—I'm an American woman—hear me roar.

The first mortar explodes, filling the sky with a fantastic orange plume. I stand ramrod stiff, watching the orange embers float to the lake surface. I'm ready for anything. I can do anything. Bless it, I feel like I have crazy eyes. This feels awesome!

The blasts come closer and closer together. Multiple mortar explosions rain from the sky—blue, orange, white, red, and purple. Some explosions leave hearts in the night sky. No, it's much too soon for me to enjoy those this year. Smiley faces, those are cool, and ones that explode then trail off making crazy circular motions as they buzz like angry hornets. "America the Beautiful" blares through every boat's speaker.

A gray fog floats out over the surface of the lake. The smell of spent black powder tickles my nose and makes me smile. I love the smell of gunpowder at night.

I lift my Solo cup and find it empty again. Wobbling to the back of the boat, I push down the spigot of the cooler. One more won't hurt.

Pressing the rim of the cup to my lips, I turn as the number of rockets zinging into the air increases to a dizzying pace. Explosions burst within explosions before having time to begin their downward arc toward the lake. "The Star-Spangled Banner" pounds across the water's surface.

The veil of smoke now so dense the light of the explosions refracts in hundreds of different directions. Ten—twenty blooms explode high in the sky simultaneously. There is one continual rumble, pow, and sizzle at a terrific pace for a full minute. The last mortars release their charges as we yell at the top of our lungs, "Land of the free and home of the brave." Our voices reverberate across the lake as the final bloom rains from the sky.

A loud chorus of clapping and yelling rises from the boats as we show our appreciation for yet another spectacular show.

The headlights of cars stopped on either end of Guntersville Bridge turn on. Their drivers steer slowly onto the highway.

Boat motors turn on randomly, and I can make out silhouettes pulling in anchors.

Yes, the celebration that has been special to me my entire life has ended for another year. But it increased in a few brief minutes the strength I'll need to move forward. I have the will, the power, and the ability to do anything I want to do. I'm an American woman. Tell me. What can't I do?

Chapter 7

I hurt so bad this morning. At first, I imagined I was involved in a boating accident and waking up in the hospital. Sitting up, I hang my feet off the edge of the bed. I clutch my head with both hands as it threatens to explode.

Carefully, I open my left eye halfway. My right doesn't seem to be working.

Puppy is sitting on his haunches, watching me with great interest. He doesn't appear pleased. He still has his float vest on.

"What are you looking at?"

He isn't talking to me.

"Don't judge me," I scold as I try to stand up and am forced back onto my mattress.

That's it. I'll have to call in sick. I know it is immature of me, but there is not enough coffee in the world to get me through today.

Considering the rest of my brain cells seem to be concussed, I'm surprised when I remember I'm the only employee at Snow and Associates for the rest of the week. Howard is driving to Mobile today for an extended weekend.

I can't call in sick. If I do, the law office will be closed.

Isn't that just peachy?

Pulling in a deep breath, I push to my feet. I'm making

progress, albeit slowly, toward the shower. See, I'll be good to go in no time.

As I reach my bathroom, a sharp pain stabs my brain, and my stomach roils. I pitch forward, grabbing hold of the porcelain sink.

My word, what was in those bullfrogs? Anti-freeze?

If I can just get a shower. A shower will make me all better for sure.

I turn the water on and wait for it to warm.

This will work. My gut feels on fire and bubbly, but the longer I stand, the better I'm feeling.

With more effort than I believe it should take, I manage to pull off my nightgown. I nearly fall on my keister as I kick free of my panties.

I can do this. I've felt worse and had to do more. All that's required of me to be successful today is driving to the office, sitting, and answering the phone if it rings. That isn't too hard.

The warm water feels refreshing as I allow it to sluice over the back of my head and over my face. Turning, I take in a gulp of water to get the horrible metallic taste out of my mouth.

See, I'm feeling better already. A quick shampoo, pull on a skirt and blouse, and I'll be as good as new. There's a chance I'll even get lucky and snag a cup of coffee if Chase is already awake.

Steam tendrils rise, and I draw the hot, moist air into my lungs. I reach for the soap bar, and my stomach lurches. Oh no. What is that?

My mouth waters profusely as my stomach cramps tighter. No, no, no. I can't be sick. Yet, it seems inevitable. I grab hold of the soap holder to steady myself.

Violent contractions wrack my body as if someone is ripping my spine out through my stomach. Each spasm leaves muscles I didn't even know I had torn and bruised.

Never ever am I drinking again. I know I've said this before, but this time I swear it. This is beyond stupid. How is this fun?

Another convulsion grips my body and leaves me sputtering

the last of the poison, I hope, out of my body. I'm too blessed old for this. Besides, I have responsibilities now. Not the ones I wanted or asked for, but people are counting on me all the same.

I finish the remainder of my shower without further incident. I'm forced to brush my teeth three times to kill the vile taste in my mouth. The mint flavor of the toothpaste threatens to throw me into another spasm, but I catch myself before it triggers.

Wrapping a towel around me, I pad into my living area. Puppy is still glaring at me.

"Come here," I say as I squat to his level.

He snorts, walking as slowly as possible to me.

"Mommy is sorry." I unbuckle his float vest. "I promise I will never do that again. Okay?"

He favors me with a low growl and sits back on his haunches.

He isn't just going to take my word. Puppy plans to make me earn his trust back.

As I pull into my parking space in front of our law office, I've convinced myself I am suffering from a bleeding ulcer. I'm not positive about that, but something in my stomach is shredding my insides, causing me excruciating cramps. I have heard ulcers are painful. So that must be what is wrong with me.

The tummy spasms and burning sensation continue to worm their way further down my digestive tract. I'm trying to block from my mind, unsuccessfully, the scene in *Aliens* where the snake-like baby burst out of Kane's chest.

I unlock the law office, turn on minimal lighting, and sit gingerly at my desk. I don't even turn on my laptop. I need calm and quiet. I must center my Zen to patiently allow my body to recover from the damage I have inflicted.

The phone on my desk rings, disturbing my meditation. I puff out an aggravated breath as I roll my eyes. Of course I can't have a few peaceful minutes to gather my senses.

I look at my cell phone. "It's six forty, people," I say as I snatch the phone from its cradle. "Snow and Associates."

"April, is Howard in?"

"Good morning, DA Jameson. No, Counselor Snow is out of town for the rest of the week."

Lane Jameson is our local District Attorney. He and my uncle are personal friends. Snow and Associates contract with the county to cover overflow from the public defense attorney's office. They always seem to be understaffed.

Lane is serious about his job and mostly a good guy, though he has a narcissistic flair that sticks out like a sore thumb in Guntersville. The entire town notes his propensity to wear expensive tailored linen suits, Fendi loafers, and his perfectly coiffed salt and pepper hair. Lane never is aware that he is an itsy bit overdressed, even for court, in North Alabama.

"Why in the world would he leave the day after the Fourth?"

"I don't make the schedule, sir. I just follow it." Whoops. That was a slip. I blame it on the alien baby I'm about to give birth to.

"Are you okay, April?"

"Yes, sir. Why?"

"I don't know. You sound—grouchy."

Splendid, then my tone matches the way I feel. "Sorry, I was distracted. I came in early to take care of some loose ends."

"I understand. Listen, I know you are shorthanded, but could you be so kind as to cover an arraignment this afternoon?"

Yesterday I would have begged for a case to kill my boredom and self-loathing. That was before the bullfrog massacre that has left me with gut rot. "I suppose. What's the case?"

"Your defendant is Jethro Mullins. He called in a nuisance report on his neighbor last night for loud music. His neighbor is Micah Holland. The police went out to the Whispering Pines trailer park and asked Mr. Holland to turn down his music. Later the music worked its way back up, and Jethro decided to go tell Micah he was going to make him turn it down."

I know where this story is going. If I had a dollar for every time loud music and two numbskulls poking out their chests turns into something violent, I could buy a cute new handbag with matching shoes.

"Micah took Jethro's threat as an invitation to throw the first punch. It was a beauty. Knocked both of Jethro's front teeth out."

"Lane, you said Jethro was my client, not Micah." I'm confused.

"No, that is the odd thing. Jethro refused to press charges. But the reason why was he had his heart set on revenge. It wasn't an hour later that some folks at Micah's house saw a Molotov cocktail flying toward them. It hit one of the pines in front of Micah's trailer."

Bless it. Some boys don't know when to just let it go. "No one was hurt?" I ask.

"Jethro has second-degree burns on his hand, and his trailer went up in flames."

"That's awful—" wait a minute. Lane must not have had his morning coffee since he got the two men confused. "You mean Micah's trailer was destroyed. You said Jethro threw the Molotov, Lane."

"He did. Seems he had some residual gas on his hands when he lit the fuse. Plus, when he threw the bottle, he didn't account for the twenty miles an hour headwind he was dealing with or the bed of dried pine needles between his and Holland's trailer."

I want no part of this three-ring circus. "This is a joke, right."

Lane snorts. "I wish. Can you cover for me? We're slammed. All the public defenders are already carrying a full load plus."

"Do I have a choice?"

"Not really. It would be Monday before I could hope to free up counsel for him. Which would mean I'm forced to let him out temporarily. You wouldn't want that on your conscience, would you?"

"What, that he accidentally sets himself on fire while he is out and kindly removes himself from the gene pool?"

"Cute. See, I told you that you are grouchy this morning."

"Quit saying I'm grouchy!" I just don't do stupid well. It makes my head hurt, and the men in this town excel at being morons. "Is he in the city jurisdiction?"

"Yes."

"Who was the arresting officer?" I ask.

"Jacob Hurley."

There is my silver lining. At least I'll be able to get the straight scoop from Jacob. "Okay. I'll give you an update before and after the arraignment."

"Thank you, April."

So much for restful healing. I scan the clock on my phone to determine if Jacob will already be asleep since he worked the shift last night. Doesn't matter; he can tell me to bug off if he is sleeping. I press his speed dial number.

"Hello?" Jacob's voice is thick.

He has been sleeping. I decide to press forward anyway. "Hey, what are you wearing?"

There is a pause, the phone on the other end of the line is dropped, and I hear a grunt, "Umm ... at the moment Thor boxer briefs."

The visual popping into my head makes me giggle. "Oh, is that your favorite superhero?"

Jacob, fully recovered now, responds in his characteristically slow drawl, "Nah. I'm partial to Wolverine. But I do carry a big hammer like Thor."

Oh my. I don't have anything for that, and I just had a hot flash. It serves me right.

A deep, ultra-sexy laugh fills my ear. "I'm catching on to your silly games, girl. I got you. Admit it."

Yes, you did. "I don't know what you're talking about, Jacob Hurley."

He laughs again, and I swear I'm going to melt. "Alright then. What do you need? I know you didn't call for an underwear check."

Oh right. "I was told you were the arresting officer on the Mullins case last night."

"Yeah. Another case of two hotheads meeting in the night."

"Mullins has his arraignment today. Is there anything I should know?" I ask.

"Absolutely. Keep him away from matches."

"Seriously? Not funny."

"No, all kidding aside, I was surprised by both of them. Micah and Jethro have lived next to each other for five years, and there's never been any trouble between them before last night. They're both good dudes. Other than the usual speeding tickets and I believe one drunken disorderly on Holland, they're only normal working guys."

"That knock each other's teeth out and try to burn each other out of their homes."

"And then there's that. Jethro should have let me take Micah in after Micah knocked his teeth out. That vigilante stuff is just bad karma all the way around."

"That's it?" I ask. "Two good ole boys getting sideways with each other?"

"I'm afraid so. If I thought there was anything else, I would tell you. But it's just a case of things getting ramped up until they are out of control."

"I understand. I appreciate you sharing the info. I'm sorry I woke you."

"No worries. Oh, April?"

"Yes?"

"I'm actually not wearing anything," Jacob laughs again as my face flushes with a rush of heat. "Have a good day." The line goes dead.

I have a hangover, and now I've got these perverted visuals of my best friend nude in bed. Today must be some cosmic test to see how much April can handle.

The front door opens, and a tall, middle-aged blonde wearing sunglasses with lenses resembling bumble bee eyes strolls into the office.

You have got to be kidding me. We're not even supposed to be open yet. "Can I help you?"

"I certainly hope so." She tosses a fretful glance over her shoulder.

Concerned, I follow her line of sight to see if someone dangerous followed her into the office.

"First, I must know if your firm practices strict confidentiality protocol."

What the heck? "With our clients," I respond.

She stares at me, motionless through her bug-eyed sunglasses. Her lips, which resemble two pink tractor tires laid on top of one another, purse as if she has recently smelled something quite offensive.

I become uncomfortable and decide to explain myself. "You're not presently a client of ours. If you were to say something incriminating, I would have to report it just like any other witness."

"Why would I incriminate myself?" She pushes her chin into the ample loose skin of her neck as she asks the question.

Oh boy. I have a live one here. "Hopefully, you wouldn't. I was just making sure you understood."

She stands frozen in front of my desk as we stare at one another once again, my visitor through her bug-eyed sunglasses and me through bloodshot eyes I'm sure I have. It occurs to me we are playing some game of verbal chicken and the first one to speak loses the game. Personally, I feel it is a tedious game and decide to put an end to it.

"Is there something I can help you with?"

She sighs heavily while tilting her head. "I suppose."

"Since it's customary to start with names. I'm April Snow, and you are—"

The woman snatches her sunglasses off and glares at me. "You don't know who I am?"

Besides unbalanced and scary? "No, ma'am, I'm afraid I don't."

"Savanna Tate."

I'm not clear if she is asking me or telling me. "Okay, Ms. Tate. Now, what can I do for you?"

"'*Loves of our Lives*?'"

"Excuse me?" Yes, siree. That migraine is coming on strong. I rub my right temple as I consider why she threw out what sounds like a random title for a romance.

"The afternoon women's series I star in."

Ha, so I hadn't killed all my brain cells. I guessed it was an overly obvious soap opera title. I've never heard of the show before now. But why was she—oh. "You're a soap opera actress."

Savanna's too-tight face screws up violently. "You have some nerve. I'm a serious actress."

Any other day I might be able to get some amusement out of this conversation, but my head hurts too much. "So, Ms. Tate, now that we have your occupation clarified, why are you here today?"

"Indeed. My neighbor has been taking photos of me."

"Without your permission?"

"Of course, without my permission!"

After the Crystal Raley case, where she was teasing her neighbor by exposing her lady parts, I believe it a valid question.

Savanna points toward the front door. "And those worthless police officers won't do a darn thing about it. Then they told me to see if you might be able to help with a case against him."

"You want a restraining order against your neighbor?" I ask incredulously.

She stomps her foot. "No! I want him to rot in jail."

Fair. We all want things. I want Savanna to turn around and leave. But that's not happening, either. "Ms. Tate, has your neighbor posted pictures of you on the Internet?"

"Heavens no." She lays a hand across her chest.

I narrow my eyes as the pain of a starburst migraine slams the back of my skull. "So, you know he's taking pictures because—what?"

Savanna puts her hands on my desk and leans close to whisper, "Because I see him watching me."

Oh boy. I didn't realize Bryce Mental Hospital was giving day passes again. "All right, Ms. Tate, the first order of business will be to set up the restraining order. That way, if your neighbor comes on your property, you can call the police and they will arrest him.

"I'm going to go ahead and warn you it's problematic with him being your neighbor. You can't just arrest somebody for looking in your direction."

"Why not?"

"I don't know, I guess because it's not against the law?"

"It should be against the law."

"I'm not arguing with you, ma'am. But if you really think it needs to be a law, that would be something to take up with your state representative. They make the laws in Alabama. Not me."

Ms. Tate finally agrees to place a limited restraining order on her neighbor.

I promise her I will have it written up and filed by the end of business tomorrow.

Something in my gut tells me Snow and Associates should have passed on those five hundred dollars of income.

Chapter 8

At nine thirty, I put our "Temporarily Out" sign on the front door and walk the block to the city jail.

My legs are working fine now. The bright sun on my face is quite refreshing. My stomach? It still feels like I sucked down a bottle of pepper sauce that can't decide if it wants to come up or go down.

As bad as I feel, I can't help but smile when I see the extra healthy girl behind the jail reception area. "Jade, are you keeping them straight today?" I joke.

"Only the ones that'll listen. The rest, I just play like they're field mice, and I'm Little Bunny Foo Foo"—she slams a meaty fist into the palm of her hand as she flashes her white smile —"and I'm boppin' them on the head."

It's a struggle to hold my gentile smile. As fond as I am of Jade, her enthusiasm scares me. "I suppose somebody's got to train them since their mama didn't."

"You got that right."

By female standards, I run on the tall side. Jade is a head taller than me and is twice as broad. She also has this look when she's aggravated that makes me want to wet my pants.

For that reason, she is a natural for jail keep. There is never any trouble on her shift.

"Which one of my bad boys do you need to see today?"

"I'm here to see Jethro Mullins."

Jade pushes off the counter she's leaning against and pulls her pants up. "That boy is the opposite of bad. He's just sad"—she raises her hands—"comes in with his hands all burnt up, missing his front teeth like he's living on the street. All the while, he's crying that they're locking up the wrong man."

Yep. That sounds like the client Lane described to me. "That's him."

"All right. Give me a few minutes, and I'll set you up in room two."

"Thank you, Jade."

I enter room two. Jethro is wearing ankle chains, and his wrists are handcuffed to the table. I'm all for safety, but it seems excessive since Jethro might be five foot five with high-heeled cowboy boots on, and he weighs in at a hundred and twenty-five pounds.

If he were to start anything, I believe I could wipe the floor with Jethro and not break a sweat. I've been wrestling brothers twice his size my entire life.

"Hi, Jethro, I'm your court-appointed attorney, April Snow."

"I didn't do it."

I rock back in my seat. I had noticed the busted lip, but the gap where Jethro's two front teeth used to be catches me off guard despite my prior knowledge.

"Fortunate for us, we don't have to worry about proving your innocence today. This is your preliminary trial. The judge will hear mostly from the DA and then make a decision if there is enough evidence to try you."

"Try me for what?"

"My guess would be reckless endangerment," I say in my most patient voice. After all, he could be concussed from Micah's punch.

"I don't know what you're talking about." He leans back, his chin jutting up.

I take a closer look at his bandaged hands and his busted lip. "A disagreement with your neighbor? Does that ring a bell?"

"Nope."

Okay, denial is the first stage of grief. Denying reality is also a particular variety of insanity. I can't get a solid read on which case accurately describes Jethro.

It is essential, too. A grieving client is a lot easier to defend than an insane client.

I'm not feeling charitable, but I muster enough professionalism to slow the process down. I match Jethro's nonchalant mannerism and slouch in my chair. "How about you just tell me what happened last night, Jethro?"

"The whole night?"

"You can if you want. But at least start with what was going on when you made the first call to the police."

Unbelievably, he appears ready to deny placing the call to the police. But he clamps his mouth shut and peers down as if he plans to keep his own counsel.

"Jethro, do you understand I am your court-appointed defense attorney?"

His features draw together as if I asked him to solve the quadratic equation.

"Do you understand that means I work for you? I am trying to help you stay out of jail or at the very least keep your sentencing to as short of a time as possible."

"But you work for the government."

I shrug my shoulders. "The government will send me a check, but I work for you."

He measures me with his eyes. He still has severe reservations.

"Of course, if you checked your last paycheck, I bet it looks like you work for the government, too. That big old reach around they call taxes?"

Jethro's brow furrows as he stares at me. He lets out a

startling bark of laughter. "Dang straight."

Yep. Crazy. But I've dealt with enough conspiracy theorists from both sides of the fence to be able to navigate these waters comfortably.

"So why don't you go ahead and tell me about last night." I lift the printout of what Lane emailed earlier. "I already have the police account. I want your version of last night."

He bobs his head in agreement. "I guess I have to go back to the start of it all so you can understand last night."

Please, Lord. I'm not a psychiatrist. If he goes back to his childhood, I might hurt myself. "Go back as far as you need to, Jethro."

He grins and bobs his head again. "See, there's this woman. Ruth. She told me three years ago she couldn't stay with a man who partook of spirits. Now I hope you don't think ill of me, but I used to enjoy going by Jester's and having me a couple of two fingers of whiskey. Just blowing off some steam, if you get my drift. But Ruth, she wasn't having none of it."

I'm having one of those moments. Where I'm listening to someone and making excellent eye contact with them. Still, I'm worried to death my eyes will appear glazed over or suddenly cross. The struggle not to bang my head on the table out of frustration is real.

"But I love Ruth. I'd do anything for that woman. For her, three years ago, I gave up spirits altogether."

"That's a huge commitment, Jethro. It's difficult for some people to give up alcohol altogether."

Jethro favors me a "have you lost your mind" glare. "I said spirits. I didn't give up beer."

"Oh, of course not." How stupid of me.

His eyes drop to his chained wrists on the table. His features darken as his busted lip trembles. He looks up, and tears are welling in his eyes. "Then I lost Ruth Saturday."

Oh, Lord. How callous of me to be calling this man crazy. Who wouldn't be acting insane if the love of their life died just a few days earlier?

Here I am struggling to get over Pat, and he didn't die. I just decided our relationship wouldn't work out.

Jethro sounds as if he was honestly in love with Ruth. No wonder he was on edge and got into a fight with Micah Holland. In my experience, men are always doing stupid things when they lose purpose in their life.

"I'm so sorry, Jethro. When is the funeral? I want to make sure that the judge takes that into consideration," I say.

"Funeral, who said anything about a funeral?"

"You're having her cremated?"

His head jerks back so severely his chin rests on his chest. "What are you talking about?"

"Ruth. You said you lost her Saturday."

"At the flea market! Geez, what's the matter with you, lady? Talking about burning people up."

The irony that he threw a Molotov cocktail, cooked his hands, and burnt down his trailer is lost on Jethro. The absurdity of it all is not lost on me.

Knowing it is my responsibility to mitigate the consequences of Jethro's poor judgment brings on another wave of starburst pains at the back of my neck. I press the palm of my hand at the base of my neck, which sometimes helps alleviate the worst of the pain.

"Are you okay.? You look sorta green." Jethro's eyebrows pull together.

"Yeah, I'll be fine. Please continue."

Jethro rubs the back of his neck, mirroring my motion. "Like I said, I lost Ruth. It's not the first time she's disappeared while we're at the flea market. She tells me that sometimes she just needs alone time."

Presently, I can empathize with Ruth on that point.

"Then usually she finds me before I leave. But this time, she doesn't. No Ruth that night or the next evening." He shrugs as his eyes open wider. "Five days later, still no Ruth."

His ability to wait five days before becoming overly concerned, while mildly interesting, is not relative to our case.

Still, I understand we'll have to talk it through before dealing with the pertinent details of the case.

"Jethro, have you filed a missing person report or at least a BOLO with the police yet?"

"She's not missing. Her car is over at her sister Sarah's house."

I now realize Jethro is a card-carrying member of the "can't take a hint" club.

"I kept calling Ruth's phone, but she wouldn't answer. When I seen she was at her sister's house, I gave Sarah a call. Sarah told me not to fret, but Ruth wasn't ready to come home yet. I figured I'd give her some room.

"But by the time Independence Day came around, I got angry. Explain to me, if she's a no-show at the house, why do I have to keep my promise about staying away from spirits?"

I favor Jethro a nod. It sounds like astute logic to me.

"I headed on down to Lakeside Liquors and told Ahmir to hook me up with a liter of whiskey."

"Jethro, would it be safe to say you were drunk at the time everything became heated with Micah?"

He shakes his head fervently. "No. If I were drunk, the loud music wouldn't have mattered. I would've just walked down there and had a good time with him.

"Micah is all right most time. He's a UT football fan, which is odd, but I don't have nothing against him outside of that.

"The problem was I was sad because Ruth wasn't home. Plus, I had an awful headache and felt sick to my stomach from having drunk that liter of spirits that afternoon. That loud techno music Micah had on was drilling a hole in my head."

"What time did you start drinking?"

Jethro looks up at the ceiling as if the time were written on the drop-in ceiling tiles. "Let's see, Ahmir opens up at eight—I'd say about ten after eight that morning."

He frowns. "I don't know if you've ever been on the downside of a spirits binge, but it leaves you on the cranky side."

I give Jethro another reassuring nod. I feel his pain and am full of empathy.

"As mean as I felt, I knew if I went down to Micah's, I'd get in a fight. So, I did the responsible thing and called the po po."

He stops and seems to consider the rest of his story. "I think Micah did turn the music down, but before long, it was as loud as it could be again.

"You know Micah can disrespect me by playing his loud music, but he doesn't have the right to disrespect the police. People have to understand, you got to respect the law. Tell me I'm not right?"

I'm sitting across from a man who is minus his front teeth, chained to a table, charged with the attempted arson of his neighbor's home. He is explaining to me his neighbor doesn't have the prerequisite respect for law enforcement. I live in a special kind of hypocritical lunatic land. I smile pleasantly as I fight my overwhelming desire to leave.

"It was up to me. Somebody had to teach Micah some respect for the law. I marched down to his trailer and told him to turn that music off and send everyone home, or I would kick his butt. Then he hauled off and popped me in the mouth." Jethro said the last with indulgent indignation.

"Why didn't you have the police take him in when you called them the second time?" I ask.

"I didn't call them. Micah did."

I'm wondering what's the best plea deal I can get Lane to offer. I'm sure he will press for jail time. If Lane is feeling charitable, possibly he'll offer a probation deal. We best make that extended probation with a hundred hours of anger management training. We'll throw in a contingency for required couple's counseling if Ruth decides to take him back.

That sounds reasonable to me.

"You see, they shouldn't have arrested me."

I snort. "What about the firebomb?"

"I don't know nothing about no firebomb."

My jaw drops open. I stare at Jethro for effect. "Are you for real? You're going to feed me that line?"

"I keep hearing everyone talking about a firebomb, but I didn't see nothing."

I point at Jethro's hands. "How did your hands get burned? Your trailer? I understand it was a total loss."

His eyes widen. "I know. Crazy, isn't it? I go to sleep and, the next thing I know, my house is on fire."

Now he's getting under my skin. Liars, thieves, and cheats. Things I just can't abide by.

"I can't help you if you don't help me, Jethro."

"What do you mean?"

I stand, making a point to gather my folders and tap them loudly on the table to straighten them. "Our relationship has to be built on trust. You will not lie to me, Jethro."

"I'm not lying to you. My mouth hurt, I got some ice, I laid down on my bed to go to sleep—"

I raise my eyebrows and give him my best "I'm about to slap you out of your chair" glare.

He stops in midsentence, his mouth open. He exhales in defeat. "I don't know what got into me. To be honest, I'm glad the wind blew it back in my direction. I would have been tore up if I burned Micah's house down. Or worse, gotten someone hurt."

"Okay. That's sensible. We all make mistakes. For most of us, nothing as drastic as burning our house down and being arrested, but errors in judgment are a part of life. And you are correct. You being the only person injured by your poor decision should lessen the prosecution's resolve to sentence you to an extended sentence."

Jethro sighs. His expression relaxes. "Thanks."

I want to tell him he's welcome, but he smiles. I'm forced to look away. I don't care to embarrass both of us by laughing at the gap where his teeth used to reside.

Chapter 9

Jethro and I continue our conversation for another twenty minutes discussing his past relationship with his neighbor, Micah. It is a long shot. Still, Micah called the police after he hit Jethro. That could have landed him in jail rather than Jethro. I hope he has a soft spot for his neighbor and understands why he was agitated.

If Micah would be a character witness for Jethro, it could work to defuse the charges.

It's a big ask, but stranger things have happened. Without Micah's assistance, the best we can hope for is a charitable plea bargain from Lane. Frankly, we don't have any leverage. I'm sure we are looking at jail time if this goes to court.

The arraignment shouldn't be an issue today since Jethro doesn't have any prior felonies. Bail should be set at a reasonable rate. That should give me time to untangle this ball of yarn.

As Jade leads me down the corridor toward the exit, I notice my gnawing hunger pain. Given my gut-wrenching morning shower, I would have thought it would be at least a day before I wanted anything to eat other than saltine crackers.

On autopilot, I find myself at the entrance to Jerry's Deli. I hesitate at the door. The last thing I need to chance a queasy stomach on is a huge Italian sub or a Rueben.

Remembering Jerry's also offers a limited soup selection, I grin and pull the door open.

Staring at the soup selection for the day, I'm not grinning anymore. I know better than to order the mystery meat vegetable soup. That leaves me with broccoli cheese, the safe bet except for the odd greenish tint or the spicy hot gumbo I am craving.

If I'm willing to chance my delicate stomach on a bowl of gumbo, I might as well go whole hog and order that yummy Philly cheesesteak I'm eyeing. Bless it. If my paranormal abilities don't end me, my eating habits surely will.

The irony isn't lost on me. I've spent fifteen minutes trying to decide between two types of soup and a sandwich. A week from now, I will be hard-pressed to remember which one I ate.

In contrast, it didn't take me fifteen seconds to decide to walk out on Patrick once I met his son Robert. I feel I should have apologized to Robert too, but my call to Patrick was awkward enough. Besides, hopefully, Robert has already forgotten about the crazy lady who ran out of his house.

If I ever change my mind about being part of a ready-made family, I can't even broach the subject with Patrick. How can I expect him to believe me if I were to say, "Oh, I would love to be your son's second mom, Patrick."

Nothing quite shows you care like fleeing from the first sight of your love interest's adorable mini-me.

"Stay away from the meatball sandwich. There have been reports of a pack of neutered dogs stalking around town."

I know the voice before I turn, "Does your girlfriend have a contract with Jerry's now?"

"Now that is just wrong."

Randy Leath and I dated for a few months back in high school. Before his present fiancée and my nemesis, Jackie Rains, stole him away from me while Randy and I were "taking a break."

I like Randy, but our relationship never would've worked long term. I still hate Jackie for stabbing me in the back, though.

Jackie is taking over the vet clinic in town from Doc Tanner. Hence the joke about male dogs missing body parts.

"Good to see you, Randy. I'm surprised Jackie let you off your leash."

Randy slaps his thigh. "Oh! Ha ha, you're killing it, April. Instead of aiming for the circuit court, you should be on the comedy circuit."

"Whatever." I don't care to argue with Randy. I do want to snatch his girlfriend baldheaded, but I don't have anything against him.

"Did your family have that big Fourth of July shindig they normally do?" Randy asks.

"Yes."

"Did you go out to the lake for the fireworks?"

"Yes."

"How's the job hunting going?"

I shove my fists onto my hips. "Aren't you concerned about talking to me?"

Randy appears shocked. "Why?"

"Because your girlfriend hates me."

"No, she doesn't."

Men can be so dense at times. "Listen, I'm sure she's not gonna come right out and tell you this, but that's where she and I are."

He shakes his head while keeping the silly grin plastered on his face. "Y'all were best friends in high school."

"*Were* being the operative word. As in past tense."

"No, we all live in this town. We need to get along. Jackie knows that, and I'm surprised you don't."

Fine. "I heard you are engaged. When is the date?"

Randy lights up like a thousand-watt lightbulb, "September twenty-first."

"Just around the corner, congratulations."

"Thanks, I'm really excited about it."

"Have you sent out invitations?"

He smiles even broader. “We did. We sent them out about four weeks back. They were so cool. Jackie’s mama did this calligraphy thing on the envelopes. They were really fancy.”

“Sounds like it, Randy. I wish I had seen it.”

He gives a nervous chuckle. “You didn’t open it?”

"I didn’t get one, Randy.”

“But you are on my list.” His brow furrows. “It must have gotten lost in the mail.”

I’m looking at Randy and thinking about Jethro. Is it a good or bad thing men are so blind when they are in love with a woman? I suppose it depends on if you are anyone other than the woman who is the object of their affection. The point of view in these situations is everything.

The line moves forward, and I leave Randy contemplating the mystery of my missing wedding invitation as I play it safe and order the broccoli cheese soup.

Chapter 10

Drawing Judge Isaac Phillips is less than ideal for Jethro's case. Where Judge Rossi has a soft spot for the opposite sex's wayward ways, Phillips is a hard lesson, Old Testament bible-thumping disciplinarian. His theory seems to be if you make the punishment twice the value of committing the crime, you can stamp out the evil in the world.

Lane takes mercy on Jethro. He doesn't use his usual colorful and flamboyant statements about the transgressions of the defendant. Instead, he shares the bare minimum of facts. There was an altercation, and eight citizens witnessed Jethro throw the Molotov cocktail at the Holland residence.

Looking at my client, I wonder how you can't have mercy on him. Whether it's the indent of his front lip where his teeth used to be, his chained burnt hands, or how the oversized orange prison jumper swallows him whole, Jethro is the perfect cover model for a novel titled *Remorse*.

Judge Phillips shifts his small dark eyes to me, "Counselor Snow, is there anything District Attorney Jameson said that you disagree with? Or are there extenuating circumstances you believe might persuade me not to continue to trial with this case?"

I stand. "Your Honor, I would like to present to the court that my client was under a tremendous amount of stress at the time of the incident. His wife had recently abandoned him with no explanation."

An uneasy silence hangs in the courtroom. I get the idea Judge Phillips is waiting for me to finish my point. A point I thought I had already made.

"Counselor Snow, the law of these United States of America is built on exactness. Where exactness does not exist creates the need for higher courts to decide what people mean when they speak. Would you say this is an efficient or inefficient manner of dispensing justice?"

I have no idea what this old coot is talking about. "Inefficient?"

"Exactly. When we fail to communicate clearly and concisely, we leave matters open for interpretation. Topics that must be interpreted by other people who have paradigms quite different from our own.

"Case in point, you report your client's wife has left him. Very well. Enlighten me, counselor. Is there a statute whereby if a man's wife abandons him, he is excused from liability or criminal conviction when he does his neighbor bodily harm?"

"No, sir."

Judge Phillip's beady eyes flatten as he leans forward. "So why, pray tell, are you bringing up this man's marital status? I am certainly pleased as punch that it's a sunshiny day outside, and I certainly like pastrami sandwiches. Still, I'm not wasting your time with these details, Counselor Snow. Do you know why?"

I pause, hoping it's a rhetorical question. It's not. "You don't like to share?"

The judge releases a sigh that lasts an impossible length of time. "No. I don't *share* those details due to the fact they have zero relevance to the case. As does your client's marital status."

"Yes, sir." I'm so angry Lane didn't offer a plea bargain before the arraignment.

"I understand you are a first-year attorney, Counselor Snow. I believe it is incumbent on the more seasoned legal professionals to instruct our newer members on how best to effectively argue cases.

"Now that we have relativity covered, I'd like to ask you again. Do you have any information that would benefit your client before the trial?"

I know I am being dismissed and realize the prudent course of action is to take a seat. The judge's decision was determined before we set foot in his courtroom. Still, I'm compelled to verbalize a weak defense for Jethro's inexcusable actions. I don't want to appear like a total loser. "He's very remorseful that it happened, your honor."

Judge Phillips shares a grin that chills my spine. "Counselor, do you know why it is safe for me to assume every defendant who appears in my court is full of remorse?"

I hold my tongue for once. This is the correct decision since this question does prove to be rhetorical.

"Because every one of them is remorseful they were caught." He wags his finger at me. "Go on and sit down if you don't have anything better prepared for the defense of your client."

Now I'm irate. I'm not sure what makes me angrier. That Lane requested me to handle Jethro's case on short notice or Judge Phillips dressed me down for not having a suitable defense for Jethro's indefensible action.

I scowl at Lane, giving him the well-deserved evil eye.

In response, Lane holds up a finger to signal we will discuss the matter as soon as we are done with "King Solomon's" court.

"Mr. Mullins, will you please stand, sir?"

Jethro's eyes dart to me. I attempt a poorly executed reassuring smile.

Judge Phillips takes his time appraising Jethro, "I see your hands are bandaged, son. Are you preparing for a boxing match, or are you injured?"

"I'm burned," Jethro mumbles.

"You're what? Speak up. I can't hear you."

Jethro stands at attention stretching his five-foot-five height to its maximum. "I said I'm burned, sir."

"Burned, you say?" the judge rests his chin on his teepee hands. "That brings to mind a verse from the good book. 'It shall be that the one who is taken with the things under the ban shall be burned with fire, he and all that belongs to him, because he has transgressed the covenant of the Lord, and because he has committed a disgraceful thing.' Does that verse mean anything to you, son?"

Jethro rocks from one foot to the other. "That I've done a bad thing?"

Judge Phillips chuckles. No mirth reaches his eyes. "That's right, son. That's right. You've done a *bad thing*. You can take a seat now."

The room remains eerily quiet. Judge Phillips scans from Lane to me, then back to Lane.

"My assistant will enter a court date on the docket as there is ample reason to move forward and ensure the laws of the great state of Alabama are enforced. I set bail at five thousand dollars. With the condition, if the defendant posts bail, he must notify the authorities of the address he will reside at pretrial.

"Given he recently destroyed his permanent residence." Judge Phillips lifts his gavel high in the air and slams it solidly against the sounding block. "Adjourned."

"Jethro, I'll need Ruth and Sarah's number. I want to make sure they know how to bail you out."

He won't look me in the eye.

"Are you okay, Jethro?"

"Is the judge saying I'm going to hell?"

"What?" A shiver runs up my spine.

"He said I would be burned with fire and all that belongs to me."

I make to grab his hand but pull back before I touch his burns. "No! That is not at all what he was saying, Jethro. He said the fact you got burned and everything you own was destroyed when your trailer caught fire reminded him of that verse. It has nothing to do with your situation. It has to do with people not following the laws of God."

"Are you sure?"

I'm sure it's Joshua 7:15. I was a superstar in summer Bible school until I hit high school.

And I'm also fibbing because Judge Phillips piling on right now is less than helpful.

"I'm positive. But what you need to be concerned with is giving me those phone numbers. I don't want you sitting in jail and cooking up any new guilt trips to give yourself. You've got enough serious issues, like no place to live. The last thing you need to be worrying about is what Judge Holier Than Thou wants to tie around your neck."

Jethro's jaw drops open. "Oh man! Ruth is going to be so mad everything is burnt up."

Yes, that is a high probability bet. "Jethro, if she can't just be happy you're alive, and you still love her, I feel you two have other things you may need to discuss."

Jethro jots Sarah's number on my yellow legal pad. The bailiff cuffs him. As they walk to the back exit, I say to his back, "It'll all be okay, Jethro."

I hope that's not a lie.

The heels of my red polka dot sandals make a wicked clicking noise on the gray marble as I walk through the oak double doors into the hallway. I raise my eyebrows as I come at Lane waiting in the hallway.

"You could've at least warned me about Judge Phillips."

Lane holds both hands palm out. "You are one hundred percent correct. I have no excuse. You did me a favor. The least I could've done was warn you about his quirks. I'm sorry. It totally slipped my mind that you had not been in his court before."

His sincerity disarms my fury. A humble Lane looks entirely different from the ordinarily arrogant Lane. It short circuits my brain as I try to reconcile the dramatic change in his physical appearance.

"Let me make it up to you? Let me buy you dinner tonight?"

I can't help my reaction. I step back, tilting my head as my lips tighten in exasperation.

"A simple business dinner, Counselor. If it makes you uncomfortable, I understand, and I will find some other way to show my appreciation for the favor and apologize for my gross oversight."

Now I feel ludicrous. I'm acting like I need to guard my femininity like it's Fort Knox because every man obviously wants me. "No, that actually sounds pleasant."

"Great. Can you meet me at Black Angus around seven?"

Black Angus is definitely a date restaurant. Besides, it still has Patrick memories attached to it. "Let's go to Rex's instead."

Lane looks like I asked him to eat colored modeling clay. "Rex's?"

"Don't wrinkle your face like that, mister. It's fried chicken night. You do eat fried chicken, don't you?"

"Yeah." His voice falters.

Lane probably eats fried chicken with a fork and knife.

Chapter 11

I lock up the law office early and don't feel the slightest bit of guilt over it. Seeing as I have the excuse of a business dinner tonight and will also be working on Savanna Tate's restraining order until I fall asleep. Howard better be prepared to come off some serious overtime pay when he returns.

Walking to my apartment, I spy Daddy sitting in a lawn chair on the dock. Puppy is sitting in front of him, watching as if Daddy is the most exciting subject in the universe.

I have a few moments to spare before getting ready for my business dinner, so I walk down to visit with them. I squeeze Daddy's shoulder and plop down in a lawn chair catty-corner to him. I do a double take at the unusual sight of a cigar in his hand.

"Does Mama know you're smoking that?"

He cuts his eyes sideways to me before directing his attention back out to the lake. "Your mama and I have an agreement."

"What sort of agreement?"

"I pretend I don't smoke cigars, and she pretends she doesn't know I smoke cigars."

"So, how's that working out for y'all?"

He takes a dramatically long drag on the cigar holds the smoke in his mouth. I become suspicious of what species of "tobacco" he is smoking.

"Surprisingly well."

Puppy's body is quivering, and he shakes side to side as he continues his vigil of staring at Daddy. He lets out a low whimper of impatience.

In response, Daddy bends over and blows a white puff of smoke into Puppy's face. Puppy snaps at the smoke and growls.

"Stop it. You'll give him cancer from second-hand smoke," I complain.

Daddy chuckles. "That dog is too tough to catch cancer."

I'm convinced if Puppy were human, he would be a Navy SEAL. He is already proficient in demolition; all you have to do is look at my apartment to prove his destructive capabilities.

"How's the job hunting going?" Daddy asks.

"Are you that eager to get rid of me?"

"No. It makes no difference to me one way or the other. But I have gotten used to Bear here, and I might want to get me a dog when you head out to New York or LA or wherever it is you think you have to go."

"Bear?"

Daddy points at Puppy. "He looks like a bear, doesn't he? Besides, you Alabama fans are always naming your dog something stupid like Bama or Crimson, so Bear is as good a name as any for an Alabama alum's pooch."

"I'm not naming my dog Bear."

Daddy takes another drag off his cigar. "I guess you could call him Nick, but I still say he looks more like a Bear. He's too tall for a Nick."

"You can't just up and decide to name my dog, Daddy."

"I didn't name him. I asked him." Daddy leans forward again, blowing another puff of smoke at Puppy.

Puppy snaps at the white billowing cloud.

"Do you like the name Bear?" Daddy asks.

Puppy wags his tail, yaps once, and spins twice in a circle.

"See?"

Whatever. I'll just have to show the "canine whisperer"

that Puppy will bark to any question. He's simply excited that Daddy is talking to him. He's excitable like that.

I squat to his level and coax, "You like the name Puppy, don't you?"

Puppy gives a low grumble and turns his back on me as he develops a renewed interest in the lake.

"I don't appreciate you turning my dog on me."

Daddy laughs. "That dog loves you. He just doesn't appreciate the name you gave him."

The three of us sit in companionable silence and watch the slight ripples on the lake surface caused by the summer breeze. The sun setting lowers the temperature causing the hairs on my arm to stand.

"You didn't answer my question. Have you got any leads?"

"I had an interview last week. But it ended up not being what I was wanting. I have to be honest, Daddy. I got the offer from Master, Lloyd, and Johnson so easily coming out of Alabama that I never thought it would be this hard to find another position."

He sighs, slouching lower in his chair. Daddy points out across the water. "You see that sunset there?"

It would be impossible to miss. Salmon, fuchsia, and pastel pink streaked with bruised purple, it's a natural work of art. "Beautiful."

"Back in the prehistoric days, when I was just a boy, I always knew I would sit on my dock and watch sunsets like this. That was always my goal besides convincing your mama to marry me.

"But you know, as much as I wanted it, and as hard as I focused on it, we didn't get this place right away. There were a few lake properties we almost bought after we married. But if we had, we would've spent too much money.

"Then one day, this property came available, and it was everything we wanted. We knew it was where we would raise our boys and daughter."

He flashes me a dopey smile. "And they all lived happily

ever after. The end." He laughs as if he has just delivered the punchline of the century before taking another puff off his cigar and blowing a perfectly formed smoke ring.

"I'm not looking for a lake house, Daddy. I'm just looking for an opportunity."

"I know, baby. All I'm saying is all things in due time. If the door is not opening for you right now, take heart. Maybe the right job is not available just yet." He shrugs. "Or perhaps you're learning something right now about yourself that you'll need later in life. Some critical information you can't learn far away in Boston or San Francisco."

It is sweet of Daddy to try and make me feel better about my train wreck career. But the fact remains, I need to hurry up and leave Guntersville. The longer I stay, the higher the chance I get "sticky feet" and end up being a lifetime resident. I have dreams of grandeur that can only be accomplished in a big city, and I'm not prepared to give them up just yet.

"That reminds me. I've got a business dinner tonight that I need to get ready for." I point to Puppy. "Do you want me to take him to my apartment?"

Daddy shakes his head. "No. He's fine where he is for now. We might go for a walk along the lake before we lose the light. He enjoys our walks."

"Thank you for babysitting him for me."

"Thank you for sharing the sunset with me."

My daddy is one of the sweetest men I know. I lean over his shoulder and give him a kiss on the cheek. "Have a good night."

Chapter 12

I see Lane waiting for me outside of Rex's when I pull up. He has changed into blue jeans and a golf shirt. I think it's the first time I've ever seen him not in slacks.

"Counselor Snow."

"DA Jameson." I roll my eyes at the formality. "Are you prepared to eat five thousand calories in one sitting, Lane?"

"You only go around once."

His humor surprises a smile out of me. "You better make it count."

He opens the industrial-grade metal door for me. The cloying scent of frying oil and cabbage greets me.

Rex's is an old-time buffet. Rex Cooper, an Army cook from the first Iraq war, is the sole proprietor.

Most of his side dishes come straight out of a gallon tin can with no seasonings added, aside from salt.

Still, there are three things Rex has mastered. He is a wizard with meatloaf, mashed potatoes, and fried chicken. Mashed potatoes are always served on meatloaf night and fried chicken night.

I pile my plate high with half a chicken and what would be three enormous Idaho potatoes if they weren't creamed to a fluffy smooth consistency. The dinner lacks in color, but I know the flavor will more than compensate.

I can't help but grin as I evaluate Lane's selection. One chicken breast, a dab of mashed potatoes, green beans, and carrots.

"Watching your figure tonight, Lane."

He raises his eyebrows. "I can always go back for seconds. I need to try it first. There's no point in wasting food if I don't like the taste."

"No harm in that, I suppose."

"I really want to apologize about Judge Phillips today."

I've been raised to be gracious when apologies are offered. "It's truly water under the bridge, Lane."

"No, it's not. And I've been thinking about how I failed to prepare you."

I look up from my fried chicken. His pause is too long for my liking. "And?"

"I realize it's part that I have become so accustomed to Phillips' draconian methods and his pontification from the bench it no longer offends me. But, more importantly, the caseload you have handled for me recently makes me feel as if you've been working in our court for a few years, not weeks. I simply forgot you have not been before him yet."

I finish chewing the massive piece of chicken I bit off. "Lane, it's all good. I'll need to learn how to deal with all types of personalities anyway."

"True. Speaking of that, how is your job hunting going?"

My word. With the number of people asking me about my career status today, I feel like I'm not paying the lack of progress enough attention. "It's all quiet now. But, hopefully, there will be an opportunity before too long."

Lane stares at me so intently I become self-conscious.

"What, do I have mashed potatoes on my chin?"

He shakes his head. "No. I just—is it totally out of the realm of possibility that you might consider staying in Guntersville?"

"Why Lane, I had no idea you cared for me like that."

His face flushes red. "I uh. It's only—as you can see, I'm sure

—we need new talent in the county. Everybody's aging out, and there's going to be opportunities for judges, district attorneys, and more soon."

Why did I imagine I would be allowed to enjoy a free chicken dinner? Wasn't it Nana who always says there's nothing free in life? The worst part is Lane is stepping way out of his comfort zone for this conversation. He seems sincere, and the compliment is flattering. Still, he might as well be offering a snowman a heat lamp.

I have zero interest in what he's peddling.

"Lane, it is a terrific opportunity for someone. But, unfortunately, it's just not my opportunity."

Lifting his fork, he flicks one of his carrots over. "I understand. But I feel it is important you know where you stand in this community. You need to know that you have already made a superb impression on your peers. If something changes in your plans, you just give me the word."

"Thank you, Lane. I appreciate you saying that." Mashed potatoes taste better when slathered in flattery.

Chapter 13

I arrive early at Snow and Associates to have some "April" time to search the legal position job boards. After everyone's concerns, and offers, I feel the need to pick up the pace with my career search.

It is my lucky day. There is a defense litigation attorney position available in San Francisco and another in Miami. Culture and mild temperature or multi-culture and hot. At this point, they both sound like a marked improvement over no culture and nothing happening.

I fire off my résumé to both firms and lean back in my chair, crossing my arms over my chest while visualizing the companies fighting over my services. There will be a monumental bidding war that will drive my initial salary to an embarrassingly exorbitant amount with any luck.

I may even be offered a substantial sign-on bonus. You never know. Right?

It is rare a law firm can hire a new associate who already owns a winning defense record. So don't think for a moment this girl isn't going to get miles of play out of the fact I have successfully defended two murder suspects.

Besides, I earned those victories—the hard way.

It is difficult for me to decide which of the two positions I would prefer. San Francisco is on the cutting edge of all things "new" in this fast-evolving world. It would be an adrenaline rush to be an instrumental part of the licensing of an emerging software product that eradicates disease or hunger from the face of the earth.

I'd make a few million dollars by the time I'm forty, retire, and take on pro bono work for worthy causes. It would be a tremendous opportunity to help make the world a better place.

Still, the heat and energy of Miami intrigues my primitive id. I can imagine blowing off steam nightly after a grueling litigation schedule by dancing the night away with hot, half-clothed men in a rainbow of colors ebony, mahogany, and sandstone, all glistening with beads of perspiration. I already smell the musk of their sweat as our hips grind on the dance floor.

It's a conundrum. A difficult decision I welcome into my life. A decision that will lead to an improvement over my current state of nomadic employment regardless of which opportunity I take.

The front door of the law office opens. The sexy men on the dance floor leave to dance with someone else, and my mind floats back to Guntersville.

The only thing worse than having an amazing fantasy interrupted is the person doing the interrupting to be somebody I don't care to see. I bite my upper lip as Chuck Davis steps into our office.

"I was right"—he glances around the office as his eyes narrow—"where's all your help?"

"Holiday week. I let most of them off. It's usually quiet on Fridays anyway."

He sits down in the chair across from me, uninvited, leaning forward. "Good. We need to talk."

"About what?"

"About my divorce."

"No offense, but I doubt I would find it of any interest, and I'm a particularly lousy relationship counselor."

Laughing, he wags a finger at me. "I forgot how witty you

are."

He stops laughing and clears his throat as I give him my "I'm so not warming up to you" blank stare.

"No, silly. I want you to handle my divorce." He clasps his hands together, "What information do you need from me to get started?"

So not happening. "We're not starting anything, Chuck. You have an attorney."

Anger flashes across his face. He regains his composure disturbingly quick. "I used to have an attorney."

"Firing your counsel in the middle of proceedings is inadvisable, Chuck. That's even if we were interested in taking on your divorce."

"I didn't fire him. He quit."

From my estimation, Chuck had retained an intelligent attorney. I plan to be the second brilliant attorney Chuck must deal with by refusing his case. "I hate you two had a difference of opinion. Still, I'm sure you'll be able to find suitable counsel."

"The only difference of opinion we have is that Carolyn offered him three times his normal rate to leave me high and dry. But, unfortunately, the slimy leach didn't have the decency to inform me until this morning right before our court appearance."

Fair. Chuck's attorney is intelligent and an opportunist.

I struggle to conceal a smile as I consider the intestinal fortitude displayed by Chuck's wife. He should've thought twice before he married a girl who plays that rough. I'd like to buy her lunch sometime.

"Did Judge Rossi at least give you a continuance given your predicament?"

Chuck rolls his hands palms up, making a pleading gesture. "That's why I'm here. She advised me if I needed local representation to look you up."

To be horrified or flattered, that is the question. In Judge Rossi's defense, she is unaware that Chuck Davis's hands have been on numerous failed reconnaissance adventures in my panties in the past. I feel confident if she had known that she would never have sent him in my direction.

It does warm my heart she thought enough of me to send a client my way. Even if he is a spoiled turd of a human being.

"Are you telling me the truth? I know Judge Rossi personally; I will ask her."

"Honest, she gave me your name. I admit I remember your brother saying you were a defense attorney. But it never occurred to me you could do a divorce decree."

I pinch the bridge of my nose as if it will help me think. "In smaller towns, your attorneys are more of jack of all trades. We do a little bit of everything."

"Sure. I guess I never thought about that. That sounds good for breaking up the monotony. You don't want to get bored doing the same thing every day."

Yes, but sometimes occupational diversity comes with a steep price. "What new date did Judge Rossi set for the hearing?"

"Two weeks from today."

That sounds like a lot of time, but I would be starting from ground zero. Chuck's wife Carolyn, on the other hand, had not only done her prep work, she successfully ambushed Chuck's case. Chuck underestimated her determination to win, but I won't.

Bless it. I'm considering his case. *Why, April? Why?*

Because I think that much of Judge Rossi. I wouldn't want to have to explain why I turned away a client she referred to me.

"I'll need your tax attorney's contact information and the company's comptroller's information." I open the drawer to the right of my leg in search of a form folder.

"Why do you need all that?"

I push a power of attorney agreement toward Chuck. "You'll need to sign this, too."

He lifts the form and mouths the title, his face turning white. "This is a power of attorney."

"Yes, it is."

His arm drops, rustling the paper against his thigh. "My last attorney didn't need this."

"Then your last attorney wasn't worth half his fee. But, of course, that is before he made the unscrupulous bargain with Carolyn." Then, narrowing my eyes, I tilt my head. "Do you think it's possible the two of them were in cahoots from the start?"

Chuck's jaw falls open. "Do you think? Why that egg-suckin' dawg. He probably didn't do any of the necessary work because he knew he was abandoning me from the start."

"I'm just saying."

A shudder wracks through Chuck, "I'm going to beat the tar out of him the next time I see him."

"I request you wait until the end of the proceeding. It needlessly complicates things if you attack your ex-wife's counsel." I point to the form. "You still need to sign the line and give me the contact information."

Chuck signs the power of attorney form and writes down the contact information I requested. His face continues to darken from red to an alarming shade of purple while his jaw muscles flex. "Anything else," he asks tightly.

Full disclosure, I asked for a power of attorney in hopes of making Chuck walk. Still, the more I consider it, the extended privilege will come in handy when I make requests of the company comptroller and Chuck's CPA. "Nope. This should do it. If I do need anything else, don't inconvenience yourself with an office visit. We can handle almost anything via a Teams meeting or over the phone."

Chuck takes the hint, to his credit, and appears unsure if he should thank me for my thoughtfulness or be hurt by my dismissal. "Thanks."

"My pleasure." I favor him an extra-sweet smile to soothe the sting.

Chuck stops at the door and adds, "I want to nail her hide to the wall, April. Whatever it costs."

"Nailing hides to the wall is what we specialize in, Chuck."

He flashes a lopsided smile before exiting the door.

Chuck's genuine smile is much more attractive than his usual cheesy fake one.

Chapter 14

I complete the protection order against Savanna Tate's neighbor. It is a simple template, cut-and-paste project. As I pull the final draft from the printer to walk it to the courthouse for filing, my cell phone rings.

I hit receive as I continue to examine the protection order for errors. "Hello?"

"Have you eaten lunch yet?" Dusty asks.

This is a novelty. It is rare-to-never that either of my brothers calls me at work. "Not yet. What time is it anyway?"

"It's almost eleven thirty."

Chuck's unannounced visit ate up more of my morning than I thought. "What do you have in mind?"

"Pizza, maybe?"

My stomach grumbles, daring me to suggest anything healthier. "Torino's?"

"Perfect. Do you want to meet me there at noon, or do you want me to pick you up?"

"What are you driving?"

Dusty chuckles. "I can bring the Nova."

"Then pick me up."

"Okay, I'll see you in a few minutes."

What? So, I like cool muscle cars, sue me. I drive a ragged-out Prius because I am environmentally conscientious. But that doesn't mean I have to turn down a ride in a primo muscle car. That carbon footprint indiscretion is on Dusty.

The large pizza Dusty orders us is nearly consumed. He hasn't said more than ten words.

I'm not stupid. Sure, it would be nice to think one of my brothers would call to take me out to lunch just for the sake of my excellent company, but I know better.

"What is the favor you need to ask your kid sister?"

Dusty looks like I goosed him. He sighs as if the world weighs on his shoulders. "That obvious, huh?"

"Dusty, you buy my lunch and dinner when I'm working for you. It seems overkill for you to feel the need to feed me when I'm not working for you."

"Touché. At the expense of being 'that guy,' I do need to ask for your help."

"Okay." Understand I'm alarmed at this point since Dusty is typically a family member who gives help. He doesn't do much in the way of asking.

He examines his hands and scrubs them with a paper towel. "I hate to admit it, but I think this thing with Bethany has really got me in a bad sort.

"I need to finish my edits this month on the next volume so I can get them into Mara. This volume is essential since it's the last one on contract. If it's good, I'll get a contract for another five additional books. If it sucks"—he shrugs—"it may be back to blogging and self-publishing.

"It's just with all Bethany's demands, accusations, and drama I can't focus on my books."

"I know a guy who knows a guy. You want me to have Bethany bumped?" I ask.

Dusty's eyes widen as his nose flares. The color drains from his face.

I meant it to be funny. Maybe my delivery was off? "I'm just kidding, Dusty."

He frowns. "Don't even say stuff like that. What would you do if she were suddenly killed in a car accident?"

"Honestly? Throw one heck of a party for you."

"April!" Dusty hisses.

"What? I'm still joking." Mostly.

"Well, don't. Besides, there's nothing you or I can do to help my divorce settlement. That's in the lawyers' hands now." He frowns. "I really thought this book was good. Possibly my best."

"It should be. You have some excellent material for it, thanks to your spectacular research team." That earns me a welcomed smile from him.

"I know. But it's not coming together for me like the other editions. Instead, it's like a pile of disconnected, moderately interesting notes. None of it dovetails into the gripping narrative I know it needs to sell."

Dusty's declared literary capitulation is impossible for me to accept. Dusty is the career superhero of our family unit. Whenever I am plagued by self-doubt and worry that I've set my goals too high, I remember all he's accomplished at such an early age. It gives me great courage to know a Snow can do anything they put their mind to attaining.

I'm convinced the only thing that can hold a Snow down is their own self-generated negativity. Listening to my brother, he might as well be wolfing down a kryptonite burrito.

"Is there anything I can do to help?"

"That's what I want to talk to you about. I'm wondering if you would mind critiquing chapters of the book for me?"

I'm dumbfounded. I try to conceal my shock, but I'm sure my facial expression is stuck awkwardly between perplexed and horrified.

"You'd be a natural beta reader, April. You have a critical eye for correctness yet still enjoy reading fiction. Think of it like reviewing a contract, making sure that it's all in order."

If Dusty is trying to convince me to help, he's doing a lousy job. I despise contract review.

"Why don't you have Miles or Liza do it for you?" My voice sounds whiny to me.

Dusty sighs heavily. His expression changes to disgust. "Because Miles would panic if he thought for a second I have lost my ability to write effectively. Liza is more—let's say visual. She can tell remarkable stories, but she's not about writing events down in detail.

"You're the one person I know who appreciates the written word and understands the visceral experience of what we do."

Dusty's insistence that I appreciate the written word is a complete newsflash to me. I've never considered myself a voracious reader since I only read a couple of novels a month. Still, I should accept my brother's compliment graciously even though it is praise not well earned.

I stare at him while considering what he is asking of me. It scares the daylights out of me. What if I mangle his book? I couldn't live with myself if I cost my brother his book contract.

"Please, April. I'm serious. I need your help to get through this."

Refusing my brother is not an option. I mean, we're talking about Dusty. The big brother who encourages me to be brave and chase my dreams and consistently defends my methods. This despite me marching to my own unique drumbeat that nobody, including him, understands.

"Okay, you know I'll help. But I need a favor, too."

He leans forward, his expression eager. "Name it."

"I need you to explain something to me. Why didn't you tell me about the research trip to the cave in Kentucky?"

His brow furrows. "The cave?"

"Miles, Luis, and Liza are going to a cave in Kentucky. Right?"

"Yes, they are. But I don't understand why you're asking me about it?"

"Why not?" My hands are shaking at my side. "Why wouldn't you ask me to go, too?"

Dusty laughs and then covers his mouth. "I don't know. I

guess I didn't want to burn you out. You're too important of a resource during the actual investigations to have you running around researching sites. I can put you on the clock and let you go if it'll make you feel better. Or if you're just looking to burn a weekend off. But I'll warn you, most often, these turn out to be a whole bunch of nothing. You may end up driving ten hours to enjoy a bunch of state highways and collect a few chigger bites in areas you don't want them."

"That would be a novelty. I think I would rather get paid for collecting a few chigger bites than being knocked about by a poltergeist."

Dusty's smile is so intense it crinkles the lines showing around his eyes. "It has been quite wild since you've come aboard."

"So, I get to go?"

"Knock yourself out, Tink. You know I'm not going to stand in the way of you doing something you want to, no matter how silly I think you are for wanting it. I'll have Miles call you with the particulars."

"And the book?"

"I'll email you the Word document this evening."

Chapter 15

Dusty gives me a ride to the courthouse to file the protection order against Ms. Tate's neighbor. I ask Dusty to drop me off at the front stairs of the courthouse, and I take my time getting out of the Nova before shutting the door. I want everyone to see me getting out of that beautiful black beast.

Now that the idea has had time to marinate, reviewing my brother's novel intrigues me. I figure it will be an excellent opportunity to learn the mechanics of taking a book from a collection of notes and weaving it into a coherent story that readers will enjoy.

Who knows, I might want to publish my own book someday. I know I can write a credible non-fiction book explaining how to effectively destroy a relationship in three simple steps. To be fair, I can do it in one step, but I would spend a day researching two additional steps so readers would feel as if they got their money's worth.

I file the protection order with the clerk. As I exit the courthouse, I run into Lane.

"That's quite fortuitous," Lane says. "Do you have a moment for me?"

"Yes, Sir."

He frowns. "There's no need to call me sir."

Lane has told me that numerous times. Yet I won't stop

because I see how he flinches each time I call him sir. If I venture a guess, he'd prefer not to be reminded that he is twenty years my senior. That must be damaging to his narcissistic nature.

"I wonder if you might have a mind to discuss a plea bargain in the Mullins case?"

I thought you would never ask! "I suppose so. If we could find some common ground. But regardless of what you offer, I'll have to do some major convincing since he was adamant about clearing his good name."

A wry smile graces Lane's face as he shakes his head. "We both know he could be looking at some serious time if this goes to trial and Judge Phillips determines the sentencing."

Checkmate. "What deal are you proposing, Lane?"

"I would consider criminal mischief in the first degree."

No way. "That's a class C felony, Lane. I can't propose he take a felony in good conscience."

"You're serious?" Lane snaps his head back as if I slapped him. "What were you expecting?"

"Reckless endangerment, tops."

"Judge Phillips will never go for a misdemeanor," Lane says.

"Oh, you're impossible. Jethro didn't hurt anyone."

"By the grace of God."

"By the grace of a pine tree, heavy wind, and a bad throwing arm." I add a topnotch eye roll for punctuation.

Lane waves his hand dismissively. "Fine. You want to take Jethro before the judge, I'm not going to argue. I was attempting to save the guy some extra time in jail."

"Admit it. You have holes in your case, Lane." He doesn't. The only way he loses this case is by missing the court date.

"No. I'm feeling compassion for your client's plight. He is sad and pathetic. The last thing he needs in his life is a long jail sentence, which you appear intent on earning him."

"But a felony, Lane? Think about how difficult it will be for him to get a job—a legal job."

"I didn't throw the Molotov cocktail"—he points at me

—"you didn't throw it either. He did. And for all your cute commentary about a bad throwing arm and a pine tree saving the Holland trailer from being destroyed, I want to ask you something. Would we even be discussing this if he hit Micah's trailer and folks had been trapped inside and burned to death? No, we wouldn't. As I see it, your client is already fortunate."

We glare at each other. When Lane rubs my fur the wrong way, my ability to speak disappears.

"Criminal mischief first class, six months in state prison, and five years' probation." He punctuates his sentence with a grunt.

Not having any leverage in this non-negotiation makes me want to scream. The circumstances make it impossible to do my job. All I can do is go along with Lane's plan and drop in a few objections.

"You can keep your felony, but I say thirty days in the county jail, one year probation, and two hundred hours of community service." It's a fool's bargain, and we both know it. The felony is what counts. Still, other than taking our slim chances in front of Judge Phillips, there is no avoiding it.

"Sixty days instead of thirty. I believe I can convince Phillips it's more than adequate punishment for the crime."

"I would hope so, considering it's excessive, Lane. For Pete's sake, he just lost his house. Have a heart."

"I am. I'm giving Jethro room and board for the next sixty days. He will have ample time to develop a plan for the rest of his life."

Lane humor. I consider arguing the point further and decide to keep my mouth shut. But, unfortunately, there is no way to keep Jethro out of prison.

"Fine. We have a deal."

"Excellent. I'll have my assistant draw up the papers." Lane makes a show of looking at his Rolex. "If you will excuse me, I have some papers to file before my weekend can start."

I watch His Royal Smugness make his way into the courthouse.

I'm not even going to count Jethro's case in my win-loss record. It was a setup from the jump. Lane knew it was a loser when he assigned the case to me.

If that's true, why do I feel like a quitter right now? Why am I questioning my decision to take the deal? I don't see a path to keep Jethro from serving time and having the stench of a felony, like roadkill skunk, hung around his neck for a moment of uncontrolled rage.

I need a pick-me-up. I need something to make me happy and quick.

My cell phone rings. "Hello?"

"Boss man said you want to come out and play in the cave with us this weekend?"

I can't remember a time I appreciated Miles's voice more. "Yes, I definitely do. What time are you leaving?"

"It's not a particularly long drive, but we want to leave at five in the morning. Are you sure you're up for that?"

"Yes." I'm thinking maybe.

"Great. This is so exciting that you are coming with us. We've always had a blind spot if we ran into black magic. But since you can sense it."

What? "I don't sense black magic."

"*Right*. Why don't you tell that to Montel Bryant? You flushed that jerk out of hiding. If it weren't for you, he might have gone undetected."

Montel Bryant was a newbie dark warlock who tried to kill Liza and me on our last excursion. Until now, I never considered how the mortal battle that ensued once we located Montel must have looked from the rest of the team members' points of view.

"Well, I'm not a witch. I just feel stuff." And sometimes create things I don't understand.

"Oh," Miles pauses, "creating stuff sounds like someone might be—*a witch*."

"Whatever, Miles."

"Liza tells me you are working on controlling your magic."

Now that just gets my goat. I'm so ticked off now.

I can't believe Liza mouthed off about our "magic" conversation. What really aggravates me is Miles just reminded me I still haven't called Nana for guidance. She is the only person who has been able to help me with my paranormal affliction in the past.

If I were an adult, and today is shaping up to be one of those debatable days, I would call Nana. For the safety of the team if no other reason. Yep, I'm already beginning to regret asking Dusty for this assignment.

The thought of another boring weekend with plenty of time to flog myself over my decision with Patrick convinces me to move forward. "Are you picking me up?"

"You know it. I'll be in the 'love cube.'"

"What?"

"The new van," Miles says.

"Please don't ever call it that again."

"Why? You don't like the 'love cube'?" he exaggerates the nickname.

"Miles, I will most certainly hurt you when I see you."

"You can't threaten me when I'm in the 'love cube.'"

"I'm hanging up now."

"Okay, see you in the morning."

Chapter 16

Next on the call list—Nana. I'm so dreading this call.

I could skip it. That's what I want to do.

With effort, I can even convince myself I don't need Nana's help. But after our last paranormal case, I know I need to understand what happened before I end up accidentally hurting someone.

On many fronts, my aversion to Nana is unjustified. She has never been anything other than generous and kind to me. I have no doubt, in her own odd way, she loves me. It's just she's so blasted weird.

She used to tell me that back in the olden days, healers and soothsayers were coveted and not ostracized. Personally, I think she's full of baloney. All I need to do is point out the Salem witch trials, and I've totally proven my point that witches have always wigged the heck out of people.

It's not like she can't go about her business and keep quiet about her beliefs. I don't believe the average neighbor would care that she is unusually fond of candles and constantly cooking foul-smelling soup in her kitchen. But when she feels the need to inform the good citizens of Guntersville she lights candles to conjure souls and the soups are warding potions, people naturally are wary. They either hurriedly move across town or report her activities to the police.

Given her past run-ins with the general population, you'd expect a sane person to fly under the radar. That's the rub. Nana doesn't care what *anyone* thinks about her.

She advertises in the weekly newspaper "Love Potions by Pauline" for two hundred dollars. Scarier yet, they work. Her potions make octogenarians commit acts of carnal knowledge while parked in the handicap section in front of the grocery store—on a ninety-degree afternoon—with the windows rolled up.

It's a true story. Jacob was forced to write the Greens a citation last month.

Don't think for a moment I haven't considered scratching up two hundred dollars to share the potion with an attractive man. I just can't shake the romantic gene I inherited from my parents. While the sex would be fun, I want my partner to love me on their own accord. There is the *real magic* in a relationship.

I don't have Nana saved as one of my speed dial numbers. Go figure.

I'm forced to scroll through my contacts and pass by it twice. I had forgotten I saved Nana's number under "Grand Dragon." Old joke, long story.

Nana answers before the phone rings. "Boo?"

It used to freak me out when I was younger that Nana knew when I was calling her. But, now I've convinced myself, her phone rings a split second before mine. Her bird-like reflexes allow her to answer before the chime completes its circuit back to me.

"Hi, Nana."

"Please tell me nobody's died, child."

"No, ma'am. At least if anyone has nobody bothered to tell me."

"It sounds like you might be on the outskirts of the family circle too."

There is more truth to her comment than I care to admit. The Snows are a tight-knit clan. I occasionally wonder if I'm a touch too odd to be included as a full-time member of their club.

"I'm sure being gone for seven years didn't help my standing."

"Possibly. It may also be because they know your plans. That you don't intend to make Guntersville your home."

And then there is that, too.

"What is it you need to talk to me about? Don't hold any secrets back from your Nana."

"I just haven't called you since I've been back. I thought I might drop in and visit for a spell. If you have time for me, that is."

"This wouldn't be about what happened last weekend, would it?"

No. I refuse to believe Nana knows anything about what happened at Sloss furnaces. "I don't understand."

"Me either, but I felt something last weekend, and it scared me. Are you all right? I would have called, but I figured it wasn't my place to intrude."

See. This is what I'm talking about. There's no way Nana can know I accidentally generated a magic protective bubble last weekend.

If Dusty weren't up to his neck in editing issues, I might think he discussed it with her. Both my brothers are exemplary people who visit both grandmothers regularly. Without Dusty's input, she could only be aware of the troubling occurrence through—her powers.

Go ahead, tell me that wouldn't freak you out.

"Well, there might've been a tiny incident last Saturday I could use your help in deciphering."

The light static on the line is my solitary answer for the longest time. "First answer my question. Are you all right?"

Physically, sure. Mentally, not so much. Thinking about it stretches my brain like a bungee cord being pulled too far. I feel like one more stressor, and it might snap. "I think so, but I have a lot of questions."

"Which is to be expected. I told your mama this day would come. She didn't want to listen to me. I just wish she had allowed me to start your training when you were a toddler. It comes much easier for the young."

"I'm sure it's not like that, Nana. If I have any abilities at all, I'm sure it doesn't amount to much."

"I won't argue with you, dear. But I'm an excellent judge of latent energy levels."

"I've already checked it out myself. There's just not much there," I offer.

"And how would you know?"

Now I feel stupid. But if I'm in for a penny, I'm in for a pound. I've already made the call, the most challenging part of discussing anything with Nana, so I might as well get what I need.

"I've been trying to move pencils with my mind."

I hear her chuckle. "Oh darling, that doesn't mean anything. If magic worked like that, I would wake up to a clean house every morning."

I release a frustrated breath, and tears pop into my eyes. "Nana, can I come to talk to you? I really need to figure this out. I'm afraid it's driving me crazy, and I'm so scared—"

"Take a breath, Boo."

Hearing her nickname for me stops my rant. "Yes, ma'am."

"Darling, you can come to visit your Nana anytime you want. You're always welcomed in my home."

"Tonight?"

She doesn't respond immediately. I feel the need to explain. "I'm going on another paranormal excursion tomorrow, and I must know how to prevent something spontaneous from happening again."

"No, it's not that. I wasn't expecting a guest, and I haven't cooked anything for dinner."

Nana is partial to poke salad, wild mushrooms, and other scavenged vegetation that I can't identify. Consequently, her lack of dinner preparation is a relief to me. "I'll pick up some sandwiches on the way, Nana."

She hesitates again before answering, "Alright, I'll make us some fresh sweet tea."

"Good, I'll see you in about an hour."

I grin as I disconnect the call. I know Nana's sweet tea recipe by heart. It is the same one my mama used until fifteen years ago when she became concerned the family was consuming too much processed sugar.

Steep six tea bags in a quart of water just brought to a boil. Add a level cup of sugar and pour the sugar tea base into a gallon jug—top off the container with water—sweet tea Southern style.

The irony of tea being exiled from the Snow household is not lost on my brothers and me. Mama replaced the liquid refined sugar poison with a plethora of diet coke flavors. If lab rats are good indicators, we should be expecting to lose our toes any day now due to the aspartame. I'm just saying.

I buy a turkey sandwich, a chicken sandwich, and some chips from Jerry's. My emotions fluctuate by the second as I make the drive to Nana's.

Like Granny, Nana lives out in the boonies. But where Granny lives on what used to be a working farm, Nana lives in the woods. *Deep* in the woods.

Her double-wide trailer sits in the middle of an oak grove. The oak trees are ancient. Their bases are as wide as my car.

The gravel trail leading up to her lot always has deep ruts and is severely narrowed by the encroachment of younger trees yearning to find the sun. Her trailer might be "mobile," but it will never be able to squeeze down the path again without a long day's work with a chainsaw and backhoe.

As I take a left off State Highway 79, the sun drops below the horizon. Ten more miles out, I turn onto County Road 13. It's pocked and the shoulders are crumbling, so I take my time.

I'm pleased to see the old covered bridge as I come around the bend. Since there is no cell coverage out this way, GPS is useless. Landmarks are king.

The old Willoughby covered bridge is a reliable landmark. It is one of twelve covered bridges remaining in the entire state. It's a big deal in our county that we have one of the bridges to our claim.

It's a big deal to me, too. Because it tells me I'm only three miles away from Nana's house, and I managed not to get lost.

The sun is fully concealed as the tall trees on the shoulder of the road screen any remaining sunlight.

I slow to a crawl as I approach the bridge, aware that it is only wide enough for one vehicle at a time. Before I enter, I scan the road on the opposite side of the bridge for oncoming cars.

It's all clear, and I enter the bridge.

My car rocks from side to side as I drive across the old wooden planks. I swear it feels as if the entire structure sways. I grip the steering wheel tighter.

The movement of a shadow on my left catches my eye. She appears five feet in front of my vehicle.

Slamming on my brakes, my seatbelt bites into my waist and shoulder. The bridge lurches forward, then back, swaying from the abrupt motion.

She is wet. Her light pink dress clings to her stick-like legs, stringy black hair dripping rivulets covers her pale face. My gut tightens as her blue lips part. She gestures for me to come toward her.

Instinctively I close my eyes as the wave of evil she emits covers me like raw sewage.

She's not real. To clarify—she's there, but she's not alive. She's just another spirit drawn to me.

I open my eyes. To my dismay, she hasn't moved. I'm not sure if this bodes well for my future or not.

Her lips continue to move. I'm struggling to roll down my

window as my muscles are all too tense. I want to know if she is saying anything audible.

"I have to get home. I'll be late for dinner. Maw will be mad that I got my dress wet." Her voice is loud but garbled as if she has a preponderance of mucus in her throat she needs to clear. "Please give me a ride home, pretty lady."

I pinch the bridge of my nose, praying not to be afflicted by a migraine.

From her size, I guesstimate her age to be eight years old. The style of her dress, out of date by more than a few decades, is reminiscent of the early nineteen hundreds. As if I need further confirmation an actual human isn't blocking my progress—a live one at least.

If I thought for a minute I could slam my foot on the gas pedal and speed through her, I would. Something warns me that would be unwise.

Every hair on my body stands on end and vibrates as I monitor her movement. This diminutive ghost is genuinely creeping me out.

Why this time? I've been over this bridge a hundred times. I've never seen or felt the presence of a ghost here before, and I've never heard any local stories of a death at the bridge. If there were, considering the bridge's notoriety, it would have been readily bolted onto the lore of the bridge.

This makes no sense.

Bright lights emanate from behind her. She disappears.

The truck, only two car lengths away from entering the bridge, flashes its lights. I continue through the bridge at a slow pace. My nerves are shot.

I wave to the truck as I pass. The driver waves back at me. I'm eternally grateful they came along.

If the drowned girl ghost hopped in my car for the ride home she requested, my only recourse would be to abandon my car in the middle of the bridge and run down the road as if my hair were on fire.

It's a long run back to town.

Nana's drive has become even more treacherous since my last visit. I'm forced to proceed slower than usual, so I don't end up hitting a tree.

Branches and thorn bushes scrape at the side of my car.

There are warding emblems carved into the tree trunks. Spirit catchers hang freely from bushes and saplings, dancing in the humid breeze.

I have always wondered how spirit catchers know to capture ghosts and not the souls of the living. Nana insists they would never take a soul from a righteous person. I want to believe Nana. Still, I keep a healthy distance between me and the peculiar string and wood artifacts.

My slow progress up the gravel path allows my mind to drift to the first time I visited Nana at her home. As my mother approached Nana's home that day, the visceral fear that plagued me is forever available for instant recall.

It was not a fear of Nana. She was a regular visitor at our lake home. Despite her oddities, I had always been inexplicably attracted to her.

The fear came from knowing what the purpose of our visit was that day. The knowledge that something had gone dreadfully *wrong* with me, and I was changed.

I had become part of something I wanted nothing to do with.

Crazy emblems carved into the side of trees and spirit catchers whipping in the storm-laden winds as we approached served to fan the fire of a young girl's worst nightmare—the nightmare of being different.

It came about because of my brothers. Approaching their thirteenth birthdays, they had received their first natural boost of testosterone.

That summer, they were busy daring each other to take on increasingly dangerous stunts. These ranged from bicycle jumps over an ever-increasing number of concrete blocks, skateboard rides down small mountains, and on the Saturday my life changed, dives off the roof of my current residence, the boathouse party room.

I have reconstructed the events many times over in my mind. We were sunning ourselves on top of the boathouse roof after a swim in the lake.

This had become a favorite activity of ours once we understood our parents couldn't see us on the roof from the house.

It seems silly now. But we reveled in doing the forbidden. The thrill was often in knowing Mama wouldn't approve or Daddy would be concerned for our safety.

Dusty started it. He bet Chase five dollars he wouldn't jump off the roof. Dusty has always had money, even in those days. Chase still hasn't met a dare he won't accept.

Chase didn't hesitate. He stood up, pulled the legs of his swim trunks to full length, then ran off the side of the roof before I could ask him not to take the dare.

He had surfaced by the time I crawled to the edge and looked over the edge of the roofline. He swiped his unruly wet hair from his eyes, spat a water plume into the air, and pumped his fist victoriously into the air.

"I feel bad about taking your money, brother. That was the easiest five dollars I ever made."

Dusty stood and peered over the edge. "Did it hurt?"

"No. But it's just the right amount of height to make your stomach flutter. Come on. Give it a try. Don't be a chicken. Bock-bock-bock!"

Chase has always been a kidder. It is impossible to ever know if he's telling the truth or pulling your leg. That's why I was equally alarmed when Dusty's expression hardened.

I reached out and touched his hand. "You don't have to, Dusty. I know you're not a chicken."

The right side of his lips twitched upward. He looked at me as if I were crazy. "I want to try it."

I pulled my hand back as he took two steps forward, pounding the roof and launching into a somersault. Dusty landed in the cannonball position "danger close" to Chase.

Chase attempted to get further away but was swallowed by the tidal wave Dusty created.

Dusty popped up and shook his red curly mane while pointing at Chase. "Chicken that!"

Chase gave his usual good-natured laugh. "I thought my head was going to end up your poop chute."

They both giggled hysterically while treading water below me.

I remember watching them from above and thinking how beautiful they were and how much I loved them. My brothers were my heroes. The world was always perfect when I was with them.

Chase was the first to look up, and he motioned at me. "It's getting too hot up there, Tink. Climb on down. Let's swim for a while. We'll even get the canoe out and paddle out to the island. You'd like that, wouldn't you?"

Brave is not the first word that comes to mind if someone asks me to describe myself. But suddenly I had a wild hair.

"Scoot back. I'm gonna jump!" I hollered down at them.

They shared a concerned expression. Chase yelled back at me, "No! Just shimmy back down and take the stairs like we normally do."

My mind was made up, and my brothers were not going to deter me. "No. I want to do this." I waved them back. "You clear the way."

Chase's expression turns serious. He took me at my word and said something to Dusty I couldn't hear.

Dusty gestured with his hand for me to stay put. "If you get hurt, Dad will whip the stew out of us."

I knew that to be a lie. I don't recall Daddy ever whipping us. Mama? Mama could be a wildcard.

"You both did it. Now I want to."

Chase shook his head, adding helpfully, "If you're going to do it, at least make sure to clear the dock."

I peeked over the edge of the roof and saw what he was talking about. If I didn't launch myself two feet out, I would be slamming into pine boards instead of water. I took two additional steps back to get a running start, hoping I would clear the dock.

My muscles tensed, preparing to spring into my run off the roof, when Dusty offered one more bit of information, "Make sure to go in feet first and keep your legs and body perfectly straight. That way you'll slip into the water with the least amount of impact."

The last instructions absorbed and committed to memory, I ran the five steps to the edge of the roofline and leaped into the air. I had an epiphany as the soles of my feet left the gritty shingles. I don't have a fear of heights.

Flying through the warm summer air, I felt completely free and in love with all the possibilities of this beautiful life.

My momentum slowed, and I realized what I do have is a genuine fear of falling. I looked down in panic. I couldn't see my brothers.

My descent gained velocity, and I remembered the last thing Dusty told me. I went ramrod stiff, making sure to correct my angle so my feet would pierce the lake surface first.

The cold lake water engulfed me in a full-body embrace. My momentum slid me quickly downward as my arms extended above my head, trailing behind my missile body. My toes, then knees, then hips met the frigid cold of the deeper layers of water, and still, my body continued downward.

My toes struck the spongy lakebed. My momentum slowed. I was mid-calf deep in the silty bottom of the lake.

The sudden encasing of my feet in muck caused me to panic. My eyes opened as I accidentally released the last of my precious oxygen. I watched in dismay at the vast number of bubbles racing to the surface.

Kicking violently to free my legs from the lake bottom, I stroked toward the light with all the force my arms could exert. My lungs were on fire from oxygen deprivation.

Within three feet of surfacing, something grabbed my ankle and jerked me to a stop. I kicked and yanked to free myself.

Whatever latched around my ankle would not let me go.

Then my direction changed. Something was drawing me away from the light. Pulling me further away from the oxygen my body so desperately craved.

Looking down into the shadows of the lake, I couldn't see what I was caught on. I twisted my leg up toward my chest, closer to my line of sight, so I could determine what was entangling me in hopes of pulling loose from it.

That is one vision that will haunt me until the end of my days. It terrorizes my dreams and is the first thing that crosses my mind when I become frightened.

Long, decaying gray fingers wrapped around my ankle.

Initially, I froze as the mottled hand pulled me further into the frigid depths below. I screamed, flooding my lungs with water. Last, I did the one last act of defiance left to me before I drowned.

I clutched the disgusting swollen fleshy fingers and yanked them backward with all my remaining strength. There was a satisfying sensation of something popping free, reminding me of a chicken drumstick being pulled apart from a thigh.

My world went dark.

I woke with a sputter. Chase was giving me mouth-to-mouth resuscitation. He pulled back, panting as he stared at me. He was scared and angry. I turned my face from him, so I would not have to endure his intensity any longer.

Dusty was running down from the house with Mama and Daddy close behind.

I think I was a lot closer to dying that day than any of the family will admit. I knew it was a close call because the blood had rushed out of Dusty's face leaving his skin the color of an Ivory soap bar.

Likewise, Chase had slipped into what we often refer to as his "Iceman" mode. The place he goes when someone is injured and he needs to help them. It allows him the uncanny ability to handle a crisis efficiently devoid of all emotions.

The knowledge I almost died paled in contrast to the vision

of what was pulling me under. Some things are far more frightening than the possibility of death.

Mama crushed me against her chest while peppering my brothers with questions. I doubt she realized it, but she was yelling at maximum volume. They were both backpedaling away from the scene.

To his credit, Dusty saved all our skins by telling Mama we were swimming together, and I suddenly went under. He conveniently expunged the high-diving portion of our escapade.

I didn't realize I was telling Mama hysterically that a man's hand had pulled me under until I heard her say, "Don't be a foolish girl, April. You must have gotten your leg caught between a branch and a log is all."

My tears stopped immediately. It always hurt my feelings when Mama would call me her foolish girl.

"No, Mom." Chase was coming back toward us. He was pointing at my ankle. "I've never seen a branch make finger marks like that."

I followed his line of sight down my leg to my ankle. The four long, linear red welts on my skin were indisputable evidence that what I saw was not imagined. I felt dizzy, followed by a bright flash of light.

When I came back, Mama and Daddy were bickering. I couldn't make out what they were arguing about, but since both continued to gesture in my direction, I assumed I was the topic.

My head lolled back, and I realized Chase was holding me. I knew I wanted to ask him something, but I couldn't remember what for the life of me.

Later, when I was tucked in bed, Mama came into my room and explained I had passed out. She told me it was expected given all the new things I had experienced today.

I was confused.

Then she told me we were going to pay Nana a visit that night. At her house.

Mama said there were things Nana could explain better than her. Including what I believed I had seen in the lake.

Mama is a forthright person. You don't have to worry about her ever sugarcoating a situation. Her hesitation and meticulously chosen words were as disconcerting as the incessant itchy burning sensation around my ankle.

Bless it. Nana's trailer has seen better days. I suppose they're not designed for thirty-plus years of habitation.

Chapter 17

I park next to Nana's 1984 Nissan Sentra held together precariously with duct tape and Bondo.

A twinge of guilt stings my heart. I'm ashamed I've been complaining about the delay of my future high-income career like it's the end of the world.

As far as I know, Nana has never had much in the way of material wealth. I've never even considered where she gets her money for the necessities.

Things I didn't consider when I was a bratty kid and still failed to recognize until just now since my thoughts often revolve around my needs and wants.

Trying to not feel ashamed, I fake a pleasant smile and tap on her screen door.

"It's unlocked. Come on in."

I guess with all the warding on the trees, Nana has no need to lock the door. I grin at my own witch joke as I pull the screen door open and step into her trailer. Hot, humid air infused with the scent of sulfur offends my nostrils. "Nana?"

"Back here, Boo. I'm in the kitchen."

Stepping through the connecting wall of the double-wide, I spy her tending three pots simultaneously. She gives each a quick stir with the wooden spoon in her hand as she smiles at me over her shoulder.

"My goodness, you get prettier every time I see you, Boo. I have never been partial to the light eye and hair color of your daddy's people, but I have to say it sure looks striking on you."

Old people say some of the darndest things. I've learned it is best just to roll with their comments or ignore them altogether. "I hope you're not cooking, Nana. I told you I was bringing sandwiches."

She rolls a shoulder. "I know how you love greens and beans, so I went ahead and made you a mess you can take home with you."

I wouldn't claim that I love them. I will eat greens and beans, especially if my alternatives are acorn soup and char siu. The meat on the char siu skewers at Nana's is as likely to be squirrel or opossum as it is pork.

"Oh, cool. Thank you. What's in the third pot?"

After an abbreviated laugh, she says, "It's a batch of a new energy potion I'm advertising on Craigslist."

"You know you used the same spoon to stir all three pots." I pay attention to these things when I am at Nana's.

"Did I? I guess the greens and beans will pack an extra pow tonight."

That just sounds dangerous. I still remember eating some lima beans in eighth grade Nana brought to the lake house for a Sunday night family meal.

They were delicious, and I ate three bowls. I also sounded like an old trail horse for the next three days at school whenever I was walking. Deadly sulfur gas bubbles escaped me at the most inopportune time when I was near my friends between classes.

It was a humiliating week.

"Pull up a chair and stay awhile," Nana says.

I lay the sandwich bag on the table and sit.

She turns the pots down to simmer and lifts her apron over her head. "I was wondering if you would be able to find this place in the dark. It seems like it's been ages since you've been out here."

"It's probably close to ten years." The pang of guilt stabs at me again.

She freezes in place as she pulls the sweet tea out of the refrigerator. "Wow, that long?"

Nana's hair has a few more speckles of gray in it than when I last saw her at my graduation. Her olive skin is as luminescent as ever. Her dark chocolate eyes are strikingly bright for a woman quickly approaching seventy years of age.

Please let me have inherited that Hirsch female gene. The one that makes it a common occurrence for people to mistake my mama as my older sister.

"Nana, is there anything weird about that old, covered bridge?"

She cuts her eyes to me as she pours our glasses of tea. "Why do you ask?"

No. We're not gonna play the "what do you know" game. "Because I want to hear what you know about that bridge."

Pursing her lips, she makes a show of twisting the pitcher top closed. "I told your mama, and I told your mama." She is visibly shaking, and she steadies herself against the counter. "Vivian always has to do things her way."

"I don't know, Nana. I'm not convinced that's such a unique characteristic compared to the rest of the females in our family."

"I suppose you're right, Boo. But Vivian believes that what you don't know can't hurt you. I can tell you for a fact, what you don't know can kill you. Kill you dead.

She added the last as if I didn't understand that you're dead if something killed you.

"Then she ups and marries that Ralph boy?" She raises her hand. "Mind you, I've got nothing against your daddy, child. He's a right good man, and there's many a day I prefer him over that bobcat of a woman I raised. And far be it from me to get into people's love lives."

But she's about to give her opinion. I'm struggling to hold a poker face since I want to laugh over her assessment of my mama.

"You know the heart wants what the heart wants and all. But mixing Snow blood with Hirsch blood? Everyone knows that's just tempting fate."

I'm not laughing on the inside anymore. "What do you mean tempting fate, Nana?"

She crosses her arms. "Doesn't matter anymore, child. It's old business. Besides, if she hadn't married Ralph, I wouldn't have you or your brothers. I should learn to keep my trap shut."

"But what did you mean, Nana?"

"Was it a young girl, say about ten years old, looking like she went for a swim in her Sunday best pink dress?"

You might as well have hit me with a taser. My body involuntary convulses when she describes the apparition at the bridge flawlessly.

My reaction is not lost on Nana. "That's a remarkably faint energy spirit, Boo. She's incredibly old and nearly burnt out. You shouldn't be able to see her. Not without summoning her."

"Uh, there was nothing low-energy about what I saw. The girl was solid, dripping water, and vocal."

"Goodness." Nana rests her chin on her fist as she gawks at me. "Did you try to block her?"

"No." I wave my hands in frustration. "I might have if I was expecting to see her. It would have been helpful if someone had mentioned her to me. A person who was just preaching about knowing about stuff, so it doesn't kill you. Dead."

Nana raises her eyebrows. "She doesn't normally appear. I've been living out here for the better part of forty years, and I've only seen her six times."

Our conversation is making me increasingly uncomfortable. It's bad enough to be unique because you're a witch like Nana. Being a "special" witch will be double sucky.

"I'll give you a charmed warding coin before you leave. With that and you blocking your mind, you'll be able to get through the bridge without another incident."

I just can't yet. "Chicken or turkey?"

She exhales loudly as her eyes seem to look past me. "Chicken."

I pull the sandwiches out and give each of us a bag of chips. I unwrap my turkey sandwich and stop. "You say I shouldn't be able to see the ghost at the bridge. Okay, but if I did, why is that so alarming to you?"

"From the day you were born, I told Vivian you have the strongest natural power I have ever sensed. Think of natural power as intelligence. Then I want you to imagine what happens when you mix high intelligence with an unhealthy state of mind. Say borderline psychosis."

"I don't have psychosis."

Nana shakes her head. "No. Hold on. I'm trying to give you an analogy. If you have a brilliant person that is not mentally stable, that can be a very volatile situation. Can we agree on that?"

I'm no psychiatrist, but smart crazy people do seem quite a bit more dangerous than dumb crazy. "Sure."

"You have all this natural ability. In the Wiccan world, our stability is our ability to control the 'veil.'"

I have endured this speech several times over the last twenty years. The "veil" means different things at various times. Regarding spirits, it is the ability to move from the living's reality to behind the "veil." Into the spirit realm.

The "veil" can also mean the separation between white magic and black magic. At times a blurred line, according to Nana.

The "veil" also refers to the distinction between strict control of magic versus random outbursts of magic. To be in control is to be faithfully "veiled."

My random outburst of magic while in Birmingham classifies me as poorly "veiled."

"The 'veil' is different with each of us. We have different strengths and influences on the distinct aspects of it. I have always feared after your encounter in the lake that your 'veil' is fragile. Possibly even torn."

Her words settle heavily on my heart as their meaning codifies in my mind. Torn. That's exactly how I feel at times during our team's paranormal excursions.

"What does that mean for me, Nana?"

She unwraps her sandwich and picks at the lettuce. "It means you have to be careful. Understand there are some benefits. It should allow you to easily move into the spirit realm and be able to discern spells, charms, and potions quickly. And with your powers, they should be more effective."

That all sounds wonderful for someone eager for a profession as a witch. Given I'm a lawyer by trade, these skills sound like more of a liability than an advantage.

"On the negative, there might be times you can't block spirits out because of the permeability of your 'veil.' You must remain vigilant against dark magic.

"Everything you do must be full of light. I can't emphasize this enough, April. With the level of power you possess and your compromised 'veil,' it would be too easy for you to slide to the dark."

This is the opposite of what I want to hear. I could refuse to believe her, but everything Nana says rings true.

It irks me to no end. I don't have time for this coven wives' tales. Mark my word, if I could do magic, I'd snap my fingers and rid myself of these powers Nana speaks of right now.

What was I thinking coming to Nana's? What had I expected to get from this visit?

I hoped she had a more robust method of closing my mind to go about with my "normal" person's life and not have to deal with this hocus pocus horse puckey. This visit is so not going the way I hoped.

"I think there's something else you need to tell me, April. I've shared what I know. Now tell me what has brought you to me tonight."

I don't feel like I'm in a sharing mood anymore. I think my best option is to forget the Birmingham incident even happened. I'm sure it was an anomaly that will never happen again—an actual once-in-a-lifetime event.

I look Nana dead in the eye and work up the nerve to float a doozy of a lie.

Nope. That's not going to happen. I'm the world's worst liar. Plus, Nana has a built-in tall-tale detector.

I resign to tell her. What's it going to hurt anyway?

"The last excursion with Dusty, we were down at Sloss furnaces in Birmingham. I was with my field partner, Liza.

We spotted something on one of the brick walls that, at first, we thought was a mirage. It turned out to be a warlock who had cast an amazingly effective cloaking spell. The short of it is, he knocked Liza out. Then he summoned a fireball he planned to throw at her.

I moved in front of Liza to shield her. Then presto, I created a blue protective bubble surrounding us. A blue dome that deflected fireballs thrown by an angry warlock."

Nana's eyes open comically wide. "The shield of Hervor."

"If you say so."

Nana's lips thin into a tight frown. "That is an extremely complicated spell."

"I didn't cast a spell," my voice rises an octave. "I don't even know what an herbivore shield is."

Nana cackles so unexpectantly I lean away from her. I reciprocate her laugh as she sobers.

"Hervor," Nana says slowly. "She was an ancient shieldmaiden."

Nana waves her hands as she shakes her head. "It doesn't matter. What does matter is the spell should have taken you years to master.

"Then, for it to deflect a direct magical attack? It's designed to ward metal objects. For it to be effective against magical attacks would require—well too much energy to comprehend."

"It didn't take any energy, Nana. Liza had to convince me she didn't cast it before I entertained the idea it was me."

Nana collapses into the chair next to me. Her look of concern is not making me feel better about my predicament.

"I don't know just yet. You're telling me something that shouldn't be able to happen."

"Just my luck that I have to be special," I say sourly.

Nana reaches out and takes my hand. "Magic or no magic, you've always been special."

Lately, I have felt "special" for all the wrong reasons. I want to feel special because I'm pulling down seven figures a year in my chosen field. Hawking magical energy potions for a living doesn't have the same pull in the social circles I want to have in my future.

"There's no straightforward way to block this?" I'm whining again.

"You can ignore it mostly. But—"

"But what?"

She cups her chin as she stares at me as if I'm a lab rat. "Typically, once casting powers show up, they only become more powerful. I'm afraid the next time you are in a stressful situation, it will happen again and—"

Nana's pregnant pauses are driving me nuts. "But what?"

She favors me with a smile that doesn't reach her eyes. "On the bright side, you conjured something defensively. To protect a friend. I believe that would be solidly in Team Light's camp."

"So that's a good thing."

"Sure. This time. But next time what will it be? Safety is in training."

"Training?" My stomach, as if composed of butterflies, takes flight in a thousand directions.

"You didn't believe something this monumental would be a simple fix like a breathing or concentration exercise did you?"

Well, yes. That's what I was hoping. "I guess not, Nana."

"That's right. This is serious business. But you're used to training. You've always been a dedicated student when you needed to be. How many years did you spend earning your law degree?"

"Seven."

Her eyes pop open wide. "Goodness, I didn't realize it was that long. There's no telling how good you would be at the craft if you dedicate that much time to learning."

I know it's silly the conversation is getting under my skin, but it has the same feel as when people say, "Wow, you could've been a doctor."

"Yes, but I always wanted to be a lawyer, Nana. I've never wanted to be a witch."

"Now you'll get to be both." She says it with the most extraordinary delight as if it is every girl's dream. Save for me.

Nana lifts her chicken sandwich, opens her mouth like an anaconda, and takes a huge bite.

I don't care to admit it, but she is right. I'll be both whether I want to be or not.

My appetite has left me.

I tense as I near the covered bridge. Reaching the other side of the wooden structure, I breathe again.

I'm thankful the evil drowned princess didn't want to come out and play. I think I'm teetering on the edge, and she might have pushed me off the sanity ledge.

It could have been the warding coin Nana gave me that looks suspiciously like a 1976 bicentennial quarter that kept the ghost away. Or maybe my effective mind-blocking techniques now that I know she exists.

She may be too tired to come out and play since, according to Nana, she is a low-energy spirit. Whether it was the precautions I took, or she needed to charge her supernatural battery, I'm glad not to have to deal with the drip-dry pink princess.

I have more on my plate than I can say grace over.

Just three months ago, a carefully crafted life came undone. Every time I believe I have reached a new low, a new level of misery, there is one more thing added to this train wreck I call my life.

Recounting the humiliations I have suffered since graduation is depressing. It's enough suffering to make Job feel sorry for me. Saints have done less and been canonized.

But is destiny done poking me yet? Of course not.

Now I'm the weird girl who's also a witch. No worries. It only means on top of working at Snow and Associates and Dusty's ghost research team, interviewing for "real jobs," and trying to raise a well-adjusted puppy, I'm now forced to spend hours each week learning how to control magic. A skill I never asked for nor wanted.

Given the recent track record, I shouldn't say this, but I believe there is no way this girl's life can get any more dreadful.

Chapter 18

It's fifteen minutes after midnight when I pull up the lake house driveway. It means that if I hurry, I can manage a four-hour nap before Miles picks me up for the trip to Kentucky.

After this evening's revelations, I now have severe reservations. Still, Dusty says the trip will be a bore. It will get me out of town to decompress and look at all these new aggravations from a fresh perspective.

Well, that's the optimistic take on the situation. I know, given how sorry I feel for myself, the only thing that will ease my mind is a hug.

Unlocking my door, I am anxious to pull Puppy into my arms and squeeze him to my chest as I bury my face in his soft fur. I know our relationship is new, but I have already come to depend on the calming effect massaging him has on my overactive mind.

I open the door and call out his name but am not greeted by a welcoming bark or disgruntled growl. I check under my bed and in my closet—no dog.

The dreadful fact settles in on me. Puppy is gone.

It is hardly even tangential. I'm aware my feelings are not rooted in logic. I don't care.

Tears well in my eyes as suffocating loneliness steals my breath.

Not because of Puppy. I know he is likely safe with Daddy. Which given I'll be leaving early in the morning is best for all of us.

I believe I may be terminally heartbroken.

It's part Randy being excited about his pending marriage to my nemesis ex-best friend, part Shane having more interest in fishing tournaments with my brother, and part Patrick having more people attached to him than I bargained.

All these facts mean April will be sleeping alone tonight. Not by my choice, just by the way circumstances played out.

I am so pathetic.

I'm aware I don't need a man to complete me. I'll never be the woman who must have a man in her life to feel like a woman.

Still, I do *want* a man. I crave the roughness of calloused fingertips gliding across my skin, the salty taste of him on my lips, and his hot breath against me as he nips my tender flesh.

No, I don't need that to complete me. But if it makes me less of a feminist to want that, I guess I'm lousy at that, too.

Chapter 19

I'm relieved when my phone's alarm sounds. I've spent four hours in pure torture.

If I'd had a bottle of tequila in my bedroom, I would have self-medicated and slept. If I had some chips and dip, I could have induced a carbohydrate coma.

I might want to be an adult and get my own groceries. My parents' kitchen is effectively closed when they go to sleep, putting a damper on late-night snack excursions. Hence, I stared into the darkness, wired awake by the anxiety brought on by my conversation with Nana.

Miles, Liza, and Luis will be picking me up in thirty minutes, and I'm starving.

I pad over to my fridge in case the elves filled it during the night. The arctic blast from the old-time refrigerator the family used to use for extra cokes and adult beverages brings goose flesh to my thighs.

There are two half-drunk bottles of Diet Dr. Pepper that I know are flat and half a quart jug of milk I meant to pour out last week. Sitting prominently, centered in the middle of the fridge, are two large pastel-colored plastic containers I brought from Nana's.

I briefly consider the idea of beans and greens before an extended road trip. Thankfully, I come to my senses before giving in to the thought.

The two amber beer bottles, both resealed with wax stoppers, behind the beans and greens, catch my interest. I had forgotten about the potions last night during my extreme need for anything to dull my mind.

Nah. Nana's concoctions would have only made my insomnia worse. She said they are energy potions. They're likely loaded with caffeine and ginseng. I needed something that would have calmed my nerves last night, not added to my "live wire" state.

Still, this morning is a different situation. Now I need to stay awake.

They're just homemade energy drinks. Nana can't have put anything dangerous in them if she's selling them.

I'm not feeling particularly peppy. I didn't get any sleep last night since I was busy concentrating on being lonely, heartbroken, and harassed by an undersized scary wet ghost. Also, because Nana wants me to spend Thursday evenings with her for Wiccan training each week.

Yeah. I'm sure that's all it is—some imitation energy drink.

I grab one of the bottles and peel the wax off with ease. The cork inside the bottle is stuck.

I don't have a corkscrew in my makeshift kitchen. Why have a corkscrew when you don't have any wine? I'll have to improvise.

Pulling out a steak knife, I cut around the edges of the cork, attempting to make it smaller and thereby pull the seal free. I manage to rough up the surface of the stopper but am forced to stop because I cut my finger. I stare at the blood with incredulity.

I need a smaller knife. I check all four of my kitchen drawers. I don't find what I'm looking for—a grapefruit knife.

This is absurd. I can't believe Nana makes it so challenging to get into her potions.

I'm losing precious time. I already decided to travel without makeup today, but I'd at least like to brush my teeth and comb the rat's nest out of my hair.

The obsession with getting into the bottle consumes me. What can I say—I'm the daughter of an engineer.

I ransack through the four drawers in desperation a second time. Skewers? Why do I have metal skewers? No grapefruit knives, but I have skewers.

There's a case study on why you bring your own utensils when you rent a vacation home. You'll need the knife, and instead, they provide you with metal skewers.

I force a skewer down between the lip of the bottle and the side of the cork. My plan is to leverage against the plug and pop it free. A quarter-inch of the cork pops out, bouncing off my nose.

Brilliant. There's no way I'm getting the cork out now.

I give a hurried glance at the time on my phone. Forget it. We're past subtleties now.

With both hands, I position the skewer in the middle of the cork. I press all my weight down to push it into the bottle. The tip of the metal skewer makes a clinking noise as it strikes the bottom of the bottle. The cork remains.

Bless it. Did Nana use a magical, human-proof cork?

I know she didn't. But it hurts to imagine armed with above-average intelligence and more education than the average person can tolerate, such ancient rudimentary technology is besting me.

Never surrender. That's my motto. At least this morning.

I make multiple punctures in the cork. A sizable portion of it breaks off into the bottle. Satisfyingly, I can pull a large part of the Swiss cheese cork from the bottleneck.

I'm glad I'm alone. I feel my crazy showing as I rejoice in my triumph.

With a madman's expression Dr. Jekyll would appreciate, I take a sip of Nana's concoction. It isn't bad; it also isn't good.

It tastes a lot like flat orange soda with a hint of cedar. I spit random bits of cork out of my mouth. That may be the cedar taste. I turn the bottle up and finish half of the thick liquid in one long swig.

Hmm. Nothing.

My morning coffee has more of a punch than Nana's potion. Coffee, something else to be said about this morning. I need to add it to my grocery list. When I get around to making said list.

I carry the half-empty bottle to my bathroom. Looking in the mirror, I ponder how to tackle my next engineering problem of the morning. My hair looks like a family of mockingbirds has set up in it.

If I had my druthers, I'd as soon try opening the second potion as try to untangle my hair.

Taking another drink, I hold it in my mouth. The taste isn't too bad. It is just odd enough to pique your interest. I wish I could figure out if that's peppermint or horehound I taste. Either seems like a bizarre flavoring to put with orange.

Then again, it was made by Nana.

Oh well, it's a bust as far as an energy booster, but I think it's loaded with enough sugar to power me through to our first fast-food stop.

I toss the empty bottle into the trash can and return my attention to combing my hair.

What feels like an hour later, my hair is sticking straight out. I work some mousse in to slick it down. Then I work some more in.

It's still not right, so I tease it with a comb. I whip my comb through it more.

Hysterical laughter bubbles out of me as I realize my hair looks like I belong in an eighties MTV music video. I like it. I spray it in place.

Is it flat on top? Yes. I tease the top, adding body. To be sure it doesn't flatten again, I spray it twice.

That looks good. I need eyeliner.

No. I want Egyptian eyes today. Yes. Perfect with my hair.

Hair and makeup complete, I brush my teeth. I grab my backpack as I twist the knob lock and pull the door closed behind me.

Chapter 20

Standing in the driveway, I tap the toe of my hiking boots at a furious pace. I check my phone. Four fifty seven, so where the heck is the van?

I can't believe Miles isn't here yet. He said he would pick me up at five. It was his idea to leave this early; the least he can do is show up on time.

Here I am, standing in my parents' driveway in complete darkness, looking like I'm preparing to run away from home. Thank you, Miles.

The company van turns up the driveway with a box trailer in tow. My three team members wave at me from inside the vehicle. Miles takes the loop in the driveway to point the van back toward the road.

I open the side door of the van, throwing my backpack on the back bench.

"Whoa?" Liza's eyebrows lift as she stares at me.

"Did I miss the memo about an eighties punk rock party tonight?" Miles asks.

"I think big hair is sexy." Luis looks me over from head to toe.

Eww. What is that about?

I pull myself into the van, catapulting into the back, landing next to my backpack. "Glad you could make it, Miles."

"Good morning to you too, April," he chirps.

"It would've been if somebody had been thoughtful enough to pick me up on time."

"It's four fifty nine, April." He points at the digital clock on the dashboard of the van. It's obviously broken—such shoddy workmanship and on a brand-new vehicle, too.

I check my phone. It also is wrong.

"I like what you did with your eye makeup today," Liza offers.

"Thanks?" Awkward. Why is everyone acting so weird?

If Luis doesn't stop looking at me like I'm a twenty-four-ounce porterhouse steak, I'll have to break his nose. "What are you staring at?"

A gleam sparkles in Luis's eyes as he says in a low, slow voice, "*Eres deslumbrante.*"

I'm not sure what he said, but it sounds dirty. This is unusual for Luis. Typically, he is quiet and extremely polite. "You keep looking at me like that, Buddy, you'll be looking on the floor for your Chiclets because I knocked them out of your mouth."

He laughs as he runs his hands through his thick, dark hair. "*Me gustan locas.*"

Miles and Liza join in the laughter. Miles adds, "You'd be looking at the right one, then."

I tap Luis on the shoulder. "Hey, Enrique Iglesias. If you got something to say to me, say it in English."

He sobers. "Relax, April. I am only paying you a compliment."

Now I felt like a heel. "Oh, okay." I really do need to learn some basic Spanish.

Miles drives slower than a kid taking their first driver's education course. It feels like two hours before we clear the city limits of Guntersville.

I'm convinced something is wrong with both the van clock and my phone. They both indicate only five minutes have elapsed since I got in the van.

I yank my hands back as I realize I have been scratching at

my arms and legs. It isn't my fault; ants are crawling all over me. Not literally, of course, but my skin is tingling something fierce.

For heaven's sake. Can Miles drive any slower?

"When are we stopping to get something to eat?" I blurt.

Miles looks at my reflection in the rearview mirror. "I can run through a drive-through if you want."

If I want? If I had the munchies any worse, I would be gnawing on the armrest of my bench seat. "What's out here?"

"There's a Burger Time right before we hit the interstate."

Their breakfast is a slight improvement over those sandwiches packed in the plastic triangle-shaped containers I can pick up at a gas station. Still, desperate times call for desperate measures. Like curtailing my taste buds for the sake of filling the massive hole in my gut.

"Sure. That'll work."

"Did you get by your Nana's yet?" Liza asks.

"Yeah, that was a hoot. I scored some beans and greens that should be good and ripe by the time I get home."

"But what did she say about your magic?" Liza rotates to be looking directly at me.

"In short, she said I'm screwed, and I'll end up turning to the dark side. She also made me commit to coming out to her place every Thursday night from now until eternity to hopefully improve my control issues."

"Dark side?" Miles asks. "I don't see that, April. You have to have some evil in you to go to the dark side."

"Yin and Yang," Luis says. "Even the most perfect of us have at least a small measure of evil we hide from the rest."

"And we all know I am far from perfect," I say.

"Did you consider she may have said that to make you understand how serious the situation is?" Liza says. "You have to admit you still act like an unbeliever at times."

I can't help but laugh at the absurdity. "I think the drowned pink princess knocked the last of my disbelief out of me on the way to Nana's. Oh, that reminds me. Miles, you don't have to go all the way to Kentucky to do research on a ghost. There is a very creepy one at the old Willoughby covered bridge."

"Nah, that one's not real, April. It's just an old campfire story," Miles says.

"Trust me. She's real all right. She's also a full apparition that speaks."

"Get outta here," Miles says dismissively.

"If I'm lyin', I'm dyin'."

"What did she say?" Luis leans into the back of the van.

"She said she needed to hitch a ride home with me. Something about she is late for dinner." Man, my skin is crawling, and it must be a hundred degrees in the van. "Can you turn the air up, Miles?"

"It's full blast."

"I'm practically melting back here."

"It's actually chilly," Liza says.

Of course, she's freezing. Liza is skin and bones.

Luis studies my face too long again. I have a mind to threaten him again, but he says, "What are you on?"

"I'm not on anything, but I'm gonna starve if Miles doesn't learn how to drive this van faster." The severe munchies afflicting me and the random hot flashes are putting me in the most irritable mood.

Liza makes a circling motion with her finger. "Back to the training with your nana. Does she think she can help?"

"Of course she can. But it's gonna take a lot of study time on my part. Time I don't have to put toward something that means absolutely nothing to my career path."

"I don't see how you can complain, April. I think it's freaking cool." Miles steals a glance in the rearview mirror.

"Maybe to you. You think it would be cool to make a career of studying all things that go bump in the night. But I have other things I want to do with my life."

Miles pulls us into the drive of Burger Time and swings around to the drive-through menu. Notably, their sausage egg biscuits are buy one get one free. I tell Miles to order four sausage egg biscuits, a large hash round, and a large cup of coffee.

"Thank you, but I don't need one, April. I ate breakfast before I left the house," Miles says.

"They're all for me." I gesture for him to place the order for me.

"Are you sure you haven't taken something?" Luis asks again.

My stomach rumbles as I unwrap my first biscuit and take a bite. My nerves' rough, raw edges calm when the first hint of fat from the butter biscuit coats my palate.

I catch Liza casting a concerned look in my direction. "I'm just hungry."

She nods and turns around, leaving me to eat sans audience.

I quickly devour three biscuits and the hash rounds, pausing at the fourth biscuit. I eye the white wax paper warily.

When I ordered, I thought I was hungry enough to eat everything in the restaurant. Now I am confident it is physically impossible for a human to eat four biscuits in one sitting.

There's no harm in keeping something in reserve. I crinkle up the paper sack and slide it under my seat.

Satiated, I sit back and watch the world pass by my window. The intensity of the foliage color amazes me. The sun is so brilliant I fish my sunglasses from my backpack. As we reach Interstate 65, the sun hides from view above our roofline as we travel north.

This trip is undoubtedly a new dynamic without Dusty and the audiovisual team. It feels more like a group of friends getting together for a weekend of hiking. Far more personable as if we're part of an extended family.

Of course, we are part of an extended family: the one I refer to as Dusty's Spook Geeks and Freaks, LLC.

Miles and Dusty started out as scholarly rivals. Sometimes, the enemies you win over are the people you trust the most in life. It doesn't hurt that the two of them have the highest geeks factors I have ever known.

Dusty trusts Miles's opinion completely. He should. If Miles says something exists, it's safe to believe it does since he will have researched it to death before making that determination.

Liza is the most fascinating anomaly. If I met her on the street, I'd be apt to believe she is the leader of a female-only biker gang. But that's what happens when you judge a person by their looks.

I know her to be exceedingly empathetic. She is also fearless and resourceful in a fight. Traits that can come in handy when you are fighting for your life.

Luis is a mystery to me. Like Liza, I'd never met him before I joined Dusty's team. Unlike Liza, we haven't had the opportunity to work closely together. I still know virtually nothing about the man.

His copper-colored skin, dark hair, and dark eyes, I'll admit are strikingly handsome. The fact he looks better in his skinny jeans, with his ridiculously tiny waist, than I will ever look knocks him way down on my attractive guy scale.

I lay down on the bench seat to take a nap. It seems like the prudent thing to do considering I got no sleep last night.

Something is wrong with my eyes. I cannot shut them. I attempt to get comfortable taking turns on both sides, my back, and finally my stomach.

Nope. Naptime is not happening.

The least I can do is start the other massive task at hand. I'll need to edit Dusty's book eventually.

Flipping my laptop open, I load his manuscript and read the opening page of the book. I read it a second time.

My word, Dusty wasn't kidding. This is garbage.

The facts are all there, but it's a collection of disjointed sentences and random thoughts. It is aggravating to read, at best.

What am I supposed to do with this? I feel like I'm reading a drunk man's outline of a book he plans to write later.

This is not the work of the Dusty I know. Dusty is precise. He can be slothful at times, but his singular goal is perfection once he goes to work.

I've never told him, but I have all four of his earlier books on my e-reader. I enjoyed reading them immensely.

When he published his first book, he sent me a first-print copy. He signed it *to the sister who opened my eyes.* A reference to the first time he saw a ghost and we were together.

Dusty can be sweet like that.

I came home for Thanksgiving dinner shortly after the book was released, and he asked me how I enjoyed the stories. I answered truthfully and told him I didn't read the book.

My paranormal experiences by this time had dropped off to nonexistent. I was concerned that reading anything to do with the supernatural might trigger a relapse. A prospect that frightened me.

The crushed look on Dusty's face still pulls at my heart when I think about our conversation. He had been genuinely interested in my opinion of the stories.

He tried to conceal the hurt I caused, but it was all too evident by his expression. Dusty commented that it was callous of him to suggest I read his book considering my near-death experience on the lake as a child.

Even with finals coming up, I finished reading his first book before returning home for Christmas break. I found it to be fascinating, and I read it two more times before spring break.

Dusty has a rare flair for writing about each excursion as if it were a carefully crafted piece of fiction. Where Dusty could simply list the facts of the research and write an explanation of his findings. He masterly weaves the haunting's historical details into the fabric of the excursion's details. It culminates in a crescendo where the ghost is freed, the demon expelled, or the team exits the premises at the last possible second in fear of losing their life.

The first book, just like the subsequent three, is built on the structure of thirteen separate excursions. Dead center of the novel, at story number seven, was our scare at the Freeman plantation. The night I almost lost Dusty through a portal to the eternal fires of Hades.

Understandably, it is my favorite story in the first book. Still, it's his writing that makes the stories so captivating, not the facts. He describes the scenes so vividly I can feel the evil swirling in the air again like we did that night so many years ago. I still get goosebumps every time I reread story number seven.

The funny thing is, I'm proud of that story. I'm pleased that my brother was so eloquently able to capture it and that I was there that night to lead him to safety.

Dusty never sent me another book. I bought the next three on preorder.

It's safe to say I won't be preordering number five. This is—well, it's garbage.

I get it. His soon-to-be-ex-wife, Bethany Roberts, is a selfish, worthless excuse of a human being. Still, I'm surprised he has allowed her to distract him so completely. No, she's not just distracting him, she is ruining his talent.

Wait. Now there's something that might make the Thursday training sessions at Nana's worthwhile.

If Nana could teach me a spell I could use to make Bethany's hair fall out, how awesome would that be? Or how to make a hex bag that will give her terminal IBS. That would be a handy tool in my arsenal, too.

Perhaps I have been shortsighted about the advantages of training with Nana. Sure, it will require time I don't have to give, but if I can learn a few helpful tricks, it might prove beneficial to me.

Reluctantly, I turn my attention back to the document on my screen and roll my eyes. Bless it. This is his contract-extension book, too.

No matter how popular the first four books were, his publisher will assume he's lost his touch and drop him if the fifth one bites. I can't let that happen to Dusty.

Besides, no matter how fun it is to imagine, I don't want to have to do anything mean to Bethany.

Chapter 21

The van slows. Looking up, I see we are exiting the interstate. On a hill to the far left of me sits a thirty-foot tall, poorly rendered version of a Tyrannosaurus Rex.

"Where are we?" I ask.

"A few minutes from the cave," Miles says.

I compare the van clock to my phone and see they are still synced up. They both read ten in the morning.

"We're going to meet with Sicilia Olivet. She's the manager of the attraction. After that, we'll go on one of the guest tours," Miles informs me.

"Are we going to go by the hotel first? I could use a potty break," I say.

Miles and Liza both give a short laugh while Luis turns and looks at me with an amused smile.

"What did I say?"

"We're in the hotel," Liza says with a smirk.

My lips part. No words come to my confused mind.

Luis offers a sympathetic smile and explains, "To keep the cost down, and because the three of us like it, we camp out when we go on scouting excursions."

"Camp?" I feel my face contort. "Like outside?"

"What other type of camping is there?" Miles says too merrily.

"Like a cabin."

"That's not exactly camping, April," Liza says.

It's close enough for me. "Are we sleeping in the van?"

"No. We have tents in the trailer." Miles continues to be entirely too amused. If he keeps it up, I'll be forced to hurt him.

"It'll be fun, April. Just wait and see," Liza says.

"I don't need to wait. I know from personal experience that camping is the worst."

"Wonderful. When we change your mind, it'll make it that much more special for you," Luis says confidently.

Luis has obviously done entirely too many drugs in his younger years if he thinks he can get me to buy into that Zen with nature bull. No matter how well you set up your tent and how tight you zip up your sleeping bag, there is inevitably at least one creepy crawler that gets by your defenses. That nasty little booger will invariably find its way to the middle of your face.

That's before we consider the wild animal noises in the middle of the night amplified to gargantuan status. A squirrel can sound like a rhinoceros running through the woods when you have nothing but thin polyester separating you from the great wild.

Yes, somebody let this small yet significant factoid escape the conversation. I bet Dusty is back home laughing so hard he can't catch his breath.

April May Snow doesn't do camping.

We pull the van and trailer alongside a two-story faux log cabin. To the side of the front door is a plaque that says "Office."

A group of twenty students mill about on the oversized front porch. A tall boy in his late teens coaxes them into a single-file line.

We step past the line of students and enter the office. A young woman snaps to attention. Her glare is as fiery in appearance as her red-dyed hair.

"The line's outside, folks. You don't want to miss your tour."

"We're with Perfect Paranormal Publications. We're

supposed to be investigating the site for a future story." Miles sounds more like he is asking than telling.

The woman, she might be twenty years old, raises a finger. "Oh, that ghost hunting group."

Miles grins. "That would be us."

Her smile turns sour, and I realize it never was meant to be a welcoming gesture. She points toward the door. "The same thing applies. You need to do a tour first. Calvin will be taking his group any minute. Come find me when you are done, and I will set you up for the night."

Miles's expression turns hostile. I wait for him to smart off to the rude woman. Liza grabs his arm and says something in his ear.

"Come on, guys," Miles says as he exits the cabin. The rest of us follow him to the front porch.

The group has already left. I see the tail of the line at the top of the ridge, and we hustle to catch up with them.

In my youth, I enjoyed going through caves. Daddy had hooked the three of us on a game he played back in the day called Dungeons and Dragons. Daddy is a superb Dungeon Master.

My brothers and I naturally took it to the next level. We soon had investigated every storm drain in our neighborhood. It was an unfathomable number of hours spent bent over in the dark, following my brothers through all manner of wet and smelly passages.

It was a complete hoot.

This began a family tradition. When we took our family trips, we would research if there were any nearby caves. If there were, we begged Daddy to take us on a tour.

It was just our thing.

This will be my first time back in a cave since I discovered Lulu White's skeleton in the cave outside of Atlanta. While it was as happy of an ending as possible, under the circumstances, it has knocked some of the shine off the spelunking activity.

As we trailed the students following Calvin, the moist, chilly air of the cavern caresses my arms, coaxing the hairs to stand on end. My mind, and consequently my solar plexus, relaxes as we walk further into the darkness.

My cares have dissipated. I'm enjoying the pleasure of a slow walk on the packed earth floor.

I hear bats somewhere in the distance, but the cave, aptly named "Monstrous Cavern," is indeed huge. I have no way of determining where or how far off the bats may be gathered.

Bats don't concern me. Leave them alone, don't stir them, and everything will be fine.

Voices, murmurs at first, begin to resonate in my head. They are not intelligible. The best I can discern, they are not directed toward me.

Nothing has felt my presence yet. Their attention is not on me.

My left hand instinctively moves to my chest. I clutch my T-shirt and the Orthodox cross it covers. The cross Liza gifted me on our last excursion.

I believe the voices are speaking English, yet the dialect is peculiar. Even as the volume of their voices increases, as we move deeper into the maw of the cave, I can't identify the accent or the words.

A cave this large offering shelter from the elements would have been priceless to a nomadic tribe. The high roof and wide sides would allow for the dissipation of smoke from campfires. It would also enable more inhabitants than a single-family unit. There is safety in numbers.

The line stops abruptly. I step to the side to improve my view and see Calvin gesturing to a hole in the floor. The throng of students form a circle around the opening as Calvin descends a ladder into the earth.

As Calvin's legs disappear below ground level, I move forward and look between the heads of two of the students. The mouth of the hole in the floor is slightly larger than the rim of a fifty-five-gallon drum. The ladder is reminiscent of the ones with "fall guards" used in industrial facilities.

Nudging between the two students, I look directly into the dark opening and spot Calvin's flashlight forty feet below. His face turns upward, and he calls for the rest of us to follow him one at a time.

Too cool. I step my foot on the ladder first, barely edging out a thirteen-year-old boy for the honor of being first in the hole.

This is what I love about caves. They are unique, like fingerprints, and you never know what you will experience.

I've ridden elevators before, but I don't recall ever having to climb a ladder straight down into a hole. I'm grinning like a loon when I step off the last rung onto the dirt floor.

I follow the beam of the flashlight as Calvin moves away from the ladder. There's a click followed by a blinding light that forces me to shield my eyes.

Geez. A little warning there would have been appreciated, Calvin.

"Sorry," he says when he notices my expression.

"No worries," I respond.

As my eyes adjust, I'm busy taking in the sights. I'm amazed at the height of this secondary cabin. It's difficult to fathom how much water must have been needed to create such a chamber.

The thick layer of dust on the packed dirt floor resembles gray talcum powder. It stands in stark contrast to the jet-black stone walls of the cavern.

I toe the floor's surface, stirring up a healthy gray cloud. This must be decades of falling dust. This floor is an excellent example of what happens if you don't dust your house.

Initially, I thought the black walls were coal, but the pores are too tight. Whatever the stone is, it's in stark contrast to the limestone of the upper level.

I press my hand to one of the walls, and the murmuring voices stop abruptly. I remove my hand as if that's what caused them to turn silent. They don't begin speaking again.

Or they are silently watching me now.

In my peripheral, I catch the movement of something large. I feel despair from a brooding soul. I turn, but there is no shadow on the wall.

It's my overly active imagination playing tricks on me. I shake my shoulder to throw off the heebie-jeebies.

The last of the students reach the bottom, and Liza begins her descent. I'm glad she will be the first of my team down. I'm anxious to ask her if she heard or felt anything paranormal in nature.

Liza's skill set is different enough that she occasionally gets a read that varies from mine.

Calvin wastes no time breaking into his well-rehearsed speech. The tall young man has a decisive geek factor to him. Still, I can tell that he'll be a real heartthrob when he has filled out in a few years.

He shines in his element as the small group of younger students are apprehensive of their surroundings. He has all the knowledge. I suppose we all migrate to the areas where the spotlight shines on us, and we can perform our best.

Liza and the boys work their way around the group of adoring middle schoolers. They gather silently with me as we listen to Calvin's history lesson.

It is nearly impossible for me not to be rude and ask Liza if she heard the voices. I desperately want her confirmation.

Calvin is soaking in the attention with his animated history tale. I know even a whisper from me is liable to echo loudly and disrupt the attention of his rapt audience.

As I listen to Calvin's recount of this chamber, I satisfy my curiosity by taking a more comprehensive study of the room. This section of the cave is an elongated oval that is easily the size of half a football field. The ceiling must be an incredible thirty feet high.

Calvin milks his story for all it's worth. He explains this part of the cave during prohibition had been a speakeasy for the locals. Events were held every Saturday night, including live music, dancing, and the locally distilled moonshine.

He relays the danger of being intoxicated this far down and how patrons ran the risk of passing out as they scaled the ladder out of the club. As the atmospheric pressure decreased during the climb, the inebriating effects of the moonshine increased.

For real? How ignorant must you be to climb your butt down a forty-foot hole to drink moonshine only to risk bodily harm when you climb out of the hole?

I cringe inside as I recall the dives I frequented in Tuscaloosa and not remembering how I got home on an occasion or two. I guess every generation has its own variety of ignorance.

Calvin's anecdote describing how the owners disassembled a piano and a chandelier to lower them through the small hole, so they could play music and create a ballroom atmosphere is intriguing. My thoughts float to how it must've been. A time before social media or even the interstate system allowed easy travel by car.

This part of Kentucky is still moderately isolated. During the early twentieth century era, a person might be born and live out their entire life never to travel more than a few miles from where I'm standing.

Funny, once I change my perspective, it doesn't seem so irrational people risked severe jail time to bring some manner of recreation into their lives. I'm sure many of them lived for Saturday nights in this hole.

All this thinking about the prohibition era has put an old tune in my head. "Five Foot Two, Eyes of Blue" was a song Dusty and Chase worked on for a barbershop quartet talent show in middle school. "Has anybody seen my gal?" could be heard booming from the living room nonstop for a month. The harmony of the male voices held my interest over the years, as did the snappy tune.

I still know every verse by heart. Secretly in my room, I sang along with my brothers as they practiced.

Of course, at the first mention of prohibition, the song pops into my head. It's only natural.

The music's volume increases. I smell the biting scent of "white lightning." Turning to locate the origin of the moonshine, stale perfume and sweat mix with it forming an overwhelming cacophony of odors.

I'm not sure if it's the odor, being underground, or the three biscuits I ate, but I don't feel right. Something weird is happening.

Chapter 22

A sudden bout of vertigo has me stumbling backward. At the same time, the sensation of déjà vu warns me I have been close to this before. I need to stop whatever odd sequence is moving into motion.

My muscles go limp, and all my joints unhinge simultaneously. Yet I don't fall to the dirt floor.

I should be concerned as my feet rise from the floor. Instead, I'm oddly relaxed, even amused.

Tilting back into a prone position, my arms swing out to the side of me. I'm floating. I'm on my back, suspended in the air, unable to even wiggle a finger.

The correct response is to be entirely freaked right now. Instead, I'm in awe of the new experience.

It is reminiscent of floating in salt water along the coast with a gentle tide pulling me further from the beach. Like those lazy moments floating in the gulf, my breathing slows, and all my senses turn inward.

The music increases in volume, more insistent now, with a wild sexual hunger as a mistuned piano bangs out "Sweet Georgia Brown." People are having loud conversations, shouting over the music to be heard. Energy thrums through me.

I'm aware I am caught up in a paranormal event of some sort

as the pitch dark swallows me. But for once, my reaction is to lean into the experience. I want to see where this will lead. This is unlike any event ever explained to me.

As suddenly as it began, my feet settle back on the floor. In a blurry, monochromatic vision, the world starts to reveal motion with no firm outlines of the shapes I see. Yet it is as if I am looking through a lens that obfuscates my normal vision.

My muscles contract and my joints lock in place to support my weight, starting at my ankles and flowing up my spine. The din is so great the first thing I want to do is cover my ears and close my eyes.

But I don't. I think to cover my ears, but my hands stay at my side.

The odors continue to intensify. Something brushes against my back. In alarm, I turn.

The world bursts into vivid color now—a flash of adrenaline courses through me. I watch in wonderment at the couples dancing on the dirt floor. The dancers jostle and bounce off other partiers as they attempt to create enough room to dance with their partners on the makeshift dance floor.

Looking up, my vision still with the peculiar "goggles" effect, I take in the grand view of the chandelier. Hanging thirty feet in the air, it is six feet across with four layers of softball-sized crystals. In this subterranean dance club, it appears as bright as the sun.

A pianist, his head shiny and as bright as a cue ball, pounds the piano's keys against the far wall of the chamber.

Well, butter my butt and call me a biscuit! I do believe I time traveled. How in the world did I do that?

How I did it could be a particularly crucial bit of information ... like for returning home.

Panic grips me. I need to get back to my time now before I lose my way.

"What will it be, beautiful?"

Despite the incredible noise, I understand the voice is directed at me. I turn and gasp at the handsome man tending the bar I'm leaning against. "Me?"

The laugh lines at his eyes deepen. "You're the only beauty I see here tonight."

What's the rush? I can hang around and visit for a while longer. It's not every day I can research history by living it firsthand. Too bad the man showering me with the lovely compliment most likely died of old age before I was born.

"Do you hit on all of your customers?"

"Only you."

"Do I know you?" He looks familiar. Perhaps he's the source of the déjà vu I felt a moment earlier.

"Now who's teasing whom, Ms. Callaway? If you don't remember my name is Henry, I should have stopped serving you last Saturday." He looks around as he pulls out a glass. "I see your husband hasn't finished his business in Glasgow yet. Tell me you didn't venture up here on your own again tonight."

Intriguing. I don't want to blow my hostess's cover, so I play along. "You know I did."

He shakes his head. "You're a nice lady, Ms. Callaway, and I like talking with you. But I'll be glad when your husband takes you back home to Lexington. This is a dangerous game you are playing. I wouldn't want to see you get hurt."

A nervous giggle escapes me. I vicariously feel the excitement building in my hostess.

"Do you want that drink?"

"I suppose, but I think I would rather you come out from behind the bar and favor me with a dance."

He smiles, diverting his eyes to the bar counter. "You're a tart one." He fills a tumbler with clear liquid and hands it to me. "Don't think I wouldn't like to take you up on the dance. But you know the local boys don't take kindly to black Dutch dancing with the girls. I'm way too young to die."

"Better to live a short, exciting life rather than a long, dull one," I tease.

That earns me a full smile from him, revealing dimples. His jet dark hair and ruddy brown complexion hint at Shawnee or

Cherokee heritage, both tribes having once occupied the area.

He's a handsome man, and I stare too long. Henry shakes his head as he picks up a bar rag and wipes out glasses that have been returned.

Moonshine is not something I typically mess with anyway. Seeing Henry clean the used glasses with the same towel repeatedly convinces me I won't be sampling the moonshine in my tumbler.

Of course, running down that rabbit hole, it's not necessarily a lack of hygiene from an earlier generation. There wouldn't be any running water available down in this pit for washing glasses.

Which, following the same logic, means there are no bathrooms. Wow. The commitment to having fun demonstrated by my great-grandparents' generation makes my generation look like a bunch of weenies.

I'm drawn to the piano across the room. Working my way through the crush of sweaty bodies, I manage to spill half my moonshine before reaching the heavily scarred upright.

The pianist passionately caresses the worn keys and does not notice me until "Ragtime" ends. Lightly he taps the first notes of the next piece. He rotates his head slightly to the left, favoring me a toothless smile.

The shock of seeing his severely disfigured face makes me retreat a step. He offers a quick shrug, returning his focus to the piano keys.

I jerk around in a half-circle to the touch on my shoulder. The last of the moonshine sloshes out of my tumbler onto the dusty floor below.

The young woman in front of me leans forward. "Pardon me."

"No, my fault," I yell. My voice echoes through the room. I realize too late the couples are slow dancing to a subdued love song.

The young woman, attractive in a wholesome manner, grins as if I've said the most amusing thing. She snugs her arm in between the crook of mine, pulling me to her side. "Now tell me, where are you from? I know you're not from around here."

Daddy always says it's better to tell the truth than tell a lie. You must hope your memory is better than the memory of the person you're speaking to if you tell a lie. Then, in jest, he would add, but if you must lie, make it as close to the truth as possible.

I'm unclear if that advice will apply to paranormal conversations as well as regular human interaction. Still, it seems like a solid plan, and I decide to go with it.

"I'm from Alabama."

Her eyes light up. "Alabama. That's so far away! What brings you here?"

"My friends and I were told this is the happening place. We thought we would come and check it out."

Her giggle is intoxicating. "You speak so strangely. I love it. 'Happening place.'" She extends her hand to me. "I'm Lauren. Lauren Ramsey."

Her hand is as calloused as any construction worker's I have ever shaken. "I'm April Snow, Lauren. I'm pleased to meet you."

She laughs again. "That will be easy to remember. April from Alabama."

The isolation of this out-of-the-way town must drive a social woman like Lauren crazy. I have only known her seconds, but I believe she would wither and die if forced to remain in such a small community where every day is the same as the next. I feel an immediate connection and empathy for her plight.

I know it's not polite, but my curiosity typically overrides my politeness and ask, "The pianist." I gesture toward the broad-backed musician.

Lauren cocks her head to the right. "Terrence?"

"Is that his name?"

"Yes." Her eyes squint as if she is translating my speech.

She clearly is not going to answer the obvious. I raise a hand and cover the right side of my face, moving my hand in a circular motion. "His—"

Her full lips form an "O" as her eyes open wide. Leaning into me, she whispers, "His face?"

Speaking of faces, I can feel mine burning as the blood of embarrassment floods it.

"Explosion, during the Great War. He helped the French turn back the Germans."

Wow. The Great War. Speaking of talking funny. It's easy to forget the word "great" with this generation has more to do with being monumental. It is not used to describe that which is simply better than good.

It is equally ironic to me that in fifteen years, this generation will send their own sons into a war exponentially horrific to the one they experienced.

My long-held perceptions shift dramatically. It is as if the bedrock stone my life is built on turns over. My world of missed employment opportunities and heavy debt load is a minor inconvenience compared to the burden these folks have and will endure. They just lived through what they believed to be the near end of their world and have no way of knowing how close they will come to that total destruction during round two of their "great war." Point of view can change everything.

"Where are your friends. Are any of them men?"

I'm relatively sure Luis is a man; I think the jury is still out on Miles. "Two of them are."

The left side of Lauren's lips hitch up, forming a lopsided grin. "Where are they? I would love to meet men from Alabama."

Yeah, if the locals have problems with a bartender with a hint of Native American ancestry, they will just love Miles and Luis. I stand on my toes, making a show of looking through the crowd even though I believe I made this journey through time on my own. "I don't see them right now."

"You must introduce me."

I recognize the desperation I hear in her voice. I don't know her situation, but I trust I understand her motives. That anywhere must be better than where she is now.

If her only means of leaving this town is to captivate a stranger enough to marry her and lift her out of this town, she is willing to do that. She will do whatever is necessary to leave these woods.

"Are you happy here, Lauren?" I should kick myself in the head.

She screws up her face. "Of course I am. This is home."

I've finally found someone who is a worse liar than me. I consider suggesting that she should go see Alabama for herself when a man no taller than her spins her around by the arm.

"There you are. You need to come dance with me."

Lauren pushes the man's hand off her arm. As she is pulling away from him, he grabs her wrist and yanks her violently toward him. "You need to learn some respect, girl."

"Leave me alone, Mason. I don't want to dance."

"You're going to dance because I want to."

"Sir, the lady said she didn't want to dance, and you interrupted a conversation we were having." I try to keep my tone even, but my anger is building due to the rough manner with which he is handling my new friend.

Mason glares at me, his eyes bloodshot red and hateful. Returning his attention to Lauren, he jerks her by the wrist again, pulling her off her feet. "It's more important to take care of your man's needs than spend time with stupid woman talk."

"You're not my man," Lauren growls as she gets off her knees.

"You're lucky to have me."

Lauren throws her arm to the side with such violence that her wrist comes free from Mason's grip. She turns to run, but Mason grabs a handful of long brunette hair at the base of her skull, jerking her back toward him.

Without thought, I shove into Mason's chest to push him away from Lauren.

He stumbles to the left but clinging to Lauren's hair allows him to keep his balance.

"You need to mind your own business, floozie."

I'm standing, slack-jawed, processing how severe of a slight the word floozie is while developing a plan of action to help Lauren escape this fool. The back of his hand catches my face.

Now, I've been in a few catfights.

They can be brutal. Hair pulled from your scalp, scratches across your face, and bites on your arms, but I have rarely felt the immediate pain caused by the back of Mason's hand whipping across my face. It feels as if somebody took a two-by-six and swung it like a baseball bat catching me right in front of my right ear.

My head jerks hard to the left, and the momentum carries my right foot over my left as I end up with my back to Mason. Immediately, I bend over and cover the right side of my face protectively with my hands. I'm positive he has just knocked my face off.

My ear is ringing, and my teeth feel loose. As I pull my hands away from my face, blood pools in my palms.

Chapter 23

The ringing in my ears is untenable. I move to stand. Something pushes against my buttocks, and I fall face first into the alkali powder floor.

"Leave her alone!" A female screams.

Attempting to spit the gritty dust from my mouth is futile. I struggle onto all fours. An incredible pain below my tailbone jolts me; I faceplant into the dust again.

Boots stamp past my blurry vision in the direction of the ladder exit. I swipe my fist against my eyes to rub the grit away. My hand only adds more dust.

"She didn't do anything!" The female, I believe it's Lauren, screams again.

"Someone has to teach her to mind her own business."

Being the quick learner I am, I roll onto my back rather than rise onto all fours again. Mason is preparing to kick me in the side while he grips Lauren's hair tight.

I put my hands out as if to block his boot. "I'll go if you just leave her alone!"

Mason's upper lip curls. "You ain't worth the trouble anyway." He puts an exclamation point on his eloquent statement by spitting on me. True class, this guy.

Black boots step over my legs. My view of Mason is blocked by a man's back. My sight is still blurred, but the dark hair is unmistakable.

"Let her go and leave now, Mason."

Thank goodness. At least there is one other person who doesn't cower to this bully.

"Or what, Injun?"

"You will wish you made a better decision."

"I don't think so, half-breed!"

Henry sidesteps to the right. I see the glint of steel as it is driven into his left rib cage. The big man grasps the side of his chest, dropping to a knee next to me. His eyes, shocked wide open as he struggles to comprehend what has just happened. The blood runs freely between and over his fingers pressed against his wound.

"April. April, come to me."

I'm still woozy from the blow to the side of my head. Now my brain is further addled as I watch a kind man bleed out by my side.

My hands. I can heal Henry like I did Dusty and earlier Trent.

"You killed him!" Lauren yells.

I roll to my side and place my hand on Henry's wound. Not wanting to be kicked again unexpectantly, I look up.

Mason still clutches Lauren's hair as he pulls her into his arms. He holds her back to his chest as he waves the bloody knife in front of her face menacingly.

Something is wrong. I don't feel any power flowing in my hands as I press them against Henry's wound.

"Everyone stay back. Or you'll get the same as the half-breed."

"April. April!" I can't tell who is hollering my name, but it isn't helpful. The amount of blood pouring out Henry's wound is frightening. It turns the gray dust into muddy red clay.

The remaining patrons, who have not already evacuated the party, form a corridor for Mason as he drags Lauren toward the ladder.

I can't help her. I can't save Henry either. Lord help me, I made a mess of this.

My attention goes back to the beautiful bartender. I wipe the trickle of blood from the edge of his mouth. His struggling gasps further apart now.

"April!"

I caress the top of Henry's head, his coarse black hair gliding between my fingers. "I'm here with you. Don't be afraid, Henry."

His dark, solemn eyes meet my gaze. His face, racked with pain, softens as his eyes struggle to focus on me. I swear a faint smile appears.

"I won't leave you," I promise.

The laugh lines around his eyes crinkle. "You are my salvation. Thank you." Henry's voice is just above a whisper.

Pain and sadness wrench my body. The side of my face feels like it has collapsed. My lower back and tailbone feel so damaged I wonder if I can walk.

Worse, my heart hurts for the loss of life in front of me—knowing that I unintentionally caused this disaster. There can be no heavier burden.

I just can't. This is too difficult to weather.

My eyelids, so heavy now, close. My chin dips, falling to my chest.

The world goes dark.

Chapter 24

"April, I need you to wake up. Come on now. You're spooking me. Come on, April. Come to me."

The voice echoes as if coming through a tunnel. It's familiar.

My body is floating. I'm on my back, arms spread again, and it's pitch dark. My troubled mind quiets. I have no care where the current carries me.

"April May Snow, you get back here right this instant."

My body lurches and swivels, changing direction. The darkness turns to hazy light. Something warm presses against me. My eyes pop open, and I recognize Liza's concerned expression.

She exhales and pulls me to her chest. "Thank the Lord."

A dry laugh tears at my throat. "You sounded like my mama calling me."

She pulls back and squints at me. "Did I now?"

I laugh and choke. Smacking my tongue, I swear I can still taste the alkali powder from when I took a nosedive on the ballroom floor. "Something to drink?"

Luis leans over me. "There's nothing down here, but I'll buy you as many cokes as you want if we can get you up the ladder."

"Is she okay? Please tell me she's okay." Calvin looks prepared to have an aneurysm at an incredibly early age.

"She's fine. The change in atmospheric pressure just made

her faint."

Even in my compromised circumstance, I am in awe of Liza's ability to develop impromptu plausible lies and deliver them expertly.

"Thank goodness," Calvin croaks.

"Amen to that," Miles agrees.

The intense pain of the beating I took did not transfer back into my world. Still, it does not diminish the startling violence I experienced.

I'm not sure why, but I decide not to share what happened with the rest of the team. Liza might empathize with my plight, but I know it will only add concern for the guys. I now have a personal stake in what is going on at the cave. The last thing I want is for the team to call the trip short on my account.

We arrive at the log cabin office. Luis buys me the promised soda. Strangely I have a powerful desire for root beer. I hate root beer.

"Are you sure you don't want to take her to the hospital and have her checked out?" Sicilia asks.

"She'll be fine once we get some sugar in her," Liza assures Sicilia.

Miles gestures over his shoulder. "We would like to see where we can set camp for tonight. We need to set up so she can rest."

"Of course. I'll have Calvin take you to the campground," Sicilia replies as she steps out of the office.

"Are you sure you're okay?" Luis asks, kneeling next to the sofa.

I'm touched by the sincerity of his concern. "Yeah. I just had a moment. It was like there wasn't enough oxygen down there."

Liza pulls my hand into hers as she sits next to me. "Did you feel anything while you were down there?"

Boy did I. Now how do I not tell my partners? "Did you?"

"No. Some faint echoes, but they were low energy."

Then you were on the wrong frequency, Liza. There is a whole party happening down there, complete with a piano.

It's not a total surprise. Liza has an easier time picking up things of a religious nature. There is nothing even remotely Godly about what I saw. It was simply good old fashioned human debauchery, lust, jealousy, and homicide. No demons, angels, or crosses to see here. *Move along, Liza.*

All the same, if she had told me she felt something, I might have shared my experience with her in private. So we could compare notes. Since there is nothing to share, I think it best to keep quiet. "No. I didn't hear a thing."

Liza's left eye narrows as she cocks her head. "Are you sure about that?"

"Positive," I say as I fight to keep a grin off my face.

"All right." She stands. "But if you remember something, you will tell me—right?"

"Sure I will." She's going to hate my guts when she finds out. But the way everyone is looking at me as if I'm a shattered plate of glass that will fall out of its frame with the slightest breath of air convinces me if I mention the event, they'll send me home.

Calvin bounds in through the door distracting Liza's skeptical glare away from me. I like that boy more and more.

"Sicilia said you are ready to set up camp?"

"Yes, we just need to know where she wants us to locate our tents."

Calvin develops an awkward grin on his face. "She said you wanted to set up over where folks have been seeing the Lady of the Shadows."

Miles holds a finger up to his lips. "It's best not to talk about what we might expect. Sometimes the mind will see what it's told to see."

Calvin's eyebrows jump into his bangs. "My bad. I wasn't thinking about that."

"No harm." Miles tries to put him at ease.

"Just follow me, and I won't say anything else."

I start to rise as Calvin opens the door. Both Luis and Liza motion for me to stay.

"You stay, *angelita*."

I don't know what Luis said, but it doesn't sound dirty, so I smile and nod at him.

"You rest and let us get camp set up. Then we'll eat lunch," Liza adds.

It's in my nature to argue. I want to tell them to quit treating me like I'm some frail flower that will break apart if handled too roughly. Truthfully, I am feeling quite fragile. Some time to myself in the quiet is a perfect prescription.

"You don't mind?"

"Of course not," Liza says.

"You're probably saving yourself a bunch of rework anyway. I really stink at putting up tents," I say.

Luis laughs. "We were pretty sure of that."

I can't help but laugh, which only encourages him to smile broader.

When they leave the room, it is just me and my memories of what happened. Before I can deal with what transpired, I must numb myself to the violence I witnessed.

I fear for Lauren. It makes no sense to worry about someone who has been dead for a few decades.

My heart aches for the oh-so-handsome and brave Henry. Whose life was cut short because he did the admirable thing, the hard job of standing up to a crazed bully when no one else was willing.

Is that how the world really was? Is? Where the good and honorable are laid to waste on the altar of evil? Is that a world worth living in?

Or is the glory realized in having done the right thing even though it brought on disastrous consequences?

Henry died with a smile on his face. Even in death, he had love in his heart. Love Mason could never feel.

I feel Mason won the battle but lost the war. He's just too ignorant to realize it yet. He could only be celebrating a Pyrrhic victory.

I'm not a theologian or a philosopher, but I am a firm believer in the commandment of "What comes around goes around." In my book, Mason has a whole lot of hurt coming his way. Still, that's not for me to judge.

I'll have to be content with the knowledge that Henry was a brave and honorable man and hope he will be rewarded accordingly. It will have to be enough.

As terrible as my heart aches about what transpired during my journey, I'm elated about the actual travel. Even the excruciating pain I felt when I got my butt kicked by Mason can't quell my excitement.

Who hasn't dreamed of traveling back in time? I'll grant you a big cave in Kentucky during the nineteen twenties wouldn't have been my first choice, but it demonstrates the possibility exists. At least for me.

This is the first time one of my unusual skills seems to have a benefit for me. Never again will I sit bored, clicking random videos in hopes of landing on something interesting.

If something interests me, say Viking agriculture, I won't have to get the particulars from scholars. I'll just pop into Norway during the ninth century and have a look-see for myself.

Forget Vikings. I prefer to have coffee with Hemingway and Fitzgerald for real in a 1920s café in France. With any luck, Picasso will join us. The possibilities are endless.

Of course, this will mean more time with Nana. I'll want her to direct me on how best to select when and where I'll travel. Lord knows I would hate to end up in Spain during 1478.

It doesn't just stop with my entertainment. This could be a complete career changer.

I won't have to rely on the word and recollection of my

clients any longer. I'll be able to travel to the day and time a crime happened and witness it myself. I know my clairvoyance can already assist, but that's dependent on what my client saw and how they perceived it.

Besides, if I use that skill without their permission, I feel I'm violating them. Which I am.

With my new skill, I can gather the information without it passing through anyone else's filter. This is thrilling.

I planned to call Nana later after a nap, but I can't contain my excitement. I pull out my phone and search my contacts for Grand Dragon.

With our new regularity of communication, I'll be forced to put her on speed dial.

"What are you excited about, April?"

How does she do—never mind. "Nana, we're up here in Kentucky searching for spirits in Monstrous Caverns."

"And that's fun?"

Hirsch family members don't share the same fascination with caves as the Snow side. "So, we went down into this secondary chamber. It was about forty feet below the main cavern."

"Uh-huh." She sounds distracted, and I hear water running.

"What are you doing?"

"Cleaning some mushrooms I found."

"Are you making spaghetti?"

She laughs. "No, Boo. These are not eating mushrooms."

"Oh—"

"Right. Now tell me the rest of your story."

"Oh, yeah. We're down in the lower cavern, and suddenly I hear music."

"Uh-huh."

"Then the next thing I know, I've gone limp. But instead of falling to the ground, I'm floating."

The water stops running. I hear Nana shift the phone. "What do you mean floating, April?"

"I guess it wasn't like really floating. At least nobody said I was physically floating when I came back. It just felt like that."

"April, you have to slow down. I can't keep up with what you are saying. Explain that part to me again."

I don't care for the tone of her voice. She obviously doesn't understand nothing wrong happened when I did this.

"Okay. I heard music, then pretty much everything went black. It was sorta like I was passing out. But I knew I was still standing. And then it felt like I was floating on my back."

"This is really important, April. I need you to think and tell me. Did you float straight up and down, or did you feel like you were floating like—"

"Like on the ocean, when the tide pulls you?"

"Yes," her voice cracks.

"Anyway, forget about that. The neat thing is a few seconds later, I'm still in the cave, but it's nineteen twenty-five.

"To be clear, I don't mean like I could see ghosts from that era; I was interacting with them. I was there, in their world. It was nineteen twenty-five in a cave in Kentucky, and I was at a dance party."

Nana doesn't answer.

"Did you hear me, Nana? I think I can travel back in time."

"April, tell me how you got back."

She apparently isn't as stoked about it as I am. It is a downer to my excitement. Nana is the one person I knew would genuinely appreciate a skill this high on the weird scale.

"I don't know. I sorta started floating again."

"And you just ended up back where you started. Just like that?"

I'm becoming irritated. "Sure. I was floating like I did the first time."

My sudden remembrance of the details sends an icy chill up my spine. There was the jolt followed by a change of directions the second time. "The second time Liza was calling to me. I followed her voice back, Nana."

"You need to tell Liza thank you. She saved your life."

I snort a laugh. "How's that?"

"Location displacement is a complicated spell, young lady. If you don't remain focused on your destination, you very easily can float out to the unbroken shadow."

Nana must already be eating those shrooms. "Unbroken shadow? You're pulling my leg now."

"I don't joke about these things. You know that."

The smile fades from my face. I'm feeling nauseous.

"The unbroken shadow is the darkness that exists between time and places. There is far, far more darkness than there are time and places. You're a fortunate girl. You need to give your friend a hug. She might not have known what she was doing, but her instincts are strong and she must have felt what had happened to you."

There is more truth to that about Liza than what Nana would know. Liza is the one person who might recognize my passing out to be a paranormal event.

"Are you still there, April?"

"Yes, ma'am," I whisper.

"If you ever feel that sensation again, you have to fight it with everything in you. I'll try to find you some information on it, but even then, I'm not sure it's something you will ever want to utilize. I think I would rather hang myself than be floating out in the dark void for all eternity."

No. That doesn't sound like a happily ever after to me. "Yes, ma'am."

I hear her exhale. "Is there anything else you care to share?"

"No, I'm good. I'll talk to you when I get back."

"Okay. But, April, please be careful."

"I will."

As I disconnect our call, all I can think is what a killjoy. Here I thought I had an incredible new skill, and instead, I almost floated out into space. How do I make sure it never happens again?

Chapter 25

Sicilia pulls up short as she enters the office. "Oh. I didn't realize you were still in here."

Her comment makes me self-conscious, and I stand. "I can leave."

She waves her hand at me. "No. You just surprised me. Are you better now? Calvin said you gave everybody quite the scare."

"Sorry. I think the change in atmospheric pressure must have gotten me."

She gives a curt nod of her head as she shuffles paperwork on her desk. "I've talked to management until my lungs have turned blue about closing that portion of the tour. We've had tourists afflicted by vertigo and claustrophobia in the past. I swear it's just a matter of time before somebody hurts themselves coming down that ladder."

"It wouldn't be too difficult to open the entrance wider and build a stairwell into the lower chamber," I say.

She shakes her head. "The Historical Society won't have anything to do with it. They want it maintained exactly as it was the night it was closed."

I know Dusty and Miles must have researched the history of the cave. Before we go on a typical excursion, we are given extensive briefings on the case.

As Miles explained to me, we didn't receive a briefing before this trip because he didn't want anything from his report to color what Liza or I felt during the scouting excursion. I want to be true to Miles's requested method, but one teeny bit of information isn't going to hurt.

"What year was it closed, Sicilia?"

Her brow furrows. "You know. I should know that. I'm not sure, but before the depression?"

"Nineteen twenty-five?"

"It could be. That sounds about right. I'll try to dig that up for you by the time we have our debriefing tomorrow."

"Do you live in the area?" I ask.

"Born and raised. One time I thought I was going to get out of this town. But this is a sweet gig, and I inherited my grandma's house last year."

"Oh, I'm sorry to hear that."

She scoffs. "No. She's not dead. Grandma decided to take off for Florida early last year. She said it was better to get out of this town late than never."

"She sounds like my kind of gal. I wish I had the opportunity to meet her."

Sicilia's expression lightens. "She's a pistol. Way too wild for someone her age."

"I pray my grandkids will say the exact same thing about me when I'm old. Assuming I have kids," I say.

The smile fades from Sicilia's face as she returns her focus to the paperwork. "Something to aspire to, I suppose."

The front door opens. Miles pokes his head in the office. "Are you ready for lunch?"

I hadn't realized how hungry I was until he asks. "I'm famished."

"Good. Luis put together a huge feast for us." Miles considers something carefully. "Sicilia, would you like to join us?"

Looking up, she graces him with a smile. "I would love to, Miles, but I'm running too far behind for lunch today."

"Okay, but if you decide you want to come by and grab a

quick bite, please don't hesitate."

"Thank you again for the invite."

As we walk onto the porch, I can see the van and trailer past the entrance to the caverns. They sit on a knoll two hundred yards away from the office. The path is formed by a thin strip of gravel.

The heat and humidity here are as bad as they are in Alabama this time of year. But I notice there are fewer flying biting bugs. This time of day, down on the lake, you're liable to walk through a cloud of gnats, or worse, no-see-ums, those ferocious, microscopic flies that try to eat you alive.

There are some impressive, old-growth hardwood trees throughout the property. A few gnarled hickories look to have survived a couple of centuries, and at least three oak trees have six-foot diameter bases. It is rare to see this much old-growth so close to civilization these days.

"Calvin said there's a lady ghost in the campground?"

Miles faces me with a frown. "I'll ask you to forget about that, April. Music and screams have also been reported at the speakeasy, but neither you nor Liza sensed anything in there. If I were a betting man, I'd say we came up to Kentucky to see a big old hole in the ground and enjoy the night around a campfire."

Miles has no idea how wrong he is, but that's because I'm not currently doing the job I was hired to do. "Will this set Dusty back on his projects?"

"No. Dusty has plenty of material for a few more books. The tough part is we need at least one if not two excellent excursions in each book. The other eleven"—he wobbles his hand—"eh. They need to be professionally written. Still, there doesn't have to be a major find."

"It seems like they would want all thirteen stories to be like our Birmingham excursion."

Miles raises an eyebrow. "Uh, no. People say they want to be scared. But they only want to be scared to a certain point. If you give them thirteen stories like the Birmingham one, they wouldn't be able to finish a book. It is better to slide five powder puff campfire-type stories in and then hit them with one that makes them stay up all night with the lights on. They can only take so much."

It still amazes me how my brother and his team have developed a strategy for success. I know it took years of dedication and trial and error, but they truly have come to a point where they can produce a product he knows will sell. All they do is tweak the template outline occasionally.

Every team member has their role, and everyone at least appears to enjoy their job. I'm the notable exception to the merry band of ghost hunters. That's why I'm the part-timer passing through.

This part-timer is the only team member who sensed anything in the speakeasy. The part-timer also must emulate the master storyteller's writing style so his greedy estranged wife doesn't kill his career.

Here I thought I was coming along for the ride. Instead, I'm having to steer the boat and keep it off the rocks. It doesn't seem entirely fair.

There is a large tent, twelve foot by twelve foot, pitched near our trailer. The small, lit campfire is in a round trench. There is a grate over one corner of it with a skillet of refried beans. The grate also holds a rectangular-shaped stoneware piece with aluminum foil over it. Whatever is in the stoneware smells spicy and makes my mouth water. My stomach sounds off an appreciative grumble.

Liza comes out of the tent and straightens her back. "There you are. I just finished filling your air mattress. Will you lie down and at least try to rest?"

Luis walks back from the truck carrying another rectangular piece of stoneware. He favors me with a broad smile. "You might want to get some enchiladas in you first. They always make me sleep like a baby."

Luis is attractive, considerate, and an accomplished electronic guru. From the smell of it, he can add accomplished chef to his accolades as well. His future wife will be satiated long before they make it to the bedroom each night.

"Here, have a seat." Liza opens a lawn chair for me.

"Thank you, but all of you need to stop. I just got momentarily overloaded down there in the hole, and I'm fine now. You don't have to baby me."

Luis, squatting next to the fire checking one of the casserole dishes, looks over his shoulder. "We know. We're simply thrilled you are okay."

Some days it's still difficult for me to transition back into this lifestyle. Not the paranormal. The lifestyle where people genuinely care about you, your health, and your state of mind.

I spent the last seven years as a member of a large organization where we talked about love and sisterhood. Only to have too many of those "sisters" stab me in the back the moment being my friend was either inconvenient or blocked them from something they coveted.

I'm slowly realizing how jaded I have become. My cynicism outright embarrasses me somedays.

Gently, my family and coworkers are coaxing my trust in humanity back to life. It feels good.

"What are you hiding under the aluminum foil, Luis? The smell is teasing me."

"Chicken enchiladas for the mild-mannered and hot tamales for the wild at heart." He wiggles his eyebrows, accentuating the word "wild."

"I don't think I've had hot tamales before," I say.

Liza sets a lawn chair down next to me. "Luis makes the best. They are spicy." Liza waves her hand in front of her mouth.

"What's life without more spice?" Luis counters.

Miles appears with paper plates that he hands to Luis.

"The enchiladas are my mother's recipe, But the hot tamales are from my abuela."

The pride in Luis's voice is readily apparent. I think about the greens and beans my Nana made for me waiting in my refrigerator.

I reckon how the hot tamales are Luis's comfort food and heritage; beans and greens are my comfort food. I should have Nana teach me how to make them.

No. That's a stupid idea. Besides, I need to learn how to make something besides ramen noodles and no-bake cakes before I venture into Southern comfort food.

Miles comes back around the edge of the tent holding several dripping water bottles. He passes them out, handing me two. "If you plan to try those hot tamales, you're going to need two bottles to put the fire out."

"Y'all are gonna scare me off if you keep talking."

Luis hands me a plate with beans, two enchiladas, and two hot tamales.

"I can't eat all this, Luis."

"You say that now. We'll see what you have left on your plate afterward."

Well, he's cocky enough about his culinary talents. I'll just see.

They do have me disconcerted talking about how hot the tamales are, so I opt for the enchiladas first. My shoulders relax, and I lean back and chew.

Luis's enchiladas are pure heaven. I'm ruined for the rest of my life. None of my favorite Mexican joints can ever measure up to this recipe.

Intense, distinct flavor caresses my palate. "You are so in the wrong profession, Luis. You should open up a restaurant."

He waves his hand at me as he passes Liza her plate. "It would never be as good. Cooking for friends, it always ends up tasting better."

Miles points a finger at him. "Don't you say it. Don't you dare say it."

Luis grins as he spreads his arms wide. "Because it's cooked with my love in it."

Okay, that sounds sorta wrong. But these are too good to stop.

"Man, he just had to go and say it," Miles complains.

"Here you go, my friend." Miles doesn't have an issue accepting his plate despite Luis's comment.

I'm still marshaling my courage to try the hot tamales. Instead, I sample the refried beans. I find them to be excellent, too. "Who gave you the recipe on the beans?"

"Old West Texas."

I have no idea what Luis is talking about. He must have recognized my expression for confusion since he bends over and lifts a large can at his foot. It has a bold red label with "Old West Texas Refried Beans" prominently stenciled on it.

It's silly, but we both burst into a laughing spell.

"Are we agreed that the caverns are a bust?" Miles asks in between shoveling food into his mouth.

Liza stops eating and stares at me pointedly.

"What?"

"Nothing. I'm only curious what your thoughts are."

"You're the one who said you might've heard something."

Luis lays his fork down and has a pained expression. Our eyes meet. He sighs heavily. "I didn't want to mention it because, as a rule, your senses are better than the electronics. The electronics can pick up on energy patterns that don't necessarily mean we have a spirit present. Especially when we're down in a hole like that. I'm not positive what effect that has on the equipment."

"What are you trying to say?" Miles asks.

"When you two were trying to help April, after she passed out, the EMF was going crazy."

"Why didn't you mention something, Luis?" Liza frowns.

"We had more pressing matters. We didn't know what was happening with April. Then honestly, I forgot until just now. Besides, if neither you nor April felt anything, I would write it off as the equipment going haywire."

"That settles that. We'll have to go back tonight to at least confirm if it was a false positive," Miles announces.

Fear grips my heart—Nana's words about the unbroken shadow course dread through my blood. "I'm not going back in that hole. Especially at night."

"No. Of course not," Miles says. "The atmospheric pressure is messing with you. We don't need you passing out again."

That keeps me out of the speakeasy, but I don't like the idea of any of us going back into it. "I thought the real ghost was supposed to be in the campground. Why waste any more time in that hole?"

Miles and Luis exchange glances; Luis just shrugs.

"What are you two not telling us?" Liza says.

"I guess it won't hurt since we've gotten your initial reading," Miles begins. "One of the more prominent sightings has been a large male ghost in the speakeasy."

Henry. The brooding spirit I felt must have been Henry.

I'm conflicted by this news. On the one hand, I'm relieved selfishly that I had not caused the argument that ended Henry's life.

I have been feeling guilty that I altered some historical event and got Henry killed. It seems he would have died even without my foray back in time.

Still, I'm sad to know Henry died in the manner I saw. Sticking up for a woman against her abusive suitor.

I should tell my team what happened—all of it.

Still, after talking to Nana, I know they will insist on taking me home. I don't want that embarrassment.

I will wait until after the excursion. Then I will confide the truth in Liza.

"I suggest we hang out for the next hour, hour and a half, and let our food settle. Then we can take a hike around the property.

"The last tour is at four o'clock, and we can take our time going through the caverns. Then come back and do a good scan of the campsite," Miles says.

The two hot tamales sit on my plate daring me to bite them. They look tasty, and if they are anything like the enchiladas, I will regret not trying them.

I cut off a portion of one with my fork and put it in my

mouth. The flavor is intensely bold and satisfying. I have not tasted anything like it before.

With each chew, additional heat emanates out of the tamale burning the inside of my cheeks. I swallow the first bite. It feels like Luis used napalm for sauce. Grabbing my open water bottle, I down half of it in one gulp.

Luis is grinning at me. "Good?"

Oddly, yes. It is so friggin' hot I'm sweating profusely. Still, the taste is unique, and I crave another bite. "Delicious."

"I told you they were outstanding," Liza says.

Cautiously I take a second bite, and my mouth warms to a new level of hot. I would not be surprised if this evening I have blisters inside my mouth.

I swipe at the sweat beads popping up on my forehead, knowing the back of my head is already soaked in sweat. But the tamales are too addictive for me to resist. I shovel a third bite into my mouth.

Luis better not ever cook for a woman he isn't interested in. If I weren't determined to move far from Guntersville, I'd consider proposing to him on the spot just for his cooking skills.

I finish my second tamale and hold icy water in my mouth to soothe the damaged lining. Man, that was good.

Luis can do with enchiladas and tamales what my brothers do with a grill. "Luis, thank you so much for lunch. That was delicious."

"The pleasure is mine," Luis says.

Enjoying my full, contented belly, the warmth of the sun on my skin, and good friends, I nod off in my chair. I can use some rest after the earlier paranormal event.

The thought makes me jerk back to consciousness. "Luis, Miles, did you bring any equipment besides the EMF into the hole?"

"No, we usually don't bring any visual in until we have confirmation. It's too bulky to carry around. We go in first with only the EMF and the tape recorder," Miles says.

"You had a tape on you?" Why didn't anybody mention this earlier?

Luis shrugs. "Yes. But none of us heard anything."

"Have you listened to the tape?" Certainly they gave it a listen. These guys have been on too many adventures not to check all their equipment.

Miles rolls his hand. "Protocol sorta went out the window when you went down, April." He turns to Luis, "We do need to check it before we return to the lower cavern this evening."

Luis stands. "I'll go get it. We can listen to it now."

"I'm sorry. I'm silly," I say to Luis's back. I hate he must run another errand after he just cooked for me.

Miles frowns. "No, not at all. We're supposed to check all readings and collaborate. Understand, Luis just got done telling us the EMF was going off the chart when you fell out. None of us had a clue why. This is good."

Luis returns with the recorder and a small speaker. He hooks the speaker up and presses play

Calvin's voice is prominent as it echoes off the walls. He's telling the story about the chandelier and the piano.

I notice I'm holding my breath. Staring down at my hands clasped in my lap, I focus on listening to the recording.

The first five notes are incredibly faint. The subsequent ten increase in volume, and I cut my eyes to meet Luis's. His jaw drops open on "What those five feet could do."

"What is that?" Miles asks.

"A piano," Liza says.

The music gets louder then stops abruptly.

Only I know why.

I was at the bar. Having already passed through the "veil" and skirted the unbroken shadow. I was in the past, and there was no further need for the music to call me.

"Play it again," Liza urges.

Luis goes back to the start on his recorder and plays it again.

Liza scoffs as she shakes her head. "That's exactly what I heard. How crazy is that?"

"That would fit with the timeline. The speakeasy was closed in the twenties because a man was knifed to death," Miles says.

Something cold turns in my stomach. Miles knew all along.

I understand the purpose of not letting Liza and me in on the history. Still, sometimes it seems it can make the job more dangerous than necessary.

That's not true. Even if I had known a man was stabbed to death on the premises, I wouldn't have known I would be pulled through a time warp. I still wouldn't have known who was stabbed and been able to help Henry.

What if I had known? If I had been able to warn Henry and saved him, what disastrous chain reaction might I have caused by stopping the murder?

"That settles whether or not we have to go back to the speakeasy tonight." Liza looks at me. "You should stay at the top of the ladder and let us know if you hear or see anything."

It's a kind suggestion by Liza. It's still closer than what I want to be, but it keeps me out of the subterranean club. "Thanks, that'll work."

"Are you okay? Your color doesn't look right." She lays the back of her hand on my forehead. "I think you might have a touch of a fever. Go lie down and take a nap. We'll let you know before we head out on the hike and see if you're up to it."

I would argue that I'm fine, but the stress of the day is wearing on me. The lack of sleep the night before is only compounding my mental fatigue. A nap is an excellent suggestion.

Liza leads me into the tent, where there are four air mattresses. Each has a sleeping bag on top.

"This one is yours. Just lie down and rest until your coloring looks better."

"Hey, Liza."

"Yes?"

"My Nana told me I need to thank you."

"Thank me for what?" she asks.

"I can't tell you right now. But I promise you I will."

Liza frowns at me as her eyes narrow. “You’re an odd bird, April Snow. Now get some sleep.”

Chapter 26

I wake to Liza shaking me. The interior of the tent is darker.

"How long have I been asleep?"

"About five hours. Do you feel better?"

I sit up too quickly. The blood rushes to my head. "What time is it?"

"It's almost seven," Liza says.

My heart sinks. I've let the team down. We were here to do a job, and I've been in the tent asleep. "I'm sorry."

"For what?"

"I feel like the sick kid that's holding the team back. I wouldn't have come if I thought I'd be so much trouble for y'all."

Liza snorts. "You can be a pain in the butt. But you're our pain in the butt."

"Thanks. I guess."

Liza grabs my hand as her expression hardens. Our eyes lock.

"We need to get something in the open. If there's anybody here who can understand that sometimes you need to work things through in your mind before you share them"—Liza taps her chest with her finger—"you're looking at her. There's a lot of times I don't share things right off because I'm not sure how to explain them. But we never dodge a direct question. Are we clear?"

My shame bubbles to the surface in the form of a loose tongue. "I didn't mean to—"

Liza raises a hand to stop me. "I'm not asking for an apology, and I don't want your excuses. I want to know I can trust you. That means that if I ask you a direct question, you give me a direct answer even if it's 'I don't know what happened.'"

Great. I should've known better than to think I could conceal my secret from Liza. Miles and Luis, no worries. Liza can sense such things.

"Now your team is going back into that speakeasy, and I need to ask you. Do you think there might be anything there that means to do any of us bodily harm?"

Good question. The only hostile energy force during my episode was Mason.

The apparition reports were of a large male figure, which wouldn't be Mason. He is a below-average-sized man. I must believe that ghost was Henry.

Besides, unless another team member decides to take a time-traveling walkabout in the 1920s like I accidentally did, I don't feel they will encounter Mason.

"No. I'm almost certain there's nothing there that will harm us." I add an exaggerated nod of my chin for extra confirmation.

"Good." Liza inclines her head toward me. "See, sharing is not so tough."

"I guess not."

Liza clasps her hands together. "Now, in reciprocation. Are you feeling anything odd about this campsite?"

I wasn't before Liza asked. "No."

"There's something here." Her lips thin. "Watching us intently."

Hearing spirits speak in my head, and worse seeing them occasionally, gives me the heebie-jeebies. Yes, I've gotten used to it over time, but I'm still not desensitized to the point it doesn't make the hair on the back of my neck stand up. Ghosts and spirits are what I sense the easiest.

Liza, on the other hand, senses what I consider to be the genuinely creepy. Stuff like satanic blood rights, demons, and contractual soul transference. The major league of all creep factors.

I don't really want to know, but of course, my curiosity isn't going to let me rest until I ask. "A demon?"

"I wouldn't have let the boys set the tent up if that were the case, silly. No, there's some sacred agreement that's been broken here. Something of profound sadness."

I lean forward. Liza has my full attention. "Like what?"

"And that's why we are here. Right?" She smirks.

Man, that's just not right. "You can't be dropping in a Perfect Paranormal Publications commercial break in the middle of a statement like that, Liza. Tell me what you're feeling."

"See. This is why you and I sometimes don't speak up right away. We're still trying to figure it out." She pushes up on her left hand and extends her right to help me up.

"I thought you needed to know because you might be able to reach out and better understand what is only tickling my senses."

She points at the end of my air mattress. "Get your boots on. The boys are about ready, and they're not going to wait forever."

I consciously push out with my mind as I tie the laces of my boots. I didn't feel anything during lunch and apparently while I slept. But if Liza felt something, maybe it is here.

I stand and open my senses fully—searching, stretching, listening for the faintest of energy.

Nothing. I bet Liza made this up to appear like she was sharing something. I know I deserve it for having kept my secret about time traveling.

"Hey, hey, sleeping beauty has woken up," Miles says as I emerge from the tent.

"Sleeping beauty? I want to know what it says about you two that Liza had to kiss me awake rather than y'all?"

Luis and Miles exchange a quick glance.

Luis points to Liza and then me. "You two are a couple?"

"She was joking, Luis." Liza lifts two loaded backpacks and hands me one before strapping hers to her back. "Dinner, water, and a couple other survival items. You never know how long we'll be gone from camp."

I grab the lantern light off the side clip of my backpack. Even though there is still enough light to light our way. I turn it on, curious to see how bright it is. It cuts a broad path through the dusk. "Cool."

"Yes. But be careful not to blind yourself with it," Miles says as he leads us toward the hiking trail. "I've got point. Liza, do you mind taking up the rear?"

"Sure," she says.

Miles leads us back toward the mouth of the cavern. The guys pull ahead, and I walk side by side with Liza. I notice the amused grin on her face.

"What are you up to?" I ask.

She points at herself. "Me? I'm not up to anything."

"Tell me."

She licks her lips and points at the guys in the lead, "Do you see anything wrong with this picture?"

I don't know what she is driving at, and I write it off as I'm still foggy from my nap. "Not really."

"Those two would walk through a ghost before they saw it. One of us should be in the lead."

I start to giggle. "Why don't you mention it to the men?"

"What? And fracture their male ego. No. I'm not that concerned about it. If I felt something nasty earlier, I would mention it. But I'm with you; I don't think there's anything malicious in that cavern."

My giggling subsides. It occurs to me that although Liza and I have saved each other's lives, we haven't bonded on a personal level. Given neither of us are the biggest "sharers," that is not surprising.

I decide it is time to start and go first. "Hey, Liza, what do you do for a living? I mean when you're not working for Dusty?" The question sounds awkward, and I cringe on the inside.

"I work at an assisted living home in Scottsboro."

I could've had a thousand guesses and never gotten that right. "Really? How long have you been doing that?"

"Since high school," she says.

"I can't imagine doing that. Do you like it?"

Liza shoots me a sideways grin. "I didn't know we were going to play twenty-one questions tonight."

"I'm sorry." My face heats.

"And how many times are you going to say that today?"

I start to explain myself and take note of her eye roll.

I'll try the social bonding some other time. I remain quiet the last few yards to the cavern. Being silent is not exactly my strong suit.

Reaching the cavern, I feel the difference. It's difficult to explain since it's all relative. It has to do with energy levels.

As a rule, the more definitively good or evil a spirit is, the stronger the energy level. Likewise, the younger ghosts typically give off more energy than older spirits. If there is no white or black magic involved.

There's also the factor of multiplicity. It is rare to be in the city and not feel some current in the air. The more populated an area, the higher the number of spirits present. In the woods, it is common to find areas of complete bliss where there is not any energy in the air.

The mouth of the cavern is utterly devoid of energy.

"Alright, let's keep the group tight," Miles says over his shoulder, leading the way into the cavern.

I turn to Liza. "There's nothing in here."

"I know. But it will keep the boys busy, and we're on the clock anyway."

There is a novel thought I hadn't had on my own. We are going to be here until Sunday afternoon regardless, and we must be doing something. Why not go double-check the caverns even though we are positive there is nothing in them?

I guess some days it's about showing up, clocking in, and clocking out, so you get paid.

Luis pulls out his EMF meter and swings it in an arc as he walks. No tweets or flashing lights emanating from it. The needle is buried on the left-hand side as if it needs four more AA batteries.

The bats stir in the distance, and I hope they fly out a different exit than the mouth of the cavern. It is evident by their sound that there is a small legion of them, and I'd rather not get in their way. When we reach the mouth of the speakeasy, Miles turns. With an expression of concern that is comical, he addresses Liza and me.

"I need you two to focus before we go down the ladder. Do either of you feel anything malicious?"

"That delicious hot tamale I had is feeling pretty mean about now." Liza and Luis laugh. I'm horrified I said that out loud.

"This is serious business, Snow."

"I'm not making light of it, Miles. But I'm not feeling anything at this point. I think we're fine."

He pins his eyes on Liza. "You?"

She purses her lips. "Same as earlier today. Nada."

"All right, then. We'll go down and do a sweep. If we don't find anything, we can come back up and walk the grounds." Miles places a boot on the first rung of the ladder. "It will be a shame if this is a bust."

I suppose that would depend on the definition of a bust. Lord knows I've already had my fill of paranormal for the day and am enjoying the reprieve.

After Miles and Luis disappear down the ladder, Liza asks me, "Are you sure you're going to be okay up here? By yourself."

"Sure. It's not like I'm afraid of the dark or anything. Besides, I've got this handy-dandy lantern light here, so I'm not really in the dark."

"Unlike some of us." Liza points down the ladder and grins.

"Now that's downright mean of you, Liza."

"Oh, like you didn't already think it," she says as her head disappears down the hole.

The chatter of the bats increases exponentially. I suppose they are heading out for the night. I try to remember that they are excellent at clearing bugs out of areas. It's why earlier I noticed there were so many fewer flying bugs around the cave.

There isn't much for me to do except stare into the darkness and wait. I can imagine Miles and Luis walking around the walls of the speakeasy with their EMF equipment. Liza, playing the part, will be acting like she is attempting to feel electrical currents that we both know are not down there any longer.

It is just a theory. I don't really know how all this works yet. But, when the bartender said "thank you" to me, I knew there was something monumental about it. In my heart, when he spoke the words, I believe he let go and moved on.

Henry's smile and the ease washing over his face even though he was in incredible pain told me it wasn't about the physical being anymore. He was telling me thank you for releasing him.

That is incredibly sad if I think on it too long. In some ways, it's even more disturbing than the handsome man having been killed. He was forced to wait a century for someone to come along and release his spirit. I guess I should feel good I was able to do that for him.

Good gosh, how long does it take to look around a hole in the ground, guys?

I feel as useful as a trapdoor on a canoe up here by my lonesome. Not to mention I've got an extra-large serving of boredom.

To amuse myself, I devise an experiment to see just how dark it is in the cavern. Turning off my lantern, I'm immediately engulfed in the pitch dark. I lift my hand but can't see it.

My finger is on the lantern's switch, but I never turn it on. I realize for the first time in months it is tranquil; nothing is clawing at my brain. It is complete bliss.

In several ways, it is like this morning when I was floating in between the endless shadow. The one significant difference is that I know I'm sitting still right now. Earlier I was moving, and something was pulling me out and away from my body.

The thought of accidentally traveling again crosses my mind. I flick the lantern back on.

I wonder if there's a safe way to travel. Surely someone figured out how to minimize the risk.

I'm stupid. It's not like driving a car. From Nana's reaction, too few people have the skill for much to be known. It's not like I'm going to find a *How to Minimize the Danger of Time Travel* text. If there was, everyone would think the author to be a complete nut.

That's what's going on. I'm just nuts. My life is driving me nuts.

For Pete's sake, come on, Liza. You know there's nothing down there. I'm bored out of my skull up here.

If I'd been thinking ahead, not a strong suit of late, I would have brought my laptop. At least I could be working on Dusty's book.

What a mess. If I sleep only two hours a night for the next three weeks, I can complete Dusty's book, arbitrate Jared Raley's divorce, convince Jethro to take the plea bargain, and start on Chuck's divorce.

Lucky me. That doesn't leave any time for job hunting or social activities with the other sex. This is fine since I have the same amount of offers on both counts. Zero.

Is this how people get old? It's not really an age thing; it's wearing out by lack of getting what you want and need. You can only get pumped about your pending opportunity so many times. Following Granny's beliefs, if you have your dreams dashed enough, you come to expect it and thereby bring about a self-fulfilling prophecy.

I have a self-fulfilling prophecy. I've got to use the little girls' room. I move closer to the entrance of the speakeasy and look down over the edge of the hole. I can see an occasional flash from one of their lanterns.

"How much longer are you going to be?"

It was quiet. A light blinds my eyes. "Sorry."

"Dang, Miles. I think you shot my eyes out," I grouse.

"Sorry. What do you need?"

"I'm wondering how much longer you're going to be?"

"Not long. I think it's just wishful thinking now that we'll find something." His voice has an uncharacteristically disappointed tone.

I watch Miles's shadow move away from the base of the ladder. I settle in at the top of the ladder with my feet braced on the first rung.

I wonder if Lauren ever made it out of this town. Escaped the clutches of that creep Mason.

It is irrational, but given my situation of being stuck in Guntersville, I need to know she traveled the world and lived a fulfilling and adventurous life. I can endure anything if I know we all get our happily ever after.

It would require a high level of research to find out unless she was somehow tied to this property. I would have to go to the county courthouse and see if there are any records of her after 1925. If she were lucky, I wouldn't be able to find anything because she left.

Why was Lauren tolerating a man like Mason? Especially since they weren't married.

It wasn't only Lauren's reaction that bothered me. A sizable portion of the town was having a grand old time, and then they scattered as soon as Mason went crazy. Why would an entire community put up with his bullying?

I'm wired so differently. If someone like Mason ever tried to lay claim to me, I would beat the holy tar out of the little sucker. Then if that didn't get the job done, I'd get my brothers to help me stomp a mudhole in his butt.

I might even ask Nana to sick a haint on him or make a hex bag that will leave him peeing fire and blood every time he mistreats a woman for the rest of his life.

See. If I can convince Nana to teach me cool stuff like spells, I will be her star pupil.

Unfortunately for Henry, Mason has already escaped my wrath on this side of the "veil."

"Come on, guys. If it hasn't happened yet, it's not going to," I holler into the black hole.

"Just a few more minutes, Patience."

Liza's sarcasm brings a grin to my face. I appreciate her fearlessness about calling it as she sees it. If anyone were to ask me when we first met, I would have bet money we would become mortal enemies.

I was the team member only participating in the ghost excursions because I needed cash, and my brother bribed me. I have skills. Still, skill with no training and a prominent level of apathy toward it can be more dangerous than helpful.

Liza was on the complete opposite end of the team spectrum. Task serious and an incredibly well-seasoned hunter complete with the equivalent of a black belt in spiritual castings and a paranormal knowledge base second to none. Her body, covered in tattoos of demon warding chants, demonstrates her higher commitment to the paranormal calling again.

Liza's fanatical desire to protect her team, even if it means putting herself in harm's way, is in direct contradiction to my motives. My goal is always to get through the project as unscathed as possible. Still, we've been able to make it work so far.

The older I get, the more I realize opposites do attract. I suppose I appreciate a friend who can fill in the holes of my personality.

A thumping noise emanates up from the hole. Looking down between my legs, I make out the white of Miles's eyes as he climbs up.

"Well, that's a bust," he says in a rush.

I stand, dusting the rocks off the back of my jeans. "We should listen to the recording before we write it off totally. We might have captured some more music."

"No. We took a listen to the recording while we were still down there in case we were lucky. There's nothing." Miles exits the mouth of the speakeasy and looks deeper into the main cavern. "I suppose we could walk the rest of the cave and then make another round on the nature trails."

Liza pulls up out of the hole. "There's nothing on those trails."

"We still have to do our due diligence and double- check them." I enjoy throwing Liza's words back at her, and it earns me a "glare of death."

"Before we go on the trail, I want to get those cameras set up in the campground," Luis says as he joins us.

Miles nods in agreement. "True. The equipment isn't going to do us any good in the trailer. If you got it, you might as well use it."

Miles pulls his phone out and checks the time. "It's nine thirty. I figure if we get everything set up at the camp by eleven, the trail in the dark should take about an hour and a half.

"Then we can get some shut-eye at one o'clock. We'll debrief Sicilia as soon as she's in tomorrow morning and just head home. I don't see much point in running up the expenses on a dry well. Agreed?"

We all agreed in unison, but as we did, I had a significant déjà vu moment. Perhaps Monstrous Caverns wasn't ready for us to leave just yet.

Chapter 27

The walk around the property is enjoyable. To be fair, all pressure is off now.

Liza walked the trail with the boys earlier, and she didn't sense anything. Taking Miles's words to heart, we're on the downside of this investigation. He is working on the checklist for this trip he has stored in his memory.

My two previous excursions with the team have desensitized my scare trigger. I hear a couple owls as well as a plethora of small creatures scurrying away through the brush as Liza's lantern illuminates the way. It's a moonless night and approaching midnight, two things that historically would have been sufficient to make my hackles rise.

Instead, I'm taking a leisurely stroll with my friends through the woods.

Miles stops our progression in front of a small family cemetery. It consists of a dozen modest chipped tombstones, the etching faded smooth by decades of rain. The wrought iron fence has been meticulously cared for by someone in the area.

"Do you sense anything?" Miles asks.

Well, duh. It's a cemetery. Even when the spirits move on, their bodies give off slight residual energy, including favorite sayings and traumatic moments in their lives, whether joyous or tragic.

Standing in a cemetery, if you're clairvoyant, can cause you to go insane. It's like listening to random thoughts of a drunk person on a constant loop. Forget waterboarding; standing in a cemetery is absolute torture.

Even so, there is no opportunity to capture any of the items of documentation required for Dusty's stories here. "I heard voices in my head" doesn't make for a very compelling ghost story. However, it might earn you a stay at a psychiatric facility.

Liza and I share a glance. "I got, nada," Liza says to Miles.

"Me too," I lie. Move along, nothing of interest to see here.

We reach a crest, and I can get a better scope of the shadowed property. The silhouette of the camping ground to the office and the hill face I know to contain the cave I estimate to be four hundred acres. On the north side, a small cluster of new homes is lit by the white glow of streetlights.

A sizable block of trees has been razed near the houses. Cut down for the next phase of the subdivision.

Progress can be good. Still, when you take a pristine piece of property that has survived the centuries, it seems a shame there isn't a push to maintain its original character. If nothing else, a place for school children to see what the forest looked like before the Europeans came to America. Once it is replaced with thirteen-hundred-square-foot, vinyl-sided homes, you can never get it back.

I frown to clear the thought from my head. That's the country in me talking. Folks need affordable housing, too.

We start down the incline as the trail continues toward the campgrounds. Unbelievably, with each step, I become giddy with excitement. I am consumed with the hope that Luis will restart the fire so we can make s'mores before we turn in for the night. It's like I'm turning into "camping girl" or something.

The LED lights on the cameras Luis set up earlier turn from red to green as we enter the campsite.

"Can you check the footage before we turn in for the night?"

Miles asks Luis.

"Turn in? What happened to s'mores?" I ask.

"I didn't hear anything about s'mores," Miles says.

Liza shrugs her backpack off, letting it land on the ground. "We don't have any supplies for s'mores. You have to plan ahead for stuff like that, Princess."

Whatever. "If somebody had mentioned this was a camping trip, I could have planned ahead."

"You wouldn't have come," Luis says in a matter-of-fact tone.

There is that, too. "We're really going to bed?"

"Yes"—Miles flips open the tent flap—"some of us didn't get a five-hour nap."

"I had a traumatic event."

Liza puts her hand between my shoulder blades and pushes me toward the flap. "Which is why you need more rest."

"Yes. I'm too tired. I'll just check the cameras in the morning," Luis says as he follows us into the tent.

Miles sets a ridiculously huge LED lantern in the center. I'm positive our tent's glow can be seen by passing airliners.

As everybody unrolls their sleeping bag, I want to giggle. This is like some adult kid slumber party.

Assuming Luis has closed the flap completely to keep the creepy crawlies out, this camping thing might not be as bad as I remembered. Tonight might even be fun.

Miles kills the light once we are settled in our bags. We are plunged into immediate and complete darkness.

I'm too amped to sleep. Staring into the darkness, out of boredom, I reach out with my energy. I feel and hear nothing.

The night air feels thick and stale—the silence presses in on me.

I hear the slow, steady breathing of one, two, and then three of my friends. I'm the only one awake.

My mind is in overdrive. My only hope is it will eventually tire, and I'll fall asleep like everyone else.

My thoughts keep circling back around to what happened to

Lauren. I know myself well enough that I'll have to research her history and hope to discover what came of her.

If we hadn't already decided to leave early, we could swing by the courthouse in the morning. I would love to investigate marriage and death records. No. They won't be open on the weekend.

While an excellent research tool for current events, the internet is useless for happenings before the late nineties. A young woman from a small Kentucky town in the 1920s, unless she became a celebrity or politician, will not be found electronically.

I clutch the back of my neck as a migraine pain shoots up my neck causing me to gasp in pain. Quick and brutal, it stabs at the base of my skull.

Then it's gone. The sensation of pain remains tingling on the skin above the afflicted area.

There is something at hand. Something is awfully close to us.

I roll over on the air mattress to face the tent. I listen intently with my ears and paranormal senses. I can feel it, but I can't hear it.

I squash down my fear, pull in a deep breath, and open my paranormal thoughts fully. The words of Liza, "Are you feeling anything odd about this campsite," force me to shudder.

Everybody's definition of odd is admittedly different. Liza specifically said it was sadness over a broken pact.

Me? I just feel an all-powerful spirit dangerously close. Just as disconcerting, it is attempting to remain quiet for now.

"Liza," I whisper. "Liza." I don't dare say it any louder. I couldn't if I wanted to since fear is crushing my lungs.

Okay. I can do this. I clear my mind and ask using my paranormal energies, "Who are you?"

Nothing. Total silence. Still, I felt a jolt in the energy. As if I had startled the entity.

The energy level increases with every passing second. The air between me and the tent wall feels as if it is crackling with electricity.

"What do you want?" I ask under my breath in case it can't understand my paranormal attempts to communicate.

It has no better effect. Still, I get no answer.

I pray this spirit isn't malicious. The power it is giving off feels like standing in front of a live uranium rod. It's so forceful the energy is blowing right through me.

The energy field moves to the left and circles the tent. I sense it ends up in front of Liza. She does not wake.

My mental clock ticks. The entity stays inches away from Liza for ten minutes that feel like an eternity. Still. I wait for it to make its first move.

Slowly, the energy slides to where the boy's mattresses are against the wall of the tent. The spirit spends scant seconds observing Luis, then Miles. It is uninterested.

Again, on the move, the power stops in front of the tent flaps. I freeze in terror considering what I might do, besides die of a heart attack, if it decides to enter our tent through the flaps. I know it's stupid to believe it would use the entrance to come into our tent. I'm sure an entity of this strength could just pass through the tent wall anytime it wanted. It's not like polyester is some powerful ghost-deterring fabric.

I pick up my phone to check the time. To the best of my recollection, the spirit has been circling us for thirty minutes.

In paranormal terms, that is an eternity. Not just because of what it does to your gut by scaring the living daylights out of you, but the fact that it takes an incredible amount of energy from the spirit. I wonder what passion could possibly give it so much available power.

And why in the world is it circling our tent? What is its intent?

Every time I believe I'm becoming accepting of the visitor, it makes another move, and my fears are renewed. When it comes back around to stand in front of my mattress, I have this overwhelming desire to pull the bed away from it.

But I know that won't fix anything if the spirit's habits have already displayed any indication. It will simply circle around and stand in front of Miles's side.

Still, that would put Miles between me and the spirit. That does seem like a marginal improvement.

I decide to be brave and push out to the entity again in case it wants to communicate now. It still doesn't respond. I sense it is confused about something. Something sad. Why won't it just tell me?

It calls to me. Not with words. I sense its energy wrapping around me and pulling me toward it.

The energy warms me and beckons me to follow. A peace so magnificent washes over me as I am coaxed to its side.

No!

I need to be careful. I can't go on another walkabout in between the endless shadows. I've got a lot to live for.

Besides, who would feed Puppy. Never mind. We all know who would feed Puppy. But I don't need to be suckered into doing something stupid by this ghost.

Truthfully, I'm becoming irritated. If it isn't going to communicate with me, it needs to go away and let me sleep. I've noticed my eyelids have become increasingly heavier during the last few minutes.

I focus my mind and blast the pointed message, "Go away."

The spirit's power glow grows even more potent. I turn my phone's light on for comfort.

The side of the tent indents. I gasp, swallowing an air bubble that hurts like a mule kicked me in the chest.

The polyester fabric stretches inward, and I make out the rough facsimile of a face. Still, the polyester strains like Saran Wrap extending closer toward me. The head appears grotesquely misshapen.

I crab-crawl off my air mattress, heading toward the center of the tent. I want to scream, but it's caught in my throat, and I can no longer breathe.

"What is that?" Liza hisses. Her eyes locking onto the red polyester face with the gaping, disfigured mouth protruding into our tent.

She pulls her boots on, lacing them in a flash.

"What are you doing?" I gasp against the pain in my chest.

"You don't want to see what it is?" Her tone is incredulous.

Uh no. I have a healthy curiosity, but there is no way I'm going out there. For that matter, there's no way I'm letting Liza unzip the tent flap. It's held so far; there's no reason to give the female spirit an open door.

Liza crawls toward the tent entrance. I grab her wrist. "Don't. You might let it in."

"Don't be silly." She waves at the mouth that is now opening and closing. "If it wants in, it will let itself in. It doesn't need my permission."

The scream startles us. We snap our attention to the red face before we realize Miles is screaming like a child,

"Oh, holy baby Jesus, what is that?"

Luis wakes with a start. "What—what—what?" The heel of his left hand pushes against his forehead

"Shhh..." Liza holds a finger to her lips. "Don't scare it off. I want to go see what it is."

"How is the tent stretching like that?" Luis asks as he turns the center lantern on while rubbing his eyes. "Polyester isn't supposed to stretch like that even on full-figured people."

When the ghost's hands stretch the polyester, too, I become so frightened I become dizzy. Perfectly formed hands encased in red fabric enter our tent. Wrists then forearms follow until the hands are directly over my pillow.

It is irrational, but I dive for my pillow and pull it off my air mattress. I might need it for later.

A baby's cry echoes through my head. It is deafening.

The ghost's mouth works itself open and closed like an overgrown red goldfish.

The baby's cry pierces my skull again. It's as if it is right next to my ear. Or in my head.

A blood-curdling cry of desperation emanates from the red mouth, "My baby. Let me see my baby!"

"Where is that baby cry coming from?" Luis protests as he spins about.

I'm dumbfounded. "You hear that?"

"Of course, I hear that. It's about to split my head open."

That is interesting. The cry is not only in my mind. I'm not sure that knowing that is helpful to our current predicament. In fact, I think it might make it worse.

"I don't like what it's doing with the tent. It's not going to hold." Miles's eyes bug out in an unnaturally large manner. I'm concerned he may fall over onto his side from fright like a baby goat.

The baby's cry pierces my mind again.

Ghostly red hands part further and cup upward. "Let me see my baby!"

"Maybe it's just me, but I'm concerned that whatever it is outside is going to be quite upset when she gets in this tent and there's no baby." Luis is struggling to remain calm.

Me? I'm one part grab the lantern and start swinging it at the face protruding over my bed, one part run out of the tent like a bear is trying to maul me, and a small portion is praying not to pee myself.

"I'm going to see what it is," Liza insists, moving toward the zipper.

"Don't be stupid. It's a ghost. And if you unzip that zipper, I might have to jack you up!" I yell at Liza more aggressively than I intend.

Her mouth drops open as if I just insulted her heritage. She continues to gape at me as if expecting an apology.

I shrug my shoulders. "What? We don't know if it's dangerous. I don't want anything to eat you."

"We can't just stay in here like trapped animals," Liza insists.

"I'm pretty good with staying in here as long as it doesn't get in," Luis says.

Miles nods his head so many times he looks like a bobblehead doll. "Yeah. Don't open the tent—whatever you do—don't open the tent."

Liza slams her fists onto her hips. "I can't believe you are turning into a bunch of scaredy cats."

"Discretion is the better part of valor," Luis recites.

"Oh, stuff your valor." Liza reaches for the zipper again.

The baby lets out another agonizing wail, and the hands protrude further into our tent.

Liza points at the hands. "The tent is going to tear any minute anyway. You might be wanting to think of your plan B."

Fair. The side of the tent is stretching preposterously as the entire front half of a female form is stretched out over my air mattress. An illusion in play allows the polyester to stretch unnaturally, but even illusions have their breakpoint; this seems to be reaching it soon.

All I can think is we need to get somewhere with solid walls quickly. The office would be perfect. But a two-hundred-yard run to a locked door that we will have to figure out how to unlock does not seem like the best plan.

The cave offers no protection. It doesn't have any closed-off rooms. Even if it did—yeah, no. That's the last place I'm seeking shelter tonight.

Yet, spirits can pass through walls. Why is this one going through the trouble of stretching the tent to its limit? Why not come through the sides? And where is the baby scream coming from? If I didn't know better, I'd swear it's in the tent with us.

"Let me see my baby!" The mother's screams are more bone-chilling than the cries of the baby. Either way, they both make it difficult to think.

I have an idea. "Liza, just hold on for one second."

She frowns at me. "I'm not sure if you have a second before it comes through the side of the tent."

I wasn't paying her any attention at this point. I pulled my air mattress over and undid the air plug. Laying all my weight on it, I tried to empty the air out as quickly as possible.

"What are you doing?" Liza asks.

"Working on a change of venue." I turn to Luis. "Is the trailer empty?"

His eyes squint, then he grins. "Yes."

I can't help but smile that he is amused. I'm not gonna say it's a great idea, but at least it will put a solid wall between us and whatever is stretching the tent. I tuck my air mattress under one arm, my pillow and sleeping bag under the other.

"You're all going to want to grab your sleeping bags and your pillows. I'm headed to the trailer, and you're welcome to join me," I announce.

"You think that'll work?" Miles asks.

I have no idea, but I know the tent isn't working and will fail entirely before long. "I don't know. Like Liza says, it's time for plan B. If you have a better idea, believe me, I'm willing to listen."

Miles stays silent and shakes his head.

I turn my attention to Liza. "There's no reason for you to confront the ghost. We have all the video cameras running. Why don't you just come to the trailer with us?"

The gears in her head seem to turn uncharacteristically slow. "Let me be the first one out and then bring up the tail to the trailer."

Luis nods in agreement. "That's a good plan. That way, Liza gets eaten by the ghost instead of us. Thank you for your sacrifice, Liza. I will remember you fondly."

Liza glares at Luis. "Eat me, Luis."

He points at the red apparition coming through the side of the tent. "No, that's what she's going to do if you don't come to your senses and listen to April."

"At least make yourself useful and grab my sleeping bag and pillow for me," she says to him.

It is surreal watching her unzip the tent. We have been in some dangerous situations the last two excursions, but this is different since it feels like we are trapped with no means of escape.

I struggle not to hyperventilate.

The excruciating wail from the newborn shreds my mind again. The tent fabric stretches further. The female form, wrapped in red polyester trailing back to the rest of the tent, stands in the tent's center.

This is going to be one of those things I'll never be able to unsee. Years from now, assuming we survive tonight, this image will cause me to shake involuntarily as the heebie-jeebies overtake me.

"All right, let's be ready to make a break for it, guys."

Liza unzips the interior and then the exterior flap. She scrambles out.

Crawling through with my sleeping gear, I jump to my feet, making a beeline for the trailer door without looking back.

Chapter 28

Liza will have to fend for herself on this one. I tried to talk her out of it. If she's going to be hardheaded, she'll have to live with the consequences. I pull the double doors of the trailer open and throw in my air mattress.

There are a couple of pieces of steel slotted strut on the trailer floor. I sling them out of the trailer to make sure we won't have to deal with them.

Miles and Luis are close behind me. They jump into the back of the trailer. We shut one door and wait.

Two female screams fill the hot evening air. Liza comes running around the edge of the trailer and leaps through the open door. I pull it shut and shove a cheater bar in between the two doors.

We stand, panting in the darkness.

A blinding light hurts my eyes.

"Sorry, guys. I should have warned you," Miles says.

My vision returns, and I see Miles adjusting the lantern light.

I look back to the trailer door, staring at the cheater bar. I'm not sure what I think that is going to do.

"What did you see, Liza?" Luis asks.

I turn my attention to my friend and am shocked at her bright white complexion. "Liza?"

She shakes her head vehemently. "I have no idea." She

collapsed onto the trailer floor. "I would say the Lady of the Shadows the legends reference. She's distraught she's had a baby taken away from her."

I give her a droll look. "I think we figured both of those facts out already."

"Excuse me for wasting your time with the obvious," she shoots back.

"Are you sure it's the Lady of the Shadows that Calvin mentioned?" Luis asks.

Liza screws her face up as if Luis had just asked the stupidest question in the world. "Dead lady floating six inches above the ground wrapped in gray shrouds?" She rolls her lower lip out and rocks her head from side to side. "I'm pretty sure it's the ghost we've been trying to locate."

"But why did she do that with the tent. Ghosts come through stuff, not stretch them." I'm beginning to worry about Miles. He looks like he is one more adverse event away from going to a dark place.

"It's not that unusual for spirits with high energy levels to be able to—"

The horrific scream outside the trailer stops me from continuing my explanation. The sheer agony of it grabs our attention.

We hold our breaths. In silence we wait for the next scream.

I can smell our fear in the stale air growing hotter by the moment.

A scratching noise vibrates across the trailer side. We make a collective gasp.

So help me, if the ghost bends the trailer's side panels, I might just go ahead and die of fear.

She trails something down the length of the trailer, creating a skin-crawling scratching noise. Then it stops.

I can't speak for the rest of the team, but I'm so tense I don't believe my voice box would work if I had a mind to say anything.

My legs begin to cramp from standing. Checking my phone,

I am shocked that we have been standing at attention, waiting for the next outburst for twenty minutes.

"I'm going to blow up the air mattress." Nobody moves or objects to my whispered announcement.

I find the valve and begin blowing into the mattress. I'm sure it was a lot easier for Liza earlier when she used the excellent air compressor tool. But there's no electricity on the inside of the trailer.

I watch my three partners over the top of the air mattresses as I blow. Given what we have seen on prior excursions, I'm surprised how shaken all of us are with tonight's event. Then again, we've never been cornered in a confined area. Each of them have their ears cocked toward the door, waiting for the next banshee scream.

Filling the mattress completely is impossible. As my cheeks burn, I decide it is as full as I can get it.

I pick up all our gear so I can slide the air mattress under us. It's a lot like playing Twister in a closet. Everyone remains remarkably quiet as they lay out their sleeping bags and go about the business of getting as comfortable as possible.

I lie on top of my sleeping bag. I doubt I'll be able to sleep.

The team quits moving, and I clear my mind to the best of my abilities. I push out with my energy to touch the ghost and understand what is causing the apparition's pain.

I locate it. It's standing directly in front of the trailer doors. If it's waiting for one of us to come out, it will have to wait for an exceptionally long time.

Giving up, I pull back into myself. There is nothing but pain and insanity left in the ghost's mind. This will not be easy.

Dealing with a malicious spirit is one thing. This ghost is by no means evil if I'm reading it correctly, but it is totally insane with loss. Given that, I'm sure it would hurt one of us if it got the chance.

The minutes pass. A part of me is becoming more upset with Dusty and Miles's rules about not telling us about the site's history before our scouting project.

This is a powerful spirit, and it is not young. It would've helped to know what we were dealing with before coming up against it.

There is barely enough room for our four sleeping bags to be laid out lengthwise. Miles gets into his and zips it all the way closed, making him look like the colossal wiener he is.

It's too hot in the trailer for the rest of us to do that, and we continue to lie on our sleeping bags with our arms crossing our chests so we don't encroach upon each other's space.

I can wait for the recording in the morning, but my curiosity is piqued. "What did the ghost look like, Liza."

"Just a white girl in her twenties. Except she was floating six inches off the ground. And her face appeared to be crushed."

"Like an accident?" I ask.

"I didn't exactly get the opportunity to pry," she snipes.

Something about it wigged Liza out. That's not easy to do.

"I'm going to turn the light out," Luis says.

I nod in agreement. I don't like the way the ghost is waiting at the trailer doors. But if she isn't screaming or beating on the trailer sides, everyone else might as well try to get some sleep. It seems we will be trapped until dawn.

I lie in the dark on my back. Beads of sweat pop up randomly, and I feel my antiperspirant fail.

It is a terrible shame. I was beginning to enjoy the camping thing before the paranormal psychotic started screaming about a baby. At least we now have a wall, albeit only a thin sheet of metal, between her and us.

"Liza?"

"Hmm?" She sounds almost asleep.

"What do you think is up with that baby?"

I hear her exhale in the dark. "I don't know, but it sure does get the adult ghost worked up."

I continue to stare into the darkness. Soon I hear Luis on my left begin to breathe heavily as he falls asleep. Liza, on my right, follows soon after him. Nothing in the world is lonelier than everybody else being asleep on an excursion, and you're the one fool who can't fall asleep.

She continues to float almost catatonic a few inches from the door of the trailer. She gives off such a strong energy wave I can practically sense her outline through the doors. I don't dare push back. Her insanity is unfathomable. The level of intensity can only be created through extreme worry and anxiety in solitary confinement for decades.

Living or dead, I've always had a healthy respect for crazy. At its best, it can be amusing. At its worst, it can be homicidal without even intending to be.

At first, I thought the baby's wailing was only in my head. But the rest of the team confirmed they heard it, too. That leaves me with even more questions.

Is the baby on her side of the "veil" or mine? Why can't she locate the child?

Something is screwy. I can understand why the Lady of the Shadows would go stark raving mad if she's been searching for her child for a century.

A yawn catches me by surprise. What a day. No, what a week. It's impressive, even with the ticked-off, high-energy ghost outside the trailer, how I'm still awake. Besides, if she decides to bum rush the trailer doors, there is nothing we can do to stop her.

There is another topic I need to talk to Nana about. For that matter, Dusty too. I've now been on three excursions with the team, and in all three, we've met with mortal danger and have had no way to defend ourselves.

That isn't wholly true. With Liza's conjuring abilities and my impromptu magic, we have some weapons. Still, we need some more basic means of protection that the entire team can wield in a crisis.

Possibly Nana knows of some ways to temporarily dispel a ghost. At least long enough to make an escape. The anxiety for the team right now isn't so much about seeing a ghost. That has become commonplace. The problem is our exit is blocked.

If we could just buy some space and time to make it to the

office and unlock it, I know we would all feel better. Safer.

Then again, I'm the only one awake. It could be I'm the only one concerned that the trailer isn't safe.

I yawn again. This time so wide, I feel my jaw pop.

Sleep isn't going to come, but I shut my eyes anyway. I hope by doing so I can calm myself further.

If it weren't for the intensifying smell of sweat, I maybe could lower my anxiety. But the scent is so overwhelming. There is just not enough air in the trailer, and it is a constant reminder that I am confined in a small metal box with three other people.

Trapped.

Chapter 29

The cloying copper scent of blood mingles with the musk of sweat. Good gosh, my stomach is roiling. If I can't calm it soon, there is a chance I'll be sick. It's not like there's anywhere to be ill. Just the thought of possibly seeing my enchilada dinner again is unbearable.

It's not the usual blood smell. There is something slightly off with it—an extra tang to the copper scent.

The sweat, with a sweeter aroma, is different than what I am accustomed to also. It may be mixed with—a woman's fragrance?

A baby wails, and my eyes pop open.

Fear squeezes my gut. My lungs expel out all air as if someone has punched me in the sternum.

Lauren is lying on a four-poster bed. A haggard-looking woman with skin more worn than the leather of a construction worker's boots stares at the newborn cradled in the palms of her hands.

The infant's umbilical cord, still connected to the placenta, trails into Lauren. The newborn's skin is still covered in blobs of white fat, yet the midwife makes no move to clean the screaming child. She is frozen in a trance-like state.

"Is it all right!" Lauren pants. "Is it a boy or a girl?"

The midwife shakes her head, regaining her ability to move.

"It's a girl, honey."

"Let me see her."

"Let me get her cleaned up first." The midwife lifts a towel while turning to me and lowering her voice to a conspiratorial tone. "Child, you lock the door and make sure that Mr. Riddick doesn't come through. You understand me?"

"Yes, ma'am." The body I occupy moves, and a door comes into view. I'm struggling with the vertigo effect. It's as if I'm a passenger looking through someone else's eyes. I did not choose to move.

Looking through the person's eyes, I see a feminine, youthful hand reach for an old-fashioned key resting in the keyhole. The hand, coal-black, turns the key and places both hands against the yellow pine door.

"Lauren," the midwife speaks to the new mom, "I need to prepare you for something."

My view shifts from my young hands pressed firmly against the door, panning to the two women at the bed. The midwife clips the umbilical cord, tying it expertly in a knot.

She wraps the baby in a rough towel and scrubs her despite the alarmed complaints of the child. "Shush now. You're going to have to be tough to survive in this world, little girl. You've been dealt a tough lot."

The midwife holds the bundle out to me. "Hold her for me, Sicilia."

"Yes, ma'am." Sicilia reaches for the child. I feel her face stretch into a smile as she moves to uncover the baby's face. "Hi there, cutie."

"Let me see her, Wendy," Lauren cries.

Sicilia takes a step toward the bed. She doesn't want to let the baby go. The child feels warm against her chest.

Wendy gestures for Sicilia to stay back. "Lauren, before you hold your daughter, you need to push the rest out. You'll take ill if the baby sack stays in you."

Sicilia and I are both happy about the delay. I feel our thoughts melding, and we are both curious.

We cradle the baby with our left arm as we uncover the towel from the infant's face with our right hand. We gasp in shock and nearly drop the child.

A vast blood-red mark trails across the baby's face from right forehead to the left jaw, covering half her milk-white face. Collectively, our jaw remains open as we study the unusually large facial birthmark.

A thundering knock at the door shocks me into action. Sicilia has frozen in fear. I am now in control of our shared body.

Turning toward the door, I clutch the child instinctively to my chest.

"I hear the baby. Let me see it!" the loud masculine voice booms through the door.

I turn from the door to the bed. I'm confused, but Wendy's expression of extreme fear convinces me we are all in danger.

"Just a moment, Mr. Riddick." Wendy snaps her fingers at me. We make eye contact. She points at a spindle chair in the corner. "Child, get that chair and put it up under the doorknob."

Sicilia is wholly checked out. My movement toward the chair is jerky, but I grab it with my right hand and set it under the doorknob. I give it a push with the toe of my deeply scarred black boot to ensure it is snug and in place.

"Good job, Lauren. We are all clear now," the midwife says. I turn in time to see her wrap the placenta in newspaper and drop it into the wastebasket.

"My baby now. Let me see my baby."

Wendy shuffles back a step from the bed. "Lauren, she has the mark of the Devil. She can't stay with you."

Lauren's expression of expectation crumbles into one of devasted despair. She shakes her head side to side, first slowly, then picking up speed as she begins to shout. "No! No, it can't be!"

Wendy appears to be on the edge of tears as she wrings her hands. I feel them welling in my eyes, too, as I steal another peek at the otherwise handsome newborn girl I hold.

"I'm so sorry," Wendy offers because there is nothing else to say.

Lauren says nothing, yet something dramatic changes in her expression. It's as if I witness the moment her sanity shattered.

"Lauren, do you understand what must happen?" Wendy asks haltingly. I can tell she has noticed the change in Lauren, too.

Lauren smiles at Wendy. Oddly, it is as if she is looking a few inches above the midwife's head when she says in an unnaturally pleasant voice, "It won't matter. She's our baby. He will love her anyway."

The doorknob jiggles violently. "You ladies open up. Why's this door locked?"

The male voice sounds familiar to me this time. Disappointment and despair roll over me. No, Lauren, what have you done?

"Open it up now, or you'll be sorry!" he roars.

I close my eyes as there is no doubt now. Lauren gave in to the bully and married Mason.

Each time Mason yells through the old pine door, Sicilia pulls further back into the recesses of her mind. I feel her cowering into a fetal position attempting to hide from the hostility. From her reaction, I hold no hope that Mason's ways changed once Lauren gave in to his incessant demands.

"Lauren, I beg of you. Don't let him see her. He will kill her. Let me and Sicilia take her to your grandmother's. Your people will be able to take care of her," Wendy says in a rush.

Lauren smiles sweetly. The illusion is complete in her mind. "Mason will think she's a blessing regardless of what she looks like."

"No, Lauren. He won't. I beg of you. We can tell him she didn't survive. Think of your daughter, Lauren. Give her a chance to live. "

"What are you conniving, treacherous women up to. You

better open this door and open it now, or you'll wish you had!" Mason bellows as he strikes his fists against the door rattling it in its casing.

Wendy turns to me. "Sicilia, hand me the baby and make sure that chair is up under the doorknob good and snug."

Sicilia is gone.

I can sense the danger crackling in the air, and I want to do whatever I can to help. I quickly hand the infant off to Wendy then press down on the chair seat, making sure it holds as Mason starts to kick at the door.

"Let me see her!" Lauren screams from the bed.

The door jolts violently in its frame, and I hear a grunting noise on the other side. I figure Mason rammed the door with his shoulder. That old pine door will splinter any moment now. I pull back from the chair in anticipation of Mason's entrance.

"I swear you're going to be sorry. What y'all hiding. She was cheating on me, wasn't she! I'll skin her alive." Mason's voice sounds crazed and drunk like the night he stabbed Henry.

I've had a lot of practice with drunks. Seven years of higher education trained me to identify a drunkard that is mouthing off because they're temporarily bulletproof versus a truly dangerous homicidal drunk. Mason is a card-carrying member of the latter group. He's proven it once before, and I'm afraid he intends to prove it a second time.

"Change of plans, ladies." All the color has drained from Wendy's face, and she's twitching as if she is afflicted by a nervous tick. "We have got to get out of here. All of us, right now."

The door trembles as Mason charges it again. "That's it. I'm going to count to ten, then you're going to know the real meaning of pain. One..."

"Can she move? She just had a baby." My voice is higher pitched with, unbelievably, a heavier Southern accent than usual.

Wendy pulls at her hair. "Sicilia, she's has to. She can't stay here with him that way."

Fair. I look across the room in search of anything that might double for a weapon.

Sicilia appears to be a similar physical size as me, which means we might take Mason down if we can find something to defend ourselves with.

"Nine, ten!"

His demanding voice draws my attention back to the door. The chair has begun to slip, and I wonder how much longer it will be able to hold Mason out.

With a deafening explosion, a two-foot hole appears in the middle of the door. I flinch as a storm of splinters and chunks of wood fly across the room.

A second blast destroys the spindle chair. Wooden spears fly toward the bed.

Bless it! What is this fool doing? He's blasting his way in with a twelve-gauge with his newborn and wife in the room?

More pieces of the door fall away as Mason kicks the bottom half with his boot while using the shotgun stock as a battering ram against the remnants of the top of the door.

Wendy shoves the baby back into my arms, "Sicilia, you carry her out. I will help Lauren."

I put both arms around the crying baby and bend over her as I run through the kitchen to the back door of the long row house. I reach for the doorknob.

"You better freeze right there, girl!"

I know Mason is yelling at me, but there's no chance I'll stop and put the baby in harm's way—until I hear the shotgun rack another shell into the chamber.

Never would I have thought I would stop when hearing that distinctive sound. I would expect to run faster, considering the rage in his voice. Instead, I freeze. My boots—Sicilia's boots—might as well be nailed to the floor.

The thought of hot steel projectiles punching through my flesh makes me tremble. I quit running, but that is no guarantee Mason won't fire nine pellets of double-aught buckshot into me out of sheer meanness.

I don't know how this works. But I'm worried I may be about to draw my last living breath. The fear mixes with my disbelief that my life would end in this manner.

"That's it, girlie. Turn around nice and slow."

"Let me see my baby!" Lauren screams again.

From the corner of my eye, I see Wendy attempting to quiet Lauren.

"Yeah. Me too, Lauren. I'm curious what this baby looks like." There is an evil tone creeping into Mason's voice. It raises the hairs on the back of my neck.

He keeps the shotgun trained on me as he squints his eyes. "Go on, girl. Give Lauren her baby."

I don't move. The longer I look down the three-quarter-inch barrel of the twelve-gauge shotgun, the angrier I become. I feel my crazy bubbling up, and it is all I can do not to say, "You better hurry up and shoot me now because I'm about to kill you."

If I were in my own body, I'm mad enough to let the chips fall where they may. But I'm not. I'm in Sicilia's body, and I have an obligation not to get her hurt if I can help it.

Still, this piece of human feces has already killed one good man in front of me. I assume he got off with a slap of the wrist, considering he doesn't look much older than the night he stabbed Henry in 1925. Now he is terrorizing his wife and his newborn daughter while he accuses his wife of infidelities.

Mason better be glad he's married to Lauren and not me. Infidelity would be the last thing he would be worried about. He'd need to be more concerned about waking up in a bed on fire with the bedroom door nailed shut if I was his wife.

As I approach him, the overpowering stench of stale whiskey on his breath envelops my face, forcing my gag reflex. He sweeps the shotgun barrel from me to the bed aiming it at Lauren and Wendy.

I try to slide by him. He reaches out with his left hand, cat-quick, and pulls the towel from the baby's face.

His hands tremble fiercely. He looks up to me, the dangerous concoction of alcohol and anger putting murder in his eyes.

He yanks the towel back further. The baby's face, now fully exposed. The blood-red stain seeming larger and redder as the rest of her face begins to recover from the labor.

Mason snorts a laugh. "What the devil?"

I can tell that of all the scenarios Mason's psychotic mind had given life to, his imagination did not consider what was before him now.

His head cocks to the left as his eyebrows knit fiercely. "What is wrong with it?"

"Nothing, sir. She's the picture of health." I know I was obfuscating the jerk's question.

"It's just a small birthmark," Wendy says.

He scoffs. "It's nearly its entire face!"

The anger and intoxication are mixing with two more unhealthy elements, confusion and the possibility of peer ridicule. I quietly step backward in hopes of escaping with the baby before Mason recovers his bearings.

"It will fade with time," Wendy continues.

Mason looks at Wendy as if to indicate she's either crazy or doesn't understand the workings of the world, and he will explain it to her. "Markings of the Devil don't fade! They never fade. That child is an abomination." He flicks his hand in a come here motion. "Give it to me. I'll take care of it. You women folk obviously don't have the stomach for it, and I know its no-count mother isn't going to handle it."

Wendy comes toward me. "Give her here, Sicilia."

"Sicilia, don't you dare!" Mason commands. "You give that Devil spawn to me."

I hand the baby to Wendy. As she cradles the baby, Mason reaches out with his free hand and grabs one of the baby's legs. He jerks the child toward him.

When the baby screams in pain, something deep inside of me snaps. It is as if somebody wound me too tight and, regardless of whose body I'm in, things must be set right.

I take a run at Mason and slam the palms of my hands into

his chest. It doesn't have the intended effect of knocking him off his feet, but he does release the baby to catch his balance.

"Don't you touch her, you murderer!" Lauren leaps to the foot of the bed, digging her fingernails across both sides of his face. I watch four trails of blood open from his ear to nose.

Screaming in agony, he brings the shotgun's stock around striking Lauren on the bridge of her nose. A sickening sound, reminiscent of a watermelon cracking open after being dropped on concrete, fills the hate-charged air.

Lauren collapses backward onto the bed unconscious. Mason slams the cedar stock viciously onto her face twice more.

I take a step forward to charge him a second time. To stop him from striking Lauren again.

"Sicilia!"

I turn to Wendy's voice. She's running with the baby toward the back of the house. Mason stops his attack on Lauren and levels the shotgun toward the back exit.

Breaking into a run, I chase after Wendy. To stay in that room with Mason is nothing short of suicide. I can't make that decision for Sicilia.

The blast picks me up and flings me face first toward the back door. The pain is so excruciating I can't breathe. I want to die.

Mason's boots rattle the loose, roughhewn planks that my cheek rests on as he approaches the back exit with a deliberate gait.

My ears ring as if someone has clapped them hard. There is so much blood in my mouth it feels like someone pulled all my teeth at once.

I don't care anymore. I hurt too bad. If Mason shoots me again, it might be a blessing to end this agony.

A wet blob lands on the back of my neck. If I weren't dying, I'd beat the tar out of Mason for spitting on me. Us.

"Stupid girl. Now you done got yourself killed getting messed up in married folks' business. You shouldn't have stuck your nose into it. You had no right!"

Unbelievable. Mason sounds all choked up and about to cry. As if he is the victim here. Talk about totally mental.

"It was just an accident. You should have let me in at the start, Sicilia. It didn't have to be like this. It didn't."

Please, Lord. Most merciful Lord. Please let me die now. I can't bear the pain any longer. Or at least make Mason leave so I can suffer in peace.

"It was just an accident," he says again.

Mason blows his nose loudly. "Always was a stupid girl. Nice but stupid." Mason steps over me. I listen to the echo of his boots until the door closes. He is gone.

Thank you, Lord.

Slowly, I'm able to draw more than just a ragged breath. I can feel my blood pooling under me, and I know I'm injured something terrible.

I'm scared. I'm afraid of dying.

My mind tries to reason out the time-traveling rules. If I die on this side of the "veil," what happens to my body in my realm?

Do I just not wake up. Would everyone think I had a heart attack in my sleep?

A short laugh escapes me at the thought, and it racks pain through me. It is just humorous to me. We are hiding in the trailer from a banshee ghost, so it wouldn't seem much of a stretch to believe I had a heart attack while waiting out the screaming ghost.

What has it all been about? Twelve years of perfect grades through high school and seven long years in college? For what? Who would miss April May Snow?

Something catches in my throat, and I cough. Again, the pain bursts through my body, and I pull into a fetal position. The roughhewn boards scraping like sandpaper on my legs and arms.

My brothers and my parents will miss me. Well mostly. I know they became used to not having me around after I left for Tuscaloosa. It is a short list on the "who would miss me?" parade. It's quite depressing.

And what accomplishments can I embrace for all eternity? No kids, no husband, and I didn't even get the opportunity to really use the legal skill I trained for all these years.

I must be getting ready to pass because everything is becoming increasingly dark humor. I remember how much I loved the movie *It's a Wonderful Life*, where George is shown how everybody's life would have been worse if he hadn't been born.

I have always been envious of George. At least he knew.

A laugh brews deep in me that I tamp down, knowing how much physical pain it will cause if I laugh. Still, it's like a joke twenty-seven years in the making, and somebody just told me the punchline. And it's hilarious.

Do you know what is worse than everybody's life *improving* if April had never been born? If her life didn't make anybody's life better or worse. It just didn't matter. She was a non-factor.

Now thoroughly depressed and in excruciating pain, I realize that dying takes a lot longer than I ever dreamed.

"I want to see my baby."

My thoughts aren't clear given the force of the shotgun blast and my subsequent loss of blood. I'm not sure if it's Lauren's voice I hear, or possibly she has already passed to the other side, and I'm hearing her ghost.

"My baby," she gurgles.

The despair in her voice wrenches my heart. Surprisingly, the pain of being shot did not make me cry. Now, hearing her voice, my tears flow freely.

A wet, sucking noise comes from the direction of the bed. With a softer whisper, Lauren says, "My beautiful baby."

No. Just no.

I may not have ever done something anyone would remember as selfless while I was in my body. Still, I refuse to go gently into that good night without recording at least one worthy deed, even if it is with Sicilia's last breaths.

The pain of movement forces a scream from me as I force myself up on all fours. There is no choice as the slightest movement sends hot firebrands tracking across my back. Slowly, I crawl toward the bed and lean against one of the posts to prepare for the following exertion that I'm not even sure I can complete.

"Lauren?"

She doesn't answer, and I know I must move quicker. I can't let her pass without comforting her.

Bracing my mind for the onslaught of pain, I grip the comforter and steel my mind for the last attempt. I yank myself up to a bent-over position and struggle to quell a scream emanating from deep within.

I can't stop. I must not quit. Grabbing the comforter at Lauren's feet. I pull myself onto the bed. An electrical storm of pain and fire shooting throughout the body I occupy drives me to the edge of insanity.

With one last yank of the comforter, I push off my knees. I land next to her with my left arm draping over her chest.

Blessed, that hurt! I lay next to her, panting as my sweat and blood run freely off my skin. I struggle for breath, and fear I have just expended the last one I will ever draw.

"My baby."

I rotate my head to the left to look at Lauren recoiling as I see the horrific damage Mason has done to her face. What is left of her face.

She can't see her baby or me.

Poor sweet girl. What has he done to you? I fight back a sob. I must take short, shallow breaths and fight for the strength I need now.

"You did so good, Lauren."

"My baby," her voice is faltering, weakening. How she speaks out of her ruptured, collapsed face, I can't comprehend.

I squeeze her toward me with my left arm despite the pain. "She's so healthy. And your grandma is going to do such a wonderful job of raising her for you. She will be so loved, Lauren."

Her body tenses with great agitation. "I want to see her."

"I know you do, Lauren. But here's the thing. You know how when you look at the sun, and it blinds you because it's so bright?"

Lauren pulls in a wet, rattling breath. She nods imperceptibly.

"Your daughter is so beautiful and perfect that when you look at her, it blinds you."

Her chest under my arm relaxes. She says nothing to me.

Her crushed and bloodied chin flutters up and down three times as if she approves of what I told her. She must have known the baby she carried and loved could be nothing less.

Then she is gone.

And I cry like I've never cried before.

I cry until my mind dives into darkness.

Chapter 30

Warmth surrounds me. As I have always feared, death is dark, but I feel cocooned and loved rather than cold and lonely.

I'm relieved I was able to give Lauren some peace before we died. Well, she and Sicilia died. Which dragged me into the equation, too, in this odd cohabitation.

Why am I not more upset I'm dead?

Because I'm relieved not to be feeling the pain of nine lead pellets in my back anymore. Once you have felt that sort of pain, being okay with death is just a matter of perspective.

As lovely as this feels, after a few minutes of pain-free bliss, I'm getting a tad concerned. Can this be it? Have a nice warm feeling and no other stimuli for the rest of—what—forever?

Geez. I'm going to be stir crazy before the first day is done and nuttier than a fruitcake by the end of the week.

Everybody in the afterlife must be stark raving mad. No wonder there are so many ghosts choosing to stay on the wrong side of the "veil."

That's it. I'll have to learn how to pass through the "veil." I should be able to contact Liza simply enough with her skills. Dusty, too, if he's paying attention. Oh, and Nana Hirsch, too. See, I won't be too bored.

Something is poking me in the lower back, and I wrap my hand around to move it. It feels like a—what? I freeze. I'm afraid to move.

The penis grows larger inside the silk shorts against my hand. I jerk my hand back and go utterly still.

I'm curious what my front is plastered against. I reach my hand up and very carefully pat to identify. I feel short silky hair.

Grinning, I raise my head and confirm Liza is cupped in front of me. More importantly, I'm alive!

I look over my shoulder and see that Luis is stuck to me like Velcro. Under different circumstances, I would feel violated. Still, I'm too ecstatic that I am on this side of the "veil" in my own body and alive to care about propriety.

There's no sense in alarming the rest of the team, so I remain still. I'm filled with gratitude for returning from the dead.

While I lie there with them, it feels good to be alive and touched. I'm embraced by the warmth of their bodies and not caring that I'm too warm now.

I feel naughty when I realize the heat isn't just from body temperature. I'm left with an understanding of some peoples' attraction to the ménage à trois thing.

Not for me. Definitely, not me. But I get it now.

Letting the initial embarrassment pass, I settle back into the enveloping warmth of my friends. I can't remember a recent time I have been so joyous.

I have been blessed with a gift few people ever experience. I went through death and now fully appreciate my life.

While my perspective on life has changed dramatically, my curiosity remains intact. I calm and center myself and push out of the trailer with my mind. I begin in the direction of the trailer doors.

Finding nothing, I circle the trailer with my mind—still nothing.

No sign of the Lady of the Shadows. No banshee screams, fingernails scratching on metal, or baby cries. Just silence.

It is a victory even if it leaves me with bittersweet emotions. With almost complete confidence, I'm positive the Lady of the

Shadows, Lauren Riddick, has moved on to a place of rest. A peace that sweet woman thoroughly deserves.

I will never forget how quickly we connected the night in the cave ballroom. We were two small-town girls desperate to find a way out of their hometown at any cost.

What caused her to give in to Mason's insistent overtures?

I can only wish I had the opportunity to ask my friend. But I'll never know.

Possibly, Lauren wouldn't have been able to explain how she ended up with a man who repulsed her. People ask me all the time why I make foolish decisions. More often than not, I answer, "I don't know."

I know it's vindictive of me. But so help me, when I do follow-up research on the Monstrous Caverns area, there better be a headline about a man named Mason Riddick having been executed. I know it will not make things right. But justice is the only salve that allows scar tissue to grow on such injuries.

This Thursday, I will make the trip out to Nana's. We need to have a long discussion about how I will control this new skill and remain on my side of the "veil" and in my time. In twenty-four hours, I have been thrilled by the amount of fun time travel can bring. I've also learned the hard way it can allow me to experience the worst of humanity firsthand while surviving the ultimate affliction all humans suffer. Death.

I give an involuntary shudder as the pain has not been entirely forgotten by my mind. The pain of death is a real thing, or at least the *dying* aspect. Both the fear and the pain are entirely beyond the scope of anything comprehensible.

Luis separates from my back, placing a warm hand on my shoulder. "Are you okay?"

"Yeah." I'm perfect.

Slowly, he slides his hand off my shoulder. The warmth lingers on my skin before dissipating. I miss being touched.

Lauren's daughter felt so good in my arms. She fit perfectly in the crook of my arm. It was as if she were handmade to sit there. And her big, round eyes, cute nose, and puffy, heart-shaped lips were flawless.

It was as if she was so perfect there had to be a mark on her face to make her human. Somehow it only served to accent her beauty with uniqueness.

I wonder if I'll ever have one of my own. Not that I'm in any hurry, being I'm a career girl and all. Still, I wonder if I will find the time to have a daughter.

Before I go too far down that track of thought, I might need to find a guy. In many ways, that seems more inconvenient than raising a baby.

There is another question to ask Nana. It might've been why I was so drawn to the baby girl while I was holding her. I could feel her power thrumming through my arm. Not unlike the slight electrical current I feel from Liza pressed against my chest.

Nana said she felt the power in me from the start. I want her to explain how it makes her feel. I want to compare it to how I felt holding Lauren's baby.

I now understand. To progress, to get through this life that is mine, I must keep a list of items to ask my mentors. It's not enough to ignore things and hope they improve with time. There are people in all facets of my mixed-up life who love me and are willing to share their knowledge with me.

It doesn't make me weak to ask for their opinions. I can always defer to my inclination. I'll just be doing so with more information.

How can I be so educated and just now be coming to that conclusion?

Something in the campsite moves. I hear a cover popping off one of the plastic storage bins.

The distinct sound of metal striking a rock echoes into the trailer. I push out with my mind, but there is nothing there. At least not spiritual.

Lighting in the trailer increases. Luis has turned on the giant LED lantern.

Squinting, I roll over. "Darn, Luis."

"Sorry. I thought we should put some light on the subject. Do you think the ghost is still out there?" he whispers.

"No. I believe the Lady of the Shadows has moved on now."

He flashes a goofy smile that informs me he doesn't understand. "Like moved on"—he wiggles his fingers, symbolizing somebody walking away—"or like really moved on?"

"Like went to her final destination, moved on."

"Really?"

Yes, I'm thrilled about it, too. I check my phone and see the sun should be up. I stretch as I sit up, and Liza stirs.

"Then what do you think that noise was?" Luis continues.

"I'm guessing a raccoon getting into our supplies," I say.

Luis reaches for the door handle.

"Around here, it could be a black bear, too," I add.

Luis turns. The expression on his face is so horrified I laugh. "Bears?" he says.

I roll off the air mattress and put my hands to the small of my back as I stretch. "We're in the woods. That's where they live."

Liza rubs her eyes. "What are you two talking about?"

"There's a raccoon in our supplies," I say.

"There's a bear out there," Luis answers simultaneously.

"And there's a crazy she-ghost out there, too. I guess they can all keep each other company," Liza says with a sarcastic tone. She motions toward Miles. "Did anybody check on our pet larva inside the cocoon?"

"No. We just woke up ourselves," I say.

"It bugs me. Him sleeping with it zipped up. I can't tell if he's alive or if he died of a heart attack," Liza complains.

Her statement rocks me back on my heels. I still believe that's what the team would have thought if I had died while I was on the other side of the "veil." That I had an untimely heart attack in my sleep.

Liza crawls over and unzips Miles's bag. "Who knows, we may get lucky and he transformed into Regé-Jean Page while we were sleeping."

The zipper is halfway down. Miles pokes his head out, his arms flailing. "What's the idea?" he asks as he puts his glasses on.

Liza turns back to me and laughs. "Nope. No such luck."

"Bummer."

"I know, right?" Liza reaches for her boots.

"What about the bear?" Luis insists.

"I'd say it better get out of the way. I have to pee." Liza pulls the cheater bar out from between the handles and holds it up. "Besides, I have this if that bear wants to dance."

It's apparent Liza also senses the tortured ghost has moved on. Still, I'm not sure if our campsite visitor is a bear or a raccoon. It's perfectly fine if I'm the last one out of the trailer.

As the doors open, I realize how much I missed the fresh air of the outdoors. Between my miraculous resurrection, the release of Lauren, and the beautiful sunny morning, I feel like I'm in a children's movie and am about to bust out in an impromptu version of "Hakuna Matata."

"Shoo. Get out of there," I hear Liza say as I exit the trailer.

She is rummaging in one of the supply containers as I come around the side of the van. She pulls a roll of toilet paper from the bin.

"Raccoon?" I ask.

"A bunch of squirrels fighting over Miles's Fig Newtons."

"Yuck."

Liza snorts. "Miles and rodents have the same taste buds. Why does that not surprise me?" She lifts the roll of paper as she heads towards the woods. "Don't rush out to find me. It might embarrass both of us."

I watch her stomp down the hill and measure if I can wait until the office is open for the potty break I need. The idea of poison oak in undesirable locations convinces me to try and wait it out.

"Would you like breakfast?"

Luis's voice at my side catches me by surprise. "Sure? What

do we have?"

He stretches his shoulders back and rolls his head, making a loud pop. "Ah, better."

"Won't that like make your vertebrae swell?" I ask.

Luis cuts his eyes to me and stares for a second. Deciding to ignore me, he looks away and walks to the storage bin the squirrels had not plundered. "I have some dehydrated omelet mix and precooked bacon."

I was expecting dry cornflakes, so expectations exceeded. "That sounds good."

Luis is focused on the supplies. He's speaking to them as much as me as he pulls them from the bin. "Good enough. I think they call it roughing it since, without refrigeration, you can't eat your normal foods."

Hmm. I'm reasonably sure I can successfully bring ramen noodles and Chicken and Stars camping without the need for refrigeration.

"What! Who attacked my Fig Newtons?" Miles's hair is squished to one side, adding an extra comical look to his bugged-out eyes and wide-open mouth.

"Liza said Scrat got into them," I say.

Miles straightens his back. "Who is Scrat?"

Luis laughs and presses his fist to his lip before pointing at me. "That's good. I like that little Scrat. He's always like, ahh!" Luis mimics running in place, looking over his shoulder.

"You just always want him to get the nut, you know?" I say.

Luis sobers. "I know. It's so tragic."

"It is. Everyone should be able to eat their nut in peace," I agree.

"What are you talking about? Who is Scrat, and why did you let him take my cookies?"

"Squirrels, Brainiac," Liza says as she tosses the toilet paper back into the open bin.

"Squirrels like Fig Newtons?" Miles appears to still be in denial.

"Apparently so." Liza points to the trees. "Did you take a look to see if we got any usable footage last night?"

Miles and Luis share a look of disbelief.

"I was so thrilled to be alive I forgot about it." Luis starts toward the recording device they stored in the van.

"That footage is going to be like winning the lottery," Miles says, following on Luis's heels.

I feel like I just lost the winning ticket. This means breakfast will be delayed. I vaguely remember being promised omelets and bacon, albeit an astronaut version, and a lady wants what she is promised.

There is something anticlimactic about seeing a picture or a video of a spirit after you have seen it in real life or come to understand why it came into existence. I'm not about to put a damper on the boys' excitement, but I'm merely feigning interest as they hook the hard drive to the monitor.

Luis punches Miles on the arm as the first footage of the Lady of the Shadows comes into view.

Luis had positioned the cameras expertly. Every movement of the ghost is documented from multiple angles giving us a fantastic view of her.

In total, there is an hour of perfect footage recorded by the motion-activated cameras. The shots are clear—flawless even.

The more we watch, the less enthused the boys become. I know why.

The videos are too good. Too clear and focused.

How's that for a twist.

No self-respecting paranormal hunter nor spook fan will believe the footage we are watching is anything other than a hoax. Yes, the Lady did appear to be hovering a few inches from the earth, not the easiest trick to accomplish but done regularly by fakers. The problem is the Lady herself is so well defined, so lifelike, she might as well be Liza or me wrapped in gray shrouds.

"Well, this bites the big one," Miles grumbles.

"I could try to blur it during editing," Luis offers.

Miles screws his face up. "No. Then the whole picture will

just be blurry. It's her that's too clear."

"I could try to just blur her image."

I feel for the boys. Their devastation is palpable. "If you're going to go to all that trouble, you might as well digitize her from the start. You know, to give her some extra scary characteristics to juice up her ghoulish factor. I know! Give her some exceptionally long arms with talon fingertips," I say.

Luis bites his upper lip as his brow furrows. "You think that would be better?"

Peaches. "I was joking, Luis. Sarcasm, you know?"

"I've got it!" Miles points a finger at us. "We'll just have to stay tonight and get some new footage of her."

Liza pulls a sleeve of saltine crackers from one of the bins and opens the end. "Not gonna happen, Brainiac."

"It's an excellent idea. We'll just change the clarity on the cameras tonight, and it'll be more what people will expect."

"You're not listening." Liza jams a cracker whole into her mouth.

It isn't omelets, but it is closer to what my expectations for breakfast were to start with. I sidle up to Liza, swiping a couple of crackers from the sleeve.

"I don't understand," Miles says.

Luis makes a disgusted sound, slaps the laptop closed, and walks back to where he was working earlier. I slow down on the crackers.

"You notice how we're all outside and not worried about a ghost?" Liza asks.

Miles shows his palms as he shrugs. "Yeah. It's daylight."

"It was a ghost, Miles. Not a vampire." Liza sounds like she is scolding a schoolboy who has forgotten his multiplication tables.

Miles paces as he processes the information. The rough night's sleep must have slowed his cognitive abilities. "Where is she?"

"Bruja Blanca sent her packing," Luis says as he pulls the pan from the bin.

"Who's the white witch? Is Scrat the white witch?"

"Dude, you seriously need to get back in your sleeping bag and try this waking up thing all over again." Liza points a cracker at him.

"I was able to help her, and she passed on through the 'veil.'"

Miles's eyes squint. He appears highly dubious. "But you were in the trailer. With the rest of us."

Why can't Miles just take things at face value?

"She's got this thing where she can talk to them through her mind," Liza says.

Thank you, Liza. My brain is not working at full capacity yet.

Miles crosses his arms. "If it were that easy, she would have gone into Les Blair's mind and convinced him to pass through the 'veil.'"

Fair. Les Blair was the homicidal spirit in the basement of the Paducah Hotel that nearly killed our team. It would have saved us a trip to the emergency room if I could have convinced him to simply pass through the "veil."

The issue was, Les was on this side of reality in search of vengeance. When we ran into him, his thirst for blood had not been fully quenched. "I think Les wanted to be on this side of the 'veil,'" I say.

"You're lying to us," Miles declares.

"Hey! There's no reason to get ugly about it, Miles," Luis complains.

Miles studies me intently. As my discomfort over his scrutiny grows, I feel the traitorous edges of my lips twitch upward.

"The point is, she's gone. Correct, April?" Liza locks eyes with me.

"Yes. I promise."

"No." Miles shakes his head vehemently. "You're going to have to explain to me how you can be so sure."

He points to the camera. "Because right there, I've got a grade A apparition. I just need to get the filming worked out to make this the best proof we've ever discovered.

"So, no. We're not leaving unless you explain *how* you know she's gone."

I consider staying an extra night. My time-traveling secret would remain safe, and it would only cost us a few hours of boredom.

Forget it. Once I tell the team, we'll be headed home anyway. It's not like the team can send me home early.

"I didn't want to tell you guys earlier because I thought I had a handle on it."

"Handle on what?" Liza's voice deepens.

"I may have time traveled," I say, the last two words quick and mumbled.

Liza's face somehow appears even whiter. "Did you say time travel?"

"No, she said dime Marvel." Luis turns from his cooking. His full attention is on me now. "What's a dime Marvel?" Luis asks.

"Time travel," I confirm on a huff.

Liza's mouth opens as she shakes her head. Luis has an expectant smile on his face as if he is waiting for a great punchline. Miles's expression looks like somebody passed gas, and he walked through the noxious odor.

Me? I feel like a freak—a freak who is a lousy team member.

I tend to always downplay how much taking the wrong decision will impact the people around me. It's no secret. It's because I prefer the easiest path. In this case, the easiest way is to ignore the issue and hope it passes.

Panning to each of their faces, I register their collective disappointment. I deserve it.

I understand when you're on a team, you're supposed to win together or lose together. The kiss of death for any group is for one or more team members to be flying solo.

When I didn't tell the rest of the team what had happened in the cave, I lied to them. It was a lie by omission, but a lie all the same.

The hurt concerned and confused looks on their faces are exactly what I expected. I committed the paranormal equivalent of having pain in my left arm all day and not telling my team because I hoped the heart pains would go away.

"Just last night?" Liza's tone is accusatory.

I honestly consider lying again. The thought of disappointing her more has me thinking deny, deny, deny.

It's time to come clean. "Last night and before that in the speakeasy cavern."

"I knew it!" Liza glares at me. "You had no right to keep that to yourself."

"I know. I just didn't want to mess up the trip for the rest of y'all," I whine.

"Mess up the trip? How about you get lost out there in the void and never come back to your body." Liza points furiously at the rest of the team. "And we're forced to explain to your brother and the rest of your family that you're not coming home. How's that for ruining the trip?"

There is no correct answer to that. It is probably rhetorical anyway. All I can do is stand with my jaw clenched and try not to let my eyes tear up.

Luis's voice whispers in awe, "There is time travel?"

Liza puts her fists on her hip and exhales. "There are a few people that have the skill. But the ones that are still alive don't use it. Because it's too *dangerous*!"

You know Liza has every right to be mad about me concealing what happened at the speakeasy. But the fact remains I wasn't trying to time travel. And especially the second time after Nana told me the skill was hazardous. Liza's acting like I did this on purpose.

"Okay. The cat's out of the bag. April can time travel if she's not careful. I would say I'll never do it again, but since I didn't exactly plan to do it the first two times—" I shrug and glare at Liza defiantly.

Liza points her finger at me again. If she does it again, I might just bite it off.

"You need to get a hold of your abilities. You're a danger to yourself, and you're a danger to this team until you fully understand who and what you are," Liza growls.

Who and what am I? "I'm a lawyer."

"Yeah? I don't know many lawyers who time travel," she snipes.

She has a point. "Whatever," I say.

I bow up as she scowls at me. Liza shakes her head, turning away from us. "I'm going for a walk."

Good riddance. I take stock of the boys. They are both in a stupefied state with shocked expressions on their faces.

"How about those omelets, Luis?" I ask.

Chapter 31

Liza returns for breakfast. Besides telling Luis thank you for cooking, she remains silent and ignores me. Except for the occasional mean mug I spy, that says plenty.

We break down the camp and pack the trailer. At eight o'clock, Sicilia drives up to the office. Getting out of her car, she looks toward the campground.

Without thought, I wave at her. She returns the wave before unlocking the office.

"What are we going to report to her, Miles?" Liza asks.

Miles opens the front passenger's door of the truck and looks pointedly at me. "What we always do, the truth."

Are you kidding me? "I'm not going to explain time travel to her. I don't even understand it," I complain.

"Not that truth. Just that the park won't have any more hauntings. People only want answers to the questions they've asked. If you give them too many details, it stops being reassuring and begins to be troubling."

That could be my issue. My curiosity always makes me collect too many details, and the next thing I know, I'm troubled about what I learned.

Luis starts the truck. "It's like sausage. Everybody loves sausage, but if you start telling them how to make it, they get squeamish."

I'm not sure the process of mashing pig lips and butt holes together into a membrane sleeve is the most perfect analogy. Still, I appreciate what Luis is driving at nonetheless.

Calvin is getting out of his car as we park our truck in front of the office. "Good morning." He opens the door to the office and holds it open for us.

We return his salutation and file into the office.

The smell of coffee is already in the air. I swear my hands start to shake, craving to hold a cup.

"Good morning. I see everybody survived last night." Sicilia flashes a disingenuous smile. "Anybody for some coffee. I just put a fresh pot on."

I thought she would never ask. "I do. Please."

"I sure hope you're able to put an end to all this nonsense. Our business has been down thirty percent this year since the sightings were reported.

"The business we have had is a different clientele than usual. A lot of drunk twentysomethings hoping to see a ghost. This used to be a family attraction," Sicilia complains.

"You should be able to return to your family-attraction status. You've got zero spiritual readings now," Miles informs her.

"No!" Calvin steps forward. "What about the big ghost in the speakeasy?"

"We spent two hours last night in the speakeasy and never got a single hit on the EMF." Luis backs up Miles.

"That doesn't make any sense," Calvin insists.

"It's true," Miles continues. "And the campground is cleared of all spirits as well."

"Thank the Lord." Sicilia sits down heavily in her chair. "That one in the speakeasy was more like a big shadow. But the way our Lady ghost floated, I could never explain her away to the guests, or the constant wailing of her baby."

"Wait. You could see them?" I can't believe what I'm hearing.

She gives me a look that screams "duh." "Of course we could see them. We wouldn't have allowed you here to research them if we hadn't seen them for ourselves. You can't believe half the things people say they see when they are camping."

"But you can see ghosts?" I need her to clarify.

"Of course we can. Doesn't everyone?" Sicilia asks.

"No," Miles replies bluntly.

"Not without equipment," Luis adds.

Calvin and Sicilia share a look.

Something clicks in my mind. "Are you two related?"

"She's my cousin." Calvin draws back. "Why, do we favor each other that much?"

Not in the least. "No, just a guess." Never mind the fact you both share a rare skill.

"We might still use the legend in one of the books. I want to make sure you understand that and don't have a problem with it," Miles says.

Sicilia hesitates. "I suppose. As long as you make sure to explain that you didn't find anything when you visited."

"We'll make sure to advise our readers there are no spirits now," Miles corrects her.

My curiosity still won't rest. "Has the Lady always been extremely defined to you?"

"Why?" Sicilia's lips thin.

"You said you've seen the Lady. I want to know if she recently became more detailed. Is that why you called now and not earlier?"

"She's always been around." Calvin looks down at his feet. "I think I was five the first time I saw her. She was always just sad and quiet.

"You could see through her most times. Sometimes she would appear from only the chest up." Calvin frowns at Sicilia. "I don't think she liked it when we took down the old homestead."

"We didn't take down the homestead. It fell down," Sicilia mutters.

"I didn't say we had a choice. I'm just saying that's when she became more active, more solid. The clearer she became, the crazier she acted. She was downright spooky to be around. I'm relieved she's gone."

"So, how did you take the old homestead down?" I ask Calvin.

"Like Sicilia said, It had already fallen in. There wasn't a roof left on it. I just took the backhoe and dump truck we keep for cutting paths and got busy. It didn't even take a day."

That could explain why Lauren's spirit grew in strength recently. Even why she had gone over the edge with insanity.

The house her spirit resided in for a hundred years suddenly disappeared. That would make anyone, especially someone who's blind, aggravated. Calvin must have uncovered something that held Lauren's energy that had not been exposed for decades.

"We will send you a letter to notify you if the story will be published. That way, if you want to, you can advertise the event in a promotion or just be ready to answer any questions people might have concerning the story," Miles says.

"Sure." Sicilia comes from behind the counter and holds out her hand to Miles. "And I do want to thank you for coming out and clearing this up. It will be great for us to get back to the clientele we prefer."

"You're welcome," Miles says, "and this is a huge property, so if another spirit pops up that is causing—"

"You'll be the first call I make."

I wish my mind would stop whirling. "Sicilia, if you don't mind, one last question."

She effortlessly slides back into her less-than-gracious personality. "Yes?"

"Is there anything in the town's historical records about a woman with a wine stain across her face?"

Calvin and Sicilia exchange another look and smile simultaneously. "That's Angi," Calvin says, "our grandmother Whitfield."

"She's a great healer. People used to come from as far as a day's ride to have her take a look at them. She never turned anyone away and was able to fix any ailment. Save for plain old age," Sicilia says.

Calvin wrinkles his nose. "But how could you know Angi?"

"I just remember seeing something online." I look down quickly to cover my lie.

This is the genesis I was hoping to find. This is so much more important to me than if Mason hung from a tree or spent twenty years in prison for his crime. I want the justice of knowing the angelic infant I held had a remarkable life. Even though the world was set against her from the beginning.

"She had a good life?" I ask after recovering from my lie.

Sicilia snorts. "The sole heir to half the property in town including these caves married her and treated her like a queen for the forty-eight years they were married. After he passed, she threw herself even more into helping others. Everyone loved Angi. Her birthdays were always a town celebration."

The information makes me smile. "Because she was a healer?"

Sicilia's persona brightens with considerable pride. It's the first time I recognize how beautiful of a young lady she is. "People appreciated her healing abilities. But it was the legend about the day she was born. It was a miracle she survived."

"Her Pa went and lost his ever-lovin' mind that day," Calvin interjects.

"That man was evil from the get," Sicilia says dismissively before continuing. "I'm named after the lady that saved my grandma the day she was born. She and Angi's mama were both killed by her Pa."

I feel nauseous. The pain and the violence of the day replay in my mind.

"My great-great-grandmother, who raised her, named her Angeni. It means spirited Angel."

My heart is so full I think it might burst. "That's beautiful."

"She is beautiful. She's always like"—Sicilia circles her face with her hands—"she always has this glow on her face."

"It sounds like y'all are truly blessed to have her for a

grandmother."

"She moved to Florida a year ago. Just up and said she had done all she was going to do, and she wanted to go to the beach." Calvin's tone is somber. "I miss her laugh."

"I know that must make you sad, but everyone should get some time to themselves. Especially someone with such a full life."

Calvin looks directly at me and smiles. "You would like her. I wish you could meet her."

I'm glad I got to meet her. I won't ever forget how she felt in my arms. "Me too."

Chapter 32

As we head back home to Alabama, I try to put my thoughts of Lauren, the original Sicilia, and Angeni behind me. There will be a time in the future to work through everything I learned this weekend. But it is time to put my lawyering hat back on because this week is setting up to be a brutal schedule.

First thing Monday, I must confirm the plea bargain with Jethro. I'm worried about him. It isn't that I believe the jail time will hurt him any. The man has been through a rough life, and jail will only be a reprieve from the constant grind of scraping out a living.

I'm concerned about how despondent Jethro is over Ruth's absence. Jethro seems to believe the woman hung the moon. I'm trying hard to withhold judgment on her since I have never met her personally, but let's just say she doesn't act like a very nice woman. Or at least she doesn't love Jethro the way he loves her.

How can people be so different? I hear people make comments like, "Oh, men are all the same," or "Women all want the same thing." The next time I hear someone say something like that, I want to just slap a "Fool" sticker on their forehead and never listen to them again.

Universal statements are for the lazy and defeated.

I'm presently dealing with two separate men from opposite

ends of the socioeconomic spectrum. Both are guilty of the same crime when it comes to the women they love. They put them on a pedestal.

They lifted the women into a position superior to themselves. They were so good at it the women believed it and used them as doormats.

I'm not positive who is to blame in those situations.

As Daddy always says, "If you are going to make a habit of lying in front of people's feet, you have to expect to be walked on regularly."

I can't fault the women for their actions. At least not without being a hypocrite. I dated a couple of guys in high school who acted like I was doing them a favor by going out with them. It's hard to respect a man who doesn't put himself on the same level as you.

Eventually, you do begin to think they're right. That you should find someone better to date.

I'm not proud of that fact. I'm just sharing the truth.

But let's be honest. With my recent track record, I'm a complete loser in the love arena. And I still understand that true love is built on the solid foundation of mutual respect. It must be an equal partnership.

Then there is Chuck the panty raider. Only now, he is also Chuck the cradle robber. Men like him are why the "all men are the same" statement ever became a thing.

I'm still dumbfounded that he maneuvered his way onto our client list. What was I thinking that day?

After I make positive Jethro is in as good of a place as I can get him mentally, I need to collect the comptroller books from Chuck's company in Huntsville. I also must arrange to pick up his tax information from his CPA.

It might not seem right since Carolyn is walking around knocked up by her lover. Still, she stands a chance to take Chuck to the cleaners since she holds the leverage of the perceived higher ground. At least she isn't cavorting around in public with her husband's replacement.

Unlike Chuck, who can't resist showing off his tweener girlfriend every chance he gets.

The best I can hope for is getting Chuck a "fair" deal on the asset split. That would mean I must prepare flawless documentation of the actual value of his company.

I'm confident I will be able to handle this task. Besides, those old business courses must be good for something. Right?

Blast it. I almost forgot my other doormat husband, Jared Raley. I need to set a time for the arbitration we agreed to with Crystal's lawyer.

What is the deal? How do I have so many men in my life and yet *no* men in my life? It's like I started a men's only law firm. I should make some business cards with April's Bad Boy Defense AKA April's Wayward Home for Men in Need of a Counselor and Mental Therapy printed on them. It doesn't exactly roll off the tongue.

My entire life, I have naturally attracted men to me. But drawing all these broken, rotten eggs is a recent phenomenon. One I hope is short-lived.

Speaking of bad. I crack open my laptop and take another look at the first page of Dusty's manuscript. Bless it, what a train wreck.

Okay, this is an elephant project. I promise myself I only have to rewrite the first page. Then I can put it away until we get home.

The van decelerates. I look up and am surprised to see we are at the South Pittsburg exit. That puts us about an hour away from the lake house.

I have forty pages of Dusty's manuscript rewritten. It will need additional editing, but it reads well if I do say so myself. This publishing thing is a lot easier than I thought.

"How about a pizza to celebrate?" Luis asks. "I need to gas up too, anyway."

"Celebrate what?" Miles grouses. "We came away with a big zero. The extent of the celebration ought to be we refuel the van, and we share a sleeve of peanuts and a coke. We've already blown enough of the research budget."

"We could celebrate we all came out of this alive," Liza offers.

"Yes. I admit I am pleased about that," Luis agrees.

"You two have a twisted reward system. It's like you get a reward if you win or lose," Miles says.

"We didn't lose," I interject. "We actually won so big it lost credibility."

Miles rolls his eyes. "Still, money spent and no story. That's a big negative in this business."

"I'm with April. We won. So, we get pizza." Luis clips the curb as he turns into the Pizza Shack lot.

"Careful, we don't need the cost of replacing a rim too," Miles complains.

An idea comes to me as we walk into the pizza shop. An idea only I can bring to fruition.

Chapter 33

We were only gone one night, but I'm excited to see the lake house. I'm ready to grab my gear, see Puppy, and crash on my bed for a nap.

The team will have none of that as they turn off the van and all get out with me. I'm standing with my backpack at my feet.

"We're glad Dusty let you come with us on this one, April," Miles says.

Liza gives me a quick hug. "You ask your Nana about how to control the time transference." She points the scolding finger at me. "If she says there is anything I need to watch for to help you, you let me know."

"I will."

Luis wraps me in his arms. My breasts mold to his ribs.

"I am so happy to get to know you better." He pulls me from him, his hands gripping my shoulders. "You are an angel of mercy freeing those two spirits from their torment. So, so special."

I feel all warm and buttery. "Thank you."

He releases my shoulders and graces me with another one of his sexy, lopsided smiles. "No. Thank you *angelita*."

Yeah. I'm going to have to pick up some basic Spanish.

"April." Miles walks toward me, his arms open wide.

My right hand springs forward and almost hits him in the

stomach. The disappointment is evident on his face, but he accepts my hand and shakes it.

"We couldn't have done it without you. I am going to tell Dusty we want you on all the future excursions you can fit into your schedule."

"Thank you, Miles."

I wait until they load up, wave to me again, and the van disappears at the top of the driveway turning onto the state road.

It is good to be appreciated. Even if it isn't for your chosen profession. Everybody needs to be wanted.

I grin, thinking about what I want next. I need to find my chunky, furry wrecking crew. I missed Puppy, and I want to steal a hug from him. I sling my backpack on and walk toward the sliding door of my parents' kitchen.

There is a spicy scent in the air as I open the glass door. My mouth waters. Stupid Pavlov. I can't be hungry after eating half a pizza just an hour earlier.

The aroma of garlic and tomatoes trails out toward the sunroom, and I follow it in a trance. Mama's lasagna is usually for special occasions. She is a great cook. The only thing she cooks now with her busy schedule as a real estate broker is an occasional lasagna dish.

Her lasagna is worth its weight in gold.

I hear her chatting to someone in the sunroom, and I peek around the corner. Not someone, her AirPods are in, and she is lounged back into the futon holding a bowl of lasagna. Steam tendrils float from the bowl.

Usually, when I see her, she is just Mama. Occasionally, I see her in a different light—the woman who is not just my mama.

Her bare feet brace against the edge of the coffee table, exposing all the supple muscles in her long, lean legs. Separating her long dark hair strand by strand with her slender fingers, she continues a conversation about an offer too low for her to bother her clients over.

I laugh on the inside as I feel for the poor soul on the other end of the phone line. Nobody stands a chance against Mama's negotiations.

Except for Daddy. He has always been her kryptonite.

Without warning, she turns to me and smiles. It's eerie. As if she read my thoughts. Honestly, a silly idea, but sometimes it does seem that way.

She waves me into the room.

"Listen, Joni. I have an important visitor who just dropped by my office. You need to let your clients know that we are still open to considering it when they are ready to make a reasonable offer. However, given their lack of commitment, we will be considering other bids. Sure. I understand. I look forward to hearing from you then."

She ends the call and gestures me over to sit with her. "I didn't think you were getting back in until tomorrow."

I give her a quick hug and sit next to her. "We finished up, and there wasn't any reason to stay another night." I point at the bowl. "Lasagna?"

Her eyes light up. "Jenny Marcum turned twenty-one. She doesn't have much family, and Chase asked if we could have her a birthday party."

Well heck. I didn't know there was going to be a party while I was gone.

"Is there any lasagna left?" My voice sounds whiny to me.

Mama holds up a spoonful. "We can split this bowl."

Great, and all the lasagna is gone, too. "No, I'm good."

"Are you sure?"

"Yeah. I was just thinking about a snack later."

I notice an odd smacking noise in the room. It is like a vacuum cleaner and a washing machine got together and made a new, odd-sounding appliance.

Following the noise to the far end of the coffee table, I see Puppy's butt swinging side to side with his head lowered. "What's Puppy doing."

"Fabio likes lasagna. But of course he would, since he is Italian," Mama says.

I jump to my feet and snatch Puppy up from the bowl of lasagna. A noodle is plastered to the top of his nose.

The pressure builds inside of me. I am Krakatoa, and I just developed a massive fissure in my side. "You can't feed—him—people food! Don't you know that is bad for him?"

Mama wrinkles her face. "I don't cook like I used to, but I assure you no one has ever gotten sick from something I have cooked. Much less died." She points at Puppy. "Look how much Fabio enjoys it."

I look down at Puppy, and his pink tongue whips out, curls around the top of his nose, and retrieves the errant noodle like magic. "His name is Puppy! What's with you and Daddy naming my dog?"

"Are you okay, April?" She narrows her eyes. "Did your Nana say something to upset you when you visited her this week?"

My head is going to explode. I should take my leave before I say something I'll have to apologize for later. "Never mind. I'll see you later."

"Okay, baby. But if you need to talk, I'm here for you."

I stomp out of the sunroom with Puppy squirming under my arm.

It makes no sense, but it really gets my goat that everyone is naming my dog. Geez, if you want a dog, go get one, but this one is taken. And what the heck? Everybody knows you can't feed a dog lasagna. It's got stuff in it that will kill a dog like—well, it's not good for them. I know that.

I finish unpacking my backpack in my room. Puppy is already in his bed, feet straight up in the air, making sweet puppy snoring noises.

Yeah. I used to go into lasagna coma, too. Back when I could get a slice of it.

I flip open my laptop and go back to work on Dusty's manuscript, cross-legged on my bed.

Chapter 34

Monday morning, Jade leads me into interview room number three. Jethro sits at the table. His head is hung low, and he looks like he has lost weight.

"Hi, Jethro. How are you today?"

His eyes, puffy and red, meet mine briefly before he lowers his view again. "Okay. How are you?"

"Feeling awesome. I believe we have a great deal from the DA if you want to accept it." He doesn't respond, and I try again. "Jethro, did you hear me?"

He exhales loudly. "Yes."

Alarm bells sound in my head as I take note of my despondent client. Jethro will never be mistaken for Mr. Congeniality, but this is a thoroughly defeated man. My experience has been that men with nothing left to lose are nothing to be dismissive about.

"Hey, what's up with you? You don't like me anymore?" I tease.

He looks up. His brow furrows. "Why do you say that?"

Good, at least I finally got a reaction. "You won't hardly look at me, you won't talk to me."

"Sorry. I just have a lot on my mind."

"I understand. But one thing you don't have to be worrying about is a long jail sentence. It looks like we can get you out of here in sixty days, less the days you have already spent if you are okay pleading to a lesser offense."

He nods his head but stares over my shoulder at the door behind me.

I snap my fingers in front of his face. "Hey, Jethro. Right here. That's good news. Are you okay with it?"

"If you think it is a good deal, I am."

"No. It's if *you* think it is a good deal. Are you okay with pleading and the sixty days?"

He shakes his head. "I couldn't care if it were sixty days or sixty years. It's all the same to me now."

Now. As in, something has changed. I knew it! "Talk to me, Jethro."

He simply shakes his head again.

"Is it Ruth?"

The explosion of emotion from Jethro catches me by surprise. He breaks into a gut-wrenching sob. His shoulders bob up and down as he attempts to hold the tears back, finally failing as the dam breaks.

I reach out and grasp his hand. He reciprocates, clutching my hand so tightly I grimace.

He pushes my hand away and swipes at the tears on his face. "I'm sorry," he says with a halting voice.

"No. Don't say you're sorry. Tell me what happened."

Sniffling, he leans his head back. I dive my hand into my purse and pull out a few tissues, handing them to him.

"Thank you," he croaks.

"Tell me what happened," I insist.

Swallowing hard, he takes a deep breath. "Ruth came to visit me last night. Right before visitor hours were over." He closes his eyes and comes to a stop.

"And?"

"She wants a divorce."

I was afraid we were going down that trail. Honestly, the Mullins' relationship was headed in that direction long before Jethro burned down their house.

"It will be okay. You'll get through this and be even better for it, Jethro. I know it doesn't seem like it now, but you will be good. You'll see."

His bloodshot eyes open and are wild like an animal caught in a snare ready to chew its leg off. "She told me she couldn't stand to be with a man who was the butt of all her friends' jokes. That I was the laughingstock of the entire trailer park, and she can't believe she ever got hooked up with someone as dumb as me."

I don't know where Ruth Mullins is or what she looks like, but I have half a mind to hunt her down right now and knock her front teeth out. If she still has them.

Talk about piling on. You want to break it off with a man, fine. But it doesn't give you the right to stomp on his ego while you're at it. That's just cruel, and I'm not very fond of cruel people.

"That's not true, Jethro. She was just saying those things to justify her decision. You're a good man, and she doesn't deserve you."

He buries his face in his hands. "No. She's right. I've always known I'm not as smart as most folks. I wish I were. But I'm not."

Looking up, he says, "She was the first woman to ever love me."

"Jethro, listen to me. You will be okay. You just need some time. It will all work out."

He wipes his face with the soaked tissues. "Take the deal, April. Just take the stupid deal already."

I'm silent as I study his wrecked persona. "Okay, Jethro."

He stands and walks to the back door the prisoners come through. He hammers on it with his fists. The door opens, and he turns back toward me. "April."

I perk up, eager to see any signs of improvement in his spirits. "Yes, Jethro?"

"Thank you for everything you did for me. You are a very kind person." He ducks through the door before I can respond.

The uneasy feeling I had earlier continues to grow in my gut. I can't shake the feeling that something just isn't right about the way Jethro is acting.

I'm not a psychologist, so it's not like I can quantify anything for anyone. Still, it is as if the man is irreparably broken.

On the way out, I discuss Jethro's state of mind with Jade. I tell her I have an uneasy feeling about Jethro.

To Jade's credit, she immediately presses me on if he said anything that indicated he would hurt himself. No. He hadn't. It is just a gut feeling of mine.

Jade tells me she will report it to her supervisor, and she will personally track Jethro for the rest of the day.

I'm probably overreacting, but I'm thankful she is indulging me.

After filling up my car, I drive toward Huntsville. It is a beautiful day for a drive, and it gives me ample time to work Jethro off my mind. I did the right thing by reporting his situation to Jade. It's always better to be safe than to wish later you had acted.

I double-check the address and logo on the side of the gigantic warehouse when I drive up to Chuck's company. The distribution warehouse is enormous. It is easily two hundred thousand square feet.

My expectation of some small mom-and-pop cleaning solution company is off the mark. This must be a national company and dealing in something more than counter cleaner and floor wax.

I park my tired Prius in between a Porsche and a Jaguar. I'm careful not to let my door swing too far open.

The entrance to the warehouse looks more like an art gallery than a chemical company reception area. Marble sculptures and oil paintings are tastefully displayed on black granite tile.

Yep. My assumption that Chuck is all hat and no cattle appears to be wrong.

"Can I help you?" The desk the receptionist sits behind

would serve most company vice president suites well. She covers the mouthpiece of her headset when she speaks to me.

"I'm here to see Jimmy Hughes," I say.

The receptionist arches her brow. "Do you have an appointment?"

"Yes. Mr. Davis set the appointment for me."

"One moment." She types something into her computer. Her phone rings, and she takes the new call.

I turn and examine some of the awards prominently hung on the wall between two oil paintings of what look to be Greek muses. Several of the awards are from automotive race teams. It seems D&D Chemical might be a lot more into synthetic oils, hydraulic fluids, and fuel stabilizers.

As much as I hate to admit it, I'm impressed. All the males in my family would have been impressed, too.

With that in mind, I take photos of several of the awards to see if my brothers might recognize the brands' names. It is like celebrity citing for gearheads.

"April?"

Chuck is undoubtedly a tailored suit man. In khakis and golf shirts, he looks like a total douche. He resembles a model off the cover of one of those billionaire women romance novels in a suit.

I'll never put him in the hot category, but Chuck is intriguing with the Alpha male persona he is projecting.

"Please forgive me for not meeting you. I hope you didn't have to wait long."

"No, I just got here." I'm trying to determine if this is some show he puts on for the benefit of his receptionist or if he is genuine. I'm not getting any helpful clues, so I'll roll with his sincere attitude for now.

Chuck turns to his receptionist. "Nikki, I am taking Ms. Snow back to Jimmy's office."

Nikki pulls out a lanyard with a visitor pass attached. "Her visitor badge."

Chuck waves his hand dismissively. "That won't be

necessary, Nikki. Ms. Snow works for us now."

He gestures toward the glass-paneled staircase. "Jimmy is on the second floor."

I start up the stairs, and Chuck falls in next to me.

"You make products for racing vehicles?" I ask the obvious to break the awkward silence.

He laughs. It sounds slightly off to my ears. "We like to call it our laboratory."

"How so?"

"The portion of the business I started when I got out of college was vehicle performance products. Specifically, fleet vehicles."

"Like trucks?"

He grins. This time it reaches his eyes, which light with a passion. "Yes, eighteen-wheelers mostly. I read an article in college about how increasing gas mileage can radically change the profitability model of freight companies. I thought, 'Wow, what if I could make something that could increase a truck's gas mileage by thirty percent? I bet they would be willing to pay a mint for that.'"

"You designed an additive that would increase efficiency by thirty percent." I try not to release my latent geeky side, but I recognize the advancement as a tremendous accomplishment.

"Thirty-five percent on our first product. We've improved since then. To be fair, I didn't design squat." He circles his hand in the air. "It's all these great engineers who work with me that design the product. I'm just the schmuck who had an idea."

"You're awfully modest. Transportation is a good, steady market, too. We always need to transfer goods."

"Yes, but small potatoes compared to our military contracts now." Chuck places his hand in the middle of my back to turn me toward the door opening on our right.

"April, this is Jimmy. My right-hand comptroller, college roommate, and the low-handicap member on my foursome."

Jimmy is Chuck with darker hair and a less expensive suit. Jimmy stands, offering his hand to me. "I'm pleased to meet you, April."

"April needs to see the company books so she can compare them against my taxes." Chuck's lips snarl with what I take as a joke. "To take care of that bloodsucker who has attached herself to my butt."

"Sure." Jimmy pulls a rolling chair over and pats the seat. "Let's take a look at this quarter."

Yeah. Nice try, boys. I wasn't born yesterday. Pulling a new flash drive from my purse, I hold it up. "If you could download the last five years' balance sheets, bank statements, and profit and loss statements, it would be a lot more helpful."

My audible appears to catch Jimmy entirely off guard. His smile fades quickly as he sends a pointed stare in Chuck's direction.

"Our accounting system is quite complicated, April. I'm sure it would be helpful for Jimmy to walk you through our processes. We only want to make sure you understand it. FIFO isn't the name of a dog if you catch my meaning."

Yes. I catch your meaning, you buffoon. "What would be helpful is if Jimmy could download the information I told you would be a prerequisite of me working your divorce for you. I honestly do not think your inventory system being first in first out, or last in first out will impact the operating income enough to make a difference. I'll make sure to keep it all above the tax line during the initial comparison."

I extend my arm to full length. The flash drive is directly in front of Jimmy's nose.

Chuck measures me with a long stare. He reads the situation correctly and nods his permission to Jimmy.

Jimmy takes the drive from my hand.

"Good. It's best to be thorough in these matters. The last thing we want is to miss something and give Carolyn's lawyers an opening," Chuck offers.

"I need to pick up your taxes from your tax attorney next. Am I going to have any difficulties?"

Chuck frowns. "No. Of course not. I told them you were

coming."

I fix him with a stare. "And they will provide me with your tax returns for the last five years?"

Chuck exhales as he measures me again. He lifts his left arm, checking his Rolex. "How about I run you over there and then take you to lunch."

I'm your lawyer, not your girlfriend. "How about you call them and let them know I'm coming, so they have the files ready."

"Come on, April. You're getting everything you want. Just have lunch with me so I better understand what to expect from the process."

Everything I want? How about everything I was promised, and begrudgingly at that. "I won't have the full strategy laid out until I know exactly what the liquidated value comes in at."

"Liquidated?" There is an edge of panic in Jimmy's voice.

I turn to Jimmy, who I had forgotten was still behind me. "Tell me, if you had to write someone a check for half the book value of the company tomorrow, what would happen."

Jimmy's eyes bug out. "It would fully tap our credit line. We could create some revenue by decreasing inventory fifty percent—" He shakes his head. "No. We would have immediate cash flow issues. We would be in an immediate death spiral with no way to pull the nose up."

I like Jimmy. He is a technician and has a desire to be correct and honest. That doesn't mean I trust him since Chuck is a bad influence.

"Correct. That's why we will negotiate for half of the liquidated "fire sale" value. That is what's fair. It's all anyone would be able to walk away with if we're going to split the goose that lays the golden eggs down the middle."

The men share a look.

Jimmy rests his chin on his fist. "That's good. That would give us a fighting chance to work out the cash flow."

"I like that strategy, April," Chuck says.

"Thanks."

"Let me run you by Stone and Forte to pick up my taxes and then go to lunch," Chuck continues.

Everything in my mind is saying, *Nope, not going to happen. Horrible idea.* "If you could just call ahead and make sure there is no misunderstanding about what information is required for the case, that would be most helpful."

"You're really going to turn down lunch at Pier Thirty-Nine?"

Nobody previously mentioned Pier Thirty-Nine. That is an extremely high-end steak and seafood restaurant in Huntsville with a wine selection unparalleled in North Alabama. Not that I had ever darkened its doorway. I couldn't afford to even glance at the front door.

"Come on, Counselor Snow. If you plan to be a big-time attorney, you'll have to get used to going to better restaurants with your clients. It is how commerce is oiled."

There is a lot of logic in what Chuck is saying. One of the classes you don't get in law school is "Power Lunch 101." Still, every cell in my body is screaming danger, danger.

Chuck persists with his hard press. "They have a Pinot Noir that you absolutely must try."

How did he know I like wine? "I suppose. But I can't stay long. I'm slammed at work."

"Excellent!" Chuck exclaims.

I sure hope I haven't made a mistake.

Chapter 35

It takes an hour at Stone and Forte to get Chuck's tax information together. All they planned on providing me was last year's taxes. Which were still being worked on under an extension.

We pull into Pier Thirty-Nine. The Valet greets Chuck.

"Hello, Mr. Davis. It is good to see you today."

"Hi, Bill." Chuck hands him the keys. "If you take her for a spin, please keep her under a hundred and forty."

Bill laughs as he gets in. "I'll try, Mr. Davis."

The scent of leather, oak, and grilled steaks engulfs me as we step inside. My eyes adjust to the decreased light as the maître d' acknowledges us.

"Good afternoon, Mr. Davis. Brian will take you to your table." The maître d' waves over a thin man in his early thirties.

It is apparent Chuck visits Pier Thirty-Nine with regularity and spends sufficient cash for everyone in the establishment to know him by name. But then again, most everyone at Jerry's sub shop and Ms. Bell's Meat and Three knows me by name. So it isn't really that astonishing of a feat.

The overstuffed leather chairs they sit us at are so comfortable I want to curl up and take a nap. But I resist since I'm here for a power lunch, not a power nap.

"Do you like prime rib or filet mignon?" Chuck asks.

"Yes," I reply as I examine the wonderfully detailed list of exotic entrées and side dishes. I choke when I notice the prices to the right of the descriptions.

Chuck laughs lightly. "I love your sense of humor."

I wasn't trying to be funny. Holy smoke. The entrée prices don't include anything else. Both a baked potato and a mixed green salad cost a week's worth of my grocery budget.

If I bought groceries.

"Their specialty is the sixteen-ounce prime rib, but all of their steaks have tremendous flavor. You can't make a bad selection."

Sixteen ounces? I would have to get a couple of friends to finish that.

Our waiter friend is back with our waters, complete with a slice of lime. "Are you ready to order, or would you like to start with an appetizer?"

"We'll have the spinach artichoke dip and..." Chuck looks up at me. "April, do you like calamari?"

"Squid?" I feel my face twist in disgust.

Chuck laughs again. "The young woman needs to try new things. Please bring us a plate."

"Excellent."

"Does Terence have any more of the Domaine Dujac?"

"I believe we still have three bottles, Mr. Davis."

"Perfect. Please bring us a bottle."

"Certainly, Mr. Davis."

For such a swanky place with outrageous food prices, the wine is dirt cheap. Be real, I'm not going to spend twenty-one dollars on a bottle of wine when I can get one I like for nine, but that is still cheap for such a classy restaurant.

It does surprise me nobody has caught that the decimal point is too far to the left on the price of the wine. I would have expected someone to have proofed the wine menu and seen the misprint on the Dominate Deuce or whatever at two dollars and point zero nine six cents. You can't buy a two-dollar bottle of wine, and you certainly can't be charged a fraction of a penny.

Every single wine is misprinted. People can be so lazy about details.

"So, tell me about yourself, April. I can tell you're not the same woman I went out with all those years ago."

You don't know half the story, buddy. "Not much has changed, other than getting my degree. I'm still the same old April."

His eyes hood over. "I don't believe that for a moment. You seem like much, much more now."

Awkward. If this is Chuck's way of making me comfortable so I'll open up, he is failing. If anything, I'm wondering how much I'm willing to endure for a twenty-dollar bottle of wine.

"Tell me about your dreams," Chuck says.

I struggle to quell the bark of laughter that nearly escapes me. I'm sure I would sound quite disturbed. You want to know my dreams? You can't handle my dreams, mister!

"Your Domaine Dujac, Mr. Davis." Our waiter holds the wine for Chuck's inspection. The waiter would make a great superhero with his impeccable timing.

I watch the pretentious rite of passage as our waiter opens the wine for Chuck. He sniffs it, sips, and swishes it, finally giving his approval with a nod.

I want to yell, "It's a twenty-dollar bottle of wine. Drink it already!" But, instead, I remain quiet and hold down my desire to laugh. I have seen this ritual on television before but never in real life.

The waiter fills my elegant, long-stemmed glass. Yes, he would make a splendid superhero indeed, especially after a long, hard Monday. I wonder if he does foot massages, too.

Lifting the glass to my lips—my nose notices the difference way before my lips touch the rim. The explosion of fragrances is intense. Oak, apple blossoms, cherry, and vanilla, the complexity of the scent is mindboggling.

Bless it. I sound like a wine critic now.

The first sweet nectar rolls over my lips, coating my tongue with lavish luxury. I swoon, feeling lightheaded from the incredible sensation, and I haven't swallowed any alcohol yet.

Chuck raises his glass to me. "What do you think?"

I think I am melting into a warm puddle. "Unbelievable."

"An unbelievable wine for a remarkable woman."

Even his cheesy lines can't mess up the pleasure of this wine. "I'm going to have to get me a few bottles to take home."

Chuck laughs. "Your uncle must pay you almost what you are worth, then."

Whatever. I'm not exactly destitute. I can buy a twenty—how much was it? I lift the wine list off the table.

Has your mind ever betrayed you and read what it anticipated rather than what is printed? Upon further inspection, the decimal that was one number too far to the left? It now appears to look suspiciously like a comma.

Who owns a two-*thousand*-dollar bottle of wine? More importantly, who drinks it?

It's like I'm drinking the powertrain of my Prius. Another glass, and I'll have swallowed the engine, too.

"Just kidding." I know my lie won't pass for the truth, but I'm betting on my shock to cover up any inadvertent smiles.

Chuck leans forward. The candle from our table forms shadows across his face. "I'll get you a bottle to take home if you like."

Sure. I would like that until the bill came due. Nothing in life is totally free. "I would never drink it. It would just sit in my fridge."

"April, you need to relax and ride the motion of life. Don't fight the world's love; surrender and move in rhythm with your surroundings. It will bring you more pleasure."

I stare at Chuck. My mouth is slightly open. I'm sure it's not my most intelligent-appearing expression.

He sighs. "I'm only saying your life can't be all work every waking minute. Let your hair down and allow yourself to explore the possibilities."

If my hair is ever down, it's because I got up in time to take a shower.

A plate with a twelve-ounce prime rib, an eight-ounce filet mignon, and a ridiculously large baked potato magically appear in front of me.

"I can't eat all this," I protest.

"Eat what you want and leave the rest. That's my motto."

Geez—It must be nice to have such a cavalier attitude about expensive food. I'm becoming agitated about the wastefulness. Then my glass suddenly refills, which makes me happy again.

"You said you were getting ready to go out of state to work for a law firm," Chuck says.

That reminds me, I need to recheck the job boards. "Yes."

"Is there nothing I can do to talk you out of it?"

"Why?"

His face flushes red. It looks unnatural on him. "I would like to hire you."

"You can't afford me," I shoot back. That is a doozie of a lie, and I don't even crack a smile.

Chuck tilts his head. "I don't know. I have a healthy payroll at my disposal. You are far more creative than any legal counsel, well counsel in general, I get from the rest of my team."

"I don't need to be anyone's glorified girl Friday."

Chuck shakes his head vigorously. "I need a lawyer, April. One that really understands how business works and isn't afraid of conflict."

This can't be happening. It almost sounds as if Chuck is offering me a position as legal counsel for his company.

"That's sweet of you, Chuck. But both of us know there are hundreds of qualified, experienced corporate lawyers out there for you to choose from."

Chuck pushes his plate to the side and leans forward, locking eyes with me. "But I don't want just qualified and experienced. I need creativity. That's something you have on them. I need you, April."

This is such a cruel temptation it's not even fair. From all appearances, the chemical company is generating significant revenue for Chuck. How wonderful would it be to focus all my attention on one client twenty-four seven?

Huntsville is not a terrible town to live in. It would also put me only an hour away from home. I could see my family every weekend if I wanted.

What in the world am I thinking?

This is "panty raider" Chuck. There is no telling what sort of sexual harassment I would be setting myself up for. Which would then lead to the loss of said fantastic job, but only after I saddled myself with rent in Huntsville.

Plus, it would be one of those recurring hires on my résumé to explain why I was let go.

No, thank you. My life is complicated enough without that headache.

Besides, my dream has not changed.

East Coast or West Coast, it really doesn't matter. My focus is on becoming a partner at a large law firm in a huge American city. Working for Chuck in a cubicle is not helpful toward realizing my dreams.

"I have to admit to you I'm persistent. Rarely do I not get what I want." Chuck flashes a knowing smile.

"Chuck, hiring the advisor you want is not like buying a television. You don't always get what you want."

Chuck leans back in his chair, his brow furrowed. "Are you serious?"

It is an excellent question. I empty my wine glass—again. "Seriously, Chuck. I have other plans that I want to keep for now. Eventually, when the offer is right, I'll move on to a major metropolitan city and begin work as a defense attorney."

"Why?" Chuck looks thoroughly flabbergasted.

"Because it's my dream job."

"But the cost of living is so high in those bigger cities. Anything you think you will gain financially by moving there, you'll just spend on housing."

Everybody is constantly overstating the cost of living. You can make anything work if you are frugal. "But there's more opportunity in the bigger cities."

Chuck laughs. "Opportunity? Opportunity comes from knowing people. You don't know anybody in those towns. I'm offering you an established client base and an immediate salary you can be proud of."

"But you're only offering that to me because you know me."

He smiles. "I believe you just proved my point. That's how business works. I would never offer this opportunity to a stranger. Not until they worked for me in a different capacity for a few years and proved their loyalty to me."

I'm conflicted. A lot of what Chuck says makes sense. Still, I have an overriding alarm going off in my head telling me I'm playing with a snake and I'll get bit eventually.

"Listen, I've been doing without a dedicated attorney the entire time I've been running my business. There's no rush. Take your time and think about it. Call me when you're ready. I've already made my decision. I just need you to warm to the idea and give me a yes."

"Okay. But how do I know this isn't an elaborate setup because you are attracted to me sexually?" I'm horrified as I realize that thought slipped out of my mouth.

"First, I would never lie to you. I respect you too much. Do let me say, yes, I am highly attracted to you. But that doesn't mean I can't want you on my team for your excellent creativity, too. And you know I am already happily in a relationship. My offer is strictly as a business owner. My job now is to keep reminding you of all the advantages of working for me."

"You're welcome to try, but I don't think much you say can change my mind," I say.

He exhales. "Fair enough. I appreciate the warning. But I'll repeat it's a rare day indeed that I don't get what I want. You need to be aware of that."

"It seems to me you're about to turn over a new leaf, then." The wine has an extra kick to it. I usually don't get this warm and fuzzy off the first glass. Wait, third?

Chapter 36

Chuck sends me home in an Uber with a twenty-one-hundred-dollar bottle of wine tucked under my arm. I tried to convince him I would never drink the bottle, but he insisted, and I was becoming so tired I knew it was time to leave.

As the taxi carries me home, I replay the pros and cons of the position Chuck offered me. It would be nice to have an immediate, stable income. I'm sure it would be enough for me to find my own place and move out of my parents' home.

Still, I wonder if it wouldn't create a situation where Chuck felt I owed him. He seems to be of the nature that he might expect more than a professional relationship sometime in the future.

I have a bottle of wine riding in the passenger seat with me that would be a month's wages for some people. It may be too late for me to become puritanical.

I fumble for my phone. I need to make sure Howard doesn't expect me back in this afternoon. I'm in no shape to work.

"Hello." He sounds preoccupied.

"I need to let you know I'll be working from my apartment the rest of the day," I say.

"Okay. If you will, give Lane a call. He was in here earlier looking for you. Oh, and Savanna Tate called. She said you need to give her a call."

My shoulders drop. “Did she say what about?”

“Nope. Or at least I couldn’t understand her. She sounded terribly upset, though. The woman’s voice always sounds garbled to me.”

“Anything else?” I ask.

“Isn’t that enough?”

“Yes.” I sigh.

“Oh. There is one other thing. If you are going to do a power lunch—it’s a two-drink maximum and finish out the meal with soda water.”

Gasping, I begin to deny my lunch date. Then I think better of it. “Yes, sir.”

There is no telling where my family comes up with their information on me. The CIA has nothing on the Snow clan when it comes to my business. Still, it has never ceased to surprise me when they reveal their knowledge of my whereabouts.

I thank my driver when he drops me off at my parents’ Entering my apartment, I kick off my shoes. I make a quick scan for the shoe destroyer. He is either out running recon with my daddy or in super-stealth puppy mode since there is no hint of him.

Pulling my phone from my purse, I hit speed dial seven. Lane’s cell rings once before he picks up. “Hello.”

“My uncle said you were looking for me?”

“Hi, April. Yes. Did you present the plea offer to Jethro Mullins yet?”

“Yes, sir. We went over it this morning.”

“And?”

I decide to continue to bargain even though my client has quit caring. “He still wants to hold out for a misdemeanor rather than a felony, but he is fine with the sixty-day sentence.”

“Fine. We’ll just present our cases and let Judge Phillips decide. I’m not going to give him a reason to preach to me about the dangers of giving too many concessions on a plea bargain.”

"But I told him the judge would never go for it, so he finally accepted." You can't blame a girl for trying. Besides, you never know if you don't ask.

"When do you want to take care of the paperwork?"

"Tomorrow?" I offer.

"I can come to your office now."

"I'm not there. I'm at home."

There is a pause on the line. "Oh, I'm sorry. I didn't mean to have you call me when you are out sick."

"I'm not sick." I'm stupid. "I just had some other things to take care of today. But I can meet you at the office first thing in the morning if that will work for you."

"I have court first thing. Can we meet after? Say at ten."

"That'll work."

"See you in the morning, April."

"Bye."

I pad over to my refrigerator and place the ultra-expensive bottle of wine carefully on the bottom shelf next to the last energy drink from Nana.

I'm not sure if refrigeration is the best way to keep an expensive bottle of wine. Still, I don't want to worry about it too much. Lest I think it best to drink it before it spoils.

Opening my laptop, I key in my password. I've been so busy between my caseload, editing Dusty's book, and the trip to Monstrous Caverns I hadn't thought to check if I received a response on either the San Francisco or Miami job I applied for last week.

My email account comes up, and I start deleting advertisements. Running shoes on sale, delete. New car advertisements, delete. Alumni donation request, delete. Lingerie discount, delete. Brooke, Chase, and Liggett, I've never even heard of that store. Delete—wait a minute.

Time freezes as I open the email and read the two paragraphs that change my life. The firm in San Francisco wants to set up an appointment for a Zoom interview with their Human Resources department.

My heart quickens at the prospect of moving to San Francisco. How incredible would that be?

I certainly don't want to get ahead of myself. But it is hard not to when, after several weeks of no response from my résumés, the job that seems the most attractive of all is the one that shows interest in me.

It is like destiny. I had to walk through all these hardships and self-doubt for the appropriate position to appear for me.

Isn't that what Granny and Daddy say all the time? You must walk in faith before you receive the reward.

I'm living proof. I didn't give up, and I walked in faith. Now I will be rewarded with my dream position in one of the cities I most covet.

See, things do always work out for good. You just have to be patient.

I fire off an email in response to the request. Now I just need to see what day they want to do the Zoom interview and blow them away with my wit and intelligence.

Lying back against the pillows on my bed, I begin California dreaming. My new life will be sweatshirts and cute skirts, long walks on the beach, and parties with diverse and exciting people. Goodness, I can't wait. I don't think I realized just how crazy Guntersville was making me.

Think about it. Just a couple hours earlier, I was running a benefits analysis through my mind regarding working for someone in Huntsville I know to be a sexual predator.

What was I thinking? I wasn't. I was enjoying an expensive bottle of wine bought by a not unattractive man who, I'm sorry to admit, looks impressive in an equally costly suit.

The fact is that if Chuck had kept his hands to himself, or at least acted like some semblance of a gentleman seven years earlier, it would've been enough to put the deal over the top. My gosh, I was that close to giving in right before my dreams came true!

A sudden wave of sadness washes over me. Is that what happened to Lauren? Did she give in to Mason right before the stranger passing through town appeared who would've taken her to Alabama or Florida? Had she given in just before she made her escape from Mason and that small town?

Possibly. I hope I never forget how fortunate I am.

Thinking of Lauren knocks my buzz down a notch.

Life seems to be more complicated to me now than it did a few months ago. I don't think anything has changed. I believe it's always been complicated. I just never knew it.

My nails are a mess. They look like I've been digging in the dirt or something. That probably happened while I was at the cave.

I dial Tiffany at the beauty salon.

"Guntersville Beauty College."

"Tiffany?" I'm sure it is Tiffany, but her usual cheerfulness is missing in her tone.

"Yes?"

"Hi, this is April Snow."

"Oh. Hi, April. Please forgive me if I sound a little gruff. We have a bit of a situation going on here at the school."

"I'm sorry. Is there anything I can help with?"

Tiffany guffaws. "Not unless you're an air conditioning technician. Our AC is on the fritz, and it's hotter than Hades in here. All these dryers make it like a furnace. The worst part is I can't get anybody out here until tomorrow night to look at it. It would appear business is booming for all the HVAC companies."

Well, it is July in Alabama. If your AC unit plans to give up the ghost this year, July or August are the two safe bets.

"Have you tried the company Patrick works for, Cool Breeze, out of Huntsville?" It still stings to say his name. I suppose I'm not entirely over him.

"No. Thank you for reminding me," she gushes.

"No worries. Hopefully, they can get somebody out soon. I know that must be awful working in the heat."

"Honey, I have no idea how our grandmothers did it."

Yeah, I'm beginning to understand my grandmothers were

made of stouter stuff than I ever will be. "I guess they just didn't know any better."

"I suppose. Hey, what did you call for?"

"Oh, right. I need to see if you have anything available tomorrow for a manicure."

"Would four thirty work for you?"

"Yes. That's perfect."

"I've got you down. And thank you again for reminding me about Patrick's company," Tiffany says.

"You're welcome." I disconnect the line, and Tiffany's syntax sticks in my mind. It's one of the curses of being a lawyer. Even though I keep my own speech informal, I still pick up on incorrect sentence structures.

For example, saying *Patrick's* company versus the company Patrick works for has two distinctly different meanings. Tiffany said it in a way that would lead a person to believe Patrick owned the company rather than being employed by the HVAC company.

As a rule, people don't pay close attention to what they say.

My chin drops as I remember the other task Howard asked of me. I just do not want to deal with Savanna Tate. I know I should have turned her away the day she sashayed into our office.

Don't think I don't consider taking the chicken way out by not calling her. Consequently, I'm incredibly proud of myself when I do the adult thing and dial her number.

Her phone rings six times. I begin a happy dance in my mind thinking my lucky streak will continue. She picks up. "Hello."

Wow. How is it some people can say, "Have a lovely day," and it sounds more like, "Why don't you cut your throat?"

"Ms. Tate, this is April Snow. My office told me to give you a call."

She huffs into the receiver. "It's about time. You know promptness is a virtue, young lady."

I remain silent. Which, given what I want to say to Ms. Tate, is no small accomplishment.

"I want a full refund," she continues.

"A refund for what, ma'am?"

"That defective restraining order I paid you for. It's totally worthless."

That's just silly. Ms. Tate asked me to file a restraining order, and it is now in place. She got what she paid for. Implementation of the instrument is between her, the police, and the judge. All valid points I want to make to her, but I know will not be helpful.

"Everything was filed properly. I assure you. Please explain the situation."

"The situation! I'll tell you what the situation is. I have a restraining order, and even though my neighbor came into my yard, the police still won't arrest him."

I knew this would be difficult to enforce with the neighbor being next door. "Did they just not believe he had been on your property?"

"How could they not! I showed them the recording of him in my yard."

"Did they say why they weren't arresting him?" I ask.

"Isn't it obvious? The restraining order must be faulty. I want a full refund."

Faulty? Something isn't jiving here. It's a relatively simple instrument, and it was filed with the court the same day she requested. There shouldn't be any problem.

"Are you listening to me, young lady? I want a refund!" Savanna yells.

"Ms. Tate, you received the product you requested. I can't refund you for work that was completed correctly."

"You better!"

Or what? "No, ma'am."

"That's it. You'll be hearing from my attorneys."

"Ms. Tate, I am your attorney. Was."

I hear her suck in a breath of air. "Well, I never. You know what I meant."

"I'd be happy to investigate the situation for you, or you can let me know which law firm to send your case file to, Ms. Tate."

"Are you getting smart with me, young lady?"

Smart to you, but not with you. "No, ma'am, I'm just keeping it real. You can let me investigate what happened, or you can get a new lawyer. Those are your two choices. A refund is not an option and you continuing to yell at me is not acceptable."

There is another sharp intake of air followed by prolonged silence. I pull my phone away from my ear to check I didn't accidentally disconnect her as I wait for Ms. Tate to respond.

"I suppose the key is to get a restraining order that actually works so that I can feel safe."

"We can both agree on that."

"I'd like you to check into the matter for me, then," she says calmly.

This is not a win. It might seem like it since I talked a customer with unhealthy expectations out of firing me. Except, fire me is precisely what I wanted her to do. I want her to terminate our arrangement and go away.

"Did you happen to get the name or badge number of the officer you spoke to?"

"Officer Hurley."

I choke. "Are you sure?"

"I'll never forget that worthless police officer." Her voice is full of venom.

"Okay, I'll see if I can speak with Officer Hurley. Then possibly we can better understand what the issue is with enforcing the order."

"The problem is that lousy officer won't do the job my tax dollars pay him to do," Savanna says.

Yeah, Jacob doesn't roll that way. There is something else going on. "Let me check into it for us, Ms. Tate. I'll get back to you."

"You need to hurry, young woman. There's a possibility I'll have to go back to LA shortly. It seems everyone is clamoring to give me a leading role now that they know I'm not available in town."

I will always be in awe of people who can tell whoppers and get away with them. "Yes, ma'am. I'm on it." As soon as I get done talking to the plastique movie star with the tractor tire lips.

Now I'm just being mean.

I hit speed dial number six. "What ya doin' hot stuff?"

"Sitting in my squad car playing with my baton."

My ears immediately turn hot. I hate it when Jacob gets the drop on me like that. I'm supposed to be better at this game than him. "I take it you're still on duty."

"I had to stop sitting in my patrol car when I was off-duty. It makes my neighbors uncomfortable."

"Okay, I'll just call you later when you're off-duty."

"Whoa. What's up, Buttercup. Do you need me to come kill some camel crickets in your room?"

"No, my new roommate takes care of that for me."

"Fang doesn't kill them. He eats them. That's the bug-eatingest dog I have ever seen."

"Fang? Are you talking about Puppy?"

"Thick-built, furry fellow. Acts like Clint Eastwood crossed with the Wolverine."

That would be him. "His name isn't Fang. When were you around him anyway?"

"He went fishing with Chase and me Saturday. That dog loves the water."

My dog is getting around more than me. I'm going to have to ground him for the rest of the year. "Please tell me Puppy had his flotation devices on?"

"Negative. Chase tried. But when he started to put them on Fang, he growled and started snapping his teeth at us. I guess he has outgrown them."

"Don't let Chase take him out on the boat again. Please."

"Okay. I'll try to remember. Why did you call anyway? I know it wasn't to talk about your dog."

"I have this client who has a restraining order on her neighbor, and she's upset that you didn't take him in for violation of that order earlier today."

Jacob laughs. He has the sexiest laugh ever. It shoots invisible lightning bolts from my navel to my girl area.

"What's so funny?" I ask.

"Crazy lady, looks like if she has one more round of plastic surgery, she'll have pubic hairs for a goatee, and her lips look like orange inner tubes?"

"Hey! Mean much?"

"Well?"

I sigh. "Yeah, that's her. But if you don't mind, her name is Savanna Tate. Ms. Tate, to us lowlifes."

"It's a long story, April."

"The good ones always are, and I like long stories."

"I'm going to Hot Mugs for a cup of coffee and a donut. Why don't you meet me there?"

Because I'm stupid and got drunk in the middle of the day... "You cops actually do eat donuts?"

"Everybody eats donuts. That's a stupid stereotype. Besides, that woman's tongue gave me the jitters, and sugar calms me down. Do you want to hear the story or not?"

I exhale dramatically. "I do. But I can't drive right now."

"Is your go-cart in the shop?"

"Something like that."

"I can pick you up in ten. I'll even let you ride shotgun so nobody will point at you in the backseat."

"You really don't mind?"

"No. You're not far out of the way."

Chapter 37

Jacob makes me help him select a dozen mixed donuts at Hot Mugs. He won't let me pay for the donuts, or my coffee either.

As I follow him to an available table, I take in his impressive back, tapered waist, and powerful buttocks and thighs. He looks like he could earn big money chasing down quarterbacks and running backs if he didn't prefer to keep his community safe from crime.

Jacob sits, tests his coffee, and winces. He locks eyes with me and shakes his head. "This town is going nuts."

"Tell me about it. That's why I have to get out of here."

He laughs. It is like sunshine pouring into my heart.

Jacob points at me. "You represent most of them, *Counselor*."

So I'm not the only person to notice all the psychologically challenged patrons seem to be clients of Snow and Associates. "Whatever."

"No, it's true."

"Tell me what happened with Ms. Tate. She's all bent out of shape that you didn't arrest her neighbor."

Jacob takes a bite of his chocolate glazed donut. Part of the chocolate glaze breaks off, falling to the floor. For a split second, his disappointment makes him look like an eight-year-old boy.

So cute.

"She's lucky she's not in jail for destruction of property. You know the older XJ model Jaguars that have a small Jaguar metal casting on the hood of the car?"

I know what he is talking about. I just wasn't aware it was an XJ model. "Sure."

"Her neighbor has an XJ. Mint condition. Well, it was until psycho fading-star actress decided to rip it off her neighbor's car?"

"What?" It is beginning to sound like the restraining order is on the wrong party.

Jacob grins. "Wait, it gets better. Her neighbor, Mr. Oaks, comes out to go to work this morning. Being a car enthusiast, he immediately sees the Jaguar statue is missing."

"I don't follow. How did Oaks know Savanna took it?"

"He didn't. But as he came to the driver's side..." Jacob flares his hand toward the tile floor. "Whoomp there it is."

I wrinkle my face. "Don't say that. It's so 1990s."

"Whoomp, there it is." He smiles from ear to ear.

"The statue on the ground."

Jacob rolls his eyes. "So Oaks goes to pick up the statue, and it slides about a foot away from his grasp."

Seriously? This better not be going where I think it is.

"This happens, I don't know ten or twelve more times, and then Oaks is in the middle of Ms. Tate's front yard. That's when they dispatched me to the scene."

"What's your gut on it?"

"My gut?" Jacob raises his eyebrows. "My gut is your client is nuckin' futs."

I want to scream. Why didn't I roll with my instincts the day she came to the office?

"I get there, and it is obvious the whole thing is a setup from the start, even without the magically sliding hood ornament."

"Ms. Tate meets me on the side of the street and starts trying to show me security footage of her neighbor in her yard before I can even get out of my cruiser."

"So, she was ready."

Jacob shakes his head. “The woman missed her calling. She should have been behind the camera. Not in front of it. She had every possible angle of Mr. Oaks retrieving his ornament off her lawn, right down to his plumber’s crack when he bent over.”

“Eww.”

Jacob’s chin tilts up in victory. “Gotcha. He was in a suit. He’s some sort of big deal researcher up at Redstone that commutes in every day.”

“Did you get a chance to talk to him? Do you think he might be harassing her?”

Jacob massages his forehead, deep in thought. “You know, in my line of work you never say no about such things. People will always surprise you. But he honestly seems very—” Jacob looks to the ceiling as he searches for the correct phrase. “Buttoned up? Plus, if he is harassing her, he’s an idiot. His wife came out, and she’s a complete knockout for a forty-something babe. I about tripped over my tongue.”

Jacob’s comment tweaks a spark of resentment in me. I know we’re just friends, and I know he obviously looks at women, but he can keep the crude comments to himself around me.

“I got propositioned today,” I blurt.

“Did you now?”

“Yep.”

“Who was the brave fella?”

That’s okay. Make fun of me. “That client I have who owns a chemical company up in Huntsville.”

Jacob’s face twists. “The one who was going through the divorce and was dragging the fifteen-year-old hooker around with him last weekend.”

“She’s not a hooker, and she’s just petite. Besides, Chuck doesn’t love her.”

Jacob’s body shakes as he attempts to restrain a laugh. Poorly. He’s forced to cover his mouth with his fist.

“What?”

"Girl, you think my life is dangerous? Give me a domestic dispute with firearms involved any day over your scenario."

I have half a mind to stand up and box him on the ear. "Don't be rude. He's getting his life in order, and he needs an attorney full-time at his company."

"No doubt with all the sexual harassment charges rolling in." Jacob continues to shake his head as he selects a powdered donut.

Yeah. I considered that might be the reason Chuck needed a full-time attorney, too. "Very funny. Careful with that donut. I wouldn't want you to *choke* on the powdered sugar."

Jacob presses the donut to his lips. He removes the donut from his lips, leaving them perfectly coated in white sugar. He puckers his lips and makes smacking noises. "What am I?"

"A moron," I say with a laugh.

"Sugar Lips."

Against my will, I continue to laugh as I sling a napkin in his direction. "You're so stupid."

He cleans the sugar from his lips. "Good. Then we balance each other out. You're too smart for your own good."

If I'm so smart, why hasn't my life come together yet?

Jacob sobers. "Are you still set on leaving us."

His question surprises me. I have never concealed my intentions from Jacob. "Yeah. I actually have an interview with a San Francisco firm later this week."

His brows knit together. "San Francisco? That's like the other side of the world."

"Just about."

He clicks his tongue. "If it would make you happy. I hope you get it."

"Thank you."

"It's been fun having you around, and I'll miss you. But you got to do what you got to do. I get it."

The last of my wine buzz wears off, and I feel sad. "You'll really miss me?"

"Sure I will. I won't have a female I trust to bounce girl

things off of."

"You don't have any girl things going on in your life."

"*Yet*. But when I do, I could have asked you questions. If you had hung around."

"There's always the phone."

"I suppose." He pauses.

"I really help you understand girls better?"

Jacob cuts loose with another one of his aphrodisiac laughs. "No. Your logic is as confusing to me as any other woman's logic. But at least with you, I know there aren't any ulterior motives. When I don't understand you, it is definitely a guy-girl thing and not some game where I don't even know where the rule book is hidden."

"Not that you would read it."

Jacob rolls a shoulder and grins. "It would just depend on how desperate the situation has become."

I don't want to admit it, but I'm going to miss Jacob something fierce. The dim-witted sophomoric young man I knew in high school has grown into a rock-solid man and an excellent friend.

He has filled a void in my life and broken a truism I always held close. Men and women can't ever be just friends. In my prior experience, in the "friendly" relationships, one or both were propagating the friendship because they held a deep-seated hope it would become more.

There are still moments of occasional sexual tension. Let's face it, I'm not blind to the fact that my friend is a blond version of Channing Tatum, and there are those sexy laughs of his that tickle places they shouldn't. But come on, it's Jacob. It's like noticing one of your girlfriends has exceptional hair. Right? Isn't it?

Chapter 38

Jacob drops me off at my place. It's five in the afternoon. There is a rectangular hole in the bottom of my door. Somebody obviously felt I needed a doggy door and installed it while I was out with Jacob.

Puppy's attention goes to me as I open the door. Half of a yellow flip-flop droops from the corner of his mouth like a Mafia boss's chewed cigar.

"No, Puppy!" I run toward him.

I stop short. What the heck. That one is already a goner.

Kneeling, I scratch behind his ear. He pushes into my hand with all his weight. Puppy likes it rough.

If I plan on having any shoes left in the future, I'll have to make a concerted effort to put them on a shelf in my closet after each wearing. Mama has been trying to get me into that habit for twenty-seven years, and Puppy, the self-appointed shoe monitor, has accomplished it in less than a month.

"Were you working with Daddy in the lab today? You two didn't blow anything up, I see. That's a good thing."

I have an hour to kill by my calculations before I can walk over to my parents' kitchen and see if they are cooking or if it will be canned chicken soup and grilled cheese night.

Wait—I forgot to pick up bread—just soup night.

I need to be productive with the hour. Things sure have

changed in just a couple of days. I've gone from nothing to do to more on my plate than I can say grace over.

The choices are to work on Dusty's book, begin going through Chuck's financials, or take a nap. As good as taking a nap sounds, my curiosity rules the day.

I stick the flash drive into the side of my laptop and open Chuck's financials.

As I peruse through the company's spreadsheets, all the things I thought I had not retained from my business undergraduate degree come back to me. It is scary, but items like depreciation and carried interest suddenly make sense to me. As if my mind needed four years to marinate on the concepts before I could comprehend the accounting rules.

Bless it. I hope I'm not turning into a geek.

That was my greatest fear in middle school. All the girls, except for Jackie Rains, said they couldn't do the math.

I could. I liked math. But, who wants to stick out like a sore thumb? Right?

After a few minutes, I dive my hand into my backpack and pull out the notebook I reserve for musings and to-do lists that get put away until the next time I open it. I flip to a clean sheet and begin to jot down notes as I toggle from the chemical company's books to Chuck's tax filings.

Puppy busts into his Cujo imitation when someone knocks on my door.

"Hush up, Puppy."

He looks at me as if I'm the one who's lost their mind. He goes back to barking and snarling.

"Come in."

Mama peeps her head through the cracked door. "Did you have dinner out tonight?"

I look for my phone in confusion. "What time is it?"

"A few minutes past eight."

What? How did that happen? "Crud, I guess I got wrapped up in my work."

"I have a plate for you if you are hungry."

I feel gratitude for her thinking of me. I also feel sad for having missed family dinner.

"That sounds wonderful."

Mama eases into my apartment and crosses over to the small table I use as a desk. Puppy, all friendly and attentive now, escorts her, his nose high in the air savoring the aromas.

"Your father fried some pork chops and made scalloped potatoes." She places the plate next to my laptop and turns toward my kitchenette area, opening a drawer.

"Thank you, Mama."

"You're welcome. I need to get some new silverware for up here. It looks like it all migrated back to the house." She places a knife and fork next to my plate as she pulls up a chair.

I feel self-conscious as she sits down. It's easy to read when Mama wants to talk, and it's impossible to beg her off.

The scent of seasoned pork chop makes my mouth water. The expectant stare of my mother holds me in place.

"Go ahead and eat before it gets cold." Mama gestures to my plate.

Tentatively I cut into the pork chop. I place the first bite in my mouth, and it melts. Daddy can do something magical with pork chops.

"I spoke with Nana today."

Her voice, so matter-of-fact, might as well be a sword swinging through the air. I feel the urge to duck. So that is what this pow-wow is about.

"I'm not going to interject myself into this. My mom knows a hundred times more about the art than I do. She's lived it every day of her life. She also assures me that the two of you have it under control."

I wonder if Nana believes I have it under control or considered it best to tell Mama that for now. I hope Nana does think I have control. Because I certainly am not convinced I have command of my powers.

"It's important for me to reiterate just how dangerous some of the things that have happened to you are."

There is no accusation in her tone, but I burst out in frustration. "I didn't want any of this, Mama!"

Her brow creases, and she gives a sympathetic smile. "I know that, baby. But that's not the point. You have it."

She raises her eyebrows as her chin dips. "A lot of power. I just need to know that you are going to take it seriously and get it harnessed before you hurt yourself."

I want to calm down, but the injustice of having something I not only don't want but can't ignore irritates me to no end. "I just want to be normal."

Mama pats me on the thigh. "This is your normal, April. Be an adult and own it."

That isn't helpful. "Easy for you to say."

Mama smiles. "I suppose it is."

Her eyes pan to my laptop and then narrow. "Spreadsheets?"

"Yeah." I gesture toward the screen. "I have this client going through a divorce, and I'm trying to confirm the net value of his company. I was bouncing the income statements of the corporation off his personal taxes, trying to make sure there aren't any hidden landmines before I present for the judgment."

"How's that going?"

"I suppose there's a reason I'm a lawyer and not a CPA."

Mama rocks back and releases a full laugh that makes me smile. "Baby, as smart as you are, you could have been anything you wanted to apply yourself to. You just decided early on you didn't much care for math."

"I guess that was a mistake."

"Not at all. You need to do what you love. I could do my own books for the real estate brokerage." Mama shrugs. "But why? I enjoy sales much more, and I can hire out the books easy enough."

"At the moment, it would be a handy skill."

"Why don't you see if Elsa can take a look at them for you tomorrow?"

"Elsa?"

"The CPA who takes care of my books. Elsa Long"—Mama makes a circling motion with her fingers—"I think she was a senior in school when you were a freshman."

The name finally tumbles from my memory: Elsa Long, captain of the dance team and captain of the math team. I can still visualize her in the center of the dance line with kicks so high the toes of her white boots went above her five-ten height. She was a brunette version of a Barbie doll.

"She lives here?"

"Moved back two years ago after her divorce."

There is one thing I hadn't experienced that I can be grateful for. "Do you really think this Elsa can help, Mama?"

"I'd be surprised if she couldn't. If you would like, I can call her for you and see if she can meet with you."

"That would be great."

Mama reaches down and rubs Puppy's ear. "Your father put a dog door up. Make sure to lock it at night so this one doesn't go wandering. Or accidentally let something come wandering in."

"Sure. I had already thought about that." I didn't even know it had a lock. But her statement about something wandering into our apartment means I'll be spending some time figuring out how to lock it.

"He is adorable. But he is not to be trusted," Mama says with a final scratch of his head.

Amen to that.

Mama texts me that Elsa can see me in the morning. She also sends me her address and cell phone number.

It appears that Elsa works from home. That doesn't sound like a bad gig if you can get it.

Chapter 39

The GPS takes me to the far side of the lake, and I start up a steep incline on the side of a mountain that has my Prius faltering. The road finally plateaus, and Elsa's mailbox comes into sight. It is unmistakable with its bright gold CPA plaque mounted on top if there was any doubt.

As I drive up the narrow asphalt trail, I take in the seclusion of Elsa's homesite. I sometimes complain about living next door to my parents, but this would be too isolated for my taste.

Her home, an A-frame that had been a trendy style in the area in the early seventies, comes into view between the tall pines and hickories.

Behind her home, the mountain tapers off quickly. Lake Guntersville can be viewed from the porch.

Being an accountant must pay better than I thought.

I ring the doorbell and wait. I watch a gathering of butterflies tasting her butterfly weed.

The front door opening startles me.

Elsa's face is the same, minus the heavy make-up and plus a few wrinkles at the eyes. "April Snow?"

"Yes."

She extends her hand, and I accept it. "Your Mama is one of my favorite clients."

She gestures me into her home. "My schedule is really tight, so if you don't mind, I'll need to bypass the pleasantries today."

Her personality is forceful, and there is no question that she is in control of the meeting. Her long brown hair pulled back in a band. A few silver strands have already arrived.

Stepping into her home, the primary aromas of incense, pot, and a touch of cat urine overwhelm me.

She gestures to a sofa. In front of it is a coffee table with an open laptop on top of it. "Have a seat in my office."

Yeah, this working from home thing would be alright in my book. The cat would have to be potty trained or find a new home.

I don't usually scrutinize women in this manner, but with Elsa, it is difficult not to notice her chest. Part because it seems even more prominent than what I remembered from high school and part because, surprisingly, she is not wearing a bra.

Again, a plus for working at home. Barefoot, yoga pants, and a tee-shirt with no bra seriously kicks casual Friday in the butt.

"Your mama tells me you're working a divorce case and trying to ascertain if your client's income tax reports match up to the company's balance sheets."

"Yeah. It's important to get a true evaluation of my client's company before the hearing."

Elsa leans back into the fluffy sofa. Propping her feet on the coffee table, the bottom half of her calves become exposed. An abundance of hair three inches long covers them.

"You have two things working against you. Number one, with a corporation, it's nearly impossible to tell anything between a stockholder's tax returns and the company's balance sheets. You could hire fifty accountants to work on that for a year and probably get at least twenty-six different answers."

"It's an LLC," I interject.

Elsa rolls her lower lip out. "Interesting. How many partners?"

I shake my head. "Just him."

"Okay. Game changer."

I want to be cautious, but I feel my pulse quicken, "Really?"

She nods as a subtle grin graces her face. "Pretty basic, actually. There's only so many different places to hide in that scenario."

This is good. I'm encouraged. "You said there is a second thing against me."

She raises her chin. "Yeah, that. I don't play on the boys' teams."

"Excuse me?"

"The boys already have plenty of advantages. I'll be darned if I'm going to screw one of my sisters outta her just due. She needs to get her cut for having lived with him while he built his business."

She must be kidding.

The awkward silence informs me she is dead serious.

How can Elsa say that? I haven't even shared Chuck and Carolyn's history with her.

Understand, I think Chuck is an A1 sleazeball. But Carolyn "I'm not going to bother taking my husband's name Digby," who is eight months pregnant with her lover's baby, isn't going to win any wife of the year award either.

"I know I'm his attorney, but you need to understand that this is a case of two not-nice people needing to find an equitable division so they can move on with their lives."

Elsa shakes her head as she smiles. "Spoken like a true guy attorney."

Alright, let's try another tack. "Tell you what, give me an opinion. Just an honest assessment."

Elsa's eyes narrow. "About what?"

"You've got a couple that has been married for six years. The man is running a business he inherited from his father. The wife is not employed. He's not perfect by any means, but she has just informed him she's eight months pregnant. With another man's baby."

"Okay."

"What's equitable distribution?" I ask.

"Fifty percent down the middle. Nothing changes in that

scenario."

I grin. "Then we see eye to eye." I don't bother to mention to Elsa I plan to value it at fire sale liquidation.

She wrinkles her nose. "Why?"

"Because it's fair. It'll be quick and clean, and once I talk my client into it, it will be the best deal he can cut.

"The problem is I don't trust him. I have an underlying suspicion that there might be something funny going on with the books. You, with your healthy cynicism"—unhealthy if I were being truthful—"would be the perfect person to review the accounts. The question is, will you help me?"

"How far back do these records go?" Elsa sits up.

I know I have her buy-in now. "Five years, but I can get more if necessary."

She shakes her head. "It won't be necessary. The first year is the honeymoon. If he's been hiding anything, it would've been in the last five years."

Man, this chick is sharp. I really like Elsa. "That makes sense."

The left side of her lip tweaks up in a smile that implies I don't need to affirm her cognitive abilities.

"When do you need the analysis?"

This may be a deal killer. "I hate to do this since it's a favor and all, but like I said, his wife is eight months pregnant. I'd like to get all this disagreeable business settled before she has the baby. I'm sure you can understand."

Elsa drops her feet back to the floor. She leans forward, cradling her chin against her fist. "You don't ask for much."

"I'm sorry. I'd love to give you more time if I could, but I'm sure you can understand with the baby on the way."

"Yeah, that's awkward, to say the least. If they're not getting along now, it will get really ugly once the baby is born." She makes a sour face. "Alright, April. Leave the information with me and give me two days to scan through and see what we're up against. Hopefully, I'll find a trail by that time or be able to confirm that there are no issues."

There is something about what she says that makes me uneasy. “What happens after two days if you’re not sure?”

Elsa shrugs. “I’ll give it back to you. I love a good puzzle, but I’ve got work up to my eyeballs as it is. I’ll give it two days, and with luck, I’ll be able to tell you one way or the other. Or I’ll give you the name of a large firm that might be able to help you.”

I consider looking for a large firm instead of gambling the loss of two days at this stage. But Mama trusts Elsa. To tell the truth, I already trust her, too. I don’t need to lose two days, but something tells me I have the right person for the job.

“Fair enough.” As I agree to her terms, the biggest cat I have ever seen jumps up the back of the sofa and wraps her body around Elsa’s neck. Elsa rubs the cat’s ears as I watch in shock.

“Do you like cats, April?”

That’s not a cat; that’s a miniature tiger. “Cats are okay. But I have a puppy I’m trying to raise right now.”

Elsa scoffs. “Good luck with that. They’re only marginally better than men.”

I don’t want to mention that Puppy is a boy. I might have to defend his honor if she gets ugly about him.

“What breed of cat is that, anyway?”

“Maine Coon.”

“It’s huge.”

Elsa knits her brow as she scratches under the docile cat’s chin. “No, she’s barely twenty pounds. They can get much bigger.”

Hmm. I think Puppy is more my speed. Still, if he tries to wrap himself around my neck, he’s going to be looking for a new home.

Elsa stands. The cat remains draped across her shoulders like a fur stole. “Please don’t consider me rude, but I really must get to work.”

“Oh, sure. Me too.” I like Elsa’s company, but the cat with the enormous gold eyes is really wigging me out.

Chapter 40

Driving into work, I think about Elsa's arrangement of working from her home. It seems like it would take an incredible amount of self-control to work from home every day. I know I do work after hours sometimes, but every day? I'm not sure I could manage that.

I have the Jared and Crystal Raley deposition at one. With any luck, we can find an equitable solution for them without too much fuss. I am beginning to believe the most significant obstacle, in that case, is that my client is still in denial.

I have a manicure at four thirty. After that, I will try to see how long I can hold out before I drink that two-thousand-dollar bottle of wine sitting in my fridge that keeps calling my name.

There is no missing the roses when I walk into Snow and Associates. There are twenty-four red roses with enough greenery and baby's breath to plump up the display until it to takes up half my desk.

I must hand it to him. Even though I made a fool of myself and made a hasty decision, Patrick is still extending his hand. Who knows? If Patrick keeps up the full-court press, I might have to change my mind about being a mom.

"April?" My uncle's voice echoes in from his office.

"Yes, sir?"

"You got some roses from somebody."

I move quickly to my desk and search for the card from Patrick, eager to read what he wrote. "I see that." Aren't I the lucky girl?

"You must have made quite the impression on someone."

I pull the envelope from the greenery and slice my finger open on a thorn. "Ow." I put the side of my finger to my lips, tasting the blood.

"I still expect two weeks' notice if you decide to elope."

Opening the card, I tease my uncle, "No chance. I'm going to make you and Daddy suffer through the longest wedding in history—" Chuck? The roses are from Chuck?

Wow. That is a shot to the gut I wasn't expecting. I'm having difficulty catching my breath.

Chuck. Not Patrick. It is like bad and then worse.

I must sit down as my world spins. Or is it crashing?

What did you expect April? You ran out right after he introduced you to the most important person in his life. You honestly still believed he could be in love with you?

I'm a special kind of fool.

I stare at the wall in front of me, struggling to catch my breath. My mind is scrambled eggs.

Getting just enough air into my lungs, I decide to get a cup of coffee. Not because I want one, but I need to have something in my hands.

My life is one prolonged, incomprehensible failure. It's as if there is a vast black hole in the path of my fate. It sucks all the joy out of my life.

How can I have been stupid enough to think Patrick could forgive me for such a faux pas. More pressing, why on earth did I accept Chuck's case and then have a mental lapse and go to lunch with him?

Done is done. I can't worry over spilled milk now.

The best thing to get all this off my mind is work. And I have that in spades right now.

I pull out the Raleys' case folder. Unlike Chuck, who is the man with a thousand secrets, Jared Raley has made it a point to document every asset the couple owns. He is more concerned about an equitable split than what Crystal did to break his heart.

Crystal is not too concerned about money either. She is a lot more interested in her neighbor's pecs, and other body parts that start with the letter P.

The front door opens. Lane marches through like a man on a mission. "You got time to take care of this?"

"Good morning to you too, DA Jameson."

He stops, straightens his posture, and smiles, "Good morning, Counselor Snow."

"What can I do for you, sir?"

"Honestly. Sign these papers so I can get back to my office."

It's humorous to me. It isn't very often I get to see Lane flustered. "Is your day going that well?"

He lays the folder on my desk. "You don't even want to know."

True. I have plenty of my own demons to fight these days. I pull out a pen as I read Jethro's plea bargain line by line.

"For mercy's sake, April. It's exactly what we agreed on."

"I'm just checking for misspelled words. You don't want to be embarrassed by filing a plea to Judge Rossi with a bunch of typos."

Lane slouches in front of my desk, shaking his head slowly. I finish reading the four-page document, sign it, and hand it over to him.

"Now he stays local. Correct?" I raise my eyebrows.

"It wouldn't make sense for us to go through the trouble of transferring him to the state for a sixty-day sentence."

"Good. I'm just making sure." I favor him with a sweet smile. "Thank you, Lane."

"Thank you for getting your client to see the light," he mutters.

My desk phone rings. "Hello?" I ask.

"I just checked my bank, and still no check from Snow and

Associates."

I wave goodbye to Lane. "Ms. Tate?"

"Yes, it is. Please explain why I do not have a refund yet."

The nerve of this woman. "Because there's nothing faulty with the work."

"Nothing faulty with the work? That's a crock. That worthless officer Hurley thinks there is a problem with your work, young lady."

"No. He doesn't have a problem with my paperwork."

"Okay, smarty-pants. Then tell me why he didn't arrest my creepy neighbor."

Really? She just called me smarty-pants? "Because he felt sorry for you and didn't want to make a scene and embarrass you."

"Embarrass me?" There is a long awkward pause. "You're insinuating that I did something wrong."

"No, ma'am. If I were insinuating, I'd be a lot more subtle. I'm telling you you're lucky Officer Hurley and your neighbor are kind, patient men. You could have been arrested for the destruction of private property. I don't like those pretentious car emblems either, but you can't be tearing them off your neighbor's car."

"Well, I never. You just wait. Once I tell all my friends how poorly I was treated at Snow and Associates, you will be closing your doors."

All her friends? I wonder how many of them are still on this side of the "veil" and if she ever needed two hands to count her friends.

Don't be ugly April.

Still, I have reached the point where principles don't matter anymore with Ms. Tate. If I can return her five hundred dollars to get her to go away for good, it will be a bargain I can't refuse.

I open my mouth to tell her I will return her fee in full—the line goes dead. I stare at the receiver in my hand. I'm shocked she hung up on me.

My blood pressure peaks as I think evil thoughts—the nerve

of that woman.

I come to my senses and laugh, giddy with relief. Dingdong, the witch is dead.

Leaning back in my desk chair, I stretch my arms over my head. That woman's voice makes my shoulder blades crawl into my ear holes.

My phone dings. Pavlov was correct; I pick up immediately to find I have a Gmail alert.

I open the email. My day turns on a dime. The San Francisco company wants me to interview via satellite this afternoon.

This is the start—the start of the long, positive roll.

See, everything was going negative there for a while. But the universe always wants to be in balance. I've got a whole lot of goodness coming my way, and it started with Ms. Tate hanging up the phone before I gave her any money back.

Now I've got corporate headhunters out of San Francisco after me. No telling what great fortune I can expect next.

I email them back, informing them I would like to interview at three thirty.

There's no reason to cancel my four thirty nail appointment. I'm sure thirty minutes will be more than enough time for them to realize I'm the girl they've been searching for to fill their essential position.

Howard comes out of his office and gestures toward me. "I'm meeting your mama at Rex's for lunch. We need to go over some zoning ordinances for the duplexes. Do you want to tag along?"

"As stimulating as that sounds, no thank you. I have to finish getting ready for the Raley deposition."

Howard eyes me suspiciously, then quips, "You might require some land-to-air missiles." He is referencing the drones that Raley's neighbor flew over their yard, precipitating the bad blood and eventually triggering the divorce.

"Ha-ha." It's always best not to encourage Howard's jokes.

"Best of luck with your call. I'm at your service if you need anyone to determine if it's a naked woman in any of the photos."

"You'd be the last man I'd call to confirm that."

He arches his brow in good humor. "Oh, honey. I don't think we want to compare dry spells now, do we?"

It's a bluff. Howard doesn't know anything about my personal life. "Whatever." Of course, it's like everybody in this town tells my parents my business. So, he may know.

Howard points at the roses. "Then again, maybe your luck is changing."

Please, Lord, don't even.

Howard pulls the door shut. I exhale as the quiet envelops my senses.

Three thirty seems like an eternity from now.

I'm too nervous to eat lunch. At noon I walk across the county park toward the courthouse annex where we will be holding the Raley deposition.

I can hear another of Howard's favorite jokes on an endless loop in my mind. "Your best quality, April, is high empathy for your clients, and your worst quality is high empathy for your clients."

Being counsel to someone is indeed a balancing act. You must have empathy to treat them as a human and connect with them. Otherwise, how can you negotiate in their best interest if you don't understand their needs and desires?

But you can get too close. Worse, you can personalize their predicament by comparing it to your life.

The longer I'm in the Raley case, the more I can't separate it from my current situation. How can I understand a woman like Crystal?

Sure, Jared needs to lose about forty pounds, and his hair is thinning, but you can see through that softening body and know that twenty years ago, in his prime, he was a good-looking man.

Yes, Crystal is hot. But her weeks consist of a few hours of Zumba and light exercise in the pool.

During that same period, Jared has been working eighty

hours a week at the dealership, overeating fast food, and self-medicating when the stress gets to be too much.

It's easy enough to rationalize how they ended up on opposite ends of the attractiveness spectrum twenty years later.

There is absolutely no mistaking Jared's devotion to his wife. Not only is he the last person to believe she was having an affair, but I also have no doubt in my mind that he will take her back if she would only say the word.

Embarrassment is of no concern to a man truly in love.

I don't know how I would react to a man that in love with me. I can't even be sure I would fully appreciate him over time. Still, I'd sure like to try it on for size.

Crystal's attorney out of Huntsville is concerned that it will give me too much of a home-field advantage if we meet at Snow and Associates. Most days, that would be laughable. But who knows, with two dozen long-stemmed roses on my desk, she might've been right today.

It isn't like I have to tell her who sent them to me.

I step into the municipal building and pull up short. Jared is standing in the foyer with a worried look on his face.

"Hey, Jared. Is everything okay?"

He has light beads of perspiration dotting his forehead. His eyes are wide with an alarming wildness about them.

"Sure. I just didn't want to be by myself in the room when Crystal comes in."

I glance over his shoulder, down the hall. "Are they already here?"

"I don't know." He taps his tie knot. "Does this look okay?"

Aww, Jared. You're breaking my heart, dude. That witch isn't going to care how you look today. She just wants a big check and her freedom.

I reach up and straighten Jared's tie knot. Then, pulling the silk snug, I tap him on the shoulder, "There. You look very handsome today."

"I just don't want her to think I'm a loser."

It is one of those moments where I know I should take the time and reassert to my client that these are divorce proceedings. It doesn't matter what your spouse, soon-to-be-former spouse, thinks about you anymore. Because you're getting a—DIVORCE.

Jared's mindset appears exceptionally fragile. I think the talk would be counterproductive at best. "You're no loser, Jared. She knows that. People just change sometimes."

I point down the hallway. "If you're okay with it, I'd like to go ahead and set up, so I'm not unpacking my brief as they come in."

He jolts into motion. "Oh, sure. I understand."

Crystal and her attorney arrive fifteen minutes late.

Crystal is a wreck. Her face is swollen, large black bags reside under her eyes, and she has a trail of mascara smudges from her tears. Small wet tracks cut through the thick orange foundation on her cheeks.

I'm not buying it. Alligator tears just tick me off.

As I glare at her I notice something else. Crystal's svelte figure is now padded by an additional thirty pounds.

Her attorney introduces herself to me as Laura Keys from Skelton and Keys law firm in Huntsville. Laura looks to be ten years my senior with a pantsuit instead of a skirt.

A sob escapes Crystal, and she covers her mouth as if her outburst caught her by surprise. In my peripheral vision, I see my client's reaction. I immediately want to begin banging my forehead on the conference table.

"Are you okay?" he whispers to Crystal.

She hiccups twice, then dabs ineffectually at her eyes, smearing her mascara further before she shakes her head.

Oh, she is a grade-A masterful manipulator. She is playing Jared like Elton John plays the piano on Saturday night.

I just can't figure out to what end. Surely Crystal doesn't think she deserves more than half their assets.

Counselor Keys fails to hide a frown before she offers, "Crystal learned she has a setback in her future plans."

I've never been particularly fluent in girl cryptic. I'm not sure if that's from being raised with brothers or because my mama is as blunt as any drill sergeant.

"How so?" I ask.

Laura looks to Crystal. Crystal meets her gaze, exhaling as her shoulders drop.

"The baby's daddy broke it off between them," Laura whispers.

Oh boy. And I know just the patient cuckold husband who will love to take advantage of that opening.

"You two aren't seeing each other anymore?"

All I can do is roll my eyes when I hear Jared ask about her relationship status.

"He said I was fat and ugly," Crystal manages to choke out before another sob racks her body. "I can't help it. It's the baby."

Well that simultaneously explains the sudden weight gain and changes the financial equation of this deposition.

"He's a fool. You've always been beautiful, but pregnancy has put this"—he opens his hands wide and spreads them in the air—"stunning glow all around you. You're like the Virgin Mary," Jared says.

I must stifle a laugh. I'll never be able to hear the Christmas story again without supplanting Crystal in a bikini as the Virgin Mary. That is so twisted.

She quits sniffling and lowers her hands from her eyes. "You really think so?"

"Absolutely. I didn't think you could be any more beautiful. But I was wrong."

"I was wrong too, Poopsie. I can't believe the mess I've made of everything."

Poopsie? Oh, I am going to be sick.

"No. I wasn't paying you enough attention. It was my fault," Jared insists.

At this point, I don't bother closing my gaping mouth. Nobody is looking at me anyway.

"What are you going to do now, Crystal?" he asks.

She shakes her head and puts a well-used tissue to her nose. "I don't know. I've destroyed the most important relationship in my life and am just now realizing it, Jared. I wish I had never taken you for granted."

"You can come home," Jared offers.

Crystal scoffs. "I'm sure you hate my guts now."

"I could never hate you, Crystal."

Her mouth parts slightly, and some of her sexiness reappears. "Are you positive, Jared? You would do this—could do this for me?"

He nods his head in response.

She frowns. "But the baby. It's not your child, Jared."

"I know. But I don't care. I want to adopt him—her—whatever? If Paul doesn't want to raise the baby, I would be honored to be the father."

"Really?" Crystal's voice goes up an octave.

He laughs. "Sure. I always wanted kids. You were the one worried about what it would do to your figure."

"You did, didn't you?" She perks up further as her excitement ramps up. "It's a boy."

"It is?" Jared leans forward, clasping Crystal's hand in his.

Her chin moves up and down quickly as a smile blooms across her face.

For Pete's sake, Jared is right. Crystal is glowing.

"A boy? Really?" Jared laughs with joy. "We're having a son!"

"I want to name him Jared Jr. I thought we could call him Jerry."

Jared shoots out of his chair and hugs Crystal. He turns her chair and locks his lips to hers. I begin to wonder if they're going to deprive the baby of necessary oxygen.

I suppose I'm a wee bit envious. Crystal has gotten her cake and gets to eat it too. It all ends up just swell for her.

Me, I don't have flour, milk, or even an egg. Much less a cake to worry about. I'm not getting any sugar either.

"I'm going to assume we need to put the paperwork on the backburner for now," Laura whispers to me under her breath.

I slide my laptop and folder into my backpack. "Hopefully, we won't ever need to pull it out again."

"That's a pleasant thought." Laura's tone tells me I'm not the only one who isn't sold entirely on happily ever after just yet.

She extends her hand, and we shake. I would have liked to test my negotiation skills against her. But the game was called on account of foolish love.

It's not a totally bad thing.

Chapter 41

Walking back into our law office, I pretend my flowers are from a future lover. I have no idea what his name is and don't want to jinx it by assigning one erroneously.

Granny Snow always says if you wish for something long enough, it will materialize. Well, by gosh, I have been wishing pretty hard. If he shows up tonight, he'll already be late to the party.

I sit down at my desk, turning on my laptop. I have fifteen minutes to spare before my interview. I print off the latest copy of my résumé and review it to see if I need to add any recent accomplishments.

No. I think a plea deal for a client accused of firebombing his own trailer is something better left off the résumé. Big-city folks just wouldn't understand.

Oddly, I'm not the least bit nervous. A strange calm has washed over me as if I already have the position.

My laptop rings, and I click on the join meeting button. A middle-aged woman with auburn hair pulled back in a bun appears on the screen. She gives the briefest of smiles void of any sincerity.

"Hello, April. I'm Teresa Starr, and I will be your HR liaison. Let me start by saying I'm glad you were able to take the time to interview with us today."

"Thank you, Ms. Starr. It was good to hear from BGGSC."

Ms. Starr offers me a smile that appears somewhat condescending. "Please, let's keep it informal. Call me Teresa. And by the way, it's BBGSC."

Awesome start, April. Nothing like getting somebody's company name wrong right off the bat.

"This initial interview is to explain the position at BBGSC and confirm your past work history."

I open my mouth to tell her that sounds great, but she starts back in with her speech.

"BBGSC is a firm that specializes in defense of high visibility clients. As you can understand, professional discretion is one of the most valued aspects of our firm. I'm sure you can immediately recognize why we are interested in recruiting you."

Because I can keep a secret? No. That's not it.

The long silence goes from awkward to embarrassing. Darn it. It wasn't a rhetorical question. "My class rank?"

Teresa sniffs. Now there is no mistaking it. She is definitely condescending. "No, your recent work history. Our firm is growing rapidly. The most significant obstacle we encounter when recruiting the younger generation is finding associates who already have real-world experience." She looks down, and I hear papers rustling. "It says here you have been working for Snow and Associates." Her lips twist. "Related?"

"My uncle."

"How quaint."

Oh no she didn't. I'm glad we're having this interview over the internet. I'm not sure my hand would have stayed down at my side if we were in person.

"According to your résumé, you've had three months' experience on the job. Is that correct?"

Yes. I exaggerated a few weeks. "Yes, ma'am."

She bobs her head. "Typically, after three months, recruits have progressed past finding out where the coffee machine is and how to do basic filing. You can see where the value is for a large firm such as BBGSC to skip all that remedial training."

Woman, did you read the part where I'm two and O in the capital defense arena? "I've actually had my own caseload while I've been working."

"Yes, but you can understand that cases in San Francisco are quite a bit more complicated than what they are in—" She rustles her papers again. "Guntersville."

Actually, Guntersville is in America. I'm reasonably sure the legal system works similarly in both cities.

"This is how we will proceed. I'll return to my management team and construct a pitch for you. If management approves of your résumé and what I tell them, I'll call you back tomorrow. We'll make you an offer contingent on you flying out and meeting the management team."

It seems backward to extend an offer contingent on the first face-to-face meeting, but I don't want to curse my good fortune. "That sounds wonderful, Teresa. I hope to hear from you tomorrow."

"I always call regardless of the news." She waves her hand dramatically in front of her face.

I'm left staring at my laptop as her image disappears—what a peculiar conversation.

I really want this job in San Francisco. But I can't dismiss the awkwardness of our chat. I'm sure that's just how they talk in Cali.

I wonder if there is an online course I can take to master speaking West Coast.

I'll cross that bridge when I come to it. There is no knowing how the application process will turn out since I can't even pitch in person to the partners. I'll have to be content with the knowledge that if it is meant to be, it will happen.

Scanning the bottom, right-hand corner of my display, I perk up. I have a relaxing manicure in thirty minutes. It's difficult not to be happy when you know you have an indulgent activity in a few minutes.

Chapter 42

Tiffany is at the front counter when I enter the beauty college. I shiver as the light perspiration on my skin from the walk over dissipates when it meets the sixty-degree blast of air from the air register above the cash register.

I rub my hands over my bare arms. "I see you got your air fixed."

Tiffany's heart-shaped face lights up. "Yes. Thank you so much for reminding me about Patrick. He came out after hours and fixed me right up."

"You certainly can't argue with that service," I say.

"I know. Right?" Tiffany raises her hands above her head and wiggles her hips. "Feel that blessed arctic breeze."

I could do with a little less blessing as it is genuinely freezing in her shop.

"Come on back, and let's see how much damage you've done since your last visit."

I tuck my nails into my palms.

"Come to find out, Patrick's son plays baseball. My son Wesley has been on me to sign him up for baseball. Isn't that a crazy coincidence?"

Tiffany has this expectant look on her face. All I can think is that it isn't that unusual to find two boys that like baseball.

"Because of the boys, we're going to get together on Tuesday and Thursday nights. Alternate between Huntsville and Guntersville so the boys can get a chance to practice together."

My left eye begins to twitch uncontrollably. I push the heel of my hand against it as I decipher what Tiffany is saying.

"Then go out to dinner"—she points the nail file at me—"the four of us."

I nod in a stupor and hope I don't appear to be studying her as hard as I am. Something is off about her body language, and I can't put my finger on it.

"You don't mind, do you?" Tiffany asks. She bites her lower lip.

"Mind?" I can't breathe! "Mind that the boys play baseball together?" The end of my question tails off as I run out of air.

Tiffany shakes her head. "No. That Patrick and I are seeing each other."

Yes. I have a full-blown panic attack coming on. Possibly a heart attack. "You're just catching a bite to eat with the boys. I wouldn't exactly classify that as dating."

She shrugs as a sheepish grin graces her face. "I don't know what it is. We just seem to have so much in common. There is this real solid connection between us." Tiffany clenches her tee-shirt at her heart.

So much in common? Besides both raising boys, I don't see where they have anything in common. Of course, having sons is one more thing in common than I had with the man.

Her lips thin. "You're not saying anything. Do you have a problem with this? If you do, I don't want to make it hard on you. You know how I feel about you, April."

"Oh no." I wave my hand at her as I lie, "Patrick and I were never an item. I'm happy for you if he's what you think you need."

She giggles as she rolls her eyes. "Time will tell about that. But I'm hopeful. You just don't understand what it's like to be lonely for a long time."

Define a long time.

"Now, let me see those hands."

"You know what? I just remembered a conflicting appointment with a client. It totally slipped my mind, Tiffany. I'm going to have to do this at another time."

I stand. "I'll pay for the time slot if you need me to."

Her lips part. "No, don't worry about it. We'll just reschedule later."

"You sure you don't mind?" I feel bad, but I just can't. Not yet, at least.

She sighs. "Not at all, April. You go take care of your client."

Leaving the shop, everything is off balance. I still can't catch my breath. It's impossible to walk a straight line as I wander to my car.

Leaning against the Prius, I burn my hand. It feels like a hundred degrees today and a hundred percent humidity.

Foolish girl. It's Guntersville in July. It probably is a hundred degrees and a hundred percent humidity.

I'm also a hundred percent humiliated by my actions again. *Get a grip April.*

Steeling myself, I brave the even hotter interior of my car. Blessedly I'm able to start it on the first attempt.

I sit, watching people I know walk down the town square as the eighty-degree A/C air blows in my face.

If I were to be a silver-lining girl, at least I know for sure the whole Patrick situation is done. He has moved on.

Which is good.

I don't want to be a mother yet. And I certainly don't want to be a mother to someone else's kid. Someone still in the picture who I'll be constantly compared against.

That's not the altruistic training I received as an undergraduate. I guess I'm just not as good of a person as I would like to be.

The big question is, if I don't want to be with Patrick, why does it hurt so bad to hear he is hooking up with a friend? Why does that even matter to me?

Because I'm a freak and I can't make up my mind.

Okay, this is April trying to be mature about this. Patrick is a friend, and Tiffany is a friend. If they can make each other happy, that should make me happy. I'm glad for them. Ugh—I lie so badly I can't even convince myself.

I put my car in reverse. I would rather be unhappy in my apartment than on the street in my car. It's the prudent thing to do. Especially since I feel on the verge of breaking into an uncontrollable snot bubble sobbing fit, and I don't want to concern anybody who happens by my car.

I'm still sulking as I turn onto Gunter's Landing, then I remember. I have a bottle of wine chilling in the fridge.

That two-thousand-dollar bottle of wine doesn't stand a chance when I get home.

I'm sitting cross-legged on the floor of my apartment with half the bottle consumed. Puppy struts through his new dog door.

He tilts his head to the right and studies the situation. Sighing in resignation, he trots over and plops down beside me.

I knead the thick fur at his neckline. My blood pressure eases, and I can finally breathe again.

I'll be okay after all. I am strong, and I will survive this pain. Besides, there isn't an option anyway.

Chapter 43

My phone wakes me. "Hello?"

"April, did I wake you?"

"No." I look at the time on my phone. It is three forty-five in the morning. Who the heck calls at this hour? "I was awake."

"Good. I have slight insomnia, and sometimes I call too early."

"Who is this anyway?" I ask.

"Elsa."

I must clear the cobwebs from my brain before I can remember. "Oh hey."

Puppy protests as I get up from the floor. My back feels like someone took batting practice on it.

"I think I have your project figured out. Check that; I know I do. We need to complete some additional legwork to prove the facts."

She is talking so fast my head is beginning to ache. "You do?"

"Are you sure you're up?"

"Of course, I am."

"This would be easier for me to show you in person. What time do you think you can be here?"

"Seven?"

"Oh." The disappointment is evident in her tone.

"Six?"

"I guess that's better."

I'm not offering five in the morning unless she proposes to make me pancakes and fresh-squeezed orange juice for me. "Okay. I'll see you in a little while."

The mirror doesn't lie when I check my appearance. I desperately need a shower, even if I'm going over to the cat lady's home.

More importantly, I need something to wake me up. That fancy wine must have like ten times the alcohol of regular wine. That's probably why it is so expensive.

I pad over to my kitchenette to make myself some instant coffee. I know, it tastes like mud, but beggars can't be choosy.

Remembering my secret weapon stashed in my refrigerator, I grin. If there is ever a time to partake in Nana's witch brew—now is as good of a morning as I'll ever find.

I'm gripping the steering wheel so tightly my forearms are cramping as I pull out of my parents' drive, freshly showered and wired, forty-five minutes later.

I lock up my brakes twice before reaching the bottom of the valley leading to the ascent up Elsa's hill. The early morning fog plays tricks on my vision. At one point, I swear I see a human crossing the road naked.

My eyelids feel like they have been duct-taped open. I can't blink to save my life. It's the most bizarre of sensations, but I have become used to it.

I rap on the door. Elsa answers immediately. She must have been waiting behind it for me to arrive.

"I knew you wouldn't be able to wait that long."

Yeah. It was something like that. "Inquiring minds want to know. Is Chuck clean or dirty?"

Elsa smiles. Her eyes have a disquieting wildness to them. "Silly, I wouldn't have called you over this early if he were clean. I would have just called you once you got in to work."

"Chuck's been lying to me. I knew it!"

"Not only has he been lying to you, but he also doesn't think much of you."

I lurch back. "How do you mean?"

"He barely attempted to cover his tracks." She laughs. "Chuck must have thought you had no chance of understanding what he was doing since he gave you the files in their entirety."

I could have done without her snide commentary. I don't need to know yet another man thought he could play me with a steak dinner and a bouquet of flowers.

Elsa motions for me to follow her inside.

The living room is changed as a large projector screen has dropped from the ceiling, and there are two spreadsheets juxtaposed on display. I recognize them to be the balance sheet and personal income tax forms from Chuck's files.

"You see these entries here?" Elsa points to some highlighted cells.

"Yes."

"OSBA. What do you think that stands for?"

"Other savings and business accounts." I'm not sure if I'm correct, but it sounds good.

"Not bad for a first guess. And, not far off the mark."

I smirk like a first grader who just answered the teacher's question correctly and got a gold star in front of the class.

"But how about offshore business accounts?"

I like that much better. It has a markedly more nefarious tone to it. "Chuck is moving money out of the US. Is that a crime?"

Rolling her eyes, Elsa says, "Not as long as you've paid taxes on it. But if not, it's tax evasion."

Elsa has a talent for making everything a suspense thriller. It is beginning to get on my nerves. "Well, did he? Pay his taxes."

"I can't say for sure. There's a slight chance that this is a recurring monthly payment to a subsidiary for a product or service. Someone will need to either get with the bank and follow the transaction to ground or tap into the bank servers and extract the information discreetly.

"Either way, you're going to have to find out where the money physically went and for what purpose."

"Is any of that legal? Will the bank give me personal information like that?"

"Uh, let's see—no. Not without a subpoena. I'm sure your client isn't going to be so helpful once he realizes you're smart and on to him. I'm sure you don't fit his profile of an attractive blonde woman."

"You're telling me I'm screwed." I don't know why, but now I have this burning curiosity to understand the transactions fully. "Are you sure there's not something you can do?"

Elsa switches the projector off. "Could. But no. I'm afraid I'm just a by-the-books kinda girl."

This is most disappointing to hear.

Still, I draw on my past experiences. Things are a matter of perspective. Size does matter in criminal proceedings.

If the money transfers Elsa found amount to beer and golf money, it won't impact the settlement. It will still pique my curiosity, but that's a different topic. "How much money are we talking about?"

"It's somewhat sporadic at the start, but the last two years, it's been a steady seven hundred thousand a month. I'd say we're talking about twenty million."

I believe my brain short-circuited. I take a seat. "Excuse me, did you say twenty thousand or twenty million?"

"Million with an M."

My jaw drops in wonderment of the sheer size of the gambit. "Bless it. I'm in the wrong business. Who would've thought chemical manufacturers could make that kind of money?"

Elsa massages her cat between its ears. "The numbers don't lie. But yes, I admit the earnings of the company shocks me, too. It makes me wonder if there may be something below the surface, another income stream he wants hidden. It's not uncommon for subsidiary payments to lead to some unsavory business practices." She shrugs. "But the numbers feeling shady and knowing there is criminality in play are two distinctly different situations."

I guess I have my answer. Or at least as much of one as I can get without unauthorized intervention. "Thank you for looking over the books for me, Elsa."

"Don't mention it. It was a nice break from my other projects." She pulls the flash drive from her laptop and hands it to me. "Good luck with it."

"Thank you."

Elsa lifts something from the coffee table. "Listen, I don't know how far you have to take this to get a judge to actually listen to you. But this guy"—she waves a business card in the air—"I must admit he is a touch eccentric but highly professional. He also has incredible resources. He's unbelievable at finding—let's say information people will kill to keep concealed.

"He's not always in town, but you could always get lucky."

I wonder who could be more eccentric than Elsa. "Thank you, Elsa."

I flip the card over and choke. Michael VanDerveer? Really?

"Listen, if you ever need your taxes done or just a quickie research project, be sure to look me up. Or if you'd like to have a talk while we kill a bottle or two of wine."

"You know I will." Quickie?

As I drive back down the side of the mountain, I try to decide my next move. I can wing it with what I can confirm, but twenty million is a significant amount of cash to hide. Plus, my curiosity is itching to understand how a chemical company clears an additional eight million a year that never hits the books.

There is no question. I will call Vander today. Besides, he left town before I properly thanked him for getting the information that cleared Vance Wagner in his shooting case.

Nana's energy potion has my feet dancing on the floorboard and my skin, just below the surface, crawling with tiny fire ants.

The discomfort is a small price to pay for the world going

by in slow motion. Man, Nana needs to market this stuff to athletes.

Imagine the homeruns batters could score with the ball moving at half speed. That is if their heart doesn't blow out as they round second base.

Deciding I need to call Vander is easy. Picking up the phone and calling him takes more nerves than I can muster now.

Taking a detour to Ms. Bell's for breakfast seems much more enjoyable. The case of the munchies I have developed can only be soothed by a huge greasy piece of meat sandwiched between plate-sized buttery biscuit halves.

My phone rings. I grimace. What the heck? It's not even seven o'clock. Can you folks give it a rest long enough for a girl to catch her breath?

I hit the answer button. "Hello?"

"Hi, April. This is Chuck."

My stomach tightens. "Hi, Chuck. What can I do for you?"

Awkward. As Granny says, I must have talked him up.

"Say yes. That you want to come work for me."

"I didn't exactly say no, Chuck. It's just I have another opportunity in San Francisco which is looking really attractive."

"San Francisco? There's a mass exodus out of San Francisco right now. You would be the only car in the westbound lane on the way into town."

"I'll take it under advisement, Chuck. Say, can I call you back? I'm expecting a call from one of the judges I'm presenting to, and it looks like they're trying to call in." One of the bonuses of phone calls. Nobody can see my "I just told a fib" awkward smirk.

"Sure. But promise me you'll think about it."

"I will. Goodbye, Chuck."

Walking into Ms. Bell's, the bacon grease and baking biscuit aromas calm my nerves. Happy with my decision to put off calling Vander, I exit with two fried chicken biscuits.

No. Only one is for me. They're about three thousand

calories each.

I make a beeline into Howard's office as I enter Snow and Associates. He is already working. I set a biscuit on his desk.

"I forgot to tell you. We're down one account," I say.

Howard points at the bag. "What flavor..." he draws back and stares at my face. "What happened to your you? It looks like someone super-glued your eyelids open."

"Thanks. You certainly know how to destroy a girl's self-confidence."

He points at the bag. "What did you bring me?"

I turn my back and walk out of his office. "A chicken biscuit. Don't choke on it."

Chapter 44

I realize Chuck has ulterior motives. Still, what he said about people leaving San Francisco lodges in my mind like a splinter, and I can only remove it with research.

Surfing the web, I find multiple sourced stories about people, primarily my age, leaving San Francisco. According to the articles, the cost of living is pricing many of them out of the area. That puts a significant crimp in my plans.

I'm not going to lie. The cost of living being higher in California does concern me. Then again, I'm a professional. With the salary I'll command, I know I'll have the lifestyle I want with plenty to spare.

The little voice in my head tells me I haven't done enough. This is a critical life decision, and I shouldn't be taking it based on what I think or feel. I have been professionally trained as a researcher. I should investigate the facts rather than guess.

I blow out a long breath of frustration. Why does everything have to be so blasted complicated? I, just once, want a slam dunk, no-brainer decision to come my way.

Instead, I am compelled to do deep-dive research on the area. Not just rely on reading articles and opinion pieces, but study analytics from the market.

The first two I pull up are the apartment rental sites and cost of living index comparison sites. I drop my chin to my chest and clamp my eyes shut.

How can these numbers be accurate? I must be misreading them.

Is it even possible for it to be fifty percent more expensive to live in San Francisco than in Guntersville? Never mind, that doesn't take into account I lose my free rent and frequent free meals.

I'm sure BBGSC takes that into account when they make their salary offers. Right?

"April, I'm going up to the county clerk." Howard is standing in front of my desk.

"Oh." I look at the time on my laptop. Ten o'clock? How did that happen?

"Do you have anything you need me to file with the clerk for you?"

"No, sir. The only business I have working is the Davis settlement. It seems to have gotten slow again."

"You know what I say about when it gets slow"—he walks to the door—"give it a moment, and you'll have more alligators than you can kill."

More Howard witticism. I wave for him to get out of my hair, and he smiles as he pulls the door closed.

Fudge biscuit. I forgot to call Vander.

I pick up my phone and scroll to his name. I'm glad I did it quickly. As the phone rings, the muscles in my neck tighten.

"Michael VanDerveer."

I gasp. "Vander, this is April Snow."

"Hello, baby Snow. What can I do for you?"

"Where are you today?"

There's a rush of air that may be an abbreviated laugh. "Did the hall monitor die, and you get promoted?"

What? "I need to see if you can help with something."

"I'm not too far away. What do you need?" he asks.

"You know Elsa Long, right?"

"Yes." He draws out his answer with a drawl.

"I have a client she is assisting me with, and we have hit an impasse on his bank accounts. Elsa thinks you might have the means of finding out the information she doesn't have access to collect."

The extended silence makes me uncomfortable. "Vander?"

"I might be able to help," Vander says.

Okay, that is encouraging. "There are monthly transactions in the client's business account that we want to run to ground."

Vander chuckles. I know he is laughing at me, but rather than making me angry, it makes me grin.

"What's so funny now?" I ask.

"You need to run the transactions to ground, not round," he corrects me.

That does make more sense. "That's what I said."

"Sure. Who's your subject of interest? I need to make sure I have access."

I hear the clack of keys being struck on a keyboard and realize he means right now. How cool is it to have the ability to spy on other people's business with just a few keystrokes?

"Chuck Davis," I say.

The clicking stops. "Chuck Davis of D&D Performance Chemicals out of Huntsville?"

Man, is Vander good or what? "How'd you pull up all his information that quick?"

There is another long, uncomfortable pause. Girls as impatient as I am find conversations with men like Vander unnerving. "Vander?"

"Let's meet for lunch."

His command sends a tickle to my gut. Not in a good way. Vander scares the pee out of me. "Why?"

"Snow, do you ever just follow directions?"

I like to understand things. Sue me. "Yes."

"We don't need to discuss anything else on the phone. Meet me at Sonny's barbecue in Scottsdale in an hour."

"Scottsdale?" I whine.

"Snow." His tone is threatening.

"Okay already. Scottsdale it is."

I start to say goodbye—the line is already dead. This cloak-and-dagger routine with Vander might be sexy to some girls, but it just gets on my nerves.

Chapter 45

There are eight good barbecue joints between here and Scottsdale. Can we go to one of those? No, we have to go all the way to Scottsdale.

And then to Sonny's to boot. Where they serve stupid vinegar barbecue sauce. Of course, Vander is such a weirdo he probably prefers vinegar-based sauce.

I'm shoving items into my purse while I indulge in a well-deserved mini temper tantrum when my phone dings.

It's a text from Teresa Starr. She wants to know when I can give her a call.

I consider calling her now, but what if it's a long discussion. It could be.

She might need me to hop on a Zoom call and talk to the partners to give them that final nudge to make me an offer. An offer that will cover the increase in living expenses.

I have the meeting with Vander in an hour. Lunch will take, oh I don't know, ten minutes considering it's Vander, and he's never talkative.

I text Teresa back that I will call her at one o'clock.

As I lock the door to Snow and Associates and put the "Back Soon" sign on our door, Teresa responds. She will be waiting for my call.

I walk into Sonny's, and a hand taps my shoulder. I swirl

around eye to eye with Vander. His expression is stern.

"You scared the pee out of me, Vander."

"Sorry. I didn't want to wait outside for you."

"Well, just say my name next time."

He gestures toward a table in the back of the restaurant. I lead the way.

"I hope you're not planning for me to eat lunch with you. I'm really not hungry," I say.

"That's a shame," he says as he pulls out my chair. "I ordered two racks of baby back ribs."

Blast it. Now I will end up eating. "I don't like baby back ribs."

He flashes his movie star smile as he sits across from me. "Yes, you do."

"You don't know."

"I know everything about you, April."

A chill runs up my spine. There are conflicting sexual and dangerous sensations flashing through my body. Vander has the oddest effects on me. He is the mesmerizing flame that I know is dangerous, and I am the predictable moth drawn to him.

"Relax, Snow. What you don't know is I'm a longtime friend of your uncle and your dad." He rolls his right hand over. "Naturally, I know a good bit about your family."

I didn't even know Daddy knew Vander. Why don't I know this?

Our waitress appears with a large deep dish pizza tray with two perfectly caramelized racks of baby back ribs and a basket of fries. It is a beautiful spread.

"Is there anything else I can get you two?" she asks.

"If you could just bring us a pitcher of sweet tea, we'll be good. We have something private to discuss." Vander says with his full charm on display.

Our waitress, well into her fifties, is captivated by Vander's smile, "Sure, hon. I'll be right back and then leave you two alone."

"Thank you."

"I didn't think you drank sweet tea," I say.

The edges of his lips rise. "I don't. But you do."

He cuts three ribs from one of the racks and places them on his plate—Vander motions for me to take a portion.

Fine. Whatever. I can't exactly let Vander eat alone, and it is lunchtime.

"You're going to want to drop Chuck Davis as a client." He takes a bite from a rib.

I choke on air. True, I never wanted Chuck as a client, but Vander's blunt command rubs my fur the wrong way.

He must've read my mind as he raises his hand, "It's just friendly advice. You do what you think you need to do. I'm just letting you know that he's been dabbling in stuff that will get him sent away for a long time. That is if he makes it to the jail."

"I don't understand."

A rare flash of frustration crosses Vander's face. "Snow, can't you ever just take a hint?"

"I guess not."

He wipes barbecue sauce from his fingers and exhales dramatically. "You know the woman he's been seeing lately?"

I scoff. "The tiny blonde teenager?"

Vander's expression turns stone cold. It sends another shiver up my spine as my smile dissipates.

"Katarina Popovic. She's nearly forty," he continues.

"I'd like to know her beauty secrets."

"She has a lot of other secrets our government is interested in." His eyes lock on mine, and there is no humor in his tone.

"Oh." Holy moly. Is he saying what I think he is?

"Yes. Oh, is right. You're a smart girl. Think about it. High-performance oils and fuel additives, his business close to a major military research base."

"He said his military contracts are his big money makers," I parrot.

Vander raises an eyebrow. "That's probably the only true thing he told you."

"So, are these chemicals developed with the help of the American government?"

There is a long pause. Vander dips his chin toward his chest. "I could tell you, Snow. But then I'd have to kill you."

"You've been dying to use that line this whole time, haven't you?"

Vander laughs while leaning back in his chair. "It is my favorite."

He is incredibly handsome when he is at ease. Vander is a few inches too short for my taste but still majorly hot.

"All kidding aside, you'd do best to get as far away from him as possible before his situation blows up. I'd hate for you to get caught up in it."

"This bites. I am officially out of clients," I say.

"Sounds like the perfect time for a vacation."

Vacation reminds me of the San Francisco job. "I am close to landing an opportunity with a firm in San Francisco."

"Cool town. You'll like it there. That's why your caseload has cleared. The universe is allowing you to clear your slate to start fresh. It's always best to tidy things up before you move on."

Vander's "move on" comment has me tearing up for some unexplainable reason. Moving on with my life is exactly what I want. What I need. But the permanence of it weighs in on me, making it difficult to draw a deep breath as the anxiety climbs.

"Vander, how do you do it?"

His dark eyebrows knit. "Do what?"

"I don't know. I imagine you to be this person who floats all over the world totally untethered to the places and people you see."

His full lips purse. "Mostly. But I have an advantage over you. I don't have any family."

That doesn't seem like an advantage. It sounds sad.

"What about women. I'm sure you date. Right?"

"Yeah. I date some women who interest me. But I'm not exactly long-term relationship material."

"Why do you say that?"

His facial features darken, and he looks past me. I fear I have gone over the line with the personal talk with Vander.

"I'm here on a short-term visa, Snow. I don't plan to be here as long-term as you."

"In the country?"

"Life." His eyes soften, and my heart breaks for him. "I never want anybody to have to worry about when that day will come."

My throat tightens. I can only imagine how lonely Vander's life must be. I have the strongest urge to get up and hug him. But I'm not that brave.

He stands and puts a hundred-dollar bill on the table. "Stay out of trouble, Snow."

"Thank you, Michael."

He laughs and raises his eyebrows, obviously amused by me using his first name. "You're welcome. Call me anytime you think I can be of help."

Chapter 46

I call Teresa Starr on my way back to the office. She advises me that the management team wants to extend a contract contingent on meeting them in person. So that is excellent news.

Not so great is the starting salary of fifty thousand a year. I do some quick math in my head and realize working for Howard and Dusty on the side, I'm already cobbling together that much income. Plus, I won't have free rent in San Francisco.

As much as I need to get out of Guntersville, I'm not prepared to move backward financially to accomplish that goal.

Teresa has the nerve to tell me I'm making a mistake as I thank her for the opportunity and tell her I'll have to pass.

Coming into town, I'm incredibly grouchy. I have no clients, no boyfriend, no job offers that even come close to what I need, and now even Nana's energy drink is wearing off.

It is two in the afternoon. I have half a mind to just go home and take a nap.

But no, April started this mature phase. Consequently, I find myself in front of Snow and Associates. Since I'm here, I might as well go on in and finish the day.

Who knows, some crazy client might come in and want me to do some stupid paperwork for them. I'd hate to miss out on that.

As I open the door, I'm surprised to see Lane and Howard huddled together in front of the preposterously huge floral arrangement at my desk. They both give me a startled look that turns to concern.

"What? Did somebody die?" I ask flippantly as I drop my keys in my purse.

The color drains out of both men's faces. Something is up—I stop walking.

"April honey, I think you should take a seat?" Howard says.

I take two steps back, my back pressed against the wall. "I don't want to have a seat."

Lane approaches me and holds out his hand. "We have some terrible news we need to tell you."

I push his hand away from me. "What?"

He screws his lips up and sniffs. "I'm not sure how best to tell you this. It's only the second time I've dealt with this situation the entire time I've been in this profession."

I don't care to hear Lane's work history. "Tell me what?"

Lane finally looks me in the eyes. He draws a shaky breath. This is the first time I recall seeing the man appear sad. I get an uneasy feeling in my gut. The room has begun to spin like a carousel.

"April, Jethro Mullins hung himself today in his cell."

Tears sting my eyes. "What?"

"They found him an hour ago," Lane continues.

"Is he okay?" I ask.

Lane shakes his head and whispers, "I'm sorry. He's dead."

The carousel picks up speed, and I get the sensation I may topple over. I'm going to be sick. "How does this happen? I told you to watch him!"

"We had him on watch," Lane pleads. "April, if somebody's darned and determined to take their life, short of putting them in a restraining jacket, we can't save them from themselves."

The dam breaks, and tears flow freely down my cheeks. I'm making some gosh-awful mewing sound that reminds me of an injured animal.

I can't stay here. Lane and Howard can't see me like this; I must get as far away as I can from here.

Through my blurred vision, I see Howard step toward me. He is holding a piece of paper in his hand.

"Honey, there isn't anything to be done. Jethro wrote this letter. In it, he says he was just heartbroken that his wife had left him. He felt like he was too stupid to be able to get her back. He gave up."

"He wasn't stupid," I screech. "He was just a normal, sweet man trying to get by in the nasty, mean world."

"These things happen, April." Lane moves to touch my arm. I slap his hand away.

"Don't touch me. You should have kept Jethro safe!"

"I'm sorry, April. I know this hurts." Howard's voice is a soft wind on the emotions that rage in my tired mind.

"Why do people have to be so vicious and ugly to one another!" I scream as a snot bubble escapes. "I'm sick of this!"

"It just comes with the job, April," Lane murmurs.

His face is wavering from the tears in my eyes, "Well, this job sucks!" I turn and struggle with the door.

Both men holler at me to not leave.

I run to my car. Somehow I'm in my Prius and pulling out of my space as both men stand on the curb and watch me.

I ache all over, and I can't stop sobbing.

Chapter 47

The car is on autopilot as I drive away from town onto the county backroads. I'm fighting to keep my car between the lines. My vision continues to blur through the curtain of tears.

I should've done more to help Jethro. I knew he was in a dangerous place. I knew it.

What should I have done? I have no clue. Still, that seems like a lame excuse.

There is no way for me to shake this feeling that I failed Jethro. I left him alone when he needed someone the most.

I'm not sure if I'm done crying or running out of moisture in my body. Either way, I'm finally cried out even though my heart continues to ache.

The sun is dipping below the tree line. The night will be on me soon, and I have no idea where I am.

As the road veers around a cluster of trees, the Willoughby covered bridge comes into view. What are the chances I would end up here tonight?

Nana's house is just a few minutes from the bridge. The idea of talking to her comforts me, allowing my shoulders to relax.

The fact that going to see Nana is comforting to me is a subtle clue that something in me has broken.

I pull up to the one-lane bridge.

I'm about to start across when the drowned girl ghost in her ruined pink dress appears in the middle of the road holding her dolly by one arm. Her wet hair obscures most of her glowing amber eyes. I feel the evil rage flowing from her, and it personifies all the needless hate I sense in the world.

I won't let her intimidate me. She is not even particularly scary.

Pulling my pocketbook out of my purse, I retrieve my charmed warding coin. I hold the silver coin up with my left hand as I drive the car forward.

Her lips transform into a snarl, exposing her sharp teeth as she begrudgingly steps to the driver's side of my vehicle. As I drive across the old planks of the bridge, I lift my middle finger and give her a one-finger salute.

The ghost's face transforms into the head of a rabid wolf ten times too large to be supported by her petite body.

Its fangs, resembling daggers, drip bloody froth.

I would pee myself if I had any liquid left in me.

My right foot stomps on the accelerator.

The car's tires spin wildly as my speedometer shoots up to seventy miles an hour, and I drive by the ghost slower than I can run.

The wheels catch on a dry plank, and I rocket forward. The small bump where the wood meets the asphalt sends my car into the air.

Holy moly, what did she turn into? I will never be able to unsee that.

That's the last time I pick a fight with that cranky little spirit, no matter how irritable I am.

Chapter 48

I open the door to Nana's trailer. The stress flows away from my body as I smell the heavenly fragrance of chicken soup heavy in the house—my stomach grumbles.

"April? Is that you?"

"Yes, Nana."

I'm on my way to the kitchen when she appears and unexpectantly gives me a fierce hug. I resist for a moment and then meld into her.

My heart rate slows. I'm calm now. Just sad.

"I was worried for you," she says as she rubs my back. "I had a visitor."

"Mama came to see you?"

Nana separates enough from me to look me in the eye. "Not that kind of visitor."

"Oh." I sigh as the thought of any more paranormal happenings seems like too much to deal with tonight.

She smiles and rubs a calloused fingertip over my cheek. "He said he was worried because you are upset. He doesn't want you to be sad."

I narrow my eyes. "Who are you talking about, Nana?"

"A nice young man by the name of Jethro Mullins. I think I knew his grandfather."

Jethro's name is like another gut punch. I can't cry anymore, but I feel my body tense as my lips begin to tremble. “Jethro?” I croak.

“He just left a few minutes ago,” Nana says.

"I failed him.”

“That’s not what he said. You know what he told me?”

I look away from her. “What?”

Nana puts my chin in her palm and turns my face to her. “He told me ‘Miss Snow was the first person to treat me like a real person in years. She did everything she could to help me.’“

Nana’s face beams with pride. “And I said ‘Yep, that would be my April.’“

I’m not sure if Nana is telling me the truth or if she talked to Howard and made the story up. It’s hard to be confident about such matters where my family is involved.

“I wanted to help him, Nana. I thought I could make things better for him.”

She pulls me tighter. “He knows. The thing about it is he was tired, and he had lost the only thing that made life worth the struggle to him. You couldn’t fix his relationship with Ruth. Only he and Ruth could do that.”

“I know, but I—”

“Hush now, Boo. Jethro took his decision, and he made sure to let you know he appreciated you being there for him. That’s all we can do for each other. Be there.”

“If I could have gotten her to agree to marriage counseling —”

“Poppycock, child. When will you learn not everything is about April or what April can do?” Nana releases me and moves toward the kitchen.

Her harsh words bite at my tender feelings. Yet, as I accept her wisdom, I feel release. The vise constricting my chest loosens, and my face stretches into an awkward smile.

“Now, I’ve made a big pot of chicken soup because it cures all ills,” she says from the kitchen.

“Will it cure me of all my foolish cravings?” I scoff.

“Ooh, spill the beans. What sort of foolish cravings do you

have?"

Our eyes meet as I step into the kitchen. "Handsome men and two-thousand-dollar bottles of wine?"

Nana laughs. "At your age, handsome men are a healthy craving. As to wine, that's the nectar on this side of the "veil." I've got a bottle of homemade blackberry wine that will make you forget all about that fancy wine. That is, if you are game for some wine tasting tonight."

Her smile is so infectious I laugh. "You're on, Nana."

The End

Have you read the prequels? ***Psychic Witch Hot Mess*** stories are the prequel series to the ***A Psychic Witch's Life*** novel series of April May Snow.

Click to get your copies today!

Psychic Witch Hot Mess Prequel Series

Throw the Amulet

Throw the Bouquet

Throw the Cap

Throw the Dice

Throw the Elbow

Throw the Fastball

Throw the Gauntlet

Throw the Hissy

M. Scott lives outside of Nashville, Tennessee, with his wife and two guard chihuahuas. When he's not writing, he's cooking or taking long walks to smooth out plotlines for the next April May Snow adventure.

Dear Reader,

Thank you for reading April's story. You make her adventures possible. Without you, there would be no point in creating her story.

I'd like to encourage you to post a review on Amazon. A favorable critique from you is a powerful way to support authors you enjoy. It allows our books to be found by additional readers, and frankly, motivates us to continue to produce books. This is especially true for your independents.

Once again, thank you for the support. You are the magic that breathes life into these characters.

M. Scott Swanson

The best way to stay in touch is to join the reader's club!

www.mscottswanson.com

Other ways to stay in touch are:

Like on Amazon

Like on Facebook

Like on Goodreads

You can also reach me at mscottswanson@gmail.com.

I hope your life is filled with

magic and LOVE!

Made in United States
North Haven, CT
18 September 2022

24280163R00183